WHAT HAPPENS *NEXT*?

"OUR GENERATION," SNOW, "is 'the disappeared.' We've dropped out of sight between our parents' generation—The Greatest Generation—and the baby boomers. Remember how we were called 'The Silent Generation'? Nobody knows about us."

But you will know!

Here are Snowy and Bev and Puddles, Tom, Dudley, the twins and all the Gang from Gunthwaite High School, in the next stage of their lives. How do they adjust to limitations, deal with grief, and face the realization that this is their last chance at love, success, and happiness? How do they face death?

With humor, for one thing. Like THE CHEERLEADER and SNOWY, HENRIETTA SNOW is funny, honest, and indelible.

Anticipation for ***Henrietta Snow***!

Readers of THE CHEERLEADER and SNOWY have written to Ruth Doan MacDougall saying:

"Like so many others, I cannot wait for HENRIETTA SNOW to arrive. I visit your Web site regularly and can feel the anticipation rising amongst your many and devoted fans!"

"More, I want more!"

"When is the next installment of the Snowy saga coming out? Can't wait!"

"I'm left starving to learn more of what happens to Snowy and the rest of the triumvirate, including their families—and of course the question, thirty years later, of Snowy & Tom (??)."

"Can't wait for the third book. Write faster, Ruth!"

"I am thrilled to hear about the sequel-to-the-sequel's being in the works. I cannot wait to find out what happens to Snowy next!"

"I can't wait until HENRIETTA SNOW!"

The Cheerleader

This best-selling novel about growing up in the Fabulous Fifties, in the years of ponytails, pajama parties, proms, and "parking," is a coming-of-age classic that explores the loss of innocence, the growth of passion, and the awakening of ambition.

"One of the truest portraits of an American girl ever written... Everything works in MacDougall's book. She captures the times, the attitudes, the emotions with the authority of one who was once there and knows the route back by heart."

—DETROIT FREE PRESS

"A devastatingly accurate portrait of the '50s."

—LIBRARY JOURNAL

"If future historians and sociologists are ever impelled to find out what it was like to be a high school student in America at mid 20th century, they will need go no farther than THE CHEERLEADER for documentation and enlightenment...Utterly honest, accurate, and sympathetic."

—KANSAS CITY STAR

"It's heartbreaking at times, hilarious at others, and she's got it all down beautifully."

—PHILADELPHIA INQUIRER

"It isn't often that you get to the last page of a book and are aware that you have just finished a real reading experience. But that's how you'll feel when you finish THE CHEERLEADER. A terrific book. Really terrific."

—UNITED PRESS INTERNATIONAL

"A classic."

—PUBLISHERS WEEKLY

Snowy

A sequel to THE CHEERLEADER

What happens when ex-cheerleaders grow up?

SNOWY describes how she and her friends, who came of age in the security of the 1950s, develop in the next decades, coping with college, marriage, and careers, their experiences unique and universal.

"Readers should prepare to laugh out loud and cry in earnest as former high school cheerleader Henrietta Snow grows up in this delightful sequel to THE CHEERLEADER. Set in Vermont and New Hampshire beginning in the 1950s and moving through 30 years...this novel chronicles major landmarks in Snowy's life. The portion dealing with her college years is especially funny, and Snowy's observations on the realities of sex (as opposed to what one reads in books) are sidesplitting. The novel is evocative of small-town New England and is a pleasure to read. Highly recommended."

—LIBRARY JOURNAL

"MacDougall's novel opens during a freshman year in the 1950s at Bennington College where Snowy, 'a New Hampshire hick' whose real name is Henrietta Snow, meets her glamorous California roommate, Harriet, and pulls some antics that would make today's students proud. Snowy's term as student employee in a Boston publishing house finally brings her back into contact with her two closest high-school friends...The three maintain their friendship as they marry, raise families, lose their parents, and face the 'fragility of our forties.' MacDougall's sexy, painfully true story illuminates what an endless process growing up is."

—BOOKLIST

"This is a richly detailed account of small-town love and friendship, of old allegiances and daily comforts and the pain that time and change exact. The author, whose novel THE CHEERLEADER was an intricate social map of Snowy's high school generation, brings us into the present with haunting immediacy."

—ROSELLEN BROWN, author of *Before and After*

BY THE SAME AUTHOR

THE LILTING HOUSE

THE COST OF LIVING

ONE MINUS ONE

THE CHEERLEADER

WIFE AND MOTHER

AUNT PLEASANTINE

THE FLOWERS OF THE FOREST

A LOVELY TIME WAS HAD BY ALL

SNOWY

A WOMAN WHO LOVED LINDBERGH

With Daniel Doan

50 HIKES IN THE WHITE MOUNTAINS

50 MORE HIKES IN NEW HAMPSHIRE

Editor

INDIAN STREAM REPUBLIC: SETTLING A NEW ENGLAND FRONTIER, 1785-1842, by Daniel Doan

Henrietta Snow

Ruth Doan MacDougall

FRIGATE BOOKS

Visit the author's Web site at:
http://www.ruthdoanmacdougall.com

 For informaton, address Frigate Books, 285 Range Road, Center Sandwich, NH 03227.

Cover photograph: Robert J. Kozlow, "From the Fire Tower"
Cover design: hannusdesign.com

Library of Congress Cataloging-in-Publication Data
MacDougall, Ruth Doan
Henrietta Snow / Ruth Doan MacDougall
p. cm
ISBN 0-9663352-4-4
1. Women—New Hampshire—Fiction
I. Title
PS3563.A292H46 2004
813'.54—dc.21

2004097734
CIP

12345 08 07 06 05 04

To Marney Wilde

And to Jennifer Davis-Kay and Jan Schor

And to all the other beloved bookworms
Who have asked for more about Snowy and her friends.

Here it is, with heartfelt thanks, and love.

FOREWORD

THOUGH IT SEEMS an oxymoron to say, "The cheerleader is sixty years old," Snowy qualifies as a senior citizen by the end of ***Henrietta Snow.*** The amazement she feels at being middle-aged though her "essence" has not changed cannot help but resonate with those of us who first met Snowy as a sophomore at Gunthwaite High (and with any person of a certain age). Yet this third novel's title—the first not to name Snowy by type or nickname—announces that at last she has "settl[ed] into herself," having achieved in her sixty unpredictable years the artistic and personal maturity she sought in the earlier books. In this she exemplifies a more familiar oxymoron—that youth is wasted on the young—but also that with luck and persistence youth merely prepares one for the rewards of middle age.

The novel will thus deeply satisfy Snowy and the Gang's die-hard fans, the "beloved bookworms" to whom the book is dedicated. And ***Henrietta Snow,*** like ***The Cheerleader*** and ***Snowy***, does much more. It shines a perceptive light on what Snowy and Dudley name "the disappeared": the generation old enough to have suffered the smothering conformity of the 1950s but young enough to have escaped it, as well as the high price of this new liberty. As in all MacDougall's fiction, the novel's painstaking realism portrays with haunting precision life's inevitably mixed nature.

MacDougall again renders commonplace experiences as if with a video camera, lovingly showing that the everyday is the stuff of life. For instance, Snowy's outfits, and the choice process involved in dressing, merit careful, if comic, descriptions that frankly reflect the importance clothes have for women's sense of self and adventure. More pointedly, tragedy ruthlessly punctures the quotidian with no preparation, proving Snowy's "Left-Field Theory," what the ancients called Fate. MacDougall's unsentimental but harrowing descriptions of these turning points portray vividly how we watch ourselves go through these intense moments, amazed that this could happen to us, but fully aware that nightmares can come true.

MacDougall also shows, with characteristically brilliant subtlety, that people's greatest strengths are their greatest weaknesses, and that success comes "at you sideways." Haunted by the catastrophe of Alan's suicide and the specter of her dormant agoraphobia, Snowy initially struggles with business problems and an absent muse. Tom too has lost his marriage and his original direction. But adversity seeds growth. Tom remains his own person now as he did at Gunthwaite High: aloof, unique, a breaker of tradition but genuinely modest, "cold and warm, cautious, impetuous, aging, strong." Likewise, Snowy may be, as Tom admits, "timid and clumsy and slow"—but "she [keeps] learning and never complain[s], at least not out loud."

Snowy calls her most recent poetry collection *Site Fidelity*, a term that describes birds' tendency to return to the same place, and a fitting symbol for Henrietta Snow. A native and resident of New Hampshire, Snowy cherishes a strong sense of place, and her best high-school friends—Bev, Puddles, Dudley, and Tom—remain vital to her life. Yet fans will be fascinated to see other members of the Gang reappear in or near Gunthwaite, like busty Rita Beaupre and other ex-cheerleaders, as well as Snowy's Bennington roommate, Harriet. This small but ever-changing community boasts a remarkable personal and public evolution. Bev's humorous professional competitiveness as a real-estate agent contrasts her former refusal to enter any contest she might not win; she knows now that "not trying could be failure." Dudley dares his early dream and enters local politics. Harriet—a kind of fairy godmother immersed in luxury, with lovers in different continents and a dual carer as painter and gallery owner—has conquered her inability to eat in front of men. Puddles, still outspoken and earthy, still working in a beloved vocation, struggles with weight and arthritis. But she also coaches cheerleading, marveling at the difference between her 1950s squad—which was minimally athletic but of high social caste—and these vigorous girls who master gymnastics and dance. Cheerleading, however, remains a "sensitive subject." For Snowy it not only symbolizes the fact that she has never ceased to "try out"; she, and others, still dislike the enduring stereotype of dumb sexy girls on the sidelines.

The triumvirate's daughters—even the one who cheered—mirror their mothers' advances. Better educated, ambitious as a matter of course, sexually active without fear or guilt, they make room for marriage within careers rather than seek husbands for status and support. Ironically, these young women in a sense still follow their mothers' footsteps. Bev and Roger, after the most traditional beginnings, now live apart in an "open" marriage; Puddles had an affair but stayed married; Snowy and Tom, still wary of their past, are content to pursue separate courses and be together when and as they wish. Even the steamy lovemaking of ***The Cheerleader*** and ***Snowy*** hardly appears in ***Henrietta Snow***: sex is no longer a revelation or a risk, and the Gang now sees it as an essential but private part of life. In fact, work has "replaced romance" for Bev; and Snowy's ongoing struggle to write poems does not take second place to Tom.

The conflict that threatens Bev and Snowy's enduring friendship exemplifies these shifting priorities, due not only to feminism but also the autonomy that comes with age. As teenagers they fought for Tom; as adults they fight for fiercely divergent personal and social philosophies. Bev can still be treacherous, and for all her charm she embodies the selfish American who will consume or destroy almost anything to make a buck. Snowy's love for her environment, which even worldly Harriet calls "one of the most beautiful parts of the world," is fueled by her newfound joy in hiking and backpacking. As in all of MacDougall's novels, New Hampshire itself is a major character: Yankee, obstinate, gorgeous, still rural, it symbolizes both beauty and loss as population grows and developers bulldoze fields and woods. MacDougall cannot stress this enough, though Snowy mocks her own hopeless nostalgia for the Main Street of her youth as "advancing curmudgeonliness." And while Woodcombe, Snowy's Arcadian village, remains a refuge from sprawl, even it cannot escape the fanaticism that threatens random acts of terror, arguably the world's worst problem at the start of the twenty-first century.

As a kind of antidote to such conundrums—and showing, like E. M. Forster and Bruce Springsteen, that human connections make life worth living—MacDougall offers us Snowy and Tom, passionate lovers, genuine friends, the only Gang members still lucky enough to be in love. True to form, MacDougall tempers the potential fairy-tale elements with truths that mirror the complexities of contemporary society. Each has children born from other unions; each remembers happiness with another, regrets neglect of another, and knows that love can happen more than once, and not necessarily forever. When his daughter breaks up with her boyfriend, Tom says that she's learning "how complicated things are": this is a mantra of ***Henrietta Snow***.

Nevertheless, with refreshing gusto MacDougall does not shy from a joyful vision of fidelity rewarded. Snowy's stubborn romanticism survives—contemplating her daughter's seemingly bloodless attitude toward boyfriends, she wonders, "What about passion and a world-well-lost for love?"—and finally her sexual, domestic, and artistic selves mesh into one life. Snowy deserves this success, as those who have followed her life from Gunthwaite High to the present know. May we all achieve some of Snowy's wisdom, courage, and continuity; and may Ruth Doan MacDougall take us with Snowy into old age.

ANN V. NORTON

Saint Anselm College

I

CHAPTER ONE

THE AUCTION WAS OVER. The joyous accumulation of almost twenty-six years of marriage, of living on New Hampshire's seacoast in the Old Eastbourne apartment and the Pevensay house and then in the mountains of Woodcombe on this Hurricane Farm, was practically reduced to bare necessities.

Henrietta Snow Sutherland, known as Snowy, had hoped she would now feel cleansed, ready for a fresh start. Instead, as she stood looking out one of the living-room windows at the front lawn where earlier a crowd of dealers, collectors, amateur opportunists, and busybodies had stared at and bid on her belongings, she just felt dead tired.

She asked Bev, "Can we beg off going to Dudley and Charl's for supper?"

"If we don't go," Bev pointed out, "we'll have to cook here."

"True," Snowy said, suddenly noticing that Bev, always beautiful with green eyes and once-red naturally curly hair that had become a white helmet, looked haggard. Bev had been her best friend since they were seven years old. Back in 1946, when they were in second grade at the same grammar school in their hometown of Gunthwaite, New Hampshire, they had discovered they were kindred spirits, and they had remained so right up to their present 1987 age of forty-eight, except for a gap of ten months thirty years ago and later a lapse into only Christmas-and-birthday-card communication during the distractions of domestic life, child-rearing, husband-tending. Last Saturday Bev's daughter Mimi had had a June wedding on a mountaintop in Woodcombe, with the reception held here at Snowy's Hurricane Farm, and Bev had planned to return to Connecticut with her husband and her three other kids afterward, yet at the last minute she decided to stay with Snowy, ostensibly to help.

Bev added, "Anyway, I'm all agog about seeing Charl and Darl."

"Okay," Snowy said. "Let's round up Ruhamah and be on our way."

But the phone rang. It was immediately answered out in the kitchen, by Ruhamah.

"Leon again," Bev predicted.

At the reception, Bev's younger son and Snowy's daughter had met and ignited, and during the past week Leon had phoned Ruhamah every day. Snowy could imagine only one reason why twenty-one-year-old Leon would pursue sweet-sixteen Ruhamah; she intended to make sure he remained long-distance.

From the kitchen Ruhamah shouted, "Snowy, it's for you!"

Bev changed her prediction. "Tom," she said, and went into the hallway, to climb the stairs to Snowy's office, which with its pull-out sofa was the guest room.

Snowy crossed the living room, the least empty of the rooms because before the auction the new owner of Hurricane Farm, Frank Barlow, had bought the Sheraton sofa, the tavern table, and the butterfly table, so they were remaining here, while she was keeping the wing chair (Alan's chair), the Martha Washington chair, the pedestal table, the glass-fronted bookcases, and one of the oriental rugs. She went through the echoing dining room—gone fast at the auction, the cherry dining table and oak sideboard—into the kitchen in the ell.

Ruhamah was two inches taller than Snowy's five-two and had inherited Alan's long eyelids. Otherwise, Snowy knew, mother and daughter looked alike, doomed to cuteness with heart-shaped faces, turned-up noses, denim-blue eyes, and dark blond hair (well,

Ruhamah's mane wasn't interwoven with the white hairs Snowy had discovered recently). Ruhamah wore jeans and an old T-shirt of gamboling lambs that said ARIES, while Snowy had got a bit more dolled up for the auction, light green corduroy jeans and a creamy short-sleeved blouse with ecru edging, an outfit she had last worn when Dudley took her to visit Alan's parents last month. Ruhamah said in her unique voice that always sounded like a chortle, "It's a woman who claims she's Harriet. Your roommate, Harriet?"

Snowy snatched the receiver of the wall phone. "*Harriet?*"

"Snowy?"

They hadn't seen or heard each other since their graduation from Bennington College twenty-six years ago. Harriet sounded just the same. As Snowy remembered how amused Californian Harriet used to be by her New Hampshire accent, she pictured Harriet's angular dark prettiness and wondered if the years had changed that. Ruhamah went out the door to the screened side porch.

Snowy asked Harriet, "Where *are* you?" During the wedding reception, Snowy had learned that Kristin, Mimi's roommate during their years at Rhode Island School of Design, was working at a gallery owned by Harriet Blumburg, who, having discovered the connection, had sent word via Kristin that she'd be phoning sometime. Kristin had said Harriet was off to China. Snowy said, "You can't be calling from China!"

"That's next," Harriet said. "First, a detour. I'm in Israel. How are you? I had trouble finding you; I phoned the number Information gave me and it rang and rang and finally some out-of-breath woman answered and said you hadn't moved in yet and gave me this number."

This phone was already switched to Frank Barlow's name. "I'm moving tomorrow," Snowy said. "I own a little general store in the village—that woman works there—and I'm moving into an apartment over it." The apartment's phone number was different from the store's, and Irene must've got so irritated by Harriet's persistent ringing that she dashed upstairs to answer it. "I haven't hooked up an answering machine there yet. You're in Israel? You sound so close!"

"Snowy," Harriet said. "Kristin told me what her roommate had told her. I'm terribly sorry. I remember Alan..."

Harriet trailed off.

If people had difficulty expressing sympathy about an ordinary death, they got completely tongue-tied about a suicide. Snowy tried to help, glad that Harriet couldn't see her eyes filling. "Remember the Sleepytime Motor Lodge? After he and I spent Saturday nights there, we'd come back to school to our room, yours and mine, and you'd tactfully go over to Commons while we said good-bye." She ripped a sheet off a roll of paper towels and blotted her eyes.

Harriet said, "You met him when you were doing research for your thesis on a poet, Ru-ha-who?"

"Ru-*hay*-mah," Snowy said, reminding her of the pronunciation. "Ruhamah Reed. Do you remember the portrait of her you gave me, a wedding present? You painted it from the frontispiece of her collected poems and called it 'The Matchmaker.' I've still got it, and it's going to the new apartment." Along with Alan's pen-and-ink sketch of the Ruhamah Reed House in Old Eastbourne. "We named our daughter Ruhamah; you just spoke with her." After the reception, Snowy had quizzed Kristin and learned that besides running the New York gallery and traveling a lot, Harriet was garnering acclaim for her paintings, something Snowy wouldn't have heard about in the wilds of Woodcombe, and although there were probably mentions of it in the Bennington alumni magazine, Snowy had stopped doing even a cursory flip through the pages when her career as a poet had hit a brick wall and seeing items about others' successes became too shamefully painful. From Kristin she'd also learned that Harriet was unmarried and had no children. And now Harriet was in Israel. Snowy asked, "Why the detour?"

"Oh, I make many detours. But this one was planned. I got an urge to see the Sea of Galilee. I've been to Israel before, but never here. There are some gorgeous views, with the mountains to the east—the Golan Heights."

Snowy remembered Harriet's phases at Bennington, when she first painted only fat women and later when she painted only circles of primary colors. Was Harriet now doing *landscapes?* What transitions had led to this? Snowy asked, "Are you painting the views?"

"I'm trying to."

"What time of day—or night—is it there now?"

"Half-past midnight."

"You once made a detour to India. You sent me a postcard saying, 'Am living in an ashram.' I didn't know what the hell an ashram was. I had to head for the dictionary." This was in 1971, the last time Snowy had heard from her. Harriet had never been a good correspondent, to put it mildly; at Bennington she'd driven her parents crazy.

Harriet said, "Some of my detours involve guys, and that was one of them."

"As I recall, you had a tendency to fall for jocks, so the Super Bowl would seem a more likely detour than an ashram."

"Well, it did turn out that he preferred cricket to philosophy."

They began to giggle.

Harriet added, "And I must confess there's a guy here, and he does play soccer. And Snowy, you ought to see the hunks off the kibbutzim—the kibbutzes—with rock-hard muscles from working in the avocado groves!"

Snowy whooped, and over the phone she heard Harriet laughing in Israel.

Then Harriet said, "Snowy, are you all right? How's the poetry?"

Snowy looked out the kitchen window beside the phone. Barn swallows were perched on the telephone line and soaring in and out of the white clapboard barn across the driveway. "Oh, fine. I've had a few collections published over the years." But there had been only rejections these past five years. "My thesis became a biography of Ruhamah Reed."

"Great!" Harriet said. "I'll look for all your work when I get home."

Snowy couldn't bring herself to confess it was out of print. Bev hurried into the kitchen, pointed at the clock, made an exaggeratedly urgent face and wrung her hands, so Snowy said in relief, "I'm sorry, I have to leave for a dinner date."

Harriet asked, "You're—dating?"

"No, no," Snowy said hastily. (What, however, was the term for what she and Tom were doing? They'd got their "dating" over with thirty years ago.) "Just supper with some old friends."

"Well, old friend," Harriet said, "dear old school chum, it's good to catch up. Hope to detour to New Hampshire someday. Bye!"

"Thanks for calling. Bye." Snowy hung up and said to Bev, "That was Harriet, my roommate. Kristin said she'd be in touch. After all these years, she phones when she's visiting Israel!"

"Imagine that, phoning from Israel." Bev had never met Harriet. Her own roommate hadn't done a disappearing act; they stayed in touch with Christmas and birthday cards. Ann Wilmot, Bev's roommate at Katharine Gibbs, had wanted to be a private secretary to a globe-trotting boss, but after graduation her first job had taken her to Chicago, where she had fallen in love with the son of the owner of a Ford dealership, had married him, and settled down to suburban life with two kids.

"Okay, let's go." Snowy grabbed her shoulder bag and hurried outside, crossed the side porch, and opened the screen door. She looked at the herb garden beside the steps and up at the backyard, the vegetable garden, the apple orchard. Beyond were the brook and woods, with an unseen beaver swamp in there. Two years ago she and Alan had bought this Hurricane Farm beneath Mount Pascataquac and they'd also bought the general store in the village. She had loved the farm but been unable to cope with the store. Now she had to sell the farm to save the store; after the refinancing, she was facing a thirty-year mortgage. She yelled, "Ruhamah?"

Out of the barn backed Snowy's white Subaru, upon which this spring Ruhamah had put a bumper sticker that said Native. As Ruhamah pulled up alongside the porch, Snowy and Bev exchanged a glance. A sixteen-year-old chauffeur? Snowy was used to this, for although her long bout with agoraphobia seemed to be over (knock on wood), she still hated to drive. Bev was used to doing suburban-housewife driving; indeed, when her kids were younger and all in need of lifts to music lessons and Little League, it seemed like she had spent her entire day behind the wheel, and she continued to log plenty of hours there with her youngest, Etta, age twelve. Bev made her "Oh, horrors!" face at Snowy. Bev adored making faces. Then she shrugged, and then she said, "Eek!" and slapped at a mosquito on her arm. She was wearing a new sleeveless navy-and-white striped jersey with her jeans. Because she hadn't packed enough clothes for such a lengthy stay, she'd had a terrific excuse to go shopping.

They got into the car, Snowy insisting Bev sit up front to take in the New Hampshire scenery she'd been deprived of all these years in Connecticut. Ruhamah drove down the driveway lined with the masses of daffodils Snowy had planted, now gone by.

Snowy said, "Shit, I forgot a hostess gift!" And she was the compulsive one. It was Bev who forgot things. In this instance, though, the responsibility belonged completely to Snowy, because Dudley had initially invited only her and Ruhamah. But when Bev decided to stay, Snowy had phoned to tell Dudley and Charl, feeling sure they'd want to expand the invitation to include Bev. She'd got Charl, another voice from the past, who exclaimed, "Then I'll invite Darl and Bill and we'll have a reunion," adding, "if you don't mind too many people, couples?" "It's fine," Snowy had replied.

Bev said, "You've just been through the sale of your home and an auction of your furniture. You're moving tomorrow. A hostess gift? Charl and Dudley won't expect you to be functioning at all. That's the whole idea of feeding you supper."

But, Snowy thought as Ruhamah turned left onto the dirt road at the foot of the driveway, Dudley had brought *her* presents, a hanging basket of red impatiens to attract hummingbirds to the apartment, and tubs of vegetable seedlings to replace the garden she'd slaved over and must abandon. Snowy felt awful, empty-handed, empty like the house.

The dirt road was officially named Thorne Road, but its local nickname was the Roller Coaster Road, and whenever they drove it during Bev's visit, Bev liked to pretend she was at an amusement park, shrieking and squealing as the car bumped and bounced. Today her theatrics were weary. At the main road, she said, "What a thrill," and subsided.

They drove along Woodcombe Lake toward the village. Back in the other direction lay Murray Cove, where on the night of May 9, Alan had washed down Valium with gin and swum out until he drowned. It was a quiet lake, its old-fashioned cottages hidden in the woods, unlike Lake Winnipesaukee, the lake of Snowy's youth, where motels and marinas and condominiums now abounded. A fisherman had found Alan's body the next morning, just when she was discovering that he hadn't come to bed and wasn't in the house or the store.

Bev said, following her thoughts and trying to distract them, "Tell me about Harriet. You've never mentioned her much."

"She's rich," Snowy said, and then was appalled that this could be the first description that leapt to mind. In college, Harriet's vast allowance, her new Jaguar, her casual references to her evidently palatial home in California, were so far removed from Snowy's experience that Snowy had hardly ever felt envy.

"Family money?" Bev asked. "What's the source?"

Growing up, Bev had planned to marry a millionaire. Instead, she'd married Roger Lambert, a high-school boyfriend from a blue-collar French Canadian background, who had got a scholarship to Dartmouth and then a law degree from Boston University and now, Snowy thought, seemed to be gaining fast on becoming worth at least one million. In high school, as a sophomore Snowy had been terrified by Roger, a suave senior, tall and coolly jaunty, co-captain of the basketball team, president of the National Honor Society, until she recognized how much they were the same, whiz kids with searing ambition. Roger had attained his. After she'd overcome her fear of him, she had liked Roger, but the father of the bride at Mimi's wedding, with a mustache counterbalancing a receding hairline, the grown-up Roger who had upset Bev dreadfully, was a stranger. An enemy?

"Real estate," Snowy said. "Harriet's father is in real estate in California. The New York art gallery, that was owned by a family friend, and Harriet used to work there during our Non-Resident Terms. The family friend wanted to retire, so Harriet bought it, according to Kristin."

Bev repeated, "Real estate."

Woodcombe was often called the prettiest village in New Hampshire, thanks to the old white houses and tall-steepled white church, a traditional scene saved from triteness by its location in a mountain notch. Once a little outpost on the edge of the White Mountains, Woodcombe seemed both vulnerable and courageous (or foolhardy), especially if viewed from Mount Pascataquac where the settlement was clearly revealed as a huddle of tiny houses and a spear of church spire below mountains piling back thickly green to higher hazy blue.

At the center of the village was the store, white with a long screened front porch. Some people now still sat chatting there on the deacon's bench although six-o'-clock closing time neared. Irene Mason, Snowy's helper, and Irene's nephew, Darren, were handling the store alone this weekend because of the auction and moving day. In the gravel parking lot, between a pickup truck and a Range Rover, Tom's old green Jeep was parked.

Tom would be upstairs in the apartment finishing the second coat of white paint on the walls. When Snowy had decided to turn the attic storeroom into an apartment, he'd done the preliminary work, but then Ruhamah, being a pain in the ass, had objected to his sudden appearance in Snowy's life right after Alan's death, so Tom had made himself scarce and Snowy had hired carpenters to get the flooring down, the drywall up and taped and sanded, and an outside staircase built. At Mimi's wedding, Ruhamah came to an acceptance of Tom. This past week he'd been doing some of the painting, in and around his schedule as fire warden on Mount Pascataquac, where he lived in a log cabin beside the fire tower. Last Sunday Bev had announced, "I've spent so much of my life wielding paintbrushes and rollers in the various houses we've owned that

I could qualify as a professional," and she had pitched in to do most of the painting, while throughout the week Snowy waited on customers downstairs, still learning the ropes, a faint twinge of unease at the back of her mind whenever Tom and Bev happened both to be working up there, telling herself to dismiss a ridiculous emotion left over from *high school,* for God's sake.

"Real estate," Bev said again. "Harriet's father is in real estate."

Snowy hesitated and then said encouragingly, "Just like you."

Bev looked over her shoulder at Snowy. "I'm not 'in.'"

"But you can be. You passed the exam. You're a real-estate salesperson. You can sell real estate."

"My license is for Connecticut."

This was the first time since the wedding reception that they'd discussed the real-estate exam. Before then, Bev had been distraught for weeks, sure she had flunked it because she hadn't got the result, and then amid wedding champagne her husband had produced the certificate, which he had found in their mail and had hidden until he could present it to her at Mimi's reception, framed. Snowy figured that Bev's fury over Roger's presumption, at the delay that meant Bev's mother had died without knowing Bev had passed the exam, had provoked Bev's decision to prolong her New Hampshire stay, although Bev might have done so anyway when she realized she could help with the painting and packing.

Snowy said, "Harriet's financial abilities must've improved since our school days when she couldn't budget her allowance and always ran out. Though I gathered from Kristin she's got somebody handling all that, at the gallery and otherwise."

"Her husband?" Bev asked.

"She hasn't married."

Ruhamah entered the conversation. "Lesbian?"

"No," Snowy said.

Bev said, "Just smart."

New Hampshire was a state soggy with lakes and ponds, and on the road out of town they drove past more white houses of various vintages, a field of lupines densely purple, pink, blue, and then a little green pond reflecting itself treetop deep, another field so full of buttercups it looked spread with yellow butter, and then small Lower Lake as smooth as a fresh coat of polyurethane until two ducks took sudden flight, their wakes spilling like silver bangles. When Ruhamah turned onto the main road to Gunthwaite, what lay across the way from a minimart but more water, one of the many harbors on Lake Winnipesaukee, with much boating activity at the public dock.

Bev said, "I used to know how to water-ski."

Ruhamah glanced sideways at her.

"Long ago," Bev said.

Ruhamah said, "I've heard you're some tennis player."

From Leon, Snowy presumed.

Bev gave a laugh. "I'm more astounded than anyone."

Snowy was even more astounded that Ruhamah had become an athlete. Relieved that Ruhamah hadn't followed in her footsteps and gone out for cheerleading, which was in disfavor these days anyway, Snowy certainly hadn't expected to learn Ruhamah was the relief pitcher on the high-school softball team. But Alan had played basketball at Eastbourne High School, and while Snowy had loathed gym, she'd wanted the cheerleading glory so avidly she trained her uncoordinated body in the routines, the most challenging stunt required just being a cartwheel, thank heavens. Thus Ruhamah had a basketball player and a cheerleader for parents. Still, as far as Snowy knew, Ruhamah hadn't shown any particular interest in sports until this spring.

Ruhamah said, "I've never water-skied."

"I thought it was glamorous," Bev said, "but once I got the hang of it I found it excruciatingly boring—except for the boys involved. Look at those condos, Snowy! Wasn't there a cabin colony here when we were kids? What was it called?"

The builders of this condo development of earth-tone boxes with balconies had opted for the "historic/old local" category of condo names and come up with Indian Carry, therefore managing to be both politically incorrect and, because the actual site of the portage between Lake Winnipesaukee and Lower Lake was somewhat farther north, geographically inaccurate. Snowy said absently, "The Lakeside Cabins." She remembered that during the reception, Bev had mentioned all the condos being built on the lake and remarked that selling real estate around here must be fun. In her youth, Bev's goal had been to have fun.

Bev craned her neck to watch the condos disappear behind them. "I wonder what the prices are up here."

Snowy had no idea.

Ruhamah said, "One of my friends' fathers bought a two-bedroom condo in a development in Gunthwaite after the divorce, and she says he paid sixty-five thousand but the price has gone down since then and is he pissed off."

Snowy and Bev digested this. Ruhamah sped onward.

It wasn't necessary to take the new bypasses or the Miracle Mile when you were approaching the small city of Gunthwaite from the Woodcombe direction, so the route was familiar and Snowy didn't get disoriented except by changes in the sights. More houses on this road and up the sides of hills and mountains; fields and woods were vanishing faster and faster. Overpopulation! That's all Snowy could think of whenever her shocked eyes lit on yet another change, another giant yellow machine clawing into the forest floor for yet another building lot. She had contributed one child to the problem. Bev had four, and was that what Bev was thinking about now, her children, two still living at home, and the cost of a three-bedroom condo? Was Bev thinking about a separation from Roger? To teach him a lesson for swiping her exam certificate, for taking possession of it, an action that had made Bev realize he had tried to undermine her pursuit of a career? Was Bev thinking about a divorce? Once when Bev had fallen in love with another man, she'd told Snowy that divorcing a lawyer was disastrous.

Tom had become, to all intents and purposes, separated from Joanne, his wife of twenty-nine years.

They passed a housing development built on the site of the old sandpit where teenagers used to go parking. Where Snowy had

Gone All the Way with Tom the one and only time in high school, the first of the two times they'd done it. Thirty years between fucks!

Ruhamah drove down Worm Hill, which had been given this nickname because years ago the ramshackle houses along it used to have handmade signs that advertised worms and night crawlers for sale. Now most of the houses were spruced up, and only one such sign remained.

Bev said, "Etta's horse. I'd need to find a riding academy here, where Prancer could be boarded—ye gods, that new junior high!"

More overpopulation. Snowy and Bev stared at the long low 1960s building necessitated by the baby boom. When Snowy and Bev were in school, the junior high had only taken up the first floor of one of the high school's two brick buildings on the south side of town.

Snowy said, "It's a middle school, and it isn't new anymore but it'll always be so to me."

"Junior high," Bev said. "Was that when we wore quilted skirts?"

"Yes, indeed," Snowy said. "And anklets. Or were ankle bracelets a freshman-year fashion?"

Ruhamah asked, "You wore ankle bracelets?"

Snowy said. "Over our white socks, which our skirts kept pushing down."

"So alluring," Bev said.

Ruhamah giggled, a rare sound to Snowy's ears this past month. Since Alan's death, Ruhamah had been seeing the school psychologist, and her school friends had rallied round, but Snowy couldn't gauge her state. At least Ruhamah no longer openly blamed Snowy.

Snowy said, "Take Bridge Street to North Main."

"Yup," Ruhamah said, and flicked directionals.

The houses grew closer: tall old houses, portly with porches and gables, nowadays divided into apartments; smaller houses hanging on as single dwellings; ranch houses squeezed in during the fifties and sixties. Then a corner grocery store that had become a "convenience" store, and then they were downtown, and instead of continuing along Main Street, Ruhamah turned onto State Avenue.

Before they reached the site of Trask's, a factory that had made gear cutters, where Snowy's father had been the foreman of the lathe department, the building now mostly vacant with only some fly-by-night stores on the ground floor, Snowy said, "Take Chestnut."

"Yup," said Ruhamah.

Chestnut Street entered the residential section most familiar to Snowy and Bev. In silence they looked at the sidewalk route they'd walked so many times. There was the Gowen Street corner; Jean Pond, known as Puddles, the friend who completed their triumvirate, had lived on Gowen Street. (Puddles now lived in South Carolina.) Farther along Chestnut stood the yellow house where Bev had lived from second to sixth grade before her war-widow mother remarried and the move was made to a farmhouse in the country.

Snowy said, "Take Emery."

Emery Street ran along the river, across which Main Street stores stood with their backs to the once-polluted river now canoed. The warehouses that used to be over there had been torn down, replaced with a squat building called the Main Street Mini-Mall. Here on the Emery Street side, on a sloping lawn overlooking the river, was the house Snowy had grown up in, a colonial bought in run-down condition by her parents after the War and lovingly, obsessively, restored by them over the years. After they had died in 1977, her father of pancreatic cancer and her mother of a heart attack, Snowy had sold the house to a firm of lawyers, one of whom last month after Alan's death had explained to Snowy the bankrupt state of the general store and then had handled the sale of Hurricane Farm.

Bev looked up at the handsome white house with black shutters, a version of her house in Connecticut though smaller and minus her swimming pool. She said, "The garage is gone. And your folks' little backyard." Now there was only pavement, the law firm's parking lot.

"Yes." Snowy looked at the green riverbank where in her youth she had sat under the trees and read and gazed at the view and longed with piercing intensity for something she couldn't name.

"Where now?" Ruhamah asked.

"Um," Snowy said, "keep going to the first right." Ruhamah knew the way to Snowy's old house but not to Dudley and Charl's on Water Street. Snowy had never visited them and for that matter didn't think she'd been down Water Street since roaming the neighborhood in her childhood, but she'd learned some years ago that they'd bought a white elephant, a big Victorian in disrepair, to contain their population explosion of one dozen children.

As Ruhamah turned onto Water Street, Snowy immediately knew which house was theirs. You couldn't miss it.

"Look!" Bev cried in delight. "A painted lady!"

Ruhamah asked, "A butterfly?"

"That house!" Bev said. "That's what they're called, painted ladies."

Ruhamah said pedantically, "A painted lady is a butterfly."

But this was a great ungainly red-roofed edifice painted pretty, its main clapboards raspberry-pink, its eaves and bands of fish-scale shingles powder-blue as were its turrets and pillars, and all its arched window frames, all its doors and porches, a delicate ivory with touches of gold.

Bev breathed, "Amazing."

Snowy said, "And what spectacular advertising for Dudley's painting!" Out on the Miracle Mile, Dudley owned a sign-painting business. Snowy had been friends with Dudley since their sandbox days in nursery school, and sign-painting had not been his ambition as they grew up. In their childhood he planned to be both a major-league baseball star and President of the United States, but when they reached high school he'd modified his goals to being a lawyer, then a senator, and finally president.

Ruhamah parked in the driveway.

As Snowy and Bev and Ruhamah got out of the car, the front double doors flew open and out rushed two identical women, small and quick, the style of their dark hair changed from the DAs of high school but still short, their faces flushed and eager. Snowy felt overwhelmed with affection for them, the twins, Charlene and Darlene Fecteau married to Dudley Washburn and Bill LeHoullier. Dudley had told Snowy they still dressed identically for special occasions, and this evening they were wearing stonewashed jeans with short-sleeved shirts the deep red of the rhododendron at the side of the house.

"Snowy! Bev! And you must be Ruhamah!" The twins hugged and hugged.

Snowy hugged back, remembering how she used to envy them, how she'd wanted to be a twin, the nucleus of the Gang. Charl looked at her intently, then hugged her again; Charl was the more emotional of the twins, but on top of that she had been, like Snowy, a widow. Snowy hugged her again too. Dudley had explained to Snowy that after the death of Charl's first husband, Jack O'Brien, who had been famous in high school for passing out at parties and then had left Charl with two kids and a third on the way when he passed out in a snowbank one winter night, Charl couldn't help crying whenever she saw other couples and she feared Snowy might be reacting similarly. Of Snowy's many problems, this wasn't one of them—or at least, she thought, not yet. She kept sensing that a delayed reaction might lie ahead.

Charl whispered anxiously to her, "How are you doing?"

"Holding up," Snowy said, smiling at her, no longer worrying about arriving empty-handed. "It's so good to see you."

Bev exclaimed, "The house is fabulous!"

"Yes," Charl said, whisking tears away, "yes."

Although Charl was the hostess, dominant-twin Darl took over, saying, "Come on in, everybody; we got the youngest ones fed but there are hungry teenagers getting hungrier," and she herded the guests before her up the broad blue stairs onto the porch and in through the ivory-and-gold doors.

There hadn't been any attempt at restoring the grand interior with Victorian accuracy. Kid-proof, that's what the rooms were that Darl led them past down the central hall, the walls of the various living rooms or family rooms and the dining room painted a presumably washable beige, the floors protected by sturdy mud-colored wall-to-wall carpeting, and the furniture heavy-duty. The big kitchen at the back of the house was brighter, with apple-red cupboards against white walls, and out the windows you could see the green lawn, scuffed bare beneath a battle-scarred swing set, and the river flowing past. At Snowy's old house, the street had separated the house and river, making her born-worrier mother not worry constantly about Snowy's falling in, but here the lawn stretched right down to the water so how had Charl and Dudley kept their sanity? With a dozen kids, Snowy supposed, you had to get fatalistic. Snowy blinked away the image of Alan sinking under the surface of the lake, as Darl said, "Everybody's outdoors," and they stepped out the back door onto a wide screened porch where kids were milling around, with more kids and two dogs outside on a brick patio where Dudley manned a huge grill.

Charl announced, "They're here!"

Then there were hugs from Dudley, last seen a week ago at Mimi's wedding reception, and from Bill LeHoullier, last seen sometime in high school. Dudley still resembled that rosy-cheeked little boy Snowy had played with, who had shot up tall in adolescence and whose hair was now receding fast. He and Snowy had made the mistake of dating for a hot and heavy spell in high school when she was on the rebound from Tom, but later they had returned to what they really were, friends. Evidently Charl didn't mind their long shared past. Snowy looked at Bill, who hadn't got fat over the years, exactly, but had thickened so much that in comparison he seemed a stripling in his football uniform in her memory, and she tried to recall if Bev had ever dated him and couldn't—Bev had gone out with so many boys!—but what she remembered clearly was that Tom had dated Darl after his breakup with Snowy and had once kissed Charl. Tom, the tomcat! Oh, forget these high-school romances! Yet Charl and Darl and Bev had all married their high-school boyfriends, and now she and Tom were—not dating, but what? In love. Despite having married other people, had they ever fallen out of love?

"—your typewriter," Bill was saying to her. "I met your husband when he brought it in for repairs."

"Oh good lord, you're Bill's Office Equipment! I didn't realize!"

Darl said proudly, "He's into computers now. He went back to school to learn them."

Bill said just as proudly, "Darl's the boss of the business. She's the bookkeeper."

Darl laughed. "Now, Snowy, you sit down and relax."

So Snowy did, in a canvas chair on the porch. While Charl introduced her six kids still living at home, ranging from age eight to nineteen, and Darl introduced the kid here who belonged to her and Bill, an eighteen-year-old daughter who was the youngest of their four (the total number of children each twin had produced being one of the few ways, such as Darl's job, the twins differed), Bill brought out gin-and-tonics, distributed them, and passed around a bowl of pretzels.

Dudley flipped burgers and told Snowy, "Be forewarned: The ones on the left are turkey burgers because Charl is keeping tabs on my cholesterol."

As Snowy had Alan's. Snowy said, "With onions and catsup, you can't tell the difference."

"Yes," said Dudley, "you can."

Snowy raised an eyebrow at him. "I won't argue with someone who was a champion debater."

"Ho!" Bill said. "That-a-girl, remind him of that! Help me convince him he should run for city council!"

Snowy said, "Dudley, run for city council."

Dudley asked her, "Really?"

She said, "And then for mayor."

Kids chorused agreement, all except the oldest one, Dudley Junior, known as D. J., who had brought Ruhamah a Pepsi and was walking her down the lawn to a dock, where a tethered green canoe lazed. Because Ruhamah was a fussy eater like Puddles, Snowy had often thought she ought to be Puddles's daughter; with boys, ought she be Bev's, attracting them the way Bev had? Snowy watched D. J. say something to Ruhamah. He had inherited Dudley's height and blondness, while most of Dudley and Charl's other kids took after the Fecteau side of the family. Ruhamah smiled up at D. J. Dudley had almost always been able to get Snowy laughing.

Charl came out of the kitchen carrying a big bowl of salad. "Dudley shouldn't eat some of the ingredients, but it's his favorite and this is a party, our minireunion. It's a broccoli salad, Snowy, have you ever made it? What I call it is the Frigging Salad because there's so much frigging chopping, the broccoli, onions—"

Darl continued, "And then you grate the cheese and crumble the bacon, and there's the golden raisins and the pine nuts, it goes on and on."

Bev said, "I refuse to make a recipe that takes more than one card. My daughter makes a stuffed manicotti that's scrumptious, but it's on three recipe cards!"

Darl said, "Is that Mimi? Tell us all about her wedding."

Charl said, "Dudley couldn't even describe her gown. Men!"

Bev loved to tell stories, and she launched into the saga of Mimi's mountaintop wedding.

Snowy leaned back and listened, keeping an eye on Ruhamah at the dock. The comfort of old friends, however changed; old comfort food on the grill, updated. The porch and lawn seemed in constant motion, alive with kids and dogs. Don't, she cautioned herself, think ahead any further than this.

TOM SAID, "THE very last," and came into the kitchen area from the outside staircase carrying a carton. "It's marked 'Pew.' I handled it carefully in case it's a stink bomb."

Bev laughed. "That's my shorthand for Snowy's pewter."

Snowy said, "Which I should have sold. But we use it. Well, some."

Bev said, "I've forgotten my Katy Gibbs shorthand, and Snowy couldn't have understood it anyway."

Snowy, holding a carton containing her mother's rooster collection and the carving Tom had done in high school of her Shetland collie, Annie Laurie, looked around the former storeroom upstairs under the eaves over the store. The moving van had already left; houseplants and these final cartons of precious items had been transported in the brown Chevy van that Alan had bought when he became a storekeeper. The fresh white ceiling of the apartment was so low that Alan would have had to avoid bumping his head in the doorway, and even at five-nine Tom seemed too tall here, or was that because of his entire appearance, his solid presence, the white curly hair, the white beard and mustache trimmed to a sea captain's, the blue eyes behind gold-rimmed trifocal spectacles, the capable look of him standing here in chambray work shirt and jeans? Bev was only an inch shorter than he, but she didn't make the apartment seem cramped. It'll be okay, Snowy told herself, with just Ruhamah and me here. It won't be claustrophobic. But it'll still be dark; the windows were small, and although the carpenters had installed a French door beside the kitchen sink, she couldn't afford the extra expense of dormers or skylights.

Tom said, "So this should go here?" Remembering the apartment he and Joanne had rented when they first got married, he deposited the pewter carton in the kitchen section at the back of the apartment, where cartons of dishes and cookware were stacked beside the harvest table on the rug that, he knew, had been braided by Snowy's grandmother. No wall separated the living-room section. His and Joanne's apartment in the married students' barracks at Rumford Teachers' College, now Rumford State College, had had a similar living-room-kitchen combo, as did the fire warden's log cabin in which he now lived atop Mount Pascataquac. He watched Snowy set down her carton. She looked skinny, jangled, and so pale she seemed to be fading out of sight. A muscle was jumping in her jaw, an old familiar distress signal. He said, "May I suggest you don't do any more unpacking today? Let's all go out for a pizza."

Bev said, "I'll beg off. I'm going to go collapse." Because there was no guest room in the apartment, with the pull-out sofa now lacking privacy in the living room here, Bev had rented a room at the Gunthwaite Inn, and not simply for tonight but for a week. Roger thought she was coming home tomorrow, the self-satisfied nincompoop.

Ruhamah emerged from one of the two bedrooms, the one Snowy insisted she take because it was larger and had a view across the village to the mountains. Ruhamah had heard what Tom said; you could hear everything in this dollhouse. Which had no dolls of any sort. Last week Ruhamah had given her lifetime collection of toys, mostly stuffed animals, to the village day-care center. She reminded Snowy, "I'm going to Jennifer's."

Snowy had also been invited to dinner tonight by Jennifer's mother, Fay Rollins, when Fay phoned last week to tell Snowy that the details of a planned pajama party for mothers had been worked out so it would be held the following Saturday night, but Snowy hadn't wanted to test her post-agoraphobia courage any more this weekend than dinner at Charl and Dudley's. Which pizza place was Tom thinking of? Because of agoraphobia, she hadn't eaten in a restaurant in years.

He said to her, "Or I could go get a pizza and bring it here."

Again she looked around at the remains of her belongings squashed into this attic. Remember others less fortunate, she admonished herself. Some people would consider this spacious, plenty of room for a couple of families or more! Alan's wing chair was too big, and it had no fireplace to face, not even their Jøtul woodstove. She should have sold his chair. She should have let Bev take his clothes away to the Goodwill box, but she had packed them and brought them along although she *had* sold his bureau. She glanced down at her old sweatshirt and jeans. "Can I wear these to a pizza place?"

Tom said, "Sure."

"Then let's go out."

So Tom opened the French door onto a stoop where, when the movers were finished, Snowy had arranged the tubs of vegetable seedlings and hung the basket of red impatiens, and they all trooped down the outside staircase into the June evening. The store closed at noon on Sundays. Tomorrow, Monday morning, she would have a quick commute to work, just down these stairs or the inside staircase.

Bev hugged Snowy. "I'll be back tomorrow and you can sprint up now and then between customers to direct me where to put things." She got into the Toyota she'd rented in Gunthwaite. "Bye!"

And Ruhamah got into the Subaru, and as the two cars drove off, Tom asked Snowy, his voice suddenly diffident, "Want to see the new coffin factory?"

She said, "Oh, Tom, you did rent the building?"

"Yes."

They walked across the store's gravel parking lot and past the little white post office. The next building, set farther back at the end of a long driveway, was a large gray barn, its double doors facing the street. Behind it she could see an old apple tree and a patch of field much like the one behind the store, snarled grasses and bushes, daisies and buttercups, with woods continuing to encroach.

She said, "This barn has been vacant ever since we moved here. How come? I can't remember if Alan ever knew. Does it belong to the post office?"

"No," Tom said, turning up the driveway. "It belonged to a house that burned flat back in the thirties. They saved the barn. I tracked down the owner in the town hall records. Old codger, Arthur Bronson. He lives in North Woodcombe. He must come in the store, so you probably know him by sight. After the fire he sold the house lot to the post office for parking but kept the barn and rented storage space in it. Then he got tired of the bother of the storage business, though he couldn't bring himself to sell what's left of the original family place. He still won't sell, but we had a hunker and he agreed to rent the barn to me, with me paying for renovating, and if he ever decides to sell, he'll let me know first." Tom took keys out of his pocket and unlocked a smaller door to the right of the big doors.

Wondering if having to rent, not buy, was a relief to Tom, because it wasn't permanent and he didn't know how long he was going to stick around, Snowy stepped into a haze of dust motes and a whiff of long-ago manure. The barn at Hurricane Farm had been turned into a gentleman farmer's playroom by the people who'd owned the farm before she and Alan bought it, yet the same aroma remained. The first barn she'd fallen in love with had belonged to Julia and Fred, Bev's mother and stepfather. It had been gray, looming behind the white shutterless Cape, surrounded with fields, an apple orchard, woods. Growing up, Snowy had spent as much time as possible at her best friend's house in the country. Snowy had loved Julia, and now Julia was dead, taking an overdose of sleeping pills in the Florida bungalow to which she and Fred had moved when he retired from the Gunthwaite bank where he'd been the head teller. Julia had a reason for killing herself; she was being consumed by cancer. Alan's reason was impending bankruptcy, which was no reason. Snowy tried to think of his depression as a disease, like cancer.

"—business zone," Tom was saying. "Arthur Bronson can rent or sell it to a business, so renting it to North Country Coffins won't be a problem."

"What about the noise of the machinery?"

"It's a small operation. We had no complaints in Newburgh." Tom walked deeper into the barn, and she followed, looking at the old stalls and up at the rafters and hayloft.

Alan's midlife crisis two years ago had meant going into business for himself. He had needed to get away from the pressures of working for the Old Eastbourne project of restoring historic buildings on the waterfront, a job he had gone into right at the project's inception when he graduated from UNH as a history major. She had worked there too, until Ruhamah was born, doing research and writing brochures. Before they'd bought the Pevensay house on the ocean, they had lived on the job, so to speak, in an apartment in the Ruhamah Reed House that under Alan's direction had been restored to Federal-style beauty. Tom had had *two* midlife crises. During the first, eleven years ago, he had quit his job teaching English up in the White-Mountains town of Newburgh and returned to his first love, woodworking, by buying an old coffin factory there, discovering a market for plain pine coffins. Like Alan, he had become his own boss, and unlike Alan he'd been successful. The second crisis had occurred when, tiring of the work—and Joanne?—and intrigued by the fire towers he'd climbed while hiking mountains, Tom had applied for a fire-warden job this year and been assigned to the Mount Pascataquac fire tower, which had just been reopened. Snowy had met him by chance on Pascataquac when Mimi had dragged her up to the summit to see if it would be the right spot for the wedding. His younger son, David, worked for him at the factory and now was running it alone until, everyone assumed, Tom returned this winter when the seasonal fire-tower job ended. Snowy looked around the barn, trying to imagine North Country Coffins here, and then she realized that the things Tom built in this business were created only to be burned or buried. She knew that some people bought coffins from him ahead of time, and he designed these for dual purposes if, in the meantime, a customer wanted to use one as a blanket chest or coffee table or bookcase (what a healthy or ghoulish attitude such customers had!), but sooner or later these pieces of furniture went into an oven or a grave.

Tom said, "I'll keep the stalls, to store lumber in. I'll put in a hot-air furnace. Bring the machinery and equipment down from Newburgh. Put in a blower system for the sawdust." He pointed at the open stairway on the left, which led up to the hayloft. "Living quarters. I'll floor over the entire loft, and do a kitchen-living-room combo like yours."

"Does Joanne—um, will your son be working here?"

"I gave him a call. He'll come next week for a look. He knows the town a little, from when he was on the Newburgh basketball team and they played Woodcombe."

"Does he live at home?"

"No, he rents an apartment with another kid."

So to talk with him Tom hadn't called home. So Joanne didn't necessarily yet know that Tom wasn't planning to return. Maybe, Snowy thought, I'm making this too complicated. Tom could have just plain phoned Joanne and told her; he couldn't have told her in person because he hadn't gone home this week on his days off, instead spending the time working on the apartment. At Mimi's wedding reception, Tom had said that this separation had been coming on for years. Joanne could be relieved to be rid of him. But Joanne had known him longer than Snowy had; Joanne and Tom had been classmates since childhood—Tom had given her rides home from school on his bike!—whereas Snowy hadn't met him until she started high school, and then it was Bev he had asked out. Tom Forbes, a sophomore and football player and desired by all the girls. Not until March of the next year, 1955, had he really noticed Snowy. Throughout these school years, he and Joanne had only been friends, unlikely as that had seemed, Joanne with her lovely cheekbones and dark glossy chestnut hair, Joanne a cheerleader and Queen of the Junior Prom. But when they got to Rumford Teachers' College where Joanne was an elementary major and Tom switched from shop to English, the platonic nature of their friendship changed to romantic. They married, they had three kids, they taught in Newburgh. Passion might have ebbed now, but they had known each other forever.

Snowy said obliquely, "I'd be happy to meet David. Bring him into the store for a Pepsi or something, if you want." In Tom's cabin on Pascataquac she had seen a photo of the kids: The boys had got Joanne's cheekbones; the girl, Tom's curls.

"Okay," Tom said, thinking of putting the old factory up for sale, the various costs of moving the machinery here, the renovations, moving his life from Newburgh to Woodcombe. Snowy stepped closer to him, and he folded his arms around her. At

Mimi's wedding reception, Snowy had reminded him how, when he'd broken up with her in high school because they'd got too serious too soon, he had said they ought to make a date for four years hence, when he would be through college. Instead, he had met her again by chance all these years later.

Snowy's stomach growled, as it was apt to.

They laughed, and Tom said, "We'd better get two large, loaded." In high school Snowy had been famous for her appetite. He kissed her.

She didn't have to stand on tiptoe, as she had with Alan.

Snowy was glad Tom kept his arm around her shoulders when they walked back through the barn, but outside they walked apart along the sidewalk, although Snowy figured most of the town knew that they were more than old friends, that the Widow Sutherland had abandoned her mourning in a shockingly short time, for she had been observed returning from the Pascataquac trailhead early one morning, having spent the night in his cabin. But she had climbed the mountain to him desperate with grief, after almost walking into Murray Cove the way Alan had. She and Tom had caught up in many ways that night, making love together for the second time in their lives.

She hopped up into his Jeep, and off they drove past the town hall, the church, the library, the historical society, and the old white school building that contained both junior and senior high schools, same as Gunthwaite's school system in the olden days.

Snowy said, "We've never had a pizza together."

"It hadn't been invented back then."

She laughed. "It was just reaching New Hampshire in our teens. Or Gunthwaite, at least. Julia, Bev's mother, served the first I ever had, a frozen one. Then we began making them, usually from a Chef Boyardee box. But it was really a college thing. My roommate, Harriet, couldn't believe I'd never eaten pepperoni until—I forgot to tell you, she phoned me yesterday! From Israel! She's doing landscapes now, and she's painting the Golan Heights."

"Isn't that a dangerous spot? It's always in the news."

"That was my reaction, but she didn't mention any danger." Snowy paused. She remembered that when she met Alan at Old Eastbourne the first time, to do research for her thesis, she had ended up nervously having lunch in his apartment, reciting a Ruhamah Reed poem at his request and telling him she thought the poet hadn't married for fear of dying in childbirth. Snowy had said to Alan, "Things were awfully dangerous then." He had looked at her and said, "I'm not dangerous." Then he'd said, "I'm scared," and she'd realized that the only other male she'd ever heard admitting to being scared had been Tom, scared because he missed her too much when she went away to Girls' State, scared enough to break up with her. Alan had been scared by love at first sight. Sometimes the similarities between these two men were what scared her most.

Out on the main road, Tom headed north, in the opposite direction from Gunthwaite. She hadn't been up this way in a long time. Locked in her prison of agoraphobia, she hadn't gone anywhere.

Tom asked, "Where'd we go on our first date? The movies?"

"Yes," Snowy said, undismayed that he didn't remember exactly. Men didn't. "A double feature. The first movie was a Western with Zachary Scott and the feature was a romantic romp with Tony Curtis and Gene Nelson as sailors on leave in Paris who meet Corinne Calvert, Gloria DeHaven. Then we went to Hooper's."

"Of course." Everybody always went to Hooper's Dairy Bar.

She said, "The plan was to use the coupon for a free Awful-Awful that I'd got when I drank three of those things in one sitting, but neither of us could face it. I copied you and had an English muffin and black coffee. My first cup of coffee ever."

"We went parking," he said, making an educated guess.

"On the Cat Path. I was terrified. I'd never gone parking alone before, just on double dates, and you were so grown-up. You had a car—and not any car but that cream-colored Chevy convertible—and you smoked and you drank coffee, black coffee. *So* sophisticated."

He laughed and pulled into the parking lot of a dark red building with an Italian flag flying and an upscale sign that said Parmigiano.

Oh, damn him, Snowy thought, damn men. This wasn't a pizza joint, it was a restaurant, and she *should* have changed her clothes. Then she recalled from her pre-agoraphobia years that summer people went into restaurants wearing an extreme definition of casual. Well, she could pretend she was a flatlander, but she and Tom surely looked instead like locals in work clothes. As she stepped down from the Jeep, her head spun dizzily and she panicked. The agoraphobia was back! For the past month she had been testing the depths of her reserves of strength, and this silly trip to get a pizza was what would wreck her!

She took a deep breath, counted to four, exhaled, and walked beside Tom into the restaurant's aroma of oregano.

"Nonsmoking, please," Tom said to the hostess, who led them into a dim room with rosy light from red candles on the tables.

Snowy sank into a chair.

A waitress approached, wearing red, holding menus with red padded covers.

"Beer?" Tom asked Snowy. "Shall we start with one large pizza and see if that's enough?"

She said, "Actually, these days I can only manage half a medium." Alan would go get two medium pizzas, one for him and her to split, one without onions for fussy Ruhamah.

Tom said, "Want to study the menu? There's other stuff."

"No," she said. "Pizza is fine." The waitress was regarding her oddly. Snowy knew it must be more than her moving-day clothes; her face must be sweaty, her expression glassy-eyed.

"We've decided already," Tom told the waitress. "Two drafts, Miller Light, and a medium pizza, loaded, please."

The waitress transferred the look to him. "Sure thing," she said, and went off.

"A new one," Tom said, pushing a jar of bread sticks toward Snowy.

She clutched it. "Do you eat here often?"

"No. Simpler to stay on the mountain. Did I behave myself?"

"What?"

"On our first date, when we went parking."

Snowy laughed and broke a bread stick and handed him half. As they crunched together, she remembered the parked convertible, the heated scent of Old Spice (him) and White Lilac (her). "Yes, you behaved very nicely indeed, but the windows got steamed up."

"We always had a tendency to steam up windows."

They smiled at each other.

"Okay?" Tom said.

She nodded.

He said, "It's been a hell of a weekend for you."

"Thank you for getting the apartment ready and helping with the move."

The waitress returned carrying a tray. Calmed, Snowy now registered that she was older than the other waitresses, about their own age, short and chunky, her hair too black, her eye makeup gaudy, her face showing the sharp edges of a hard life. Snowy remembered waitressing at Sweetland in high school; she'd been good at it, but she had hated it. If I didn't have the store, Snowy thought, this could be what I'd be doing to survive. If I fail with the store, as Alan did, I could be doing this. Her grandmother, her father's mother, had worked as a waitress after her grandfather died; waitressing in Manchester, Nanny had supported Daddy and his sisters.

The waitress set down their beer glasses, glanced at them both again as they said, "Thank you," and retreated without replying.

Tom said, "Does she look familiar?"

Snowy considered. "Maybe."

"You must run into familiar faces a lot, living near Gunthwaite. I'll have to get used to it."

She asked, "Then you're really moving down here to stay?" The question sounded idiotic. Hadn't he just shown her the barn he'd rented for the new location of North Country Coffins, with the hayloft for his new apartment?

He answered the question she didn't ask. "After I work out

arrangements with David, I'll tell Joanne." He reached across the table and took her hand, holding it so tightly that residual bread-stick crumbs dug in. Then he raised his glass of beer.

She lifted hers, which trembled only slightly. From anguish and despair, was she passing into the healing of time? But, as did Edna St. Vincent Millay in a sonnet, she doubted that time really did heal.

Tom said, "To your new apartment."

"And to yours," she said, knowing they were talking about new lives.

CHAPTER TWO

ANOTHER BARN. FAY and Martin Rollins's house was a converted barn, the remains of a farm out on Phinney Road, its pastures and fields overgrown with junipers and steeplebush, hemlocks and birches, through which the old stone walls crept.

Snowy had never been actually inside the house before, but she imagined that these wide open spaces of this cathedral-ceiling living room would usually be dominated by the Rollinses' three teenagers. Tonight, however, the kids were staying with friends, and Martin was confined to his in-home office upstairs (his usual habitat because he was semiretired from a computer company in the Boston suburb from which the Rollinses had moved), and the place belonged to the women invited to the brainstorm of Fay Rollins and Joyce Parker: a mothers' pajama party.

The guests included Bev, invited by Fay upon learning Snowy had a friend visiting. When Snowy and Bev arrived, Fay made only a stab at introductions because the party was getting going fast, with much laughter, music, videos, and shrieks of delight over the food provided by Fay from Indulgences, the bakery she owned in Gunthwaite. Snowy couldn't resist sampling a chocolate truffle cake, while Bev grabbed a glass of Chablis and piece of quiche, before they carried their overnight bags into a downstairs bedroom that belonged to Jennifer Rollins, Ruhamah's friend. The wallpaper surrounded them with a rain forest of dark jungle green where monkeys dangled, and Bev, looking up at the ceiling wallpapered into a forest canopy, said, "Girlhood. Remember the water-stained wallpaper in my bedroom and the way I tried to hide it with photos from our Dramatics Club plays? How I envied you your pink-and-white bedroom."

Snowy said wryly, "My folks. Every room in the house on display, including mine." Julia, Bev's mother, although a craftsperson, a weaver, had not been house-proud.

Then, as they changed into their nightclothes, Bev said, "I'm on the horns of a dilemma."

"You're horny?" Snowy buttoned her nightshirt. It was her best summer one, L. L. Bean floral-pink pima cotton, but it was far from new. Bev had put on brand-new lime silk pajamas, and in her open overnight bag lay a matching robe.

"Ha-ha," Bev said, sipping wine, "or as Puddles would say, hardeeharhar. Hey, I think we should call Puddles tonight. It doesn't seem right to be at a pajama party without her."

"What's the dilemma?" Snowy tied the belt of her pink seersucker bathrobe.

Taking her phone charge card out of her pocketbook, Bev moved toward the telephone on the bedside table. "You're unpacked and settled into your apartment, so I should go home, but today I went into a real-estate office in Gunthwaite to ask about houses for rent and if there might be a remote chance of one near a riding stable."

Snowy thought of a million implications, mainly divorce. "Oh, Bev."

"But during the discussion I couldn't help talking shop, and before we were done Geoffrey Plumley, the owner, offered me a job—if I can pass the New Hampshire exam. Another exam! I assumed when I graduated from Katy Gibbs I'd got those wretched ordeals over with forever!"

Snowy plopped down on the bed. Its bedspread design was of endangered species, and she squashed a peregrine falcon. "A job, in Gunthwaite?"

"The real-estate boom is over, he says, especially for second homes up here. Isn't my timing exquisite? But because of the slump, some of his salespeople who need a steady income have given up and got regular jobs instead of depending on commissions."

"You've been married to Roger for twenty-eight years. You dated him off and on for five years before that."

Bev picked up the receiver, and she and Snowy looked at each other. Out in the living room the noise level of the mothers would have astonished their children.

Bev said, "Puddles was ready to divorce Guy, wasn't she?"

"But the man she was having the affair with went back to his wife."

Bev tapped numbers. "Our house is rebelling," she told Snowy, "just as it always does when I'm away. Every time Roger phones me he's flummoxed by another disaster, though yet none of the magnitude of the time Etta's horse fell in the swimming pool. He insists I come home immediately and deal with everything from a broken microwave to whatever's gone wrong with the dining-room chandelier. Then there are the kids. Leon isn't doing the yard work and odd jobs he's supposed to. Etta changed her mind about the outfit I bought her for the last-day-of-school party, and she went shopping with a friend and God knows what she'll look like—hello, Puddles?" Bev held the phone out so Snowy could hear the shriek all the way from Puddles in Helmsdale, South Carolina.

"Bev? What's happened? Did Snowy get moved okay? I haven't called her because I didn't want to seem like I was interfering."

With mixed guilt and satisfaction, Snowy realized that Puddles, usually blunt and forthright, was still reacting to the shock of Snowy's hanging up on her last month when Puddles, an Advanced Registered Nurse Practitioner, had badgered her too much about starting grief therapy and phobia sessions, which Snowy had avoided doing. At Mimi's wedding, Puddles had apologized.

"I'm still in New Hampshire," Bev said, "and guess where we're calling from!" She handed the phone to Snowy.

"From the apartment?" Puddles guessed, standing in her blue kitchen-sunroom, looking through the doorway into her living room at the ornate dark furniture that had belonged to her husband's family, the lush Southern evening caressing the familiar interior through the plantation shutters. This house had been built years ago by her husband, Guy, who was a contractor. She loved it. In the beginning of their marriage, they had lived in a series of houses Guy built, moving to another whenever the one they were in was sold, and this impermanence added to the shock of moving to South Carolina, Guy's native state. When she became pregnant, she'd insisted on staying put in this house, and when she went back to work her salary had saved it through the ups and downs of Guy's business. Now, with Amy and Susan, their twin daughters, grown and gone, the house was too goddamn big but she couldn't imagine leaving it. Guy, nine years older than she, had begun daydreaming about retiring to Hilton Head to play golf full-time, and he talked of condos with no responsibilities, but Puddles didn't want to budge. She tried to imagine unloading almost everything and moving into an attic apartment, as Snowy had just done.

Snowy said, "We're at a pajama party!"

Puddles said, "Snowy? That's you? A pajama party?"

"At a friend's house. It's a pajama party for mothers, and they have one of those new things, those VCRs, and they're showing a video of male strippers!"

Bev said, projecting her stage voice so Puddles could hear, "I fail to see why women get excited at such a sight. I myself get all embarrassed and repulsed."

Puddles said, "Well, I still have that Burt Reynolds centerfold on the ceiling over the examining table, and it's still a useful distraction."

Snowy said, "And the food! Even you, Puddles, would love everything. There's a mocha mousse cake I'm going to try next, and—"

"A good sign," said nurse Puddles, "your appetite is back. You're socializing. How are you feeling otherwise? Are you still jogging?"

"Yes, around the village at five a.m." Snowy used to run the Roller Coaster Road, past the Thornes' farm. "Then I jump into the shower, and then I open the store at seven and remain on my feet until six p.m., so I'm getting plenty of exercise."

“Put a chair behind the counter,” Puddles advised, stroking Reese, the old calico cat snoozing in a kitchen chair; years ago Puddles’s daughters had chosen the orange-and-brown kitten and named him after Reese’s Peanut Butter Cups. “Give yourself a break. You aren’t working at a supermarket, for Christ’s sake, so there must be some slack time.” In high school, Puddles had worked summers as a cashier at the Gunthwaite A&P, instead of waitressing like Snowy and Bev at Sweetland.

“Slack time makes me nervous—no customers, no money—so I dust the shelves or something. It’ll get busier as more summer people come back. Winter will be full of slack time, though.” Wanting to change the subject, Snowy said, “Bev has some news,” and returned the receiver to Bev.

Bev mouthed at Snowy, “Do I?”

Snowy shrugged.

Bev told Puddles, “I’ve been offered a job at a Gunthwaite real-estate office, if I can pass the New Hampshire real-estate exam, and I’m considering it.”

“Holy shit!” Puddles yelled. “You mean, you’re going to leave Connecticut? Leave Roger?”

“Well,” Bev said, and gulped Chablis.

Puddles said, “After that stunt he pulled with your exam results, he deserves a good scare. You’ll move to Gunthwaite, with Etta?”

Bev said, “I can’t trust him ever again. I keep wondering what other stunts he has pulled. Other women.”

Puddles said, “He wasn’t unfaithful to you in high school. That time he broke up with you, it was because you were dating that water-skier behind his back, so when he went out with other girls afterwards, it was your fault.”

Bev rolled her eyes at Snowy. Pity Puddles’s patients, if they needed a gentle bedside manner! Bev said, “The main thing is, he didn’t take me seriously when I got this urge to sell houses. It may be a pathetic ambition, but he couldn’t deal with the prospect of my becoming anything more than a wife and mother.”

Puddles said, "But Bev, Roger is a lawyer. You'll get screwed in a divorce."

"Not a divorce," Bev said. "Not yet, maybe not ever. Just a time-out. The kids are gone, except Etta—well, Leon, too, but he's old enough to cope. Maybe if Leon comes to Gunthwaite, he could find a job that would suit him."

Eek, Snowy thought. Leon, not long-distance but in the vicinity? Ne'er-do-well Leon, who, unlike his older brother, Dick, didn't have Roger's ambition or even his basketball prowess? Maybe what he'd inherited was Bev's old raison d'etre: having fun. Then Snowy thought how Bev as a real-estate agent would be joining the enemy, selling and developing. Doing this down in Connecticut wouldn't have been so bad, because Connecticut seemed doomed by New York, but in New Hampshire, that was different.

Bev was saying, "If Roger is difficult, I won't be destitute. I've got what Mother left me, and maybe I'll actually sell some properties."

Puddles asked, "Where in Gunthwaite will you live? A condo? There sure are a lot of them, multiplying like amoebae, like down here. I couldn't believe my eyes. I'm thinking I ought to come up and visit Maine sometime, to see the changes in my home state, see it before it's unrecognizable." In junior high, Puddles had been a New Girl when her family moved to Gunthwaite from Portland after her father was offered a foreman's job at the Gunthwaite Shoe Factory. The homeroom teacher had asked Snowy to look after her and make her feel at home. Here in South Carolina after her marriage to Guy, a patient she'd met during her training at Massachusetts General Hospital, Puddles had felt like a New Girl much longer.

"Not a condo," Bev said, "though the *idea* of them is appealing, right at this moment in my life, because they're so contained, so compact, so—single. But the more I thought about it, the more I felt it would be easier for Etta to continue living in a house. I've got to make this change as smooth as possible for her; she'll be traumatized enough by having to leave the riding instructor she adores. Besides, any condo I could afford would be too small a stage for me and would cramp my style. The realtor I talked with, the one who's offered me a job, didn't have any rental that would suit, but he's going to check around."

Puddles asked, "What will you do with all your stuff?"

"I haven't thought that far," Bev said. "It depends on what I find, furnished or unfurnished." Her collection of pine cupboards! Would Roger notice what she took from the Ninfield house, unless he was forced to sit or sleep on the floor? Her jelly cupboard, she must have that even if she rented a furnished house. And maybe the pie cupboard and— How could she leave her beloved swimming pool? Well, she couldn't shift *that* to Gunthwaite, so she'd better take her detested treadmill. She added, "Right now, I'm simply having fun at a pajama party."

Puddles said, "Remember the last pajama party I had at my house, toward the end of our senior year? Mom had made celery sticks stuffed with cream cheese, but while we were fooling around and making pizza and telling those title-author jokes like *The Tiger's Revenge* by Claud Balls, somebody left the plate of the celery sticks on the furnace register and they must've gone bad, and Linda Littlefield ate some and threw up all over the place." There was a silence at the end of the line, and Puddles belatedly remembered that Tom, who had been dating Bev again then after breaking up with Snowy, had brought Bev to the pajama party after their date but had left with Snowy, all of which had caused Bev to end her best-friendship with Snowy until Puddles engineered a reconciliation in Boston that winter when Puddles was at Mass. General, Bev at Katharine Gibbs, and Snowy had arrived to work at Commonwealth Publishing during her Non-Resident Term.

"Linda," Snowy said, not looking at Bev, thinking of Linda Littlefield, the only girl on their JV cheerleading squad who didn't make Varsity. Linda had, however, made the Court of the Junior Prom Queen, along with the twins and Patty Nichols; Snowy hadn't been chosen. Bev had been queen. And the night of Puddles's last pajama party, Snowy had stolen Tom back from Bev, had driven away in his cream-colored convertible to lose her virginity officially.

Curiosity consuming her, Puddles said, "I wonder whatever happened to Linda. She went to Skidmore College, didn't she? One of us ought to have attended the reunions, to keep tabs on what happened. Dudley probably knows." Dudley had been president of their class every year since junior high. "Or Charl."

Bev let the awkward moment slide away. "Snowy, make a mental note to ask them." But Bev thought how she and Tom had worked together painting Snowy's apartment like old white-haired buddies. God, high school could haunt! Down in Connecticut she had created a whole new life for herself, with Roger who had been eager to shake the dust of Gunthwaite from his shoes, and with her children. What was she doing, considering a move back to Gunthwaite?

Puddles couldn't control her curiosity about Tom, either. "Have you seen Tom since Mimi's wedding? Learned anything more about what's going on with him and Joanne?" When she'd talked to him at the wedding, the situation had sounded to her like a trial separation, such as Bev seemed to be considering.

Snowy said, "He helped with my move, and he'll be making one of his own. He has rented a barn on Main Street, where he'll move his coffin business." This past Tuesday, Tom had come into the store with a young man whose handsomeness was eerie, for Snowy realized immediately, seeing him in person, how it was based not just on Joanne's cheekbones but all her beauty translated into masculine form. David was taller than Tom but had his burliness. Twenty-two, five years younger than his brother, Brandon, David had also inherited Tom's woodworking skills and had gone to a state technical college before starting work at Tom's coffin factory. Snowy didn't know what, if anything, Tom had told him about her before Tom introduced them, saying, "Snowy, this is my son David, and David, this is Henrietta Snow Sutherland. We go back a long way." That night Tom had phoned her to say David had liked Woodcombe and the barn enough to agree to make the move with him. So Tom was returning home today, to tell Joanne. Where would Tom sleep?

"Thought so!" gloated Puddles. "A trial separation, now a divorce!"

There was a knock on the door, and Fay came in carrying a plate of Toll House cookies that wafted chocolate. "Everything okay?" Fay said. "Hot from the oven!"

Snowy said, "Gotta go, Puddles. Fresh cookies."

"Wait," Puddles said, "you have to hear the brilliant thing my grandson did."

Oops, Snowy thought, Bev and I should've remembered to ask after him. Susan, one of Puddles's twins, had recently produced Guy James Cram Hammond, Puddles's first grandchild.

"He did the eye lock!" Puddles said. "You know, that moment when the baby stops gazing into the distance, drooling, and focuses on you. His eyes followed Susan all around the room. Bye!"

Snowy and Bev each took a cookie, and they went with Fay out to the living room, where the VCR was playing a video of *Hud* and Bev said, "Ah, Paul Newman, sigh and swoon," and women were sitting around on sofas, chairs, and cushions on the floor, in clothes that ranged from a ratty flannel bathrobe to a lacy negligee, with lots in between, so to Snowy's relief she fitted right in. They were partly watching the movie, partly talking, and doing plenty of laughing and eating. One woman, who wore sweatpants with a T-shirt that read Grow Your Own Dope: Plant a Man, seized Fay's plate and said, "Did you hear the one about the guy on his deathbed who suddenly smells Toll House cookies, his favorite cookies, so he drags himself into the kitchen and finds his wife taking a cookie sheet of them out of the oven and putting them on a cooling rack. With his last ounce of strength he reaches for one, the very last cookie of his life, and his wife raps his knuckles with the spatula and says, 'Don't touch! They're for the funeral!'"

Snowy joined in the laughter, which suddenly dwindled. The woman who'd told the joke looked stricken. Everybody had remembered that Snowy's husband had died last month.

At the store, Snowy had encountered straightforward condolences, awkward sympathy, embarrassed silence, and she had learned to pretend to be Puddles, matter-of-fact. Now she said, "That's okay. Alan didn't want a funeral, so what did I have instead? A wedding reception for the daughter of my best friend, with the wedding cake and other goodies from Fay's!"

And Bev took over, ensconcing herself on a cushion, telling the story of the mountaintop wedding as entertainingly as she'd told it to Charl and Darl, adding new embellishments as they occurred to her.

Snowy curled up on a nearby cushion and listened, hoping her smile didn't look so tight as it felt. Her wedding anniversary was next Wednesday.

Then she remembered how Tom had long ago asked, "What is it you girls do at pajama parties?" She had replied, "That's a secret." He'd said, "When I was a kid I really believed that all the women in the world got together at meetings at midnight to decide how to make life miserable for us. Like, they would decide you couldn't listen to *House of Mystery* because it was too scary, and if they made a cake, you couldn't have any because it was for company."

Women were laughing at Bev's story. Snowy thought of the deathbed-cookies joke and this time her laughter was genuine.

INTO THE WHITE Mountains Tom drove, his venerable Jeep chugging along the familiar route up through Franconia Notch. He turned west toward the setting sun. He knew he should have started out this morning and got it over with, but instead he'd deluded himself about work on the barn that absolutely had to be done today in preparation for moving the factory equipment. Procrastinating, dubbing around. Coward.

He reached his destination, Newburgh, a river valley town where once there had been a logging industry as well as farming. The long log drives were over, but tales were still told here about colorful characters like Axe-handle O'Grady, a logger, boozer, and general plug-ugly, but, it was said, good-hearted if stupid. Tom slowed the Jeep to look up at the Victorian high school on the hill, a beauty spoiled by a cinderblock elementary-school wing and a new gymnasium addition. Sixteen years he'd taught there, perhaps its most colorful character, the eccentric head of the English Department. He'd become famous his first day of teaching when a boy at the back of the classroom made some wisecrack and Tom, a terrified new teacher taking attendance at the front of the class, had thrown his attendance book at him, hitting him squarely on the noggin. Afterward, he realized he'd subconsciously been inspired by Gunthwaite's Mr. Foster, a College Prep English teacher he had never had but about whom he'd heard from Joanne and Snowy and other College Prep kids; amongst Mr. Foster's many antics was throwing blackboard erasers. Such discipline techniques had not been taught in Rumford Teachers' College's Principles of Education and Principles of Teaching courses, but after the attendance-book incident Tom hadn't had any trouble with any student, and apparently during the following years he'd become famous for more than that, because students returned at Thanksgiving from their freshman year at college to tell him the jump they'd got on their new classmates, thanks to him.

He drove on down Main Street past two churches, the post office, a grocery store much larger than Snowy's, the Sit 'n' Snack Luncheonette to which teachers were not permitted to go for lunch because taxpayers felt they were paid to stay in school all day, a small lumber mill, and North Country Coffins in the old coffin factory building he'd bought and renovated when he could not stand teaching a moment longer. Yet when the business he'd envisioned, doing custom work for people who appreciated the idea of simple pine coffins, had instead become mostly wholesale work for crematories, he'd got bored again. He had earlier taken up hiking and been intrigued by the fire towers on summits; this year he had found the fire-warden job. Joanne hadn't been exactly thrilled by the first of these career changes. She had been furious. But as for the second, when he'd told her that he wanted to try fire towers she had just said, "It's a worthy cause." He thought he detected in her tone relief at getting him out from underfoot.

Driving past a row of shabby identical mill houses, Tom glanced at the one in which David rented an apartment. Years ago Tom had recognized that David was a lot like him, although David's reserved nature was unmistakable instead of disguised as Tom's was by an apparently casual happy-go-lucky manner. When Tom had phoned him to come down to look at the Woodcombe barn, had explained that he wanted to move the business here, and had said, "Your mother and I, as you've probably noticed, are on the verge of an amicable divorce, now that you kids are grown-up," David hadn't got angry; he'd just gone very quiet, then said, "Oh." Tom had said, "No need to mention the move to your mother. She and I will discuss it Saturday." If, after being introduced to Snowy, David had added her into the situation, he didn't say so. Probably figured his dad was too old for such stuff, anyway, and thus it didn't enter his head.

Tom turned onto Cobble Road. Driving past woods, he upbraided himself for not phoning Joanne to tell her he'd be coming home. But she knew his schedule. But lately it had been erratic, and his explanation had been a lie about helping some guys paint a house, not quite a lie, just a variation on the truth about painting Snowy's apartment.

Was he hoping that if he arrived home unannounced, he'd catch Joanne in bed with someone and that would get him off the hook, would solve his problem, would absolve him? She would have the house to herself tonight. Their older son, Brandon (Tom's middle name, which he hated but Joanne liked), who would be twenty-seven next month, had gone into the Army, as had Tom's older and younger brothers, a decision that to Tom seemed the equivalent of choosing to go to prison, but at least Brandon had graduated from UNH first. A pilot stationed at Fort Stewart in Georgia, Captain Brandon Forbes wasn't coming home for a visit in the near future. Tom had gathered vaguely from Joanne that there was a girlfriend, a Southern belle. Libby, their youngest child, a sophomore at UNH, was a forestry major and working this summer for the White Mountain National Forest at the Pemigewasset Ranger Station; she and her high-school best friend, who was going to Plymouth State

College and waitressing at a Plymouth restaurant, had sublet an apartment in Plymouth from a couple of upperclassmen.

So Joanne would be alone. Unless, a party-giver, she was throwing a party for some reason he'd forgotten.

Snowy was at a pajama party tonight.

He braked. A female partridge cakewalked out of the bushes, paused at the edge of the road, then put her head down and made a dash across. He inhaled a scent like fresh corn silk from the roadside grasses and sat waiting to see if any babies followed. Babies. Brandon, born in Rumford while they were living in the married students' barracks, had been unplanned. Unplanned? Brandon had been the result of rape, of Tom's getting drunk and randy and jumping on his sleeping wife without bothering to use a condom, without stopping when Joanne woke up and screamed at him to stop. The pregnancy almost ruined Joanne's career, because in those Dark Ages pregnant women weren't allowed to do the semester of student teaching required for graduation. Abortions were illegal back then. Tom, desperate with a guilt that had never left him, had struck upon a solution: Joanne finished all her requirements except student teaching, took a semester off, gave birth to Brandon, and when Tom graduated that spring he found a school system, Newburgh's, that would let Joanne do her student teaching in the elementary school while he taught in the high school. Thus, Joanne could graduate only one semester late. On Saturdays, Tom had worked at the Newburgh lumber mill to pay for a baby-sitter to look after Brandon while Joanne student-taught, and he'd kept on running a molding machine there summers for extra money after she graduated and started teaching second grade. The town of Newburgh paid her a salary of $4,000 a year and him $4,200; together that added up to about what Sam Page, a high-school buddy and husband of Adele, the girl who'd been co-captain with Joanne of the GHS Varsity cheerleading squad, was making driving a Coca-Cola truck, having left the confines of a job at Trask's, Gunthwaite's main industry, where Tom's father and Joanne's had worked—and Snowy's. So that Joanne could take time out to have

David and Libby and stay home with them until they were in school, Tom moonlighted again at the lumber mill. Had he finally overreacted to all this atonement, at the end of his tether, dropping out of teaching, then running away from home?

The night of the rape, that fury of lust had been caused by remembering Snowy.

Baby partridges did not appear. Tom drove on past a field of clover and Indian paintbrush and turned up his driveway between another field and a lawn. When they moved to Newburgh they had rented the old run-down house and barn on the knoll, one of the town's failed farms. Because summer people hadn't discovered Newburgh then, real-estate prices remained low so they'd been able to buy it eight years later. He noted all his exterior work—new roof on the house, weathered rotted clapboards stripped off, insulation blown in, new clapboards painted white, new roof on the high two-story gray barn—and saw in his mind's eye all the interior renovations he'd done at Joanne's bidding. It would be Joanne's now, the house and barn, the ten acres including the vegetable garden that had once been his pride and joy. Momentarily, he wondered if the house could continue functioning without his ministrations, but then he knew this was overweening hubris. Joanne had managed fine this spring, and the house had not missed him.

There were no cars in the driveway. No party.

In the old days, as he came home from work he'd be greeted by their border collie, whom he wished Joanne hadn't named Bonnie because, unbeknownst to Joanne, Snowy had grown up with a Shetland collie she'd named Annie Laurie from that song about "bonnie" Annie Laurie. After Bonnie died, they hadn't felt like getting another dog, so without canine fanfare he now parked the Jeep in the driveway, climbed out, and walked into the barn. He glanced up at the loft, where he stored extra lumber. Down on the ground level, beneath the plank floor on which Joanne's latest Toyota was parked, he had stored his old convertible that none of his kids wanted and he couldn't bring himself to sell. Maybe sometime he could restore the famous '49 Chevy convertible. He glanced back at the Jeep, which he'd bought secondhand a dozen years ago and now, fifteen years old, was gaining on "classic" status. He was accumulating too damn many old cars.

But he would keep the Chevy. And the Jeep.

Saying a mental good-bye to the barn, he went into the connecting shed and opened the door onto the back porch that he had built. He remembered how he and Joanne had christened this porch the summer night he'd finished it, when the kids were asleep, with the soft air so warm after winter, the moths crawling outside the screens, and gorgeous Joanne lusciously spread-eagled on a beach towel she'd bought with S&H Green Stamps, her lovely smile languid. They had all the time in the world.

He took off his glasses, rubbed his eyes, put the glasses back on. Instead of going right into the house, he tapped on the kitchen's screen door. "Joanne?" he called. "It's me." When she didn't answer, he stepped into the kitchen he'd remodeled. She wasn't here, surrounded by the cupboards and cabinets he'd painted with blue milk paint, but her presence was, in the bunches of dried flowers hanging from the ceiling beams, the glowing copper pots, the blue gingham curtains. The dining room and living room were also mostly done up in what he could only think of as Country Charm, old-fashioned wallpaper, ruffled white curtains, floral slipcovers, a quilt folded across the back of the sofa, but there were some incongruous touches, such as the La-Z-Boy recliner Joanne had bought him for his birthday years ago and the big-screen TV she had bought for her own enjoyment as well as for the Super Bowl parties she gave, Joanne being the die-hard football fan in this family. His initial furniture contribution had been the rolltop desk he'd bought secondhand and restored, and then when his parents moved to Florida he had acquired the things he'd made in high school for his folks, including two bookcases and a record-player-radio cabinet. He thought: I'll keep the desk and a bookcase.

"Joanne?" he called.

Still no answer, but he heard movement upstairs. Would he actually find her with a guy? A guy who hadn't arrived here in a car?

Tom went into the hall, climbed the old staircase, and halted in the little upstairs hall. To the right were Brandon's and David's bedrooms, now guest rooms; Libby's room downstairs still belonged to Libby. To the left was the bedroom he and Joanne had shared all these years.

He stepped through the doorway, flinched, then automatically caught a Valentine chocolate box that came hurtling at him. It was a white one with red rosettes, but he couldn't remember which year he had bought it for her. Standing on a step stool, Joanne looked too slender, too ladylike, to have thrown it with such force. Strange how he always forgot how slight she was, for in his mind she seemed so large—even looming like, he thought guiltily, a goddamn Thurber woman.

Joanne considered him, surprised at her upsurge of violence. When boys started giving her chocolates for Valentine's Day, she had decorated a wall in her girlhood bedroom with the emptied heart-shaped boxes. After she and Tom were married, she moved the collection to the bedroom in their apartment in the married students' barracks, then to this bedroom, and he gave her an extravagant addition each year. She had loved these symbols of romance, had always kept them all carefully dusted, the pink boxes, and white and lavender and blue, and the true red boxes that matched the satin bedspread on the queen-size bed where lay others she'd been yanking off the walls, frothy with lace and ribbons.

She hurled another at him, sweet pink rosebuds.

He caught it and set it on the hope chest he'd built in high school. "What are you doing?"

She snapped, "Redecorating."

Shit, he thought, David told her after all. "I'm sorry," he said.

"Pizza. Holding hands. Adele has been going crazy trying to decide whether or not to phone me about it, and you can imagine how I felt when she did. No, you *cannot* imagine!" She threw another box, blood red.

Tom let it bounce off him and heard himself say stupidly, "Huh?"

"You forgot about the grapevine, didn't you. Somebody saw you and told somebody who told Adele, sure she'd tell me. Everyone feeling sorry for me!"

He stared at her. She was talking about last Sunday night, when he and Snowy had gone to that pizza place. Adele Roberge Page. Co-captains Joanne and Adele had maintained their friendship through the years.

Joanne stared back at this person she'd known all her life. He was looking stupefied. Could she give him the benefit of the doubt? Adele had told her that Snowy's husband had committed suicide this spring. Poor Snowy! Could Tom have actually been doing a good deed, being a considerate old friend, taking her out to dinner to distract her from her sorrow? Adele said Snowy's house had been sold and she was living and working in the Woodcombe General Store. Joanne asked, "Did you know she was in Woodcombe when you took the job at the fire tower there?'

"No."

"I gather she's had a rough time. Adele says her husband killed himself. It wasn't over you?"

"God, no. I didn't run into her until afterward."

Joanne came down from the step stool. The benefit of the doubt. "Have you had supper? There's some pasta salad in the fridge."

When, he wondered irrelevantly, did people even in Newburgh start calling it "pasta" instead of "macaroni" and "spaghetti"?

She said, "Just promise you won't see her again. I can stand not quite trusting you with an old girlfriend, but I can't stand people feeling sorry for me."

He said, "Joanne, hasn't this spring been kind of a trial separation? Haven't you wanted it to be one, too? You've liked it, I know you have."

He was correct, but she hadn't thought they would ever discuss it outright. She'd thought they would have this little vacation from each other until the fire-tower job ended in November, and the worn-out marriage would be fresh upon resumption. She felt a sick stab of foreboding.

"The next stage," he said. "Now we're ready for that. I'm moving the business to Woodcombe. We can work out the financial details and everything—it's all yours, whatever you want, but could I have the Chevy and—"

He ducked as she grabbed the Valentine boxes on the bed and began bombarding him.

WEDNESDAY, JUNE 24, would have been Snowy and Alan's twenty-sixth anniversary. Snowy spent the day working. School having ended last Friday, Ruhamah was working alongside her full-time, and because there were more people returning to summer homes, restored Capes on country roads, as well as more tourists detouring to see the pretty village, Snowy and Ruhamah and Irene were all kept busy selling bread and milk and vegetables and meat, potato chips and rat trap cheese, fly dope, postcards, packets of garden seeds, dill pickles dripping brine from the pickle barrel. Although the potbellied stove was cold, folks stood around it sipping Cokes and talking, and stood discussing the items on the bulletin board, and sat out on the porch on the deacon's bench reading newspapers and watching the passing scene. Snowy hardly had a moment to think of the little ceremony in her parents' living room, to remember how her hands had sweated, how the quacking ducks in the river had nearly drowned out the justice of the peace and the wedding vows.

That evening, as she and Ruhamah collapsed in front of the television, for the first time she was glad to be so damned tired her mind had shut down—or at least her emotions had.

And this was how life continued. She worked harder than she ever dreamed she could. Compulsive perfectionist, she concentrated on storekeeping, doing what she should have done when Alan bought the store instead of letting him shoulder the burden alone. When she had enough energy left to read in the evenings, she read about general stores; although she and Alan had discussed them and their role in contemporary village life, she now was really studying, belatedly doing her homework, she who had always before prided herself on doing her homework early and thoroughly.

Once upon a time, these stores supplied a town with all the necessities. But now they offered the basics, so townspeople didn't have to drive miles to a supermarket to get eggs and beer, and for the tourists there were frills like snacks and souvenirs. Identifying the types of customers and striking the right balance in fulfilling their needs was crucial, but your biggest challenge, she read, was the hours you had to put in to make a go of it. You were chained to the store all day. At night you were awakened by phone calls from customers desperate for a light bulb or a Sara Lee cheesecake, especially if you lived over the store. When you weren't waiting on people, you were doing the ordering and stocking the shelves. It was hard to hire help, and if you did, wages reduced profits. Almost inevitably, owners burned out, even in those situations in which Mom and Pop and all the kids were working. She read that divorces occurred, but the books didn't mention suicide.

Sometimes, when Tom was off-duty, he stopped work on the barn and came over to the apartment, either cooking the evening meal there—his culinary talents ran to zapping microwave food or opening cans or to making supper-time versions of breakfast, omelettes or pancakes or French toast—or inviting her and Ruhamah for a barbecue in the field he'd tidied into a backyard behind the barn, where he'd set up a picnic table David had built in the North Country Coffins workshop. Occasionally he took her out to dinner, though never back to the Parmigiano, probably thinking that a variety of restaurants gave her a chance to test agoraphobic responses in different settings. Most often they went to Peggy Ann's Place, the locals' favorite restaurant out on the road to Gunthwaite. If Ruhamah wasn't off with friends, she came along. When Ruhamah was sleeping over at Jennifer's or elsewhere, Tom walked to the apartment and spent the night, returning to the barn before daybreak. She had thought she couldn't forget and make love with him in the bed in which she and Alan had slept and made love. How strange, and how simplifying, that she could.

She didn't know exactly what had happened between him and Joanne the Saturday he went to Newburgh to tell Joanne he was moving permanently to Woodcombe. She knew he hadn't stayed overnight; she didn't jog on Sundays because of the extra early-morning chore of organizing the Sunday newspapers, and when she lugged the piles of the *New York Times, Boston Globe, New Hampshire Sunday News,* and *Sunday Monitor* in from where they'd been left on the porch by the delivery guy, she had seen the Jeep parked in Tom's driveway. After the store closed at noon, she cleaned her apartment, determined not to walk over to the barn and ask prying questions. Finally she heard footsteps on the outside staircase and Tom appeared on the stoop, annoying the hummingbirds whizzing around the red impatiens. He came in, looking drawn. She realized that he'd lost weight since they'd met on the mountaintop this spring. Not daring to touch him, she offered beer, iced tea, iced coffee, Pepsi. He declined, asking, "Is Ruhamah here?" Snowy said, "She's off playing in a village softball game." So they were alone and could speak freely. He said, "Joanne will be seeing a lawyer this week, and I guess I'd better too. What's the name of yours?" "Jason Ellsworth," she said and jabbered about the changes in her old home that would startle him when he went to the law office there, and then Tom put his arms around her and pressed his cheek against her hair, and they just stood like that for a long time.

A few days later, a laughing Tom had run into the store, saying, "Come see!" He grabbed her out from behind the counter and tugged her outdoors to show her, parked at the barn, David's pickup, loaded with boxes and furniture and towing a flatbed trailer on which sat the cream-colored Chevy convertible with the black top and the continental tire on its trunk.

Bev had also acquired a car, brought by a son. Leon had driven her Ford LTD station wagon up from Ninfield, Connecticut, with Etta his passenger. In Bev's case, Snowy knew all the details of what had gone on between husband and wife. Bev had decided to stay in New Hampshire, whether or not she passed the real-estate exam, and had phoned Roger to tell him she was going to take some time out. In high-school plays, Bev had learned she could weep at will, and she planned to use this talent if Roger got difficult, but there were none of the expected tirades from Roger, no lawyerly arguments; instead, shocked silence. Weeping for real, Bev told Snowy, "I almost lost my nerve then. I remembered how he came into Sweetland when I'd two-timed him and he said, 'That's that, that's over,' and I remembered the New Year's Eve party we got back together, where was it—?" "At Sam Page's," Snowy said, "we celebrated the start of 1956." Bev said, "And at midnight everybody started kissing. Roger and I had come with other people, but that suddenly seemed all wrong, and we—the record player was playing 'My One and Only You,'" she sobbed. Snowy said, "Have you found a house yet?" Bev wiped her eyes and replied, "Yes! Geoffrey Plumley came through with a rental this afternoon! Another broker had it listed for sale, but just the other day the owners decided to rent it until it sells. It's hideous, a two-level ranch house with a family room and a third bedroom in the basement like dungeons vile, but Snowy, it's only half a mile from Springmeadow Farm, which is a riding academy that boards horses, so Etta can walk to it and I won't have to drive her back and forth. So this ghastly house is perfect. The owners got transferred to North Carolina and are asking a high price for the place, and they're sticking to it in hopes of the market's improving. They think if they wait they can get top dollar because it's on a road to the lake. At the end of the road there's a view of Blue Island! Wait'll Puddles hears!" And Bev and Snowy began giggling over how they'd almost got drummed out of the Girl Scouts, when in eighth grade their boyfriends had crashed a Girl Scout jamboree on the island.

Following Leon and Etta came a moving van containing the furniture Bev wanted for this unfurnished house she'd moved into. Roger hadn't put up any protest, so to her relief she hadn't had to return to Ninfield and confront him face-to-face. And following the moving van came Dick, Bev and Roger's older son, a student at Yale Law School, driving Roger's toy, a Chevy Blazer (*not* his serious car, a Porsche), towing a horse van in which rode Prancer.

"Menopause," Bev told Snowy. "That's what Roger is probably chalking my actions up to. A temporary aberration he's humoring. I'm taking a cram course evenings for the New Hampshire real-estate exam. Oh, Snowy, what if I flunk?"

Snowy said, "Then you'll take it again."

"Roger thinks I'll flunk. He thought my passing the Connecticut exam was a fluke. He remembers high school, when he was like you, acing exams while I muddled along."

"Don't let him get to you."

"I've finished arranging the furniture, and the house is presentable, so can you come see it on Sunday?"

Snowy had never visited Bev in Connecticut. On this Sunday, when Snowy and Ruhamah were through work they drove to Gunthwaite, along Lake Winnipesaukee past the amusement area with its boardwalk and Karamel Korn and miniature golf, where there was now also a water slide and the once-glamorous dance hall had degenerated into a video-games arcade, past a marina, past demolished woods upon which rose Pinemere Condominium Estate, and turned onto Blue Road, where an older development of ranch houses looked confused, having become part year-round, part summer. Bev's rectangular house and attached garage had gray siding and a green rectangular lawn bordered with rectangles of bark mulch under lumps of shrubs.

It was a far cry from the newlywed apartment Bev and Roger had rented on the wrong side of Boston's Beacon Hill while Bev worked at a bank and Roger got his law degree, a basement studio apartment that Snowy *had* visited, but Snowy could feel Bev was having similar fun decorating it, each place the base for a new life, and she couldn't help comparing this with her own move into the apartment over the store. Bev's pine cupboards were arranged throughout the kitchen and the combination dining-and-living room, and out of of the Ninfield colonial had also come a lot of weaving done by

Bev's mother and older daughter, from the living room curtains to the seats of six dining chairs, and there were some elegant items like a tapestry-covered sofa and a wing chair upholstered in toile French scenes, but otherwise Bev seemed to be playing at being in a summer cottage, buying wicker furniture not only for the patio but also for indoors and choosing loon patterns on cushions, lamp shades, kitchen curtains, pot holders. Holding up a loon dish towel, Bev said, "I've begun a new collection that'll rival your mother's roosters!"

Laughing with Bev over those roosters, Snowy suddenly heard Leon suggest to Ruhamah that they go for a swim at the public beach. Ruhamah replied tightly that she hadn't brought a bathing suit. As far as Snowy knew, Ruhamah hadn't yet gone swimming this summer. Snowy didn't think that she herself ever could again, not even in Winnipesaukee and certainly not in Woodcombe Lake. To Snowy's relief, Bev sent Leon off on some errand, and Ruhamah spent the rest of the visit helping Etta finish unpacking her Barbie dolls and then walking with her to Springmeadow Farm to see Prancer. Redheaded Etta, named Henrietta for Snowy, looked so much like Bev at age twelve that Snowy's head spun in a before-and-after time warp. When she and Bev were twelve, what had they been playing with? They weren't horse-crazy girls. No Barbies back then, and they'd long outgrown their Betsy-Wetsy dolls. Boys, Snowy recalled, had been much on their minds, and now it was men. Snowy looked at the toile wing chair and thought in French: *Plus ça change, plus c'est la même chose.*

But during the visit, Bev didn't mention Roger, nor did she speak directly of Geoffrey Plumley, about whom Snowy was growing increasingly curious, though Bev did wring her hands and wail about real estate: "I'm taking the exam *next week!* I can't believe I'm deliberately putting myself through this agony again!"

And Snowy looked around the house and thought how she and Bev were single again, sort of.

Leon had competition. That evening Charl phoned to say that their son D. J. had revealed he'd been wanting to ask Ruhamah out but was nervous about Snowy's reaction because of the age difference. Charl laughed, "Dudley and I will vouch for him!" D. J. at nineteen, who'd be starting his sophomore year at Rumford State College, seemed far less an older man than Leon, a twenty-one-year-old who wasn't even a dropout, who hadn't even attempted college, which of course enraged his father, Roger having strived as Snowy had for the scholarships that would enable them to go. Snowy gave her permission and then asked Charl, "Do you and Dudley know what happened to Linda Littlefield?"

Charl said, "Linda? Remember when she and Puddles were fighting over that Mike who had an MG?"

"Puddles won."

"I wish you and Bev and Puddles would come to the reunions! Linda has come to them all. She married a doctor, and they live in Weston, Mass."

Snowy could imagine Puddles's response: "Humph, one of my daughters *is* a doctor."

"And," Charl said, "she's a grandmother at least once. I've forgotten how many children she has; two, I think. She wears the most beautiful outfits to the reunions."

Snowy asked, "Has Dudley made a decision about running for city council this fall?"

"He's talking about things like 'testing the waters' in Ward Two and 'building a war chest,' and D. J. being his campaign manager. He's joking but he means it. I don't know how he'd have time to run, even if it's only a trial run this time. Well, maybe now that our youngest is in elementary school and there aren't any more coming along, I could get a job and help out."

Snowy had long been mystified about why Dudley had quit Yale, to which he'd earned a scholarship, and returned to Gunthwaite, where he eventually married widowed Charl and began fathering a passel of kids. Then this spring he had told her how in New Haven he'd got a girl pregnant and paid for an abortion that had killed her. So with Charl and her Catholicism, he had tried to atone.

Charl said, "I'll tell D. J. it's okay. Wouldn't it be neat if they really fell for each other!"

D. J. certainly impressed Ruhamah by taking her to a music-festival concert instead of to the movies.

Sometimes when Snowy set out on her morning run, she wanted instead to jump in her car and drive to the Roller Coaster Road. She wanted to drive past Hurricane Farm and see what Frank Barlow was doing to the place, then drive on to the Thornes' hardscrabble farm for a visit, pretending she still lived down the road. Frank Barlow stopped in often at the store. Divorced and retired, he had hoped to buy the store as well as the farm in order to have something to do when he moved to Woodcombe, where his father had also retired. But she had only sold him the farm. So Frank was keeping busy by getting involved in almost every club and committee in town. Cedric, his father, a wealthy widower, was an irritable and irritating old fussbudget who spent most of his time working in his beautiful flower beds surrounding his house on the corner of Center Road and Pascataquac Road. In contrast, Frank was affable, a roly-poly man whose eyes squinted as he smiled, but Snowy hoped he'd inherited Cedric's green thumb. She managed to control this urge to go see her gardens or visit the Thornes. Whenever Cleora Thorne made her slow arthritic way into the store to shop, Snowy didn't inquire about what Cleora might have observed at her new neighbor's and Cleora didn't volunteer any information about the gardens or the house, respecting Snowy's feelings. Snowy always asked after Cleora's husband, Isaac, who had rallied from death's door last spring, and Cleora always complained, "He still wants the dang cows around. Easy enough for him, I'm the one doing the milking. If it was up to me, I'd get rid of them cows in a minute." But their presence and rhythm were necessary to Isaac. Snowy had enjoyed the sight of those Guernseys during her morning run—but she too didn't have to milk them twice a day. The Thornes were just barely hanging on, hiring young Pete Roberts to do some of the chores, such as cutting, splitting, and lugging wood, their children having escaped from farming years ago. How long could this continue? Ringing up Cleora's flour, raisins, dried codfish, and a six-pack of Bud for Isaac, Snowy could not imagine the Thornes in some assisted-living nursing-home paradise.

Bev phoned Snowy during store hours and exulted, "The mail just came and I passed the exam! No nonsense about a husband hiding the results! I'm going to earn a living for the first time in decades! Well, maybe. What if I don't sell one single place? Geoffrey says that the main thing real-estate agents have to learn is patience."

This was the first time Bev had called Geoffrey Plumley by his first name. Snowy said, "So you've phoned your boss and told him you can start work?"

"He's not really my boss. He's my broker, and I'm an 'independent contractor'! Independence! Whoopee!"

After they hung up, Snowy left the store in Irene's hands, went up the inside stairs to the apartment, into her bedroom where she stood looking at the old mahogany veneer desk she'd had since junior high. She'd kept it out of the auction, as well as her typewriter and typing table and desk chair, and in this nook she did her store homework. Could she organize a few extra minutes a day for writing poetry? Why bother? She hadn't sold anything for years. Such choking frustration, not succeeding at what you do best and love best to do.

THE TOURIST SEASON no longer ended with Labor Day. Even before the leaves began to turn, foliage seekers known as leaf peepers appeared, and whole tour buses loaded with them meandered off the main highway into Woodcombe in quest of colors. The colors came, and everybody tried to compare their brilliance with previous years', but Snowy didn't care if they were brighter or paler; she was rent with sorrow, giddy with beauty. During her morning jog, she felt as if she were running in a great big cereal bowl, the fallen pine needles like shredded wheat, the leaves in shades of peach, apricot, cream.

Depending upon summer homes' insulation, or lack of, the retired summer people stayed on until at least Columbus Day, and some waited until Thanksgiving to head for Florida and Arizona. The slack time Snowy had feared financially and longed for physically didn't really begin to stretch out until only rusty oak leaves were left, and the autumn smelled less like cider and more like red wine.

Tom phoned one evening and said, "Let's go for a walk." As they strolled down the village street to the end of the sidewalk and then along the edge of the road, they kicked at acorns and watched a full moon pop up like a beach ball over the mountains. When they reached a brook that ran under the road, Tom stopped and leaned against the little railing and said, "The divorce is now final. I had to phone my mother and tell her."

Snowy had met his parents her junior year in high school, and she still remembered the terror of the invitation to dinner at Tom's house. A New England boiled dinner. His mother had a brisk manner as well as Tom's blue eyes and long straight eyelashes. His eyesight came from his horn-rimmed father. After his father had retired from Trask's, they had moved to Sarasota, where his father died and his mother stayed on.

Tom said, "When I told her, she cried."

Snowy put her hand in his and listened to the brook's cold melodic plinkety-plunk, as precise as a music box.

D. J. returned to Rumford State College but came back to Gunthwaite weekends to help in Dudley's campaign for city councilor, and Ruhamah joined in. This was, Snowy hoped, a fine civics lesson. And she hoped with all her might that Dudley would win the Ward Two seat; she was pretty sure he hadn't really decided to run because she'd told him to, yet she felt responsible. If only she could at least cast a vote in Gunthwaite! The night of the election, she and Ruhamah sat up pretending to read, their attention on the telephone, which at last rang. Ruhamah leapt for it, listened, leapt again, punching the air with her fist and slapping the ceiling. Then she handed the receiver to Snowy, saying, "That was D. J.," who'd cut classes for the occasion. "The ballot count is finished and Dudley won!"

Dudley was on the phone now, saying to Snowy, "Remember our mock election in high school, when you and I and Bev were almost the only Democrats in the class and Adlai Stevenson lost?"

"Oh, Dudley!" Snowy cried. "Congratulations!"

"Now I'm one of only two Democrats on the council and the only person our age. Everyone else is older or younger."

"I think," Snowy said, "that our generation is 'the disappeared.' We've dropped out of sight between our parents' generation and the baby boomers. Remember how we were called 'The Silent Generation'? Nobody knows about us."

Dudley said, "Then I'd better make sure I'm heard."

Back in high school, Snowy wouldn't have had any doubt he would be. But now, after all these years of the sign-painting business and catering to customers? This other Dudley, respectable businessman and paterfamilias? Maybe, though, that was better than being the brash champion debater, or maybe the combination would be successful and was what had won him the council seat. He'd won! She didn't repeat her suggestion about next running for mayor and instead asked how Charl liked the job she'd taken in the photo department of a mall store, convincing babies and kids to hold still and look adorable for the camera.

"For Charl," Dudley said, "it's a piece of cake."

During the summer Alan's mother and father had driven up from their home in Eastbourne and visited, mainly to see Ruhamah, and now as Thanksgiving approached, Alan's mother phoned and said, "I don't know what to do, but Margaret thinks we should have a sort of simplified dinner. Would you and Ruhamah be able to come? Will the store be closed on Thanksgiving?"

Snowy wished she could go into a holiday hibernation, emerging after New Year's Day. The first Thanksgiving without Alan, the first Christmas. Because her parents had made such a big deal about holidays, Snowy had always been low-key with Alan and Ruhamah, but no matter what, these were going to be hell to get through. The other day she had cautiously asked Tom about his Thanksgiving plans, and he'd replied that he planned to keep working. With the fire-tower job over for the year, he was concentrating on the business. Snowy had said, "Um, you don't visit your mother at Thanksgiving or Christmas?" He said, "My brother George and his wife go down to Sarasota at Thanksgiving and take Mom out to dinner. At Christmastime, brother Doug and his wife go down. We—Joanne and I and the kids—went once at Christmas years ago when my father was still alive, but we couldn't really afford such a vacation, being poverty-stricken teachers. I've visited Mom some other times since. Joanne didn't like Florida. Neither do I. And with what's happened this year, I'm steering clear of family and their opinions of my actions."

Snowy realized she had to face family. For Ruhamah's sake, Snowy accepted Alan's mother's invitation, although after she'd done so, she promptly began worrying that the family get-together might actually upset Ruhamah more than soothe. Then on the trip down she forgot to worry about anything except car crashes; this month there had been light snow off and on, but today there was freezing rain. Ruhamah drove so circumspectly that Snowy knew she was frightened, too.

They arrived at the seacoast safely. On Eastbourne's waterfront they went past the sardine cannery from which Alan's father had retired after a working lifetime spent moving up from packing to sales, and through the miserable rain they looked at the Old Eastbourne village of restored houses. Often Snowy and Alan had taken Ruhamah to the Ruhamah Reed House, to show her the home of the poet for whom she was named, where Snowy and Alan had met and where they'd lived in their newlywed years. Back when Snowy's work was being published, Ruhamah had herself begun writing poems, but she hadn't mentioned any in ages.

Suddenly Snowy thought: There should be a memorial of some

sort here for Alan. He had devoted twenty-five years of his life to the creation of Old Eastbourne, saving historic buildings from a wrecking ball, raising money, keeping tabs on the accuracy of everything—right down to the correct fanlights, the correct varieties of flowering shrubs mentioned in old diaries and records!—and coping with committees and boards of directors who brought the tides of depression rolling in over him. But Alan hadn't wanted a funeral; what about a memorial here? Snowy thought of a bench with a plaque, in the Ruhamah Reed House garden... How about just a plaque in the main office, she asked Alan in her mind, and she could sense his amusement.

Ruhamah drove on into a real-life residential area, where Alan's parents lived in a nice white house whose vinyl siding, which Alan's father had had put on some years ago, added to the depression that was apt to descend on Alan whenever he arrived back here. Margaret, Alan's sister, and her podiatrist husband, Howard, lived across town in a swanky development's many-angled house built so every room could at least get a peek at the ocean. It was an empty nest now that their son and daughter were grown and married, but children and grandchildren were home for the holiday and they had all come over to the vinyl house.

Carrying her contribution of cranberry-orange relish, Snowy stepped indoors with Ruhamah into the smell of turkey and sage and found the place full of emotions as well as Sutherland generations. Phyllis, Alan's pretty mother who had adored him, had made the traditional lobster bisque that he liked, and she wept as she ladled it out of the Blue Willow tureen, then laughed hysterically as one of her great-grandchildren, Margaret and Howard's baby granddaughter, jerked a bootied foot into the basket of rolls being passed around, sending Pepperidge Farm Brown and Serve flying. Bob, Alan's father, had the long-lidded eyes that Alan and Ruhamah inherited, and he was an argumentative man, not a debater like Dudley but only, as Alan said, an asshole. There were still plenty of other victims at the table to give Bob abundant opportunities for contradiction, yet without Alan here he seemed to have lost his fighting spirit, so he just nagged. But he didn't do even that when he asked Snowy how business was and she replied, "Fine"; he didn't press for details, and he didn't tackle Ruhamah about school or anything. Phyllis had simplified her Thanksgiving menu somewhat. Peas and mashed potatoes, not squash and creamed onions too. Instead of the pumpkin and mince and apple pies, there was only one, brought by Margaret, an untraditional chocolate chiffon. Still, it was all a lot of work. Howard's contribution was wine, but Snowy stuck to water in case Ruhamah didn't want to do the driving on the way home.

Ruhamah wanted to, and Snowy, exhausted, let her. After a lengthy period of concentration on the icy road, Ruhamah asked, "Do we really have to go back there for Christmas?"

Feeling unexpected vehemence, Snowy exclaimed, "No!" She and Ruhamah must do something cheery, but what could she afford?

Ruhamah spent Friday and Saturday nights of the Thanksgiving weekend out on dates with D. J., while Snowy pondered Christmas and then on Sunday consulted Bev, who'd had Thanksgiving at her house, with all her kids there—and also Roger, whom she'd invited so she could prove what she'd accomplished, the new home, the job. "But," Bev told Snowy, "I don't think he really took it all in. He thinks I'm playing. And he wanted to play reconciliation."

"What did you do?"

"I let him spend the night. It would've been too confusing for Etta if he'd stayed in a motel. And I must say, it was kind of fun. Maybe this is like those bi-coastal marriages that actors have. Speaking of acting, I've learned there's a group in Gunthwaite these days, the Gunthwaite Summer Theater."

The man with whom Bev had fallen in love and almost had an affair had been her leading man in Ninfield Players' productions.

Snowy asked cautiously, "Are you going to join or try out or anything?"

"I'm far too busy. I'm a career woman! Roger went on and on about the 'economic downturn.' I was thrilled I could tell him I've sold some places."

"You knew you'd be good at it."
"Yes, if I could get the exam part over with. It's like acting, and it's just as tough. It's a cutthroat business." Bev remembered why Snowy had called. "What to do at Christmas, Snowy? You and Ruhamah come here! Everybody will be here again. Tell Alan's parents you have to be with your poor lonely best friend."
"Thank you, but I was wishing Ruhamah could have a complete change of scenery. I've only got Christmas itself off, though, so I don't know where we could go for such a short time."

During her lunch break the next day, Snowy walked up the street to the barn that was now officially North Country Coffins. She'd learned the names of the terrifying machinery in the workshop, so when she entered she knew that the lethal-looking thing that Tom was manipulating at a long bench against a wall was called a radial-arm saw, while David was using the thickness planer that stood in the middle of the room along with various worktables, a band saw, and a table saw. There were workbenches down one wall, and against other walls stood a joiner, a lathe, a drill press, and Tom's rolltop desk very similar to Alan's. Tom removed his ear protectors, letting them drop around his neck like a stethoscope, and mouthed, "Lunch?"

She nodded.

So he tossed the ear protectors onto a workbench, led her up the staircase, and opened the door into the kitchen. She enjoyed this bachelors' apartment. He and David had built the plain-front pine cupboards and cabinets, and Tom had also built the trestle table, but he had picked up the four mixed kitchen chairs at a secondhand store, from which had also come the many rugs thrown on the plywood floor throughout the apartment as well as the appliances. There were a bookcase Tom had made in high school and furniture from David's Newburgh apartment. Tom's double bed and mattress he had bought new at a Gunthwaite furniture store after consulting Snowy about what kind of mattress she preferred. "Extra-firm," she'd replied, and he said, "Same here," and of course jokes ensued.

Now as he opened a can of Progresso chicken noodle soup, spooned it into two mugs, and stuck them in the microwave, she asked, "I want to do something fun for Ruhamah at Christmas, but I've only got that one day off. Any ideas?"

He said promptly, "We'll go to an inn. Drive there Christmas Eve after you close the store, and come back late Christmas Day. Pick a spot, the mountains, or the ocean—not the New Hampshire coast but something different for you, the Maine coast. My present to you both, and you two can go on your own if it's too soon for me to be around on Christmas."

"I didn't mean—but what about your kids—or—"

He put a box of saltines on the table. "If you and I don't go somewhere, I'll keep working."

Same as he'd done Thanksgiving Day. "Thank you," she said, "I'll see."

That evening, when Snowy told Ruhamah about Tom's suggestion, Ruhamah said, "D. J. says we're invited to their house for Christmas. His father or mother will be phoning you."

"Do you want to go to there? Do you want to go to an inn?"

They looked at each other. They wanted Alan.

Snowy went to her desk in her bedroom and stared unseeing at a book about small businesses.

Long ago, when Snowy was in college, Julia, whose first husband, Bev's father, had been killed in the landing on Iwo Jima, had written Snowy to tell her that Ed Cormier, Snowy's first boyfriend, had died. Julia wrote, "One can eventually become used to an absence, just as one became used to a presence, though the pain remains." In her letter after Alan's death, Julia had written, "You'll never stop missing him."

The kitchen wall phone rang, and Snowy heard Ruhamah answer it, say, "Yes," and fall silent, evidently listening at length. Girlfriends, boyfriends. Then Ruhamah came to the bedroom doorway, an excited smile on her face, and said, "It's Harriet."

Snowy ran into the kitchen and grabbed the receiver. "You're back from China?"

"Been and went, there and elsewhere. But as I was telling Ruhamah, I'm back at the gallery for the big shopping season, and I wondered if you and she might like to see New York at Christmastime. My apartment has two bedrooms, and you'd get two holidays, Hanukkah and Christmas, though I recall that what you celebrate, Snowy, you pagan, is the winter solstice."

"Oh, Harriet, it would be wonderful, but the store is only closed on Christmas Day."

"It's your store, so change the schedule."

"Some summer people come back to Woodcombe for Christmas. We get extra business from them and other winter tourists, skiers, because we're so Currier-and-Ives cute. I've squeezed in a few little tables and installed a coffeemaker, and there'll be cocoa. Muffins. I'm sorry, Harriet, I've got to tend to business."

"Well, I feared that might be a problem. So how about Ruhamah's coming down on her own? You could put her on a bus and I'll collect her. Can you spend the day with some of your friends up there? I'd love to show her the sights, Snowy. I want to help, if belatedly. Shit, maybe this is a stupid idea."

Seeing Ruhamah hovering with that eager look, Snowy breathed, "It is perfect."

Harriet said, "I've found copies of your books."

Startled, Snowy blurted, "How the hell? They're out of print."

"Through secondhand bookstores, of course. I liked them. What happened to Commonwealth, your publisher? Wasn't that where you worked during Non-Resident Terms?"

"It got swallowed up in a merger and they stopped publishing poetry. I couldn't follow my editor to a new publishing house because he didn't move on to one; he found a job editing an airline magazine. No other publisher has been interested in my stuff."

"Do you have an agent?"

"I didn't think I needed one then, and I doubt I could get one now. A commission on poetry doesn't amount to much."

"But you're still writing? Still sending poems to magazines?"

"I'm running a store," Snowy said. After she'd thanked Harriet again and they said good-bye, she turned to Ruhamah. "At last, you'll see New York!"

"Awesome," said Ruhamah, who rarely used teen slang around Snowy. Then she looked uncertain and said, "But the store—"

"Irene and I can handle things."

"It'll be busy. You were just explaining to Harriet how busy—"

"I was exaggerating. You're going to New York, my baby."

"But you ought to come too."

"I've already been, when I was your age."

"Yeah, Radio City Music Hall with the Girl Scouts. Not the same." The smile, however, was back on Ruhamah's face. "What do I take for clothes?"

Snowy spent Christmas Eve and part of Christmas Day with Tom at an inn in the mountains. She insisted on going Dutch, and they agreed not to exchange presents. The Alpine Avens Inn was large enough so they were anonymous, but cozy enough so they could feel as quaint as a brochure illustration that eve as they sat with their eggnogs in front of the Yule log in the fireplace in the balsam-swagged main room, the Christmas tree lights twinkling like childhood. Snowy remembered the way her mother and father always seemed to be posing for a portrait of family life and thought how bewildered they would be by this tableau, Snowy and Tom alone.

Because Christmas Day was rainy, Snowy didn't feel too guilty sleeping late. Would she, who'd always been one of those irritating early-risers, ever get enough sleep now to ease the exhaustion? But she wanted breakfast, so finally she hauled herself out of the four-poster. Tom, showered and dressed, sat reading beside the bedroom fireplace, looking like a trim Santa Claus with his white curls, beard, gold spectacles.

He said, "Merry Christmas, Snowy."

"Merry Christmas, Tom."

After her shower, when she emerged from the bathroom in her bathrobe, she saw that a present wrapped in white tissue paper and tied with a red ribbon had appeared on her overnight bag.

"Tom," she said. "We agreed."

"Don't blame me," he said. "Old Saint Nick came last night."

"So he did," she said, reaching for the package.

"Ho ho ho," said Tom.

She untied the ribbon, unwrapped the tissue paper. It was one of those newfangled tape players that Ruhamah had, a Walkman, with a paperback—no, an audio book, a book-on-tape, and oh bliss, the tape was an Agatha Christie, *Murder in the Mews*! He had remembered that she loved murder mysteries, that she'd told him about how at Bennington she used to reward herself, studying done, by curling up with Agatha.

She said, "I'm going to cry. Thank you. I don't know how to use it, though. I've never tried Ruhamah's, because I'd just hear incomprehensible music."

He stood up, took a jackknife from a pants pocket, and slit the plastic packaging of the Walkman and the cassette. He showed her how to insert the cassette into the Walkman. Watching his clever hands, she thought of the first present he'd given her, on her sixteenth birthday, a Parker pen because her old pen leaked so much her fingers were always inky.

Tom was remembering that, too. Slipping the earphones onto her head, he pressed the Play button. The sudden look of wonder on her face as she heard the start of the reading reminded him of her expression when he had given her the little package at her house after a date and had beat a hasty retreat in the convertible, confused by mingled desire for her and for his previous fancy-free life.

He kissed her and said, "Aren't you starving? Let's get breakfast!"

CHAPTER THREE

NOW THE WINTER doldrums began. This was the time when Alan used to think aloud about how he ought to cut Irene's hours back, but he couldn't bring himself to and neither could Snowy. Letting Irene wait on the diminished number of customers and do most of the chores, Snowy worked in the store's office at Alan's roll-top, organizing the information for the income-tax return that her accountant would put together. How maddening that mere numbers, figures on paper, could make her heart pound and her stomach sick!

For Christmas Puddles had sent her a desk calendar with supposedly buoying comments. Snowy had relegated it to this desk rather than set it on her bedroom desk, and one sunny February morning she was staring at "Work won't kill you; worry will," when Bev phoned and said, "Can you play hooky today? I've finally listed a place that I think fulfills Mimi's requirements. Why don't you come here to the office, and you and I will meet her at the house and afterwards we can all have lunch."

"I didn't know Mimi was house-hunting."

"She wants a combination house and shop. Come on, it's such a lovely day."

Snowy hesitated, tempted. The prison of agoraphobia had been replaced by the prison of the store. Because early mornings were so dark and cold and the sidewalks and roads slippery, her jogging escape was reduced to a brisk walk under the village streetlights.

Remembering how after her return this morning she had looked with longing out the store's front window at the rosy sunrise through the wrought-iron lace of snow-covered branches, Snowy said, "Okay. I'll check with Irene and if there's any problem I'll phone you right back. Otherwise, I'll be along. I'm in Levi's and a sweater. Should I get dressier for house-hunting?"

"Not at all. I'm in my working duds, but that's different, and," Bev sighed, "you know Mimi. Granola grunge."

Which wasn't quite fair, Snowy thought. Sometimes Mimi wore things she wove, beautiful tops and vests, shawls and scarves. But she definitely hadn't inherited Bev's interest in current fashions.

Irene had no objection to Snowy's leaving, so Snowy pulled on her short lined leather boots and dusty-pink L. L. Bean Thinsulate parka and ran outdoors to the Subaru, playing hooky indeed, escaping both work and, she hoped, worry. She was behaving like a real person, like her pre-agoraphobia self, meeting a friend, going to lunch.

As she drove toward Gunthwaite, yesterday's snowfall freshened everything she saw, hiding the goddamn snowmobile tracks that scarred the lakes and woods, perking up disconsolate houses whose owners hadn't the energy or inclination to take down the Christmas wreaths that drooped on storm doors, tattered ribbons flopping. Winter was cheery again, with those lacy tracery views everywhere; it looked like a Valentine. She wondered idly if Tom would give her a Valentine card or present. Should she get him something? In 1956, on the first Valentine's Day since they'd started dating the previous March, he had given her a heart-shaped box of candy.

Alan was apt to forget Valentine's Day, so she had to remind him and they'd go out to dinner. Until agoraphobia.

New York City was beautiful, according to Ruhamah, and so was Harriet's Fifth Avenue apartment opposite Central Park, although it wasn't decorated with her paintings, as Snowy had expected. "These," Ruhamah had told Snowy breathlessly, "are in the big room that's her studio, and it's great, it's a total mess!

Three easels with three paintings she's working on, and stacks of canvases and paints and rags and all that stuff." Snowy remembered Harriet's turbulent half of their room at Bennington and the reek of turpentine and oil paints. Ruhamah said, "In the rest of the rooms, there are things from every place she's traveled. The walls are off-white and the furniture is beige-ish, but the rugs are a *riot* of colors, and they're from all over the world, and so's everything else, an old French vase here, a Portuguese chandelier there, an eighteenth-century Italian screen and a Moroccan inlaid-pearl chair and a brass menorah from Israel, and on and on. Of course," she added, embarrassed yet proud of herself, "I didn't know what most of them were, but I asked." Snowy said, "With Harriet, I always let her know my limitations." Ruhamah said, "The kitchen is all white. We ate out a lot, but we had real New York bagels for breakfasts in the kitchen, and Harriet made me Chicken Kiev there—she told me her dad had been the gourmet cook in her family and that was his specialty—" Snowy interrupted, "'Had been'?" Ruhamah said, "Hasn't she told you? Her dad and mom have both died, both of lung cancer." "Hell," Snowy said, and then asked, "Did she mention her brother? He's a few years older and worked with her father in their real estate business." Ruhamah answered succinctly, "She showed me photos of him and his wife and two nephews and their wives and some babies," and returned to her subject: "I had my own bathroom, and there were candles beside this big tub and a glass shower and a marble floor and the thickest towels ever. Awesome!" When the snapshots Ruhamah had taken on her trip were developed, with the interior of the apartment one of the sight-seeing highlights, Snowy agreed that it was awesome, but she was even more interested in seeing that Harriet also looked awesome. The clarity of Harriet's sharp bone structure had not softened over the years; aging had changed Harriet from pretty to distinctive.

Plumley Real Estate was located on the far end of Gunthwaite's Miracle Mile, where the clutter of the malls and fast-food joints and car washes thinned out to the classier establishments like a wine-and-cheese shop and a florist's greenhouse, and some trees remained. Snowy parked in a slot beside Bev's station wagon. The pale building in front of her was fun, sort of art nouveau with its swoops and curves. She went up the steps, opened the door, and entered a big room carpeted in svelte gray. The size of the room and the recessed fluorescent lighting triggered a twinge of dizziness. Oh God! Snowy wished she'd stayed at the store, safe in the familiar.

Three of the blond desks were occupied, by women talking into phones. One was Bev, writing as she talked. Snowy stood riveted, gaping, fears of agoraphobia forgotten in her surprise. Bev was wearing half-glasses, reading glasses! Snowy had never seen her in glasses nor had Bev ever mentioned needing them. She also wore a purple (aubergine?) turtleneck dress, with silver stud earrings that matched the frames of her little glasses. Snowy moved forward. Bev glanced up, then beckoned Snowy to the chair on the customer's side of her desk. Snowy sat down. There were no photos or flowers on the desk, just neat stacks of papers.

It dawned on Snowy that forgetful Bev must have had to learn organization while running a household of four kids and a husband. Bev had transferred the lessons to her workplace. Bev, efficient!

"Fine," Bev said into the phone, "I'll see you at the closing. Bye." She hung up, scribbled something more on the memo pad, and sat back, enjoying the audience of a clearly impressed best friend. "Well, what do you think?"

"Remember when you planned to be a secretary and said you would major in skirt-hitching?"

Bev laughed. "Like Mrs. Moulton in high school, sitting on the edge of her desk." Bev straightened some already straight papers and took off her glasses.

Snowy asked, "When did you get the glasses?"

"All this studying! I finally realized that either the print was becoming smaller or I was growing older, so I went to an ophthalmologist at the Gunthwaite Clinic. At Katy Gibbs I used to imagine myself wearing glasses like Ann Sothern in *Private Secretary.*

Remember how great she looked in those big black rims, competent and sexy and funny combined? But I didn't need them back then. Have you had your eyes checked recently?"

"No."

"You probably should." Bev made an old-crone face. "We're almost fifty, Snowy."

"Don't jump the gun. We'll only be *forty-nine* this year. Where's the owner?"

"Geoffrey? Showing a property." Bev lowered her voice. "Speaking of eyes and birthdays, I'm going to give myself an eye lift for an early birthday present."

Snowy squeaked, "Eye lift?"

"Shh." Bev stood up, putting some papers in a big square black leather shoulder bag that seemed to double as a briefcase. Around her waist was a silver belt and below her dress were high black leather boots. From a coatrack she lifted a black down trench coat, and when she belted it, covering the purple dress, Snowy was reminded of the high-school occasions when Bev wore black outfits so that her red hair would be the only color. Now the effect was equally striking, but with white hair.

As they got into Bev's station wagon and Bev drove back along the Miracle Mile, turning at the Kentucky Fried Chicken place onto the ramp to the bypass, Snowy wondered how all this had happened. Instead of their whistling-in-the-dark jokes about age, this was for real, as real as these hated changes in her hometown.

"Eye lift?" Snowy finally repeated.

"You must have noticed my sagging eyelids. I have to look my best now I'm a working woman—'working outside the home,' as they say. I've told you, real estate is a dog-eat-dog business. You need a protective lead shield over your conscience. And I need to keep my looks, such as they are. The day before yesterday I had a consultation with a plastic surgeon in Hanover at Dartmouth-Hitchcock, and I asked him about my neck, too, and he suggested liposuction. It'll all cost about twenty-six hundred dollars. The timing is tricky because I'll look so ghastly for a while, but I want to get it over with before business picks up this spring and I don't want to horrify Etta, so I've scheduled it for her winter vacation week in February. Leon is taking her home—to Ninfield, that is—to stay with Roger that week and visit her old friends."

Snowy's mind spun. Bev seemed beautiful to her as always. Dartmouth-Hitchcock Hospital? That was where Snowy's father had been operated on for his pancreatic cancer. How many trips had she and her mother made to and fro before they brought him home to die? Someday Bev would die. Alan had died two months before his fiftieth birthday, not young, but he would be forever a middle-aged version of the youths on Keats's Grecian urn, of Housman's athlete dying young. She and Bev would get older and older. Tom. He was a man, so the odds were that he would die first. But not for a long long time, knock on wood, knock on wood. She could not bear it!

"The thing is," Bev said, "they won't let you drive yourself home afterward. Your problems with driving—I ought to ask Mimi or Dudley or the twins or somebody, but I don't want anybody to see me like that except you. And the doctor says I'll need someone the first night and to help the next day, and to drive me back for a follow-up appointment on the third day."

Dizziness swirled. Snowy said, "Give me the dates and I'll arrange with Irene and Ruhamah to be away."

"It's okay? Don't do it if it would be too much and set you back in your recovery, your—what's the word?"

"The books call it desensitizing. I'll be fine, Bev. You'll have the greater challenge; you won't be able to make faces."

They laughed. Bev crossed her eyes and said, "Isn't this a milestone!"

Through the years, Snowy and Bev had kept track of various milestones: first bra, first lipstick, onward to sex, the Big Milestone.

Bev said, "Here's another. After Puddles's demonstration of her estrogen patch at Mimi's reception, I decided I ought to investigate the matter. I checked out the gynecologists at the clinic and they're still all men and I'm too used to a woman OB/GYN down in Ninfield to put up with that again, so I went to that nurse you mentioned you go to, the nurse who's an ARNP like Puddles, and now I'm wearing a patch."

Snowy tried to absorb this news, too.

Bev said, "Not that I need lubrication except for my bi-state marriage," and swung down an exit onto the road to Leicester. "I heard a saying on TV the other day: 'It takes a mighty good man to be better than no man at all.' I certainly haven't yet encountered one that would make me give up the joys of the single life I've discovered. Maybe you and Tom have the perfect compromise, two separate establishments, living closer than Roger and I are, and of course you and Tom are madly in love."

"Um," Snowy said. "This Geoffrey Plumley. Is he married?"

"Divorced."

"How old?"

"In his fifties. He came up here from Massachusetts to make money on the lake."

Carpetbagger, Snowy thought, asking, "Good-looking?"

"A wheeler-dealer. It's strictly business, Snowy." Then Bev added, "Last month I went to my first Plumley Real Estate Awards ceremony. It's a banquet held every January, with awards for sales. If you'd been there with me, Snowy, we'd've been rolling in the aisle. They all took it so seriously!"

Bev laughed, but Snowy heard uncertainty in her voice. If Bev had decided to get an eye lift to look better for business, wasn't Bev taking it awfully damn seriously herself?

Bev said, "I got the award for Most Promising Newcomer. Big deal."

"That's great. Congratulations."

Leicester was Gunthwaite's rival town in sports, blue and gold versus Gunthwaite's green and white. When Snowy had been the editor of the high-school newspaper, she had made the trip to Leicester often to the printer who produced the paper; now Mimi's husband, Lloyd Quinn, worked for this printing company, doing graphics. Bev braked before they reached downtown where the printer's was and the ski shop over which Mimi and Lloyd lived in an apartment. She parked in the driveway of a large white farmhouse, a sight from the past on this highway.

They got out, and while Bev took a sheet of paper and a key out of her shoulder bag, Snowy admired the place. The front yard had been lopped off when the road was widened, the fallen-down barn was a jumble of snow-covered rafters, and the house's paint was flaking off, but the lines of the house were still plain and true. Why did anybody build any other kind?

My God, Snowy thought, I'm becoming a curmudgeon!

A red Volkswagen Rabbit plastered with environmental bumper stickers skidded to a halt behind Bev's station wagon. Out leapt Mimi, her long brown braid flying. Age twenty-five, she had, like Bev, inherited Julia's height, but she'd also inherited Julia's gawkiness rather than Bev's grace, and in her skinny jeans and old denim barn coat and handwoven scarf, a big handwoven bag slung over her shoulder, she reminded Snowy so much of Julia that Snowy's heart wrenched with grief, with missing Julia.

Mimi hugged Snowy, then gave Bev a hug and asked, "But Mother, isn't this the place where—where they found the—?"

"Yes," Bev said, "and that's why you'll be able to afford it." She went up the rickety front steps and unlocked a new lock in the old door.

Mimi looked at Snowy. "It's time to get out of that apartment," she said. "I'm ready for a shop, my own design studio." As Julia had, she sold her weaving through the League of New Hampshire Craftsmen.

Snowy couldn't help warning, "You've seen me with the store. A shop ties you down. I've run away today."

Mimi squeezed her arm, said, "Glad you did," and loped after Bev.

Snowy followed. In the dark front hall there was a rank miasma of decay, neglect, filth. She shivered in the cold and asked, "What was found here?"

Bev and Mimi exchanged a glance. Consulting the sheet of paper, Bev led the way into the room on the right, a big living room almost empty, the sun smiling through the dirty windows onto a golden oak morris chair with tattered cushions. "A beautifully proportioned room," Bev said to Mimi. "I see it as your showroom, and across the hall—" She led them into the opposite room, completely empty. "—here's your workroom."

Mimi asked, "Where was it they found them?"

"Upstairs. Mimi," Bev said, "I didn't think it would bother you enough to pass up this opportunity. It's a steal. A prime location on a main road that's the route to I-93 and I-89."

Snowy said, "Who found what?"

Bev asked, "You don't read a New Hampshire newspaper or watch the Channel 9 news?"

Feeling guilty, Snowy said, "I see headlines when I organize the papers at the store. Sometimes I watch the news. The New Hampshire primary..."

Mimi began to prowl around the room, knuckly hands held out the width of her looms.

Snowy asked, "What the hell did I miss in the news?"

Bev had been itching to tell the story. "It was about a year ago. The old couple who lived here kept themselves to themselves, so nobody noticed when the woman stopped going to the supermarket and wherever. Finally people did notice that the man hadn't been seen, and the postman reported that mail was accumulating in their mailbox. Junk mail, that's what they mostly received, but it was piling up after a week or so. The front walk was left unshoveled after a snowstorm. So the police came and got in. Up in the main bedroom they found the man lying on a double bed, dead. Beside him was something covered with a blanket. They drew back the blanket. There lay his wife's decomposing body."

"Oh dear," Snowy said inadequately. "Had he killed her?"

"You and your Agatha Christies! No, natural causes, both of them. He just hadn't had her buried or cremated." Bev fell silent.

With Snowy she watched Mimi get the feel of the room, Mimi who had more future ahead than past behind.

Mimi asked, "What happened to the furniture?"

"They'd been selling it, evidently to buy medicine and groceries and pay bills. Farmhouse furniture would fetch antiques prices. After she died, he had enough money to keep going awhile. There are still some canned goods in the pantry and some really old home-canned vegetables. But he ran out of fuel oil and the woodshed is empty. So he got into bed and died. Pneumonia."

Snowy asked, "They didn't have any family?"

"A son in Seattle," Bev said. "He's in his sixties. He hadn't stayed in touch. Now that the estate is probated, he just wants to sell the place quickly and forget again."

Mimi shook herself like a wet dog and said, "Well, let's see the rest."

The house went on and on downstairs, in the manner of old farmhouses. Bev and Mimi worked out which rooms Mimi could expand the shop into, should business warrant, while keeping living quarters in the rooms nearest the kitchen, which had last been updated in the 1950s. Snowy was almost ambushed by nostalgia for her childhood kitchen but was saved by the dank cold.

Bev said, "In antiques stores nowadays, I see the things I grew up with. Look at that Mixmaster! It's a 'collectible'!"

Mimi said, "Won't what happened here put my customers off?"

"People forget," Bev said. "Lots of people didn't hear, like Snowy, and summer people and tourists won't have the foggiest. See, there's a nice view over the sink. Remember, Snowy, how my mother always maintained that there had to be a window over a kitchen sink or you'd go mad doing dishes? I guess that's still true in the era of dishwashers."

Snowy went to the window over the chipped and dingy white enamel sink and looked at the back pasture where the new snow had frosted humps of junipers.

Mimi said to Snowy, "I wouldn't be chained to the shop. I could close if I had to. I'm not selling essentials and being the heart of the village, like you."

"Er," Bev said, "here's the back staircase. Shall we go up?"

"Sure," Mimi said, misgivings apparently over.

Unlike the stairs in the front hall, these were almost vertical and very narrow. The smell of clammy plaster reminded Snowy of how the Emery Street house had smelled when she and Mother and Daddy had moved from a cozy apartment on a nearby street into a place so damp that Snowy had thought she might as well be living in the riverbank like Ratty in *The Wind in the Willows*. Well, her parents had certainly fixed it up, and so could Mimi. But the work!

In the upstairs hall, Bev gestured toward all the doors and said, "Plenty of bedrooms for children."

This time, it was Snowy and Mimi who exchanged a glance. Mimi had confided to Snowy that she and Lloyd didn't plan to have kids.

Mimi asked, "So, which is *the* room?"

Bev walked down the hallway and stopped at the doorway of the front bedroom. They joined her, looking in at wallpaper bleached to bone, braided rugs loosened into loops, and more furniture than in any other room, a pine wardrobe, an oak bureau, and a four-poster stripped down to rusty coils.

"Remember," Bev said, pointing out the front windows at the road, "the three most important things in real estate are location, location, location, and you've got frontage on a well-traveled highway to the interstates."

"Okay," Mimi said. "I'll bring Lloyd here after work."

Bev folded the sheet of paper and put it back in her shoulder bag. The house tour over, they all hurried down the front staircase and outdoors into the clean white day. Bev said, locking up, "Now, where shall we have lunch? Whose turn is it to choose, Mimi?"

"Mine," Mimi said, "but let's let you, Snowy. When it's Mother's turn, we go to Leicester's yuppie place, the Bouquet Garni, and when it's mine we go to the diner. What'll it be, Snowy?"

"Oh no," Snowy said, "I'm not getting in the middle of this."

"So it's the Miss Leicester Diner," said Mimi, and stepped into her Rabbit.

As they followed her downtown, Bev advised Snowy, "The Leicester diner is a leave-your-coat-in-the-car place. It'll smell like grease if you don't."

"Remember Jimmy's Diner in Gunthwaite?" Snowy said. "Going there was our slumming milestone." Roger had taken Bev to Jimmy's; Tom had taken Snowy on their second official date. "I wish it had managed to survive when McDonald's and Burger King came in. Besides atmosphere, Jimmy's had real hamburgers and French fries. Remember when everybody called them French fries instead of just fries and they weren't sliced pencil-thin?"

And when they entered the Miss Leicester Diner and settled into a booth, Snowy optimistically ordered a hamburger and French fries. Mimi went for the shepherd's pie, while Bev chose a tuna roll. Tuna fish had always been Snowy and Bev's favorite summer sandwich, but you couldn't find their wintertime favorite, marshmallow fluff and raspberry jam, on any restaurant menu because they'd invented it themselves, as kids. The waitress, like the one at the Parmigiano, was middle-aged.

Mimi asked, "Is Ruhamah still talking about New York?" Mimi called herself Ruhamah's almost-aunt, and she'd received an account of the Christmas trip over the phone, along with messages her roommate, Kristin, had sent via Ruhamah.

"It's wearing off a bit," Snowy said. "Harriet was heroic, showing her everything from Bloomingdale's to the Guggenheim and umpteen other places."

Bev said, "I'm so relieved I only had to learn Boston, though I used to yearn for New York. I envy Ruhamah, going to those plays."

"She's got a mental calendar of the trip," Snowy said. "I don't think she even has to refer to the journal she kept. She tells me that on this day such-and-such weeks ago she and Harriet were doing such-and-such."

Mimi said, "I suppose I was like that when I got home from our honeymoon." Her father had given her and Lloyd a European hiking trip. "After you and Alan went to England, did you retain one particular scene clearer than others in your mind's eye? That's what's happening to me now, and not a vast view but flowers in a field, which I'm trying to get right in a design."

Snowy said, "It was so long ago. Before Ruhamah was born. But yes, Ludlow. I *had* to go there because I'm such a fan of A. E. Housman." She closed her eyes and saw Alan. "Also, fish-and-chip shops. Alan was crazy about British fish-and-chip shops, really exotic to him even though he'd grown up on the seacoast eating plenty of fish and shellfish." At that moment their food arrived. The waitress set down Snowy's plate, and as Snowy said, "Thank you," noting that the hamburger and French fries did look like the genuine old-fashioned Jimmy-type, all of a sudden in her memory she recognized the waitress. Not this waitress, but the one at the Parmigiano. Rita! Beneath the years, beneath the war paint on that careworn woman, had been Rita Beaupre, Tom's girlfriend when he started dating Snowy.

VALENTINE'S DAY FELL on a Sunday this year. At noon, Tom came over to help Snowy close up the store, and instead of chocolates he brought a curly-haired young woman who was, Snowy knew instantly, his daughter, Libby. The photo Snowy had seen hadn't shown that Libby had inherited his long straight eyelashes, too. Also his eyesight; she was wearing glasses. Snowy had gathered that Libby had taken the divorce harder than the neutral sons; Libby had not visited Tom in his new home before.

"Snowy," Tom said, "this is Libby. Libby, Henrietta Snow Sutherland, known as Snowy."

"Hello," Snowy said.

Libby nodded warily.

Tom said, "Is Ruhamah home? Libby and I are going snowshoeing behind the village and I thought you two might like to join us. We went skiing at Cannon yesterday, and my knees aren't up to more of that."

Libby suddenly laughed at him and said with affection, "Your football knee."

"Ah yes," he said. "I'm paying now for all that glory."

Libby continued, teasing, "Up and down Mount Pascataquac all spring, summer, and fall couldn't have helped."

"Probably not," Tom agreed. "Want to come along, Snowy?"

So Snowy fetched Ruhamah, who was vacuuming the apartment, and out in the store's shed Snowy and Ruhamah located their snowshoes, unused since last winter, together with Ruhamah's cross-country skis and downhill skis, which Ruhamah had used this year, and Alan's snowshoes and skis Snowy didn't know what to do with.

Off the foursome went, out behind the store, stepping forth into the sunny windy afternoon, embossing the snow with patterned tracks across a brushy field, through some woods, onto the clear expanse of the town's athletic field. Libby and Ruhamah drew ahead. The New York trip seemed to have made Ruhamah more outgoing, and Snowy could hear her asking Libby about UNH, which Ruhamah would probably attend, Alan's alma mater. During the near-bankruptcy, Snowy hadn't touched the trust fund for Ruhamah's college, but she wouldn't be able to add to it, either. She couldn't afford Bennington, no matter what scholarships Ruhamah might be able to get, and anyway, the place wasn't the same now that guys were let in. Snowy's theory was that women should be allowed into men's colleges because they provided a civilizing element, but men ruined women's colleges. Scholarships, she thought, student loans—

Tom was saying, "Besides the times when Libby went with us to see David's basketball team play Woodcombe, Libby has only driven straight through the village before, to the trailhead when she'd hike up to the fire tower to visit last spring. This is the first time she's looked around here."

Snowy listened to Tom's use of "us," meaning Joanne. It still came naturally to him. Snowy asked, "Does Libby approve of Woodcombe?"

"Who wouldn't?"

Trying not to pry, Snowy said, "She must miss you."

"I'm getting it in dribs and drabs, but at Christmas she decided to break up with her boyfriend, one she's been serious about for some time. Not because of the divorce, she assured me. Just because it wasn't any good anymore. The gist being that she's learning how complicated things are."

Snowy lifted and set down each snowshoe, feeling buoyant, weightless. Across the athletic field, Ruhamah was leading the way up the low hill from which could be seen all of Main Street, all the white houses cowering in snow below the frozen mountains.

Tom said, "Next Sunday, how about a movie?"

"Well," Snowy said, "I'm going to stay at Bev's next Sunday to go with her to Hanover early Monday morning, and I'll be taking a few more days off to look after her. She's having a little, well, a little operation."

"What? What's wrong?"

"Nothing vital. She has instructed me that I can only tell on a 'need-to-know' basis. Promise cross-your-heart not to repeat this. She's having an eye lift."

Tom didn't look aghast or burst out laughing. He said, "Oh."

"Has—has Joanne?"

"No, but she talked about it. Maybe when Libby was through school and there might be some extra money."

Snowy had been staring in the mirror and deciding that although she couldn't afford cosmetic surgery, maybe she could afford to have her hair highlighted. But first, she had to play nurse, and she hoped motherhood had made her better at it than when their Girl Scout troop in high school had been nurse's aides. That experience was dreadful except for moments of hilarity, such as the time Puddles practiced cranking up a hospital bed containing Bev playing patient, and Puddles had cranked both ends so enthusiastically that Bev ended up folded and squashed, while Snowy almost wet her pants laughing. When it came to real patients, Snowy had hid, disgusted by their ailments. Would she be able to take care of Bev? Would she even be able to look at her, cut up and sutured? She couldn't consult Puddles. Bev had decided that Puddles didn't need to know until afterward, because she'd scare Bev to death with horror stories. Over the phone, Bev had said, "Puddles gets a fait accompli or maybe I won't tell her at all."

Snowy had replied, "But Bev, during her New Year's phone call she again mentioned wanting to visit Maine. She'll probably visit us en route."

"By then I'll just look 'rested.' That's the goal, not looking young but as if you've had a lovely holiday." Bev dropped the calm act. "Oh, Snowy, what if something goes wrong and I'll never be able to close my eyes again? What if I'm blinded? What if the liposuction causes paralysis?"

Snowy was getting scared too, now that it was really going to happen. "You can sue and win billions."

"I'll end up a wealthy mystery woman swathed in veils, wandering from spa to spa." Bev tried to giggle, then wailed, "What if afterward I simply don't look like myself anymore?"

Snowy didn't know how to reply. If she said Bev looked fine or if she said Bev needed surgery, either comment would upset Bev.

While Snowy was dithering, Bev had a thought that brought a modicum of comfort. "But," she said, "I don't look like myself anymore anyway. Therefore, what the hell."

Snowy had arranged with Fay to have Ruhamah spend the first part of February vacation at the Rollinses'. Late the next Sunday afternoon, when Ruhamah had driven off to the Rollinses' in

Alan's van, Snowy drove to Bev's house. Leon had taken Etta to Ninfield yesterday, so they had it to themselves. Snowy realized she hadn't sampled Bev's cooking since meals in the Beacon Hill apartment; Bev had got very good, and for dinner she cooked up a storm because, she said, "I may never be able to see or chew anything ever again." Worry didn't diminish Snowy's enjoyment of the artichoke appetizer, the poached salmon and the herbed rice and the broccoli—Bev had remembered her favorite vegetable!—and the brownies with vanilla ice cream and hot fudge sauce. Later, while watching *Murder, She Wrote* in the family room, they had seconds of dessert and during commercials talked about their waitressing days at Sweetland, not about tomorrow.

They took Snowy's car, because Snowy didn't want to have to cope with an unfamiliar one, Bev's station wagon, on top of everything else. Bev drove. In the trunk was a cooler with ice packs and the saline solution Bev had already bought. The morning was so very cold, zero degrees, that a cooler for summer picnics seemed ridiculous. But it was for an eye lift. Also ridiculous? Bev sped through Leicester past that farmhouse she'd sold to Mimi and Lloyd (Roger helping with the purchase; Bev giving Mimi back Bev's share of the commission; Leon hired to assist Mimi and Lloyd with renovations), on through towns to I-89 to Hanover. During the trip, Bev talked about real estate, but in Hanover she switched to the Winter Carnivals she'd gone to with Roger. They skirted the Green, arrived at the hospital, searched for and finally found a parking space.

Inside the hospital, Bev said, "Well, at least I'm not here to have a baby," and was whisked away. Snowy extracted an old paperback from her shoulder bag and sat in a second-floor waiting room trying to leave her surroundings for Miss Marple's St. Mary Mead. She remembered other waiting rooms in which she had waited, during Ruhamah's childhood ailments and then Alan's vasectomy, snip snip.

A nurse came up and said, "The procedure went smoothly. Your friend has been taken up to recovery on the eighth floor and will be resting until about two o'clock. You might want to get some lunch."

Instead of heading for the hospital cafeteria, Snowy put on her parka and went for a walk, finding the rooming house where she and Mother had stayed during visits to Daddy. Ever since her childhood there had been such a distance between her life and her parents' that even before the scornful teenage years she had viewed with detachment their earnest attempts to create the appearance of a perfect family life, with the fine house and the cute daughter. When her mother went to work in the office of the shoe factory after Snowy started high school, convenience foods had partly replaced the perfect old-fashioned made-from-scratch meals, but otherwise Charlotte and Hank Snow continued striving to present their dream, which had at first been Daddy's because he had grown up so poor in Manchester, his alcoholic father dying early and his mother also dying too young after raising Daddy and his sisters on her own. Having only hazy memories of Nanny, Daddy's mother, Snowy had called her mother's mother both Gram and Grandma; later she wondered if this was just affectionate playing with words or a need for two grandmothers. Snowy's parents had met when Daddy had come looking for work in Gunthwaite, lured there by a vision of the perfect setting, lakes and mountains and rivers, clean breezes freshening the old mill town. Back then, Gram added some money to Grandpa's wages from Trask's by renting the spare bedroom and providing meals. Daddy had happened to rent the room after he got a job at Trask's. Inevitably he fell in love with his landlady's pretty daughter who dished up delectable chicken and dumplings, and Charlotte worriedly hitched her picket-fence hopes to his vision of their future.

Looking at the Hanover rooming house, Snowy missed Mother and Daddy. In a way, she had missed them all her life.

She walked on to the Green and down Main Street to the Dartmouth Bookstore, where she browsed, avoiding the poetry section. Then she checked her watch and hurried back to the hospital. After taking the elevator up to the eighth floor, she asked for Bev. A nurse directed her down the corridor.

When Snowy entered the room, she saw that two of its three beds were occupied, one by a man, one by a woman who wasn't Bev. The third bed was empty. Empty! Bev had died!

Then a toilet flushed, and a person came out of the bathroom, a woman wearing Bev's shirt and jeans but the face unrecognizable, sheathed in a chin strap, eye area stitched with black sutures and grotesquely swollen. Bev's voice said, "Hi. They just removed the IV, so this was a test run. All okay," she told the nurse who came in. "May I go home?"

The nurse looked at Snowy. "You're driving her? Bring the car around to the front."

Snowy obeyed, and as she drew up in the Subaru, Bev appeared, pushed in a wheelchair. Bev had enjoyed the drama of such rides when she'd left hospitals carrying a baby, with an audience beaming, but now she hopped out fast and scooted to the passenger seat, saying, "Oh, what an embarrassing ride through the main lobby! Frankenstein's monster in a chin strap!"

Snowy drove off. "It's sort of like a nun's whatchamacallit."

Bev started to make a virginal face, realized she couldn't, and yanked the hood of her parka over her head. "I am *so* sorry you have to look at this repulsive sight."

"That's what best friends are for."

Bev groped in her shoulder bag, brought forth sunglasses, and gingerly put them on. "Ouch. The doctor gave me a prescription; we can pick up the pills and ointment in Gunthwaite. I'm full of enough dope to get me home, and I've had compresses on but we'll probably have to stop partway for that saline."

"Are you hungry?"

Bev made the retching noise she'd taught herself in high school. "I thought I was, but one bite of the ham sandwich they brought me and I realized I wasn't. Snowy, I swear I'm never going to eat anything with fat on it again. After I was on the table, with an IV and with a gadget attached to my left forefinger, the doctor and two nurses began the proceedings, first numbing my eyelids, and while that stuff was penetrating, the doctor went to work on my chin. I couldn't tell what he was doing, there were just strange sensations, but then he produced the lipo instrument, which I could see all too clearly. It reminded me of the opposite of Julia Child and a larding needle. The tube was clear, and I watched dark yellowish goop being sucked out. Fat! Ughy-pew!" This last word used to be a favorite of Bev's and she still employed it in moments of stress.

"God," said Snowy.

"Then things got really exciting. A buzzer began going off, and I was asked to breathe deeply. We had a few sessions of this as he began work on my right eyelid, and I started to feel as if I were having a baby after all, what with these breathing exhortations. Finally, there was a consultation amongst the doctor and nurses about how cold my hands were; the attachment was taken off my finger, my sock removed from my left foot, and the attachment put on the toe, but no luck there either, my feet were too cold. Just as he said to give me oxygen and try something-or-other, a nurse suggested trying an earlobe. I got both oxygen and the earlobe attachment, and that silenced the buzzer. After the operation was over, I asked what the commotion was all about, and he said that the buzzing machine looks at the color of blood to see how well oxygen is getting into the bloodstream and there'd been a technical problem because of my constricted vessels. Constricted in terror."

"Do you want the saline yet?"

Bev was immersed in her story. "Not quite. Anyway, things went forward. While he was suturing my eyes, he chatted about this and that, and I began to feel more as if I were at the dentist's, especially when I was asked questions I couldn't answer, because of the oxygen equipment, not because of a dentist's fingers in my mouth. Then it was over, and one of the nurses put on the chin strap. I got to ride on a gurney up to recovery. Then came these gauze pads—" She took a package out of her shoulder bag. "—soaked in saline set in ice cubes, and I sort of slept while the compresses were periodically changed. My eyes seem to shut all the way, but I can't really tell at this stage. I guess maybe I do need to stop sooner than I figured."

Snowy screeched to a stop in the break-down lane of I-89, jumped out, ran around to the rear of the car, took the saline solution out of the cooler. When she slid back behind the steering wheel, she saw that Bev was removing the sunglasses and looking in the visor mirror.

Bev said, "Eek, eek, eek! It hasn't improved since I looked in the hospital bathroom mirror. Snowy, what if I'm disfigured for life?"

"You'll be fine," Snowy said, trying to sound convincing, grabbing the package, fumbling out two gauze pads, and dousing them with the cold solution.

"Why did I do this? I must be insane!" Bev put the pads over eyes, leaned back, and promptly fell asleep.

When they were off the turnpike and on the highway, Bev awoke hurting and Snowy stopped the car to change the pads, and stopped again before they reached Gunthwaite, where Snowy parked at Bev's drugstore, not Main Street's long-gone Rexall with a little soda fountain, the only place in town that used to sell cherry Cokes, but the Brooks Pharmacy on the Miracle Mile. Snowy rushed in and got the pain pills and ointment. Then she drove on to Bev's house, wishing they'd find Puddles there, competent and professional Puddles to whom Snowy could hand over the responsibility. No Puddles, so Snowy did the best she could. Bev had readied a comforting tuna-noodle casserole for supper, but now she just wanted to go to bed with her bedroom TV and a Diet Pepsi; Snowy kept her supplied with compresses, and because Bev was supposed to sleep sitting up, Snowy brought pillows from all the beds in the house to try to find an arrangement that alleviated the torture.

Bev said wanly, "What a terrible hostess I'm being. Please, heat up the casserole for yourself."

"We'll have it tomorrow. I'm polishing off the last of the brownies."

Bev gave a feeble giggle.

During the night, sleeping in Etta's bedroom, Snowy could only doze, worrying, the door open so she could hear Bev, the hall light blurring Etta's treasures that surrounded her, riding trophies and ribbons, Barbie dolls, pictures of horses, books about horses. What if Bev died?

The next morning Snowy tapped tentatively on Bev's door.

"I'm awake," Bev said. "How do I look?"

Snowy stepped in. "Um," she hedged, "how are you feeling?"

"I look worse?"

"Well, your eyes are more swollen and you seem to be wearing *lots* of lilac eye shadow."

Bev threw back the bedclothes and marched across the hall into the bathroom. "*EEK!*"

"Can you eat any breakfast?"

Bev came out, adjusting the Velcro closure of her chin strap. "I'll phone the doctor. He said to stop the compresses today, but that doesn't make sense if my eyes are ballooning. Go have your breakfast, Snowy. Just brushing my teeth tells me I'd still better not do any chewing yet, so it'll be yogurt for me, but not for a while; I'm queasy. This is all backwards, first the labor, then the morning sickness." She went to her closet. "How I wish I could take a shower, but not for a couple of days. I'm a revolting *filthy* monster. If anybody knocks on the door, give me a chance to run and hide before you answer it. This chin strap, twenty-four hours a day for a week!"

Snowy was in the kitchen sitting on a stool at the breakfast bar, drinking tea out of a loon mug, eating an English muffin off a loon plate, and trying to read her Miss Marple, when Bev came in wearing an outfit of green zippered sweatshirt and green sweatpants that did not resemble in the least the rags Snowy jogged in.

Bev fumed, "Grammar should be a required course for nurses

and doctors. I get so irritated when they tell me to 'lay' down that my blood pressure shoots up, but I'm too polite to correct them so I blame the rise on the so-called white-coat syndrome. This nurse just told me that the swelling is caused by my 'laying' down overnight. I bet Puddles is the only person in the entire medical profession who uses 'lie'!"

Snowy stood up. "Then we continue the compresses?"

"Yes, and I'm to switch to Tylenol now instead of after the pain pills are used up, which should stop the nausea." Bev looked out the kitchen windows at the backyard, a snow-covered rectangle like the front yard. "What in the world am I doing here, in this condition, instead of home with Roger?" She turned and theatrically swept a hand at the kitchen. "Have I gone crazy, Snowy? I certainly have gone loony, haven't I!"

Suddenly afraid of this unrecognizable Bev, Snowy thought how the gestures and mannerisms of Bev and Puddles were more familiar to her than her own and how steadying this usually was. She put an arm around Bev, led her to the bentwood rocker, and took the saline solution out of the fridge. "Sit."

"Menopause. Midlife crisis."

"Or simply a delayed reaction to the big decisions and changes you made. Sometimes I wonder if I've got a version of post-traumatic stress disorder or something." Snowy handed her two soaked pads.

"Oh, Snowy, you have a reason to!" Bev leaned back and applied the pads.

"Did you take any Tylenol? Want me to get some?"

"I took a couple. The nurse said to use half a pain pill if Tylenol doesn't do the trick."

"Do you want any yogurt yet?"

"No. This is an extreme way to cut calories."

Snowy sat down again at the bar. "Your mother mentioned the stages of grief. With me, after anger at Alan came the less pure emotion of resentment, which didn't last long, thank heavens, because I've been so busy. Maybe you instinctively avoided resentment over Roger's behavior, as well as other festering emotions, by leaving Ninfield." Did that last observation sound like a batch of bullshit?

Bev said vaguely, "I think Mother would approve of my leaving, but the eye lift—she wouldn't say anything, but she'd be bemused. I wouldn't have done this if she were alive. Snowy, remember how sublime Roger looked playing basketball? Remember the time Roger won the Alumni-Varsity game in the last instant with that throw from the far end?"

"I remember."

"The owners of this house have finally dropped the price."

"They have?"

"Do I buy it? If they sell it out from under me, I'd have to make Etta move again, and Leon, but where would I find another house so close to a riding academy? And close to the lake. But otherwise, this damn house is—just ordinary! I daydream about coming across my dream house in New Hampshire when I'm listing properties, but if I did I couldn't afford it."

"You've improved this house a lot."

"Not too much whimsy?"

"Outdoors, could you get a landscape designer to add personality?"

"Yes," Bev said, brightening. "Peonies especially. In Ninfield, my peonies, my dahlias and phlox..."

Bev dozed off. Snowy sipped tea and read, keeping watch.

In the afternoon Snowy opened the glass doors of the living room's awful brick fireplace and lit a fire, and on the sofa Bev spooned strawberry yogurt and read *People* magazines. At suppertime, Snowy put the casserole in the oven and found a package of frozen peas in the fridge, to cook up nice and mushy; Bev managed to chew a small serving of both and felt up to a bowl of ice cream with the evening's television.

The next morning Snowy did the driving to Hanover, Bev in the passenger seat in sunglasses. Bev emerged from the doctor's office with tapes at the outside of her eyes. During the drive home, the story Bev told was: "The nurse took off the chin strap and looked at my eyes and pronounced me not so colorful as some people. Can you imagine what *they* must look like? The doctor came in and agreed I was doing fine and said I could have the stitches out, even though it's early, because I live far away. The nurse took them out, and it wasn't any more painful than plucking your eyebrows. Then she put on these tapes, which should be kept securely in place until Friday. The doctor said the redness in the scar area will last a month. I can start wearing makeup next Monday. After this week in the chin strap, I'm to wear it for two weeks as much as I can. Not to the office! I'll be wearing turtlenecks! And I can take a shower now, below the neck. I have to wash my hair in a sink backwards, with help. If you could help me with the hair-washing today, Snowy, I can manage the rest of the week."

"No, you can't. You might fuck things up. I'll come over after work and play hairdresser. Remember in our yearbook, so many girls put 'hairdressing' and 'beauty school' as their ambition because they were really just going to get married?"

"I feel horribly guilty, keeping you from the store and Ruhamah. And Tom."

"Bev, it's been ages since I had a whole day to sit and read as I did yesterday. You're not the only one who'll look like she's been on vacation." But Snowy was now worn-out. This was the most driving she'd done in a decade.

When they got home, Bev carefully took a shower, and after Snowy shampooed her hair in the kitchen sink Bev said, "We should do that someday. Go on a vacation together."

"We're career women," Snowy said. "We haven't got time." Nor, in Snowy's case, money. "Let's make the most of this. What do you feel like for supper?"

"I've got a craving. I'm back to the cravings stage. Remember the marshmallow-fluff-and-raspberry-jam sandwiches we used to make? I craved those when I was pregnant."

"Our favorite winter sandwiches."

"None of my children ever liked them. It has to be just peanut butter and marshmallow fluff. So unadventuresome!"

"Same with Ruhamah. You have marshmallow fluff? Raspberry jam?"

"But no Sunbeam bread. Pepperidge Farm."

"A compromise," Snowy said, and that's what they had for supper on paper plates in front of the television. Then the last of the ice cream.

Later, while they were watching *Matlock,* Bev said during a commercial, "I'm going to be okay."

Snowy understood that she wasn't just referring to her face.

"And," Bev said, "I'll buy this ghastly house. I've spent a bit of the inheritance from Mother on my face; I'll make a more sensible investment now."

ON MARCH 19, Snowy's forty-ninth birthday, a Saturday, one of the presents that Ruhamah gave her was the morning off so that she could have her hair highlighted at the Village Beauty Shop in Marge Ames's ell, where Snowy and Ruhamah usually just went for haircuts. As Snowy pulled on the rubber cap shaped like a 1920s flapper's cloche and in the mirror watched Marge pick up a sort of crochet hook, then felt the tugs as Marge pulled strands of hair through the holes in the cap, she wondered how the hell Bev could have dared do anything more drastic than this. What if something went haywire? What if the results were orange or platinum? But when Marge finished blow-drying Snowy's highlighted locks, the color only looked more scrambled up than before, with lighter blond combining with her dark blond to camouflage the white hair. Or so she hoped. She remembered how in high school she had considered cutting off her trademark ponytail, saying that she couldn't wear it forever and end up an old lady with a gray ponytail. She stared into Marge's mirror. The ponytail had gone a long time ago, and now at forty-nine she sported a highlighted pageboy, something she couldn't have predicted. Marge said, "A success!" Snowy heaved a sigh of relief.

And as for Bev, although her eyes still had a somewhat surprised look, she was almost back to normal.

Returning to the apartment, Snowy made herself a mug of tomato soup and stood at the counter gulping it, in a hurry to get downstairs to relieve Ruhamah, who would be heading off to Leicester to help Mimi and Lloyd move into the new house and would spend the night with them. Ruhamah's overnight absence was, Snowy knew, Ruhamah's unspoken present; Ruhamah had begun taking pride in being sophisticated about Snowy and Tom. The official present had been given at breakfast, a pair of silver earrings shaped like snowflakes, Ruhamah chortling, "You really should get your ears pierced again, Snowy, so you can wear two earrings in each, like me." "Maybe," Snowy said, thinking that one piercing session twenty-odd years ago had been quite enough. "These are lovely, Ruhamah."

As she put the mug in the sink, the phone rang. Puddles said, "I hoped I'd catch you now. I figured you'd be going out to dinner with Tom tonight or maybe overnight. Happy birthday!"

"Thank you, Puddles. How are you, how's everything?"

"I'm brooding about my own birthday, and I've decided to give myself an early birthday present."

Snowy almost remarked that Bev had done this, but she remembered in time that Bev hadn't yet told Puddles about the eye lift. She said, "What kind of present?"

"A trip to see Maine again, while I'm still in my forties and mobile. I'm planning to do it in June, before the tourists are too thick on the ground. This year I won't time my vacation to accommodate Guy's construction schedules or his golf."

Puddles's birthday was July 9. She was the youngest of the born-in-1939 triumvirate, with Snowy the oldest and Bev, on April

18, the middle. Snowy said, "You're planning to see more than Portland, your hometown?"

"Yes, as much of the Maine coast as I can. Now, don't answer yet but think about it: Why don't you and Bev take your vacations then and join me?"

"Nothing to think about, Puddles. I can't take a vacation. But can you come visit here on your way to or from?"

"We'll leave things flexible. So, what is it? Dinner or overnight with Tom or both?"

Snowy laughed. "Dinner." Puddles didn't have to know everything.

"Yeah, sure." Puddles sighed enviously. "Lazy old Guy, only interested in blow jobs nowadays. Why are they called that? It's suck, not blow."

Snowy shrieked, "*Puddles!*"

After dinner at the Gunthwaite Inn, when Tom and Snowy returned to Woodcombe, he said, "Well, a choice. Your place or mine?" David was back in Newburgh for the weekend.

"Yours," Snowy said, because she'd never spent the night there before.

In the hayloft apartment, Tom produced a tissue-wrapped gift, which proved to be another newfangled gadget, a VCR. He said, "You can tape the programs you can't stay up for." Snowy was awed by and afraid of it; she knew Ruhamah would be thrilled.

Like his bedroom in his parents' Gunthwaite home, his bedroom here was impersonal, but he and Snowy got very personal.

That evening Puddles phoned Bev and told her about her Maine plans, adding, "How can we talk Snowy into taking a vacation?"

"I can't take one either," Bev said, folding laundry as she cradled the receiver in her new improved neck. She thought wistfully of the Maine coast. "Snowy and I are both catering to tourists one way or another, and the season begins on Memorial Day nowadays, not the Fourth of July."

"How about just a couple of days, midweek?"

Remembering the summers after high school and her first year at Katharine Gibbs, when she had expanded her working horizon farther than Sweetland by waitressing at a hotel in Camden, Bev suddenly remembered Snowy's telling Mimi about a pilgrimage to Ludlow because of A. E. Housman's poems. Bev said, "Camden! Edna St. Vincent Millay! That might do it, Puddles, that might entice Snowy away from her store. There's an inn associated with Edna St. Vincent Millay, not the Grand View Hotel where I worked but the Whitehall Inn. Maybe Snowy and I could get away for an overnight and meet you at the Whitehall Inn."

"Edna St. Vincent Millay," Puddles mused. "Snowy wrote a research paper about her for our junior-year English class. Great idea! I'll make reservations at the Whitehall Inn and we'll present Snowy with a fait accompli."

Bev glanced at a mirror and the fait accompli she should tell Puddles about, but maybe if she waited until June, Puddles wouldn't notice. Then she wondered what on earth had possessed her to suggest Camden, where she and Roger had spent their honeymoon at the Grand View Hotel.

ON MAY 9, the first anniversary of Alan's death, the first hummingbird of the season appeared at the feeder on the apartment stoop as Snowy started outdoors for her morning run.

"Hello," she said. It was a ruby-throated male, thrumming like an entire swarm of bees. She wished she could imagine it to be some kind of sign, but no. She went down the stairs and jogged off down the street in the rapturous spring dawn.

Everybody had hinted or plain suggested that the way to handle the anniversary would be to get away, to take Ruhamah and go anywhere, New York (Harriet), a backpack (Tom), a health resort (Puddles), or just to Mimi's to help set up the shop (Bev). Dudley and Charl had invited her and Ruhamah to supper. Snowy had asked Ruhamah what she wanted to do. Ruhamah gave her a long-lidded look, like Alan's, and said, "Stay here and face it, don't you?" "Yes," Snowy said, thinking that besides, this year the ninth was a Monday and she had to work.

She considered small things she might do. She could make a Spam casserole for supper, a dish that was a family joke because Alan loved Spam in reaction to his father's banning it after having eaten too much in the Army during the War. She and Ruhamah could go to Murray Cove, which they had been avoiding for a year. Maybe next year. Today, tomorrow, she would just keep her head down in blind routine. Routine had held her together during agoraphobia. Would it now?

The day didn't get too bad. The evening did. A year ago, on a Saturday night, she and Alan had attended a Fabulous Fifties party thrown by Patsy and Nelson Fletcher. After, exhausted by the strain, she had gone to bed while Alan stayed up for a nightcap and some television. What if, what if, what if she had stayed up with him and maybe he would have poured out to her everything that was troubling him and that could have exorcised the demons—

The phone rang, and it was Alan's mother, weeping. Would this be the time Phyllis Sutherland would finally utter the unutterable, would scream that if Snowy had been a better wife Alan wouldn't have killed himself? Ruhamah, in her rage last year, had implied it was Snowy's fault, and maybe despite the school psychologist she still thought so deep down.

But Phyllis wept, "I wish he'd wanted a funeral of some kind. There's just—nothing!"

Then Snowy remembered the stirring of an idea when driving past Old Eastbourne last Thanksgiving. "How about a plaque or bench or something at Old Eastbourne? I'll write Jay suggesting it." Jay Sprague was the chairman of the board of directors. "Then you and Jay could get together and discuss what would be the best kind of tribute."

"Snowy. That would be wonderful."

After Phyllis hung up, Ruhamah came out of her bedroom and for the first time sat down in Alan's wing chair instead of on the sofa to watch TV.

Snowy sat in the Martha Washington chair and during a commercial said, "Depression is a disease." She'd said this a number of times to Ruhamah since Alan's death. Maybe she should have said it before he died.

"Yes," Ruhamah said.

Snowy suspected it could be a contagious disease. Whenever the black cloud had descended on Alan, she could feel it smothering her own natural but precarious cheeriness, and when Ruhamah was born she feared it for her as either contagious or inherited.

Snowy said, "Please tell me if you ever get pulled down like that. You know there's help for it that Alan wouldn't look into, just as I wouldn't with agoraphobia. We were stubborn."

"I know."

At bedtime, Snowy opened the bureau drawer where she kept her bottle of Valium now that she shared a medicine cabinet with Ruhamah in this one-bathroom apartment. A year ago tonight Alan had taken her bottle of Valium and a half gallon of Gilbey's gin to Murray Cove.

She closed the drawer. Instead of Valium, she would try a bedtime story. She got into bed with the Walkman Tom had given her and listened to her latest audio book from the library, a P. G. Wodehouse.

It didn't get better the next morning. This was even worse. She jogged into the green dewy glowing morning, listening to the babble of birdsong and the hectic sound of spring peepers, inhaling the soupy pease porridge smell of green, of pollen and seed froth; she passed front yards that were bouquets of pink and white cherry blossoms, lilacs fattening to bursting; she looked up at the mountains tumbled in mists. All she could think of was this morning last year when she awoke to find the bed empty.

That search through the house had been like a nightmare. She remembered it in staring flashing images, and the awful dread pounded again in her chest. When the house had proved empty too, she had run out to the barn and found the van gone. Thinking he might have needed to go to the store early, she had managed to drive the Subaru to the village. The Sunday newspapers had been delivered and sat piled on the porch, waiting to be lugged in. She had unlocked the door. He wasn't in the store, either. Then the town police chief's black Jeep Wagoneer had stopped out front.

Snowy wasn't just jogging now. She was loping, trying to outstrip the images. From the lake came a loon's tremolo, rippling.

Across a field behind a house at the end of the village, you had a clear view of Mount Pascataquac, like the view she used to have at Hurricane Farm. She looked up at the little spike that was the fire tower. Tom was on duty for a three-day spell, and in the cabin beside it he would be starting his day.

Way back when she and Alan were dating she had first recognized, nonplussed, some of the similarities between him and Tom. But not depression. Tom, though, beneath his persona (1956 GHS Yearbook: Tom Forbes voted the Friendliest Boy, the Most Flirtatious, Best Dressed, Best Line, Best Dancer, Best All-Round), was distant, aloof, detached. He was always ironic. But these traits would not ever make him do what Alan had done.

She turned and ran home toward the routine of her shower, breakfast, opening the store, work.

"THIS IS INSANE," Snowy laughed, squirting another barrier of fly dope around her head. She returned the spray can to Tom, who didn't seem to be bothered at all, either by the blackflies or the weight of the big pack on his back, although he was carrying most of the supplies and gear, including the tent.

"Sure is," Tom said, taking a plastic water bottle off his belt. "Drink some."

She had her own water bottles in her own smaller pack, Ruhamah's rucksack she'd borrowed, but she would have to remove it to get at them and after she had done this on their last stop on the trail, the worst thing yet had been putting the pack back on, not the weight (lately her morning jogs had been rehearsal hikes, training with the loaded pack and the brand-new hiking boots she ordered from L. L. Bean) but the horrible clammy chill as her cooled-off shirt made contact with her sweaty skin. It was a long-sleeved shirt, and she was wearing long pants, khakis, not shorts. Tom was similarly garbed, blackflies dictating your clothing in spring. She drank three swallows. "Thanks."

"Okay? Want some more gorp? A Snickers? Want to count the trout lilies?"

When they'd stopped she had marveled at the biggest patch of trout lilies she'd ever seen, speckled and flickering in the sun through the new leaves. Snowy said, "Nope. Onward and upward." She picked up her walking stick. Lloyd, Mimi's husband, made these sticks out of saplings; Mimi had given her one last year and recently had given one to Tom, for a birthday present.

So Snowy and Tom climbed on along the trail up Swiftwater Mountain on this Sunday afternoon, May 15, Tom's fiftieth birthday. His fire-tower schedule allowed him today and tomorrow off; she had arranged with Irene to take tomorrow morning off. After Snowy had closed the store at noon, they had driven out of the village in Tom's Jeep, bumping onto a labyrinth of dirt roads Snowy had never been on before, to an old logging road. Tom had edged the Jeep off the road, and above the new ferns' recently uncurled noggins Snowy saw in the roadside bushes a small wooden trail sign at the start of a barely discernible path that disappeared into the woods. In comparison, the trail up Mount

Pascataquac was I-93. She had hoisted her pack and followed him. They had threaded their way through the trees, slogged across a wet meadow lushly sprouted in an abandoned beaver pond, and back in the woods they'd begun to climb, the Swiftwater Brook going in the opposite direction beside them, bounding downhill in reverberating springtime enthusiasm, then quietly eddying clear amongst plush green rocks, then overflowing, pouring out again, exploding in lacy white spray. The blackflies could make you want to turn and race downhill too; they hung in front of her like a spotted veil through which she saw trillium blooming along the banks, some dark Victorian red, some delicate purple-veined white.

A few weeks ago she had asked Tom how he'd like to spend his milestone birthday, and he had replied, "With you in the woods," and suggested the overnight hike. She'd said, thinking of his job on top of a mountain, "Wouldn't it be a busman's holiday, a busman's birthday?" "We won't go to a summit," he said, "we'll go up to Swiftwater Pond. At this time of year we should have the place to ourselves—and the bugs." "Tom Swift," she'd laughed, "Tom Swiftwater."

Of course the trail didn't stay on one side of the brook. Oh no, of course not, that would be too easy. Now the trail took a notion to leap it again for the umpteenth time, and Tom stepped lightly across on some rocks. She concentrated, clutching the walking stick. Before agoraphobia, she hadn't exactly been a tightrope walker, but she hadn't particularly thought about balance; her uncertainty as she teetered across was a leftover from the years of dizziness.

Watching her, hoping his expression looked casual, not concerned or critical, Tom wondered if this birthday-hike idea was dangerously selfish of him. What if it caused her a setback? When they had come to the first crossing, she had reminded him of the way his dog, Bonnie, in her puppyhood, used to run back and forth beside a brook, whining anxiously, before daring to splash across. But Bonnie had learned fast.

Lunging up the bank, Snowy smiled. "I may arrive dry, after all!"

"What a disappointment. I was hoping you'd have to take every stitch off."

She leaned against a huge mossy boulder, like a soft green wall. "Well, I might anyway, eventually."

He kissed her.

When they continued on, the climb became a scramble over slippery lumps of granite that jabbed and scraped. At last Snowy noticed through the sweat streaming down her face that the woods were less dense. The ground leveled, and the brook decided to meander.

Tom said, "We're here."

Out of a pocket she hauled a bandanna and mopped her face. She saw blue ahead through the trees. "The pond?"

"The Swiftwater Pond I promised."

"I did it!" She had hiked three miles, approximately what she jogged around the village, but uphill with a pack sure made a difference. Thank God that because she wasn't in hiking condition and because they didn't have much time, Tom had chosen a short hike to an easy destination. She looked at her watch. Four o'clock, precisely what Tom had estimated, no doubt figuring her slow pace. "We're right on schedule."

"And now you can relax." He led the way through the woods to the shore of the pond, a brimming saucer of blue wedged down into the forest. He pointed at a log. "That's your chair." Slipping off his pack, he took a silver square out of a side pocket and partly unfolded it.

"A Space Blanket?"

"For now, a chair seat." He placed it in front of the log.

She remembered how on picnics with Alan and Ruhamah she brought along a plastic trash bag for this purpose. She and Alan had been alone on the last picnic, out behind Hurricane Farm at a beaver swamp, and the tarp had come in handy for romance. It was the last time they'd— She shoved the memory away, took off her pack, and unstuck her sweaty shirt. "Can't I help you do, what's it called, set up camp?"

"I've got a modus operandi. You sit down and commune with nature."

She swatted a blackfly, dived into her pack for her own can of fly dope, and sprayed it madly. She couldn't possibly sit still and be chewed alive! But this was Tom's domain, and he wanted her out from underfoot, just like a wife with a useless husband. Or maybe he was thinking of her as his guest. She sat down on the Space Blanket, the log against her back, tried to ignore the bugs, and gradually she grew aware of a quiet she hadn't experienced since she left Hurricane Farm and her walks in the woods there. You knew it was a busy quiet, full of creatures looking for food, which meant in many cases devouring another creature, yet it seemed absolutely peaceful. Swallows cruised over the pond, weaving back and forth, back and forth.

Lulled, she watched Tom. He had camped here a few times last year, so he didn't have to search for a level spot. From his pack he took a bundle of green material and pieces of metal that almost in a blink (or had she dozed off?) were transformed into a small tent with a top rounded by metal hoops, not the tepee she'd imagined. He had told her that his tent was a little bigger than a single-person tent: "a one-and-a-half person tent," he'd said, and they had laughed, knowing they'd manage. Now, it looked claustrophobic. Out of the magic pack came the two-person sleeping bag he'd bought for the occasion, and he spread it within. Then he took out a couple of empty water bottles and a plastic gadget.

He said, "I'm going over the outlet to get our extra water supply."

"That's the filtering thing?"

"The latest model."

As she watched him crouching in the brook, contentedly pumping water into the bottles, she remembered him at home in another world, Varney's gas station, the hangout for high-school guys, where he worked pumping gas and spent the rest of the time under the hood of a car.

He returned to the campsite and next took out of the pack a piece of clothesline, which he strung between two trees before performing a modified striptease, peeling off his shirt and T-shirt, then hanging them over the clothesline and producing from his pack a cotton navy-blue turtleneck, which he donned, saying to her as he swapped his hiking boots and ragg socks and sock liners for socks and sneakers, "You ought to change, too."

"Okay." She got up, delved into her pack, and felt the bliss of exchanging her sodden shirt for an old aqua turtleneck jersey. He'd advised a turtleneck, because of the bugs. After she draped the shirt over the clothesline, she asked, "Sure I can't help?"

"I'll join you in a minute for the cocktail hour. If you need a bathroom, it's the great outdoors, same as on the trail. Back there, away from the pond and the brook."

So she visited the bathroom, washed her hands with a Wash 'n Dri towelette, then returned to her chair, where she put on clean socks and her running shoes. He had continued organizing, bringing forth from his pack a little metal contraption that she only realized was a stove when she saw that he'd lined up a metal pot and a couple of blue boxes alongside. Kraft Macaroni and Cheese! Last year Ruhamah had gone through a phase of eating the stuff for her weekend breakfasts. He unpacked two plastic plates, two sets of metal knife, fork, spoon. She remembered how last spring and summer her hands had automatically picked up silverware for three out of the utensils drawer when she was setting the table. Looking away, back to the pond, she strove to empty her mind of anything but the hypnotic swallows.

Tom put a can of peanuts on the log, handed her a plastic glass, sat down beside her, and raised his glass to her.

She said, "Happy birthday, Tom," and sipped. Chablis.

"Now I'm a full-fledged member of the American Association of Retired People."

"They start recruiting rather early. You're not retired. Did you actually join?"

"It's cheap, so why not. I might learn something useful."

She laughed. "You're not bothered by turning fifty?"

"Why should I be? I'm just damn glad I lived long enough for this, with you."

They sipped wine, munched peanuts. The woods across the pond seemed to draw together, blending, thickening. The spring peepers began to seethe, shrill with lust, and bigger frogs popped up through the pond's surface like a percolator perking.

Tom remembered the huge birthday parties that Joanne always threw for him. If they still were married, this year's would've been a whopper, with everybody bringing joke presents for failing eyesight and hearing and memory and bodily functions. He'd get fake false teeth, Ex-Lax, nose-hair clippers. What about Joanne's fiftieth birthday, next month? He always took her out to dinner on her birthday. Would somebody else do that this year? David and Libby hadn't mentioned that she was seeing anybody, but certainly the gorgeous Joanne must have all the single guys of a certain age in the north country sniffing around, and some married ones too. Yet what if she ended up alone on her fiftieth? He hated to think of that. He'd better make sure David went home for the event and Libby and Brandon phoned...

"Dinner." He heaved himself to his feet. "If this were a decade or more ago, I'd still be cooking over a campfire."

"The stove is environmentally correct?"

"After supper, I'll show you how to do environmentally correct tooth-brushing."

She giggled, then grew nervous as he used a small container of bottled gas to get the tippy little stove going. No disaster occurred. While a pot of water came to a boil, he spread a red-and-white checked plastic tablecloth on the ground.

"This is new," he explained. "The elegant touch, just for you."

"I'm honored."

"Dual purpose, to sit on and eat off." He dumped macaroni into the boiling water. Out of a plastic container he forked sliced tomatoes onto the two plates. With metal tongs he lifted the pot off the stove to drain it. A plastic bottle contained milk, some of which he poured onto the drained macaroni before stirring in the cheese powder. "Dinner is served," he said.

She joined him, sitting on the tablecloth. Eating the marvelous meal, she wondered why she had given Ruhamah such a hard time over such a delicious sodium paste.

Snowy accepted seconds, when offered. Tom had judged that she would.

As he filled the pot with more water to boil for instant decaf, she got up and went to her pack. She had said that she would bring dessert, and she produced a Styrofoam box, which she carried over and put carefully down on the tablecloth and opened. She took out a small cake, whose white frosting almost disappeared under chocolate script that read Happy 50th Birthday Tom. "Whew," she said. "I was afraid it would either land in the brook or get jounced to bits."

He'd been expecting she'd bring something lightweight, a couple of cupcakes or Twinkies or something. But she'd lugged a whole cake, unused though she was to a heavy pack.

She said, "Fay thought a carrot cake would withstand the hike best, but I knew you'd prefer chocolate, so Fay made this dense as well as small. Custom-made." She went back to her pack and returned with a package wrapped in spring-flowers paper, tied with a green ribbon.

He kissed her, the pot boiled, and picking up the tongs he poured water into the insulated plastic mugs he preferred to tin. After he cut the cake with his jackknife and served the slices, he opened the present. A very nice leather glasses case, along with a neat little plastic kit of minitools for glasses repair.

She said, "I figured you probably have a repair kit, but maybe you could use an extra."

"I always have to remember to put it in my pack. Now I can keep one there." He took the tiny magnifying glass out of the kit. "The solution to a Catch-22: How do you repair your glasses when you can't see?" The only time she'd given him a birthday present before, in 1956, it had been typed-up copies of the poems she'd never shown anyone else. "Thank you, Snowy. And the glasses case is beautiful."

"Well, I've noticed you don't use one at night, but I hoped it might come in handy sometime, maybe backpacking when you don't have a bedside table. I considered getting you a sun visor—"

They laughed. Eating cake, she thought of how he used to take his glasses off when they went parking and hang them over the convertible's sun visor, then turn to her, becoming the other Tom, her private Tom, with his blue eyes and long straight lashes unguarded.

After they'd finished dessert, he opened a small bottle of Dr. Bronner's Liquid Soap and washed the dishes right there, instead of in the pond as she'd expected. She was allowed to dry them.

"Now," he said, "the tooth-brushing technique. The idea is to spray instead of spit."

She dug out the Ziploc containing her toothbrush and toothpaste, and he got his and demonstrated, misting bushes with Colgate.

"See?" he said. "Closer to leave-no-trace."

She said, "In Hollywood, isn't that called a spit-take? When someone is drinking something and chokes and lets fly?"

"Is it? Took me a while to learn."

Snowy, too. She brushed her teeth and tried a projectile spit but dribbled down her chin. As she tried again, he moved on to the next part of his modus operandi.

"Bears," he said, packing edibles and cookware into two nylon bags. "Just in case."

She remembered how he had faced a bear that had come to Mimi's wedding reception at Hurricane Farm. "Have you ever met one here?"

"No," he said, tying a rope to a bag. "Don't worry. Just a precaution." He flung the rope up over a branch of a spruce, hauled the bag high, tied the second bag onto the end of the rope, and lifted it up to balance. "We'll want to hang up our packs, too, to keep mice out of them. First, take out our jackets; we'll need them." He suited action to words, hooking their packs over stubs of branches. "Now we can watch night come to the pond."

They sat leaning against the log, listening to the frogs. Eventually their interest in Mother Nature became secondary to their interest in each other, and earlier than he'd planned they retreated to the tent. As she took off her shoes, he zipped the net doorway shut.

Snowy said, on her back wriggling out of her khakis, "Roomier than it looked." She laughed and rolled into his arms. "Another milestone."

No bears visited their campsite during the night. The next morning she awoke before Tom, eased the doorway zipper open, and crawled out clutching her clothes. Cold! She hopped around, putting them on, then walked down to the pond. Vapor wafted up from the gray water, and there was a smell of fresh morning, springtime, renewal. Last year at this time she would not have dreamed she could feel even partial contentment.

It was good of Tom never to ask her about the poems—or lack of them.

She heard a sloshing to her left. Without moving her torso, she slowly turned her head, and a moose seemed to fill her vision, solid in the wavering light. It stood knee-deep in the pond, its antlered head lowered to feed. It was unaware of her or deemed her beneath notice. She had seen a moose before, almost domestic in the backyard of Hurricane Farm. Here, surrounded by forest, it seemed—well, you couldn't say such a funny-looking animal seemed noble, could you? Maybe you could.

Tom's presence beside her was so much a part of the moment that she didn't feel surprise she hadn't sensed his approach. He was wearing just his T-shirt and Jockeys; Skivvies, Alan called them.

Together she and Tom stood watching in the serene quiet morning, way out in the woods.

This hiking and backpacking, Snowy thought, could get to be addictive. She'd better buy a pack of her own.

CHAPTER FOUR

BACK BEFORE AGORAPHOBIA, whenever Snowy and Alan took any sort of trip, he always kidded her, "You're either eating or planning where you're going to eat next, or both."

So when she and Bev left in Bev's station wagon for Maine on this sunny Tuesday morning, June 21, the summer solstice, Snowy immediately started thinking ahead to lunch. The prospect of fresh seafood would, she hoped, keep her from worrying too much about indulging in a vacation from the store. Puddles and Bev had trapped her into it, Bev announcing last week that Puddles had reserved a single and a double at the Whitehall Inn in Camden, and one of the twin beds in the double was for Snowy, and that was that. Lunch, Snowy thought, but still she fretted about leaving the store. For God's sake, it was only overnight! Lobster, she thought.

Bev was evidently on the same wavelength, as a best friend should be, because after Woodcombe was behind them and they were heading east on Route 25, she said, "We'll have lunch at Moody's Diner. Have you ever been to Moody's?"

"Nope," Snowy said, trying to settle down, straightening her blue polo shirt under her seat belt. With this shirt she wore her denim pants that were slightly dressier than jeans. But Bev looked more like a summer person, in a green jersey and white shorts.

"If it's still there," Bev said. "It's been there in Waldoboro forever, so let's hope it is."

"Alan and I only got as far into Maine as Portland. We had enough ocean where we were. Moody's is an old-fashioned diner?"

"A landmark, flourishing. How Mother loved the place! She and my father spent their honeymoon in Bar Harbor, and they stopped at Moody's en route, and when Mother took me to Camden those two summers I worked at the Grand View Hotel, she and I always stopped at Moody's too. We always had the fresh crabmeat rolls."

So Snowy switched her thoughts from lobster to crabmeat.

"Pie," Bev said as they crossed the state line into Maine. "Moody's has a zillion pies, with real whipped cream. Mother and I would have the berries in season, strawberry pie when she took me to Camden and blueberry pie when she brought me home." Then Bev thought of how she and Roger had had coffee at Moody's on their way back to Boston after their Camden honeymoon. Roger had also had a piece of apple pie, for a second breakfast; a New England tradition, pie for breakfast. Afterward, they'd continued down Route 1 to their new life in the basement apartment on Beacon Hill. She asked Snowy, "Do you really think Puddles won't notice my eyes?"

"I don't notice any difference anymore."

"But you're used to it. When she last saw me a year ago, I was drooping."

"I didn't notice that, either!"

They drove along a river, past a galloping waterfall, through hard-times towns, past trailers and auto-body shops and healthy-looking apple orchards fluffed out in full leaf. When they reached pulp-mill stinky Westbrook on the outskirts of Portland, Snowy felt a tug south toward Eastbourne and Pevensay and the ocean she'd known with Alan.

Then they were on the turnpike, and Bev said, "A whole year since I came to Mimi's wedding and didn't go home. Roger is expecting me to return now. I've had my sabbatical."

Snowy asked, "But how can he, when you've bought your house?"

"Actually, I haven't told him I did that."

"Oh," Snowy said. "Still stringing him along?"

"I know it's cowardly. I don't want to upset him more than I have already. I don't want to—I don't know what I want!" Bev pressed her foot down on the gas pedal.

They sped to the exit onto Route 1, then drove through Brunswick and Bath, Snowy gawking at all the sights, from McDonald's to the mammoth ship under construction at Bath Iron Works. Wiscasset was a postcard-perfect Maine town. Except for the traffic. Although Puddles had scheduled her trip to get ahead of the crowds, the tourist season had definitely begun. After Wiscasset, after Damariscotta—

Bev cried, "There it is!" She pulled into the bustling parking lot of a low building Snowy would never have guessed to be a famous landmark.

Inside, Moody's Diner felt familiar, and as she and Bev sat down in an old wooden booth, Snowy thought of the Miss Leicester Diner and of Jimmy's Diner. Opening the menu, she said to Bev, "Memories of Jimmy's Diner again. Diners each have their own personalities." And she thought of how, whenever she was shopping at one of the malls in Gunthwaite, more and more lately she felt overcome with yearning for the Main Street of her youth. Advancing curmudgeonliness.

Bev said to the waitress, "A crabmeat roll and an iced tea, and then a piece of strawberry pie, please."

"Me too, please," said Snowy.

The waitress left, and Bev leaned back and sighed. "I didn't realize how good it would feel to get away."

"Are you tired? You've been driving almost four hours. Want me to take over?"

"Thanks, no. If I were in the passenger seat, my memories would really get scrambled."

Snowy pictured Julia and teenaged Bev in one of these booths; she could see them, but then she had to overwork her imagination as she tried to see a young Julia with her redheaded bridegroom here on their honeymoon. Their wedding had been so informal, in Julia's family home down in Massachusetts, that there weren't any photographs of the ceremony, and Snowy didn't recall any honeymoon snapshots, either, in the albums she'd looked through in her youth when visiting Bev. Julia had started spending money on photos only after Bev was born. "When did your parents get married? 1938?"

"Mother was another June bride."

"I wonder what she was wearing when they stopped here."

The waitress brought their iced teas. "Thank you," Bev said to her, and then to Snowy, "It's like an old movie in my mind. Vintage clothing."

"So are *our* trousseaus."

Disconcerted, Bev said, "Eek, I hadn't thought of it quite like that. Remember my going-away outfit I scoured Jordan Marsh for? Spring-green suit and a white blouse with perky green polka dots. White pocketbook, white heels, *white gloves!* Oh God, how fifties!"

Snowy hadn't changed into any going-away outfit because she had already been wearing a suit in the ceremony in her parents' living room, unlike Bev in the fairy-tale wedding gown Bev had wanted since childhood. When they were little, Snowy and Bev had made Wedding a part of their dress-up games, but when Snowy grew up she realized that she found formal weddings silly and presumptuous. Why would you want to invite a bunch of people to witness a very personal ceremony? Yet if she eloped, her parents would be terribly upset, so she'd had the simplest wedding she could manage. However, Bev growing up still desired the drama of those Wedding games, but on her actual wedding day she'd had to float in her beautiful gown across the lawn at Julia and Fred's house instead of parade down the aisle of the Unitarian church as in her childhood plans, because the real-life groom was Roger, and although Roger had lapsed, his family was still devoutly Catholic. "Remember my suit?" Snowy said. "Pale blue piqué. We were matching our eyes." She laughed. "We still are!"

They looked down at themselves, at Snowy's blue polo shirt and Bev's green jersey.

Bev said, "Oh my God, how mired in tradition!"

They grabbed their iced teas.

Bev said, "I stopped here with Roger after our honeymoon. We sat in one of those booths near the counter, and I think I was wearing almost the same thing I am now, Bermudas and a green top!"

"Consider it classic," Snowy said.

The waitress set their plates in front of them.

Bev took a bite of crabmeat roll. "See why Mother and I always went for these?"

"Yes!"

They began to laugh.

Bev said, "This is going to be fun. Why have I been so apprehensive about Puddles—and everything?" Then that "everything" sobered her, because it included the filming of the movie of *Peyton Place* in Camden the summer of 1957. Despite her success in the Gunthwaite High School Dramatics Club plays, she hadn't dared go to the auditions for stand-ins and extras. She had made up many excuses: She didn't have time because of her waitressing schedule; she was also too busy having fun with wealthy summer boys; and anyway, she deplored the movie's inaccuracy, Hollywood's choice of beautiful seacoast Camden instead of the novel's true setting, a New Hampshire inland town. But the real reason was the same as the reason she hadn't tried out for cheerleading. If she didn't try, she wouldn't fail. Or so she'd thought back then. Now, facing Camden again, she knew that not trying could be failure.

"Fun," Snowy said, "and no cooking. I wonder what the Whitehall's menu is like,"

As they were leaving, Bev paused at the display of souvenirs. "Oh, why not." She chose a Moody's Diner T-shirt for herself.

Snowy bought a Moody's Diner coffee mug for Tom.

❧

AFTER THOMASTON (grim prison, lovely houses) and Rockland (why did its scruffy Main Street have so many places to get your hair cut?), they drove in slowing traffic into Camden, where the Route 1 Main Street was the epitome of quaintness. While Snowy tried to look at all the dear little stores and glimpse the harbor, Bev pointed somewhere and said, "The Grand View is over there but you can't see it from here, eek!" and slammed on the brake as tourists surged across the street ignoring crosswalks.

Snowy asked, "Did you spend your paychecks in these shops?"

"It was a tormenting temptation. I did buy clothes for dates on boats when my Gunthwaite wardrobe just wouldn't do. Otherwise, I saved every cent for clothes for college."

They remembered that they hadn't gone clothes-shopping together as usual that late August, because Bev had stopped speaking to Snowy after Snowy had stolen Tom back from Bev that spring, even though Snowy had thereupon broken up with him the same night. Bev and Puddles had shopped together, Bev buying the minimum in Gunthwaite and waiting to spend the rest of her savings at sophisticated Filene's and Jordan Marsh in Boston when she started Katharine Gibbs.

Suddenly, they both felt very tired. In silence they crept on along Main Street, and then the cars began to move a bit faster as Route 1 turned uphill on High Street between big white houses appearing even whiter against window boxes of exuberant impatiens and petunias.

Bev said, "Keep a lookout on the left."

Snowy spotted the sign, a dark green square bordered with white. "There!" Its gold lettering said: Whitehall Inn. Food. Drink. Lodging. Since 1901. And her exhaustion disappeared and she was shivering with gooseflesh-excitement. This really was the place. Edna St. Vincent Millay had approached this inn as she herself was doing, though of course then the road would've been less crowded and noisy with traffic. In 1912, Edna's sister Norma had been waitressing here and had talked twenty-year-old Edna into coming to a staff party during which the staff entertained guests. Edna had recited her latest poem, "Renascence." Across the front of the big white inn stretched a porch, with pillars from which the Maine state flag and the U.S. flag were flying. Behind the planters of red geraniums, guests were rusticating in rattan rockers.

Bev made the left turn and followed the driveway off to the side into a parking lot. A hefty woman, wearing khaki shorts and a T-shirt printed with lobsters, was sitting on the edge of the open trunk of her car, having some sort of tailgate picnic. Snowy blinked; the woman became Puddles. She wore her brown hair the same as she had last year, a short practical cut; her high-school and nursing-school hairdo had been almost shoulder-length, curling at its tips like soft snails.

Bev whispered, "She's put on a few more pounds since last year."

At Mimi's wedding, Snowy had seen how once-fragile Puddles wasn't fighting middle-age spread the way she herself and Bev were, and she admired her for it. Now, though, Puddles was no longer looking fit if heavier. Flabby was the word Snowy was now avoiding. How could Puddles presume to lecture Snowy—or anybody—about health anymore? Why, too, was Puddles overeating, Puddles the fussy eater whose sandwiches Snowy used to devour during lunch at school?

Bev parked beside the maroon Ford that Puddles must have rented at Logan Airport. "Puddles!" she cried, rushing to hug her.

Puddles slid off the trunk, hugged Bev back, then said, "Eye lift. And chin?"

"Of course not," Bev said. "I'm just rested."

"Sure," Puddles said, "and I'm on the grapefruit diet." She hugged Snowy and held out a bag of Oreos. "Have a cookie?"

“Thanks,” Snowy said, taking one, feeling Puddles giving her the once-over with a nurse practitioner’s eye, remembering Puddles’s effortless cheerleading cartwheels, as light as milkweed silk in a breeze.

Puddles said, “You’re looking a hell of a lot better than you did a year ago.”

“Time,” Snowy said, “the supposed great healer.”

“Time and Tom?” The minute Puddles said this, she wished she hadn’t. She glanced at Snowy’s left hand, at the little diamond engagement ring Alan had given her, at the wedding band.

But Snowy laughed. “Yes, both time and Tom.”

They stood there awkwardly.

Bev said, “Speaking of time. We can’t check in until three, so shall we walk down to the waterfront?”

“Great,” Puddles said.

With relief, they locked their cars and set off down the hill.

Snowy asked Puddles, “How has your trip been?”

“I got as far as Bar Harbor yesterday, spent the night, and turned back to get here on schedule. So I’ve done more sight-seeing than I ever did when I lived in the Pine Tree State. In Portland I visited cousins I haven’t seen since my grandmother’s funeral twenty-something years ago.”

“Gutsy, traveling around on your own,” Snowy said. “I mean, gutsy for us fifties females.”

Puddles said, “Gutsy, that’s me.”

Snowy sensed a reverse in Puddles. Once fragile in appearance and stalwart in spirit, had Puddles switched characteristics?

Bev began playing tour guide. As they crossed the road and started down the main street, she intoned, “To your left is the library, with an amphitheater behind it—”

Snowy stopped stock-still. On a little slope she saw a figure looking out toward the harbor. In a trance, she left the sidewalk and walked toward Edna.

Whereas Edna had been small, the statue was taller than life-size, six feet or more, and bronze, done with a palette-knife effect that reminded Snowy of some of Harriet's painting experiments at Bennington. Edna wore a long-skirted dress and stood with one hip slightly cocked, clasping a book in both hands behind her back. Her hair was in a bun, her neck long, her profile unsmiling, expression intent.

When Snowy became aware that Bev and Puddles had joined her, she also realized that she was crying.

Bev put an arm around her. "This is new since my day."

Snowy blubbered, "Remember how I used to joke that I was mad at Camden because Edna ought to have a statue and you'd told me there wasn't one?"

Puddles produced a packet of Kleenex from her shoulder bag and gave Snowy a tissue.

Bev said, "Later this afternoon, let's drive up Mount Battie. I climbed it on an old carriage road with a boyfriend one of those summers, but I read somewhere the road has been fixed up into an auto road. From there you'll really see the three mountains and three islands she was writing about in 'Renascence.'"

Snowy mopped her face. "I might make another scene."

"That's allowed," Puddles said, giving her a second Kleenex.

Snowy blew her nose, turned away fast from the statue before she started crying again, and Bev led them back down to the sidewalk, where they had to wriggle to move forward through the throngs, past the shops and restaurants. Snowy felt she should be trying to picture the street as Edna would have seen it during her lifetime, but she was relieved to have to concentrate simply on not getting crushed to death. Her emotions felt squeezed, wrung out.

Bev said, "Port!" and pointed dramatically to the left, and Puddles and Snowy followed her down a narrow side street of more shops and restaurants onto a big wharf. "The public landing," Bev explained.

"Holy shit," Puddles said, taking a camera out of her shoulder bag. "Anyone want to go for a sail?"

In this harbor, the air was filigreed with straight and diagonal lines, tall slender masts and rigging. The effect was so delicate that Snowy thought the boats must be as insubstantial as the sky itself. Wild roses scented the sea breeze.

"Windjammers," Bev said while Puddles snapped a picture of her and Snowy against the harbor, "yachts, sailboats, I had many an adventure when I embarked from here, me hearties. Starboard!"

Leaving the landing, up a side street to the right they went, and then Bev forged on up another street, higher and higher until Puddles gasped, "I thought we were going to *drive* up that mountain of yours!"

Bev stopped, panting herself, but she'd been too full of memories to notice. She asked Puddles, "Are you okay?" When they were climbing Pascataquac for Mimi's wedding, Puddles had kept an eye on her because Bev had recently had a heart-attack scare caused by diuretics. Now Puddles looked ready to drop. Snowy, thanks to the hikes she'd gone on with Tom since the Swiftwater backpack, wasn't out of breath at all.

Puddles said curtly, "I'm fine," but she felt all wobbly, in her knees and in her soul. "Where are we going?"

"I wanted to show you my hotel," Bev said. "Around this corner."

"Lead on," Puddles said.

Snowy said, "Are you sure?" and Bev repeated, "Are you okay?"

"Shut up and climb," said Puddles.

Bev and Snowy meekly obeyed. A high hedge curved along the sidewalk, and the scent of roses returned, sweeter and sweeter.

Then ahead past a lawn and gardens stood a great ungainly structure of gray shingles, green awnings.

Bev said, "The Grand View Hotel. It's still here."

The grand view included the masts along the waterfront, the ocean itself, and a mountain with a tower on top.

But Bev was only looking at the hotel. "We waitresses lived in that wing in the back. That little window, second from the left, no view, that was the room I shared with another girl. When Roger and I spent our honeymoon here, we had the moderate-price view, from the second floor. See the two windows in that turret, to the right? That was our room."

Puddles said, "And the next year Guy and I got married and spent our honeymoon on St. Thomas. God, how young we all were. Except for Guy. Do you realize he's fifty-eight this year? He wants to retire to Hilton Head and play golf until he croaks."

Now, on the spot where Bev had figured she herself would be the next one to need a Kleenex, it was Puddles who began to cry. But when Snowy and Bev moved toward her, Puddles backed away, digging that packet of Kleenex out of her shoulder bag. She looked at her watch and said, "After three; we can check in."

They walked down the hill.

ON MAIN STREET, Puddles recovered enough to dive into a shop and buy a darling Camden T-shirt for her grandson, Guy James Cram Hammond, whose nickname this past year had become Little Guy, which unfortunately, Snowy speculated, must be the nickname some people somewhere gave to a penis. As they went uphill again, Puddles told Snowy and Bev about his first birthday party last month and his remarkable abilities. "He's almost walking, taking these high steps as if up to a curb—" Puddles paused to demonstrate, a pantomine that Snowy hoped wouldn't startle drivers of the passing cars into crashes. "—and he's talking a blue streak, with eight words. Susan told me to give him a keyboard, and he immediately started banging away on it, bouncing up and down." Puddles bounced and banged.

Giggling, Snowy asked, "Do you have pictures with you?"

"You're asking a grandmother *that?*"

They were all laughing when they reached the Whitehall Inn, where the long porch blended the huge white structure amazingly into the green shadows of trees. After fetching their suitcases from their cars (a large suitcase for Puddles, overnight bags and vanity cases for Snowy and Bev), they walked across the porch past a group of two men and two women, sixtyish, sitting in a circle of chairs and chatting through the din of the Route 1 traffic. Snowy followed Bev and Puddles indoors, started across an expanse of oriental rugs on wooden floors, and saw a photograph of Edna on a wall near a piano.

Young Edna, looking just the way a poet should, ethereal and beautiful.

This whole wall was devoted to Edna. Holding her breath, Snowy tiptoed closer and examined Edna's framed high school diploma, more photographs, some of which Snowy remembered on jackets of poetry collections, and two framed poems, "Friends," typed, age sixteen, and "From a Train Window," handwritten with a crossed-out line rewritten.

"Jesus H. Christ," Puddles said. "You in a trance here, and Bev over there in Foxy Grandpa glasses. I've checked us in and made the dinner reservation. The bellhop is waiting. Come on."

"Bellhop?" Snowy said from her trance.

"Well, a kid."

Snowy turned and noticed that even the piano was devoted to Edna. A sign said: 1901 Steinway Piano Played by "Vincent." Family and friends called Edna "Vincent," but Snowy had always felt it would be presumptuous for her to do so even in her thoughts. Then, as Puddles hustled her across another oriental rug toward the reception desk, Snowy saw that Bev was standing in a little hallway beside it, wearing her reading glasses, studying a bulletin board. Snowy escaped from Puddles and detoured to Bev. There were photos of celebrities who'd stayed here.

Bev pointed to one particular photograph. "'Lana Turner,'" she read aloud from the label, "'in a scene from *Peyton Place* filmed at the Whitehall Inn.'"

Puddles said, "Come *on,* you two."

Snowy nudged Bev, and they joined the bellhop, a boy in jeans and polo shirt who hoisted Puddles's suitcase and asked Puddles if this was her first visit to Camden.

"I'm a native Mainer," Puddles told him, "a born Maniac. But I've lived away a long time, and I haven't been in Camden before."

"I have," Bev said, removing her glasses. "It's a charming town. Don't bother with my bag; I can manage and so can Snowy hers. We live nearer, in New Hampshire, so we're traveling lighter."

The kid looked relieved and led them upstairs. They came to Puddles's room first, and while he set down her suitcase, Snowy and Bev peered in from the doorway at an unpretentiously old-fashioned décor, wallpaper with little flowers, a white chenille bedspread.

"Thanks," Puddles said, remembering that the Whitehall's policy was no tipping; a gratuity was tacked onto the bill, which kept things simple. "The other room is just down the hall?"

"Right," the kid said.

Puddles told Snowy and Bev, "I'll be along in a few minutes."

The kid continued down the hall to open another door.

"Thank you," Bev and Snowy said.

"Have a good stay." He left.

Bev and Snowy set their overnight bags on luggage stands, their vanity cases on the dressing table, and looked around. The little wallpaper flowers here were yellow against a cream background. The twin beds had white chenille spreads, and the white cotton curtains had a bobble fringe. Snowy went into the bathroom. Seeing her face in the mirror, she remembered Alan's taking the photos for the jackets of her own poetry collections. As far as she knew, Edna had kept working despite all her difficulties. She had been wildly acclaimed and famous, and as her renown faded she nevertheless remained in print. When she died in 1950, she had been out of vogue, and she was out of fashion now, but you knew that fashions could change in poetry as well as everything else. Not to be published at all anymore, wasn't that worse than achieving fame and losing it? Stop whining, Snowy told her reflection. Stepping out of the bathroom, she reported, "Tub with claw feet. We knew those before they became vintage. In and out of fashion!"

"As long as the toilet is modern," said Bev, disappearing into the bathroom.

Two cream-cushioned rattan chairs waited at the windows, a little round table between. One was an armchair, the other a rocker. Snowy sank into the armchair and gazed out through green leaves.

Bev emerged, saying, "What's with Puddles and the tears over Guy and golf?"

"I think we're tuckered out, all of us."

"Have you had enough Edna? Want to skip Mount Battie?"

"No!"

Bev unpacked a short-sleeved linen sheath, nautical navy with white trim. Holding it up, she said, "Not much different from one I had those Grand View summers, so when I saw it at the Mall of New Hampshire I couldn't resist. Another classic? After tonight, it'll do for real estate."

"Real estate?" Puddles said, knocking and entering simultaneously. "Are you actually earning a living or is Roger still subsidizing?"

"Both," Bev said, hanging the dress in the closet. "I think of the money he sends as just for Etta and Leon. I can't support a family yet with real estate; it's not a steady income yet and by its nature probably won't ever be."

"Feast or famine," Puddles said, walking over to the window. "Like Guy's business. I've always been the steady income, and we've saved and invested enough of it so that now Guy can retire.

I never thought that would happen, because of so much famine. I didn't prepare my mind."

Not knowing what to say, Snowy unzipped her overnight bag and took out her dinner clothes, white cotton pants and the shirt of pastel blue and pink flowers she'd bought for Mimi's wedding. Bev and Puddles had therefore seen the shirt, but she didn't feel she could go buy a new one, even some bargain at Gunthwaite's outlet mall. She hung the outfit in the closet behind Bev's new dress and unpacked tomorrow's shorts and jersey.

Puddles, furiously swallowing more of the goddamn fucking tears, batted at a curtain bobble, the way Reese, her cat, would. She told herself: Concentrate on Bev and Snowy. "So," she asked Bev, "you're staying in New Hampshire?"

Bev hadn't told Puddles that she'd bought the house. Bev didn't now. Taking her hairbrush out of her vanity case and looking in the dressing-table mirror to brush her hair, which as usual was perfect already, she said, "Etta has settled in at school. She has her horse here. Leon—well, he's Leon anywhere. Of course, Roger can make a convincing case for our return, and he's doing his damnedest. It would be awfully easy. I remind myself how easy I've had it all these years. Everybody ready?" As they went downstairs, she added, "Let's go in my car. The hours I've spent chauffeuring my children were good training for driving real-estate customers around. Some couples squabble worse than my kids."

So in the parking lot they got into the station wagon. Puddles didn't take much convincing that she should sit in the front passenger seat, seeing as how she was the Maine native and should be thus honored, while Snowy rode in the back. Bev drove north on Route 1 and turned off into Camden Hills State Park. At the entrance booth Puddles insisted on paying the admittance fees, and Snowy and Bev let her because her window was handiest, and as they started up the auto road Puddles played tour guide this time, dispensing details from the information sheet she'd been given at the booth. "Mount Battie is nine hundred feet high and commands a panoramic view."

A molehill, Snowy silently scoffed, as the station wagon churned its way upward.

Puddles continued, "There used to be a hotel on the top and then it became a clubhouse and then it was torn down in 1920. The next year a tower was put up in recognition of the services of Camden men and women in World War I."

Bev said, "The tower was very romantic."

Many cars were parked at the summit. Bev found an empty space and pulled in, and Snowy changed her mind about the molehill.

Mountains and ocean.

The round stone tower with arched entrances was being thoroughly enjoyed by the tourists, but when Bev and Puddles walked toward it, Snowy veered off to a plaque set in a stone. Holding her breath, she read the opening lines of "Renascence" about these mountains and this bay. Beneath the excerpt she read: "At the age of eighteen, a frail girl with flaming red hair left her home in early morning to climb her favorite Camden Hills, where, deeply affected by her surroundings, she wrote 'Renascence.' The poem received immediate public acclaim and was the inspired beginning of the career of America's finest lyric poet."

Snowy didn't start crying again. Rage boiled up, scalding. Goddamnit all to hell! She was seized with an urge to kick the plaque, to scream and punch—

Puddles's hand grasped her arm. "Come on. We climbed the Washington Monument, remember? So let's climb this little bitty tower only twenty-six feet high."

Shakily, Snowy let Puddles tug her over to the tower. As they climbed, Snowy was reminded of visiting Warwick Castle with Alan, circling up a tower staircase. Bev tried to remember which boyfriend she had come up here with, their purpose not really the view. Puddles thought how she had wanted to be a nurse ever since she had had her tonsils out at age four and how she'd achieved her ambition and then gone further, becoming an

ARNP, whereas Snowy seemed to have quit her poems, which was incomprehensible because Snowy felt about writing poems the way Puddles felt about nursing and you didn't just stop, and granted you couldn't earn a living from poetry so Snowy had to work at the store, but you didn't need all that much time to write a damn poem, did you, so Snowy could do it in the evenings but there was no evidence that she had written anything, and writing was her real work, and Puddles couldn't imagine not going to the Helmsdale Clinic every day and doing her own work, so Snowy must be one fucked-up mess and Bev's brainstorm about Camden was making it worse. They emerged at the top. People were taking photographs of each other and of the ocean disappearing into haze on the horizon.

Snowy looked in the other direction, at the mountains.

Getting out her camera, Puddles said, "I've been pretty sure Guy has been going deaf, but because when wives suspect this it usually turns out that the husbands just aren't listening to them at all anymore, I wasn't positive. I knew he wouldn't trust me to test him, so I sent him to his doctor, who sent him to a specialist, and Guy is now wearing two hearing aids. The trouble is, he's having a problem with their fit. The Sunday before I left on my trip, we were over at Susan and Dean's house, seeing Little Guy and having dinner, and suddenly in the midst of Susan's specialty, shellfish-mushroom kabobs, Guy started choking. I gave him the Heimlich hug and out popped a hearing aid. When he was eating, it had fallen into his plate without his noticing, and he thought it was one of the mushrooms and ate it."

As Puddles hoped, Snowy began whooping with laughter, while Bev giggled but looked envious of the story.

Snowy squeaked, "A mushroom?"

"A button mushroom," Puddles said and handed her camera to a nearby out-of-stater and asked, "Could you take a picture of us three little maids from school?"

BACK AT THE Whitehall, they changed in their rooms and, as arranged, Snowy and Bev met Puddles down in the lobby at the doorway to the Spirits Room.

"Need I say it?" Puddles said. "I stopped in Freeport at the L. L. Bean store." She was wearing clothes Snowy recognized from the catalogue, a coral-colored sleeveless shirt and a pair of blue chambray pants with a comfy drawstring waist. "Nowadays," Puddles said, "clothes are my only lust, and I don't care what size they are."

"You look lovely," Bev said. "Shall we enter the Spirits Room? Will we find a séance or a bar, the specter of Edna St. Vincent Millay or gin-and-tonics?" Or, she thought, ghosts of Hollywood here to make the *Peyton Place* movie?

They found a dim snug bar, and while the bartender mixed their gin-and-tonics, Puddles said, "Remember Boston, the bar on Charles Street where we used to meet with our fake IDs—well, Snowy and I had our doctored drivers' licenses, but you, Bev, you got the bartender so hot and bothered you didn't need any ID, remember?" The words were out of her mouth before she recalled that the first time they'd all three met there when Snowy had come to Boston from Bennington for her freshman-year Non-Resident Term, Puddles had had to trick Snowy and Bev into joining her because Bev was still mad at Snowy over Tom.

Bev, thinking that trips down Memory Lane could be fraught with peril, laughed and tactfully steered the reminiscence in another direction. "Remember all the sight-seeing Snowy made us do, Chinatown, the Gardner Museum, when I wanted to spend my free time shopping, or at least window-shopping?"

"And here we are," Puddles said, "seeing sights again."

Snowy said, "But this time it's your idea."

They carried their gin-and-tonics to the front porch and settled into rattan rockers.

"God," Puddles said, "just look at me, a sweet old granny, rocking away." Out of her shoulder bag came the birthday-party photographs of Little Guy.

Snowy and Bev oohed and aahed, and Snowy said, "The cake, it's shaped like a truck!"

"Susan made it," Puddles said. "Little Guy has got the vroom-vroom gene, same as all boys, but it's extreme with him because of Cram Construction. He's used to seeing his father *and* his mother driving a bulldozer, not to mention his grandfather although Guy doesn't do much of the physical stuff anymore and was just showing off for Little Guy."

Bev said, "So Susan is back at work?"

"Oh, almost immediately after delivery."

Bev asked, "Do you ever get broody about a baby—not a grandchild, but you and Guy having another baby?"

"Are you out of your gourd?" said Puddles.

Snowy began laughing.

Puddles said, "It's exactly like that schmaltzy saying: 'If I'd known grandchildren were so much fun, I would have had them first.' It's just the way everybody says, you can enjoy them and then *leave.* Except of course for the unlucky grandparents who get pressed into service as a full-time day-care center."

Bev rattled ice cubes. "Snowy, have you and Tom ever considered a baby?"

Startled, Snowy said, "It never crossed my mind. Nor his, I'm sure. Besides, at my age it'd be a medical miracle, and Tom has had a vasectomy."

Puddles said, "Not such a miracle anymore, thanks to the wonders of modern science. Beverly Colby Lambert, are you saying *you're* broody? You were never interested in kids and then you went and had four and now you want another?"

"No, I certainly don't, so why do I stop and look at everybody's baby in the supermarket?"

"Menopause," Puddles diagnosed. "Mimi had better get busy and give you a grandchild."

Snowy checked her watch. "Our dinner reservation."

They strolled indoors, through the Spirits Room into the dining room, which had the feel of a bosky dell because green was the main color. As Snowy sat down at their table with its white cloth over a green tablecloth and looked at the green-patterned wallpaper, she wondered if the room had been much the same when Edna's sister had waitressed here. Nowadays, the staff wore white blouses or shirts and black skirts or trousers; what had Norma worn? Reading the menu, she saw "Chicken St. Millay: a Whitehall classic" and knew that she must order this even though she usually never chose chicken in a restaurant because she ate it at home far too often.

"Pork tenderloin," Puddles decided. "I've eaten so much seafood on this trip, I'm ready for a break in the barnyard."

Bev ordered, "The poached salmon, please," and after the waitress left she conferred with the wine waiter, while Puddles said to Snowy, "This Edna of yours, did she live in Camden all her life?"

"She was born in Rockland, moved to Camden, and then when she read her 'Renascence' poem here at a Whitehall's talent night, she wowed one of the guests who helped her get admitted to Vassar and get the money to go there. After college, she went on to New York City and Paris and everywhere and ended up living in Austerlitz, New York, with her husband. They fixed up an old farm. She named it Steepletop. She died there; fell down the stairs and broke her neck; age fifty-eight. Her husband had died of cancer a year or so earlier."

"Fifty-eight. Same age as Guy."

"Is Guy really going to retire?"

"Susan and her husband are ready to take over the business whenever he says the word."

"You'd move to Hilton Head? That's an island, isn't it?"

"Bridged. With many many golf courses."

"But what about your work? You'd have to leave the clinic and go to one on Hilton Head?"

"Unless we maintain separate establishments, which we can't afford. Unlike some people." Puddles flicked a glance at Bev.

Who had just finished with the wine waiter and heard. "I'm making a life for myself," Bev said.

Snowy asked her hastily, "At the Grand View, what was your waitressing uniform?"

"Same as we had at Sweetland, those white nylon numbers, but instead of the little white nylon aprons we had flowered calico with ruffles. So quaint."

Their salads arrived, strawberries and bleu cheese and walnuts on mixed lettuces.

"Yuppie lettuces," Snowy said. "I'm tempted to try growing radicchio in one of the tubs Dudley gave me, but an organic gardener in town keeps the store supplied with such specialties along with good Bibb, et cetera, so there's no point for me to do it. Except for the fun of gardening."

Puddles was still thinking about having to leave the Helmsdale Clinic. Whether or not she and Guy needed her income to supplement their retirement fund, she would find work elsewhere. She had to; if she wasn't nursing, she might as well be dead. Was Snowy, by not writing poetry, killing at least part of herself, committing suicide to be dead like Alan? Shit, no, that was too morbid. Snowy had Tom, whom she should've married in the first place. Puddles asked, "You miss your garden?"

"Well, it's partway down the list of things I'd miss if I let myself. Isn't this yummy!"

The wine waiter presented Bev with a bottle, and Bev went through the ritual that Snowy had only seen men do. After sampling, Bev nodded and said, "Delish." The waiter smiled at her and poured a California chardonnay into all their glasses. Snowy had never tasted chardonnay before.

"Yummy," Snowy said again.

Puddles said, "I'd miss my house if I had to move." Speaking of morbid! While packing for this trip, she had found herself imagining what the rooms and her possessions would look like to people, to Guy and Susan and Amy, if she were killed in a plane crash or car crash or something; she had tried to picture how these things would be changed by emptiness, finality. She added, "I'd miss my office, too."

Bev said, "Our Puddles, unadventuresome?"

"A stick-in-the-mud," Puddles said, "after leaving New England and then the constant moving from house to house at first down there. Except for Amy, my whole family is in Helmsdale, thanks to Guy's talking my folks into moving there so he wouldn't have to go north for holidays. *Both* my brothers have settled there."

Bev asked, "How far is Hilton Head from Helmsdale?"

"An hour and thirty-five minutes. I know that's not like going off to the ends of the earth, but I'm used to everybody right around the corner, practically."

Snowy said, "Couldn't you convince Guy to retire to New Hampshire? We have golf courses. In the summer. Then your family could all move back to New England."

"Hardeeharhar," Puddles said. "Here comes the food."

They ate, and the talk rambled. Chicken St. Millay consisted of a chicken breast in a sauce of shallots, mushrooms, wine, and cream, and it reminded Snowy of dishes she used to make back when she first got married. It too was yummy. So was the apple chutney that came with Puddles's pork tenderloin and Puddles offered, chutney being one of the many foods she didn't like. Bev told a story about the glamorous real-estate life, sloshing around in a marsh trying to find the survey marks for the property line, and Puddles bragged about Amy's working at a Charleston hospital, and Snowy listened, thinking of Edna and of dessert.

Bev asked, "What about Amy's love life?"

"She's still dating losers," Puddles said, "and I'm beginning to enjoy them, or at least the ones she brings home. The latest one told me his goal is to stay away from legitimate jobs. He takes 'walk-away' jobs for the money for essentials and spends the rest of his time enjoying life. Amy must find this refreshing."

Bev said, "Good thing she hasn't met Leon; she'd be a goner. Which reminds me, Snowy. How is Ruhamah and D. J.'s romance?"

"I don't know," Snowy said. "Ruhamah is reticent. Maddeningly. I do know she goes to girl-boy things at the high school with the son of the village postmaster. Vacations and some weekends, it's D. J."

Puddles asked, "Anything between her and Tom's son who's almost living next door?"

"Nothing," Snowy said, "and that's a relief. She'll probably end up getting serious about somebody completely unconnected to any of us. If she ever does. My God, listen to us!"

"Vicarious romance," Bev said. "Aren't we pitiful?"

Puddles asked Snowy, "Is Ruhamah on the Pill yet?"

"No! I mean, we've discussed birth control, but she hasn't brought up the subject on her own—Puddles, she's only seventeen!"

Puddles said, "Need I say more? I will. Besides telling my daughters to come to me when they were ready, I snooped in their rooms regularly. I advise you to do the same. Snoop, spy, pretend you're Miss Whatshername in your Agatha Christies."

After a moment Snowy said, "Okay," for the sake of peace but without the slightest intention of following Puddles's advice.

Bev said slowly, "I've never mentioned that I found marijuana in Leon's room, back when he was fourteen. I didn't tell Roger. Leon and I had a little talk. Since then, like a coward, I've stopped checking his room."

The waitress appeared. "Dessert?"

Because none of the desserts was named after Edna, Snowy chose blueberry sorbet. So did Bev, while Puddles went for the carrot cake. After their decaf coffee, Puddles said, "Let's hit the

Spirits Room for the grand finale," and they got liqueurs there and went back out to their rockers on the porch.

Snowy said, sipping Drambuie, "Every spring I reread two of Edna's poems about spring, a youthful jaded one and a later one, 'The Goose Girl,' which celebrates simplicity."

Puddles took a slug of her crème de cacao and asked, "Do they rhyme, like that 'Renascence'?"

"Well, 'The Goose Girl' does. Couplets again."

"I like rhymes," Puddles said. "Lots of yours rhymed, the ones in the magazines and collections you sent me. Seemed unusual compared with the crap I run across elsewhere, not that I run across much in my line of work."

"Fashions," Snowy said.

Bev rocked, sipping Grand Marnier. "Snowy, remember when we were driving up here and I said I didn't know what I wanted? It's now dawned on me. I should have tried out for *Peyton Place* thirty-one years ago. I'm not going to hide from the big time this time. I want to be the best real-estate agent in New Hampshire!"

"Overachiever?" Puddles said. "Like Roger?" And like Snowy used to be.

Bev said, "In our company, the Plumley Salesperson of the Year, the person who generates the most sales, wins a trip at the awards ceremony every January. This year, the trip was to Las Vegas. Lorraine Fitch is the salesperson who was the top producer. Top producer, isn't that an awful term?"

Puddles agreed, "It sounds like a prize dairy cow."

"But I don't care," Bev said. "I want to win."

Puddles said, "Win a trip to Charleston, and Snowy, you come along with her, and after touring Charleston you all come visit me at long last."

"Okay," Bev said.

Snowy pointed out, "Puddles, you just said 'y'all.' You, a state-of-Mainer!"

"Heaven help me," Puddles said.

They rocked.

IN BED, SNOWY couldn't sleep. The whir of the fan in the window shouldn't disturb her, for she'd had to install fans in her bedroom and Ruhamah's in the summer, and this one disguised the noise of the Route 1 traffic, a sound she *wasn't* used to. She kept fretting about Ruhamah's being in charge of the store. She wished she'd packed her Walkman and a book-tape bedtime story.

Finally she got up. She and Bev had decided to leave the bathroom light on behind an almost-closed bathroom door, for a night-light, and by this faint glow she opened her shoulder bag and took out her ballpoint and memo pad. Sitting in the wicker armchair at the little round table, she began to write. In couplets.

The next morning at breakfast in the dining room, after showering in the old tub, the encircling shower curtain billowing, Snowy ordered Maine blueberry pancakes. Bev and Puddles decided on the omelette of the day, mushroom and cheese, and Puddles added sausages on the side. As Snowy poured maple syrup, she thought with wonder of the work she'd done last night. Her writer's block, she realized, had meant blocking the pain of Alan's death, for she'd feared it as the subject of poems, a releasing and an unleashing of the horror, an examination of the emotions, reliving every detail even more than she did already. But last night she'd written about Moody's Diner.

Puddles was saying, "After age forty, it's all maintenance. Where did you have your eyes done, Hanover?"

Bev nodded. "And liposuction on the jowls," she said, and launched into the story.

Stories, Snowy thought, suddenly remembering that the best reviews of her collections had praised her for telling stories instead of looking up her own ass, so to speak. Well, last night she'd told the story of Julia and Bev and Moody's. Happiness flooded her, warm as syrup.

But after they'd packed and checked out, as they stood in the parking lot beside their cars trying to say good-bye, Puddles began to cry, saying, "Oh, fuck this!" and Snowy and Bev hugged her and both burst into tears too, which then convulsed them all with laughter.

CHAPTER FIVE

IN THE FIRE TOWER, Tom lowered his binoculars after scanning the forest for smoke, sat back in his wooden chair, and looked down to see two people with a couple of kids step out of the woods onto the summit. He knew from the way the adults stopped in their tracks that they probably hadn't been up here before, that they weren't prepared for the view, which even on a cloudy day like this August Saturday could hit you over the head and stun you with lakes and mountains. The two kids went scampering off to gape at his log cabin instead of at the scenery.

He hoped the weather would hold and the rain predicted for evening would wait until then. Snowy wasn't working today; she and Ruhamah were in Old Eastbourne with her husband's family for the ceremony honoring Alan. Tom had gathered that the program involved the installation of a plaque in the main building, a speech by the chairman of the board of directors, an acceptance speech that Snowy had insisted Alan's mother be the one to deliver, not Snowy herself, and then a lunch—a "luncheon." He glanced at his watch. Luncheon time, so he unwrapped the turkey sandwich he'd made this morning in the cabin. Where, he now noticed, the grown-ups had joined the kids, and the guy was knocking on the door.

It wasn't unusual for hikers to be curious about the log cabin, and therefore he kept it locked while he was up here in this little room called a cab, his home away from the cabin home, which was away from his home in Woodcombe, which he still had a tendency to feel was away from his Newburgh home, which initially had felt too far away in the northern mountains from Gunthwaite and Lake Winnipesaukee, and wasn't it interesting that four years in Rumford at the dear old teachers' college had never made that town seem like home.

What a goddamn joke, these starveling emotions about places in the Granite State! He had such a meager perspective, never having traveled. Snowy had looked back at the United States from across the Atlantic, if only during a two-week vacation decades ago. But Americans were rootless nowadays, seeking some figment of home, so in a way didn't that make them the innocents and him the more deeply experienced? He poured the last of his breakfast coffee out of his thermos into the Moody's Diner mug Snowy had brought him from her Camden trip and sipped, watching the adults and kids turn away from the cabin and walk toward the tower.

Sometimes people didn't venture all the way up, instead stopping on one of the landings on the metal stairway and snapping photos from there. But he heard footsteps continue up the last flight, so these folks wanted to show their kids the view from the top. Sometimes he welcomed company in the cab, but it depended on the company, interesting individuals or crashing bores.

A man's head appeared in the trapdoor opening. The man whooshed, catching his breath, and said, "Hi, Tom."

Getting to his feet, Tom stared at him blankly. The man hoisted the two little boys into the cab, stepped in, then reached down and helped up a panting woman. You couldn't always tell ages these days, when people were having kids later in life, but this couple looked more like young grandparents than old parents, their hair graying, lungs huffing and puffing from unaccustomed climbing, their girth encased in the "activewear" type of shirts and pants too formal for the trail, and on their feet dandy white walking shoes instead of hiking boots.

The woman smiled and said to the man, "I told you he wouldn't recognize us up here!"

Tom recognized the smile, which in high school would have featured the red lipstick then favored and now was sort of pinky. "Adele!" So the man was, of course, Sam Page. "Sam!"

Adele hugged Tom, and he shook Sam's outstretched hand. It had been a few years since the Pages had come up to Newburgh for Joanne's parties, various things interfering, but whenever Joanne was in Gunthwaite visiting her parents, she went to Adele and Sam's. (Back in the mists of time, Joanne had dated Sam, and Tom had gone out with Adele. Long ago, Tom thought, that was so long ago it was almost forgotten and if recalled, it was something that had happened to other people.) Tom hadn't kept up with pals himself, but Sam had been a friend, quarterback of the football team, a fellow amateur mechanic at Varney's gas station, and through Joanne he'd followed Sam's career, which hadn't included Sam's plans for UNH because Adele got pregnant their senior year. Sam had moved up the ladder from driving a Coca-Cola truck to sitting behind a desk at Coke's Gunthwaite branch. Very comfortable, Sam and Adele looked.

Tom fumbled for tact. "Yes, seeing you up here, that's what slowed me down a second. And these youngsters—" He rescued his binoculars from one of the boys. "They must be—" He did a frantic search of his memory and, thank God, came up with the name the Pages had given their firstborn. "—Karen's kids?"

"Taylor and Tyler." Adele lifted up the younger to show him the view, saying, "See that lake over there, the biggest lake? Your house is near it."

Sam lifted the other kid and said, "We were recruited to baby-sit today and thought we'd show them this. Never been up here ourselves, either. So, you keep a lookout for fires?"

Tom raised his binoculars. "Ever vigilant." He remembered a New Year's Eve party at Sam's parents' house, when he and Snowy watched the Times Square celebration on television and Snowy told him about sight-seeing in New York during her Girl Scout trip to Washington. He at least in college had taken a trip to New York City, for the hell of it with his roommate, but as with their similar trip to Boston they didn't have money for much more than the gas to get there and back. And then he and Joanne had married, which put an end to any extra money at all. Once he and Joanne, Libby, David, and Brandon had spent a Christmas vacation at the house in Sarasota his parents had bought for their Golden Years, enjoyed by his father only briefly before a fatal heart attack, and he'd visited his mother a few times since then, so he'd seen Boston again, Logan Airport, that is, and been to Florida. This was the extent of his travels. He recalled a term that ornithologists used about birds winging back to the same spot each year: site fidelity.

Sam was glancing at the alidade, a rotating sighting device, on the map table. "Hermit. I always knew you were the type."

Tom said, "If today were sunny, the mountain would be crawling with people. Well, how are you, how's the Coke business?"

"Doing fine," Sam said.

A silence fell, even more awkward than the small talk. Adele and Sam quickly filled it by speaking to the kids, pointing at mountains, but what really filled it was an unspoken word: JOANNE.

Shit, Tom thought. He said, "David told me how you fooled Joanne into a surprise party for her fiftieth. That was terrific."

Adele said, "This is the big year for all of us, the Big Five-O. Though you'd never know it on Joanne. Unlike me." She laughed, and jounced her grandson against her bolster of a bosom, his heels bobbing against her ample haunch.

Tom said, "You look great," and suddenly she did. These friends, these roots.

Sam said, "We thought of inviting you, but we weren't sure."

Adele said, "It's not as if the divorce was amicable."

Remembering the barrage of Valentine boxes, Tom said, "Are divorces ever, really?"

"She's still angry," Adele said. "That means she still cares."

Christ, Adele sounded like high-school intrigue. Tom reached for the CB mike. "Gotta call the warden on Belknap Mountain."

While he was on the CB, the kids began squirming and whining. When he clicked off, Adele said, "We'd better leave. We're having a Labor Day barbecue, Tom. Joanne will be there. If you feel like it, we'd love to have you, too."

"Thanks, but—"

"You and Snowy aren't married? I've never seen anything in the newspaper."

Startled, Tom said, "Married? No." Snowy still wore a wedding ring; she was still Alan Sutherland's widow.

Adele said, "Another one of us who's turning fifty this year is Rita. Remember her?"

Tom grinned. As if he could forget the only girl on their cheerleading squad who could do a split! He'd dated Rita Beaupre because of this, more than anything else, but she held out on that secret though allowing him to discover everything above the waist. God, had she been stacked! And God, had she been a chatterer! He'd guessed he could have whatever he wanted if he would go steady with her, but then he would have had to listen to her all the time and was that worth it? Ah, the problems of youth. In the midst of this predicament, he had noticed Snowy. "Yes," he said, "I remember Rita."

"You've seen her since we graduated," Adele said, "only you didn't recognize her. She waitresses at the Parmigiano, and it's a wonder she recognized you under that beard, but she did."

"The Parmigiano? She's a waitress?" Tom had a hazy recollection of Joanne's mentioning that Rita had married well. "Didn't she marry her boss or something?"

Adele said, "When she was the receptionist at Henderson's Insurance Agency, she started having an affair with Paul Henderson, even though he was married, and she got pregnant. He divorced his wife and married Rita. But when you fool around with a married guy, you ought to watch out for him fooling around after you're married to him, which is what Paul Henderson did, so like an idiot Rita fooled around too, with a vengeance, and when he found out and decided to divorce her, she couldn't get alimony, just child support. They had three kids by then. She's lucky he didn't want custody. These past years, she's had a tough time."

Sam set down Taylor or Tyler. "Okay, let's get going."

Adele said, "She'll be at the barbecue."

Sam said, "Spotted your North Country Coffins sign when we came through the village. Is David there? Maybe we'll stop and say hi on our way back."

"That's Snowy's store?" Adele said. "We could get you kids a snack, how'd you like that, boys?" She explained to Tom, "They wanted the picnic right when we got here so we ate it down in the trail's parking lot."

"Snowy isn't working today," Tom volunteered, adding with some sanctimonious satisfaction, "She and her daughter are at a memorial tribute to her husband."

Adele's and Sam's expressions went solemn. "Oh," Adele said, contrite. "What a terrible thing she's gone through." She waved the hand of the kid in her arms. "Say good-bye."

Both boys piped, "Bye!"

BECAUSE OF HER success selling coffee and cocoa and muffins during the winter, Snowy had consulted her accountant and added ice cream cones to her offerings. As she told Bev, "It's like our Sweetland summers, I'm scooping ice cream again! I've gone backward!" She, who in her youth had been determined always to go forward.

Bev pointed out, "You own the business. You're not an employee. That's an advance."

"The bank owns it."

The hot summer grew even hotter, and Snowy began changing into a dry top during her lunch break as though on a backpack. During the Sunday-afternoon hikes she took with Tom when his schedule allowed, usually alone together but occasionally with

Libby and Ruhamah, and during the two overnight backpacks they squeezed in, she thought she'd melt away into a pool of sweat, which was understandable considering the exertion, but the way she poured with sweat just weighing cold cuts for a customer could not be entirely blamed on the weather. When at night the sweat soaked through her nightgown into the bedclothes, when she began putting a bath towel on the sheet before she lay down, she finally admitted she was having hot flashes.

There wasn't time to tend to this until after the tourist season ended, nor to the other problem, eyesight. Luckily, she had memorized the price of everything in the store, so she didn't have to squint at a frozen pizza a customer set on the counter, and in the evenings, working on a poem at the typewriter, she knew what the words she chose looked like, so that wasn't difficult, but while reading a book she had to hold it farther and farther away. The books she was reading now were about menopause, the pros and cons of hormone replacement therapy.

Thus, when she mentioned to Bev that she'd decided to see Shelby Levesque, the ARNP, she asked for the name of Bev's ophthalmologist, saying, "At least getting glasses is something straightforward. This estrogen debate is making me more nervous than the Pill did. We didn't know any better in those days. Now we're aware that women are guinea pigs."

"Puddles will be gleeful that you've joined us in HRT. But I wish Mother were here to discuss it with, though she was still part of all the grin-and-bear-it generations."

"Maybe that's what we should do."

"Snowy, do you want to keep sleeping on bath towels?"

Snowy made both appointments for the end of October, on the same day, and when the time came she found herself in downtown Gunthwaite at the clinic where she'd been taken for childhood ailments, where she'd got a diaphragm before her wedding. In Shelby's office in the OB/GYN section on the second floor, she discussed the choices and gambled on estrogen-progesterone pills in the lowest dosage, at least for starters.

The choice proved more difficult in the optician's showroom in the Abnaki Mall, to which she went after her next appointment at the clinic, the ophthalmologist. What kind of reading glasses? Half-glasses like Bev's? Regular size? Spending all this money, she had to make the right decision, but she was self-conscious about vanity and afraid of wasting too much of the optician's time. Finally she asked to use the phone and called Bev at work, an SOS, and to her relief Bev was there, nearby at the Plumley office.

Bev jumped in her station wagon and sped along the Miracle Mile to the mall to rescue Snowy, plunking her down in front of a mirror, immediately deciding upon a pair of thin gold-rimmed half-glasses that "Make you look cute but not too cute and allow you to work in the store without taking them off and putting them on," but then perching most of the optician's inventory of frames on Snowy's nose to be absolutely sure that her first instinct was right. It was.

COULD THE HOLIDAYS have begun to accumulate a few new traditions, non-Alan, post-Alan? Again this Thanksgiving, which this year was clear and sunny, Snowy and Ruhamah went to Alan's parents' house for a modified meal. His mother wept again, but less. Last August, though, at the ceremony at Old Eastbourne, Phyllis had been dry-eyed and dignified, pulled together by formality; the observance, at last, of some sort of rite, gave her solace if not a reason. In her speech Phyllis told the story of how Alan had been fascinated by the history and architecture of Eastbourne ever since the day in his childhood he had visited a schoolmate whose house had a rickety widow's walk declared off-limits by the friend's parents, so of course the two little boys egged each other on and climbed up through the attic to stand on it and look down at the city, the docks, the harbor. Alan had been so awed that he forgot horseplay, which probably would have resulted in a long fall down the roof. Phyllis didn't mention the subsequent spankings administered to the friend by the friend's mother and then by Alan's father to Alan. Snowy had glanced at Bob, Alan's father, standing beside the Old Eastbourne chairman, and heard Alan's description: "The old man hardly ever hit me—he preferred sarcasm—but this time he whaled the living daylights out of me. So, unbeknownst to anybody, the first chance I had I snuck back up on that widow's walk. Wouldn't a shrink love this? Now I'm restoring them." And now, Snowy thought, I'm a widow.

Tom flew to Sarasota to have Thanksgiving with his mother and with his older brother, George, who'd come down from Massachusetts with his wife.

Again Harriet phoned and invited Snowy and Ruhamah to New York for Christmas, telling Snowy about her travels. "Back to Israel last winter," she said, "and a stay in Greece, and then this fall a spell in England."

Snowy asked, "Another soccer player in England, or cricket?"

"No, only Nathan in Israel."

"What does Nathan do besides play soccer?"

"Oh, he's a painter too, which complicates things. I sell his work at the gallery. Does he love me for myself or for my gallery? In Cornwall, it was just me and the ocean."

Feeling foolish, Snowy mentioned her little trip to Maine's ocean. But she had to beg off again from taking a trip to New York herself, before she handed the receiver to excited Ruhamah and nodded consent.

Snowy and Tom returned to the Alpine Avens Inn this Christmas Eve. As they sat in front of the main room's fireplace, Tom sipped eggnog and thought of Libby, David, and Brandon up in Newburgh with Joanne. How long had it been since he'd seen her, over a year? He certainly hadn't gone to Adele and Sam's Labor Day barbecue, and that was just as well because after Thanksgiving David had returned from Joanne's groaning board and hesitantly mentioned that there was a guest at the dinner, a man invited by Joanne, a classmate she'd met at the barbecue, Victor Andrews, who had married a girl he'd met at UNH and was recently divorced. Absorbing the news, Tom had remembered last seeing him in the summer of 1956, the summer after their graduation, at the dance hall on the lake, Victor with Snowy, dating Snowy, after Tom had broken up with her. Tom remembered the parties at Victor's grandparents' camp, most memorably the one after their junior prom. Who had been Victor's date for that? One of the twins, he seemed to recall. He couldn't recall that Joanne had ever dated Victor. David told him that Victor was working with computers for some company down in Nashua. Watching the inn's owner prod an uncooperative Yule log, Tom thought how David hadn't said anything about whether or not Victor would be joining Joanne and the kids for Christmas dinner. Victor wouldn't be there tonight, spending Christmas Eve in Joanne's bed under the red satin bedspread, would he, not with the kids in the house? The kids, Tom reminded himself, were all grown up.

In Gunthwaite, Bev's house wasn't packed with kids this Christmas because Mimi insisted that Etta, Leon, and Dick stay at her new house, not too subtly leaving Bev and Roger alone on Christmas Eve. Bev had read that women sometimes liked to have their ex-husbands around to do odd jobs, but Roger had never been useful—except with cars, thanks to his misspent youth at Varney's. And he wasn't an ex-husband. He was her husband, the guy she had known since high school, yet he was becoming interestingly unfamiliar. She still didn't think there was another woman in his life down in Connecticut, mainly because he was too busy at work to be bothered and because with her he definitely acted as if he'd been locked in a monastery. They had the house to themselves; they could make a racket. Which they did. Bev marveled at how much she'd changed, how she could find sufficient excitement this way, with Roger, when she used to dream of new men, new passions.

Then, as she and Roger recovered out in the living room in their bathrobes, sipping Grand Marnier in front of the hideous fireplace, a thought struck her: Had real estate replaced romance? Had it *become* what romance used to be for? Did it provide the thrills she sought? Oh dear God, yes! She was so surprised by this insight that she blurted out, "I've bought this house."

Roger had only been thinking lazily that it was time to put on another log. He turned and looked at her. "You're staying."

"Well, renting is such a waste of money. Buying the place is an investment."

"So you want a divorce now."

"No," she said. "Let's go on like this, at least a while longer. It suits me. And, truthfully, doesn't it suit you?"

Ever since Roger could remember, every step he'd taken had been set on a path that would get him the hell out of Gunthwaite. Bev had wanted to escape too. He stood up and added a log. "I couldn't come back and practice here."

"That would defeat the purpose of our arrangement," said Bev.

Her tone struck him. She was an actress, so he'd always been used to variety in her delivery, depending on her mood and the circumstances. But she had just spoken to him in a new way. Or had he only now heard for the first time her clear self-confidence? Had he been pretending she was a mistress he was keeping up here in the boondocks? He'd never had the time or inclination for a mistress, so he'd cast his runaway wife in that role. He looked at Bev, free of him, and laughed.

In her Helmsdale home, Puddles's knees creaked as she pushed herself up from the floor in front of the Christmas tree where she'd arranged presents. Reese the cat batted at low-hanging tinsel. Puddles and Guy would be going to Susan and Dean's first thing tomorrow, for since their grandson was born Susan wanted Christmas at her own house, and Puddles could understand that. Last year Amy had come home, but this Christmas she was on call at the hospital. Tomorrow Mom and Dad would be going from Christmas tree to Christmas tree in Helmsdale, visiting her brothers and their families in addition to Susan and Dean and Little Guy. Puddles had mailed presents to Amy, had taken Santa-Claus presents over to Susan's earlier today so that tomorrow morning Little Guy would think they'd come down the chimney, and thus these presents under this tree made the most meager showing since her early-married years. As usual she was giving Guy some golf stuff, a new coffee-table book about St. Andrews, another polo shirt, another pair of non-plaid pants, a new golf towel. At the beginning she used to have fun giving him balls, with many a wisecrack, but he never found this as sidesplitting as she did so the jokes wore thin and she'd lost her enthusiasm. As usual this year he would give her some kitchen gadget for which she'd have to make room on the counter until a suitable time had elapsed to pack it away with the other counter-crowders that he never noticed were gone. She was betting on a breadmaker this year. She flexed her knees and rubbed her right hip. Goddamn arthritis. She looked at Guy in his recliner, watching TV tuned too loud even though he had his hearing aids in. Fa-la-fucking-la.

ONE SUNDAY IN January, Bev phoned Snowy and said, "Lorraine Fitch won again, damn her."

"Who? What?" Snowy had been doing the ironing and listening to a Dick Francis on her Walkman when she answered the phone, and her mind was in England, steeplechasing.

"The Plumley Salesperson of the Year—last year, that is, 1988. The awards banquet was last night. I didn't even win the Most Promising Newcomer award this time, because I'm not new anymore. The trip Lorraine won was to Nashville. I know it sounds ridiculous, but I did well enough with my sales last year that I couldn't help having a smidgen of a hope I'd get the award, and I'd've even have liked to go to Nashville."

Snowy said, "You'll win for this year's sales."

"1989. The year we turn fifty. Eek, how did this happen? Just a minute ago I was thirty-five!"

When Snowy's milestone birthday arrived in March, she thought that it was age eighteen she felt. Or maybe even younger, back to the first birthday party she could remember, in the apartment before the house on the river, age five, dressed up by her mother in a deep pink dress with lace trim and a big black velvet sash, a black velvet bow in her hair, shyness exacerbated by the torture of being the center of attention of her kindergarten friends. Did your essence ever change, no matter how old you grew?

She knew Tom had an aversion to parties, so to circumvent any ideas that Ruhamah or Bev might be harboring about springing a surprise one on her this Sunday birthday, she announced that what she really wanted to do was go bargain-shopping in North Conway and have a pizza. Bev, with Etta, therefore picked Snowy and Ruhamah up after Snowy closed the store at noon, and they drove to North Conway, where Snowy spent the afternoon of her fiftieth in factory-outlet stores. She and Bev and the girls found various treasures, Snowy especially pleased with a Liz Claiborne blouse the remembered color of that long-ago party dress, marked down to nine dollars and ninety-nine cents. Heading back, they stopped at the Parmigiano for the pizza supper, Bev's treat. Snowy hadn't mentioned Rita to Bev, because Tom's old girlfriends were a touchy (ha!) subject, and she wondered if Bev would recognize her. But Rita wasn't working tonight.

After Bev left Snowy and Ruhamah off at the store, Snowy phoned Tom, who came over to the apartment bringing champagne. When Ruhamah discreetly went into her bedroom and turned up the volume of the music on her radio-cassette player, he produced a small gift-wrapped box, a box she knew must be a jeweler's.

Oh Christ, thought Snowy. A ring? Slowly she unwrapped the package. She found a little padded white box. An engagement ring? A wedding ring? Tom had never given the slightest indication he had marriage on his mind. But now that Ruhamah would be graduating in June and leaving for UNH this fall—

Snowy raised the little lid and saw a necklace, a bloodstone on a fine gold chain.

Relief and disappointment vied frantically within her. She breathed, "My birthstone."

He said, "I remembered the one you used to have on a charm bracelet."

"It's beautiful. Thank you." She thought: Men! Men do not have a clue, not even Tom.

Next month, Mimi threw Bev a great big birthday party at Weaverbird, her farmhouse studio, a dinner party, to which Roger came from Connecticut even though it was on a workday. The season had begun for Tom's fire-warden work, but he was off duty so he joined Snowy and Ruhamah, driving them to Leicester in Snowy's Subaru. Mimi had invited Dudley and Charl, too, and Darl and Bill, and everyone from Bev's real-estate office including the owner, so Snowy finally got to see Geoffrey Plumley. He wasn't what she'd expected from Bev's comments about the wheeling-and-dealing guy in his fifties, a Massachusetts transplant. Snowy had expected a sleazy hotshot type, but Geoffrey Plumley either possessed or cultivated a disarmingly rumpled tweedy appeal, with the added attraction of, in his tousled graying brown hair, a widow's peak (if it was called this on a man) that gave him a soulful saintly look that must be very useful in his business. Snowy kept an eye on him through the evening in Mimi's beautiful rooms, which were decorated more simply than Snowy had thought a craftsperson would, as simply as Hurricane Farm had been, Snowy's theory being that you couldn't do better than white walls, oriental rugs, green plants, to which Mimi had added woven tapestries. But Snowy didn't see any sign that Geoffrey Plumley was smitten with Bev or vice versa. Roger was the one acting captivated.

As was Leon, by Ruhamah still. At eighteen, Ruhamah didn't seem particularly intrigued anymore, yet she and Leon wandered off together away from the main rooms of Mimi's many-roomed house, and Snowy thought what a relief it would be to have

Ruhamah out of his sphere this fall, especially since Bev's marijuana revelation. She wondered who would escort Ruhamah to her senior prom, the platonic pal, son of the postmaster, with whom Ruhamah had gone to her junior prom, or another classmate, or... Snowy had followed Puddles's advice after all, when increasing worry and curiosity combined to overcome her principles, and one day when Ruhamah was in school, she'd gone through Ruhamah's room like a detective—or a thief. She had found no birth-control pills or devices and no drugs. But wouldn't you know it, her relief was mingled with another worry, that Ruhamah lacked a spirit of adventure and whose fault was this?

Come May, Ruhamah announced, "D. J. is taking me to the prom," and drove off with Jennifer Rollins and Kim Parker to shop for a dress in Manchester, at the Mall of New Hampshire to which Snowy had never ventured. Upon her return, Snowy phoned Bev and said, "It's a lapis-lazuli blue and very subtle, a long sheath with spaghetti straps. Remember our strapless gowns with all those crinolines?"

Bev said, "I'm so afraid Etta will be wearing jodhpurs to *her* proms!"

Dudley phoned Snowy and said, "I hear that my son has the honor of escorting your daughter to her senior prom."

"History repeats itself!" Snowy said. She and Dudley had gone to their senior prom and senior banquet together. "Sort of. It's good of D. J. to bother with a high-school event."

"I doubt if it's a bother. Snowy, as my political advisor, do you think I should run for a second term as city councilor?"

"When did I become your political advisor?"

"Two years ago, when you advised me to run for the council and then for mayor. I don't know about mayor, but I think I'm useful on the council. Remember how you said our generation is 'the disappeared'?"

"Oh, Dudley, you've got to run for another term!"

When Puddles's birthday rolled around in July, Ruhamah had graduated and, as a present from Harriet, gone on Harriet's return trip to Cornwall for three weeks, so Snowy had got a preview of her empty nest. Phoning Puddles to wish her Happy Milestone, Snowy cried, "I thought I was going to *luxuriate* in having this teeny apartment to myself, but it'll be—it'll be *empty!* When Amy and Susan left, how did you bear it?"

"Well," Puddles said, and lowered her voice. "I had an affair, remember?"

"That was long after they left for college."

"Yes, I don't suppose I can blame that on them. Though if I hadn't had to get a mattress for that goddamn Cram family heirloom cradle, for Susan's baby, then I wouldn't have gone to the mattress factory and met Calvin and tested some mattresses with him."

"Your house isn't really empty. Guy's there."

"He sure is, and Snowy, what will I do if he retires?"

"I've never lived on my own except in Boston. First I lived with my parents, then at school with Harriet, then Alan, then Alan and Ruhamah, and then with Ruhamah."

"Think of the benefits. You've only got one bathroom; you'll have it all to yourself. Your one TV will be yours now. When Amy and Susan left, I used to be glad to come home from work knowing I'd only have to think about dinner for Guy and me. Which reminds me: You be sure you don't get slipshod about meals and not bother just for yourself. You could invite Tom for suppers—hey! Why don't you invite Tom to move in with you and let his son have the apartment over the coffins?"

The thought had crossed Snowy's mind more than once lately. Tom hadn't suggested it, and she had an awful suspicion that she was waiting for him to ask her to go steady, just like in high school. If he did, would her reaction be any less confused than when she thought he was giving her a ring? She said, "Bev thinks we have the perfect arrangement as is."

"Yeah. She could be right. Oh, I forgot to tell you that I've joined you four-eyes; I've got reading glasses."

"Happy birthday."

Snowy didn't suggest living together to Tom, but at the end

of summer, with Ruhamah's okay, she asked him if he would go with them down to Durham to help move Ruhamah's belongings into her dorm room. He was an old pro at UNH, having done the same for Brandon and then Libby, who now had graduated and was working full-time as a White Mountain National Forest ranger. Ruhamah's room possessed the same basics as Snowy's had at Bennington, a desk, chair, bed, bureau, and closet, but whereas Snowy had only brought, besides clothes, some books in a carton and her Royal portable typewriter, Ruhamah's equipment for scholarly endeavor included her computer, her Walkman, her radio-cassette player, a new portable TV, a new VCR, and many plastic milk crates of books and tapes. Lauren, Ruhamah's roommate, had brought a microwave oven and immediately made popcorn for all.

After leaving Ruhamah there on campus, leaving with Tom who drove while Snowy wept, Snowy knew this hadn't simply been the year of the Big Five-O. It was the year when her life would once again be changed by an absence.

BUT AS THE new life proceeded onward into the new decade, the evening's solitude after a day of waiting on people became less a test and more a balm. Doing the necessary schmoozing with customers and keeping track of town gossip and relationships, Snowy found herself looking forward to the silence upstairs, to reading with her supper, then writing at her desk, and then maybe, for undemanding conversation, a phone call to or from Bev and an occasional call from Dudley, the reelected city councilor. For noise, she could choose the television program she wanted, that benefit Puddles had predicted. During one spell, she watched the evening news at suppertime, her meal cooling while she stared as unbelievingly at the dismantling of the Berlin Wall as she and Alan had stared at its construction. Their other emotion in 1961 had been appalled anger. Now, she gasped at the swift resolution after all these years of deaths and diplomacy and wanted to exclaim like Alice in Wonderland, "You're nothing but a pack of cards!"

Then she settled back into the lulling reprieve of the evening alone, after the day's demands.

"It's almost a vice," she told Tom as they lay talking in his bed one Saturday night after some rambunctious sex, a snowstorm howling outdoors. "Down in the store, working, making chitchat, I can feel the quiet up there awaiting me in the apartment and I crave it, like an opium den."

She was venturing to tell him about the feeling, because she sensed he had it too. He was often alone in his apartment this winter because David had fallen in love with Lavender Hyland, a local young woman, fresh-faced and lively, who was a certified nurse's aide at the Gunthwaite hospital, and who was also apt to be pregnant. Snowy earlier assumed that this was carelessness, with the poor little babies put up for adoption, but later she'd learned from gossip at the store that Lavender had a sideline as a surrogate mother, after having first become one for her sister and then for two other infertile couples. Nowadays it was obvious that Lavender had been impregnated again, and Tom said it wasn't by David; it was business. There must be substantial money involved, either legally or illegally; Lavender had bought one of Woodcombe's white Capes, this one out on Crescent Road, where David was spending most of his nights. Very strange, Snowy thought in fascination, but Tom explained, "David says it's something she's good at, having babies. He admires the way she wants to help people." Snowy thought of Charl producing a dozen, to keep. In her own experience, one session with the miracle of childbirth was plenty. She thought of David building coffins during the day and sleeping with a bountiful Earth Mother at night.

Libby had an apartment in Plymouth and was apt to visit Tom on Sundays, going snowshoeing with him and Snowy. Otherwise, he'd also been discovering an empty nest's peace. He wondered if he and Snowy ought to sacrifice solitude to live together before they got too set in their ways, but he didn't say anything directly because he didn't know how he felt or how she did. He didn't know how he felt about Joanne's news, either. He always avoided talking about Joanne to Snowy. Now he decided he should tell Snowy that news, but he began obliquely, running a hand along Snowy's hip. "I got an invitation to my thirtieth reunion at Rumford in May. Thirtieth!"

"Have you been to any of the others?" Snowy hadn't gone to Bennington's. "Or high-school reunions?"

"Joanne goes to them all. Back in the old days, I stayed home and baby-sat. Then I found other excuses, and she didn't mind; she had more fun on her own without me along just wanting to get the hell out. But she did drag me to our twentieth at Rumford."

"I thought you didn't graduate together. Didn't she finish the next year, because of Brandon?"

He had told Snowy how Joanne had got pregnant by mistake; he hadn't explained that it was because he had raped her. "She considers herself a member of the Class of '60, not '61."

"Are you going to go to this thirtieth?"

"God, no!"

Snowy laughed at his horror.

He said, "Joanne has a gentleman friend."

Snowy stopped laughing. "Oh?"

"It's a guy from good old Gunthwaite High she met again at Adele's. Victor Andrews. Do you remember him?"

On the rebound, Snowy thought. She herself had dated Victor after Tom had dumped her, and now Joanne was doing the same damn thing. "Yes."

"He's divorced, lives down in Nashua, and according to David and Libby he's been commuting weekends to court her. For over a year now. The big news at Christmas, Libby said, was that they announced their engagement and their plans for a June wedding.

Joanne is job-hunting at the elementary schools in the Nashua area. She and Victor will live there in Victor's condo and keep the Newburgh house for a vacation home." Libby's tone in imparting this news had been deliberately noncommittal; she would accept Victor as she'd accepted Snowy, eventually. By now, he knew, Libby liked Snowy a lot. Climbing mountains with companions showed you the stuff they were made of, and Snowy might be sometimes timid and clumsy and slow but she kept learning and she never complained, at least not out loud.

Snowy asked, "Are your kids okay about this?"

"I guess so."

After a moment, Snowy went ahead and asked him, "Are you?"

"Oh sure," he said, but now that he'd told Snowy, he still didn't know. Rage had been the first emotion, that was clear and clearly irrational, and then had come relief, and sadness, and bewilderment. It seemed like he never stuck with anything, not teaching, not the coffin business year-round, not Joanne. In 1956 he had rid himself of Snowy because he was scared of how much he loved her. He pulled her close and put his face in her neck.

Snug in the loft in a blizzard, Snowy felt like Heidi. Sort of.

ON THE HIKE up Mount Daybreak on a June Sunday, Libby was now adjusted enough to her mother's wedding the next Saturday to discuss it with Tom and Snowy. During their late lunch, sitting on the long summit ledges that bulged out over treetops, Libby described with amused affection the dress Joanne had chosen: not a bridal-shop confection like the one Tom remembered from their wedding and Snowy remembered too, having by chance seen them come out of the Gunthwaite Congregational church, but still a dazzler. "Creamy," Libby said, resettling the bridge of her glasses with a forefinger, "a very delicate print of tea roses on a creamy background. She'll be carrying an armload of roses."

Snowy took another restorative bite of her peanut-butter sandwich. After much experimentation, she had learned this was the best energy lunch for her needs, and she packed two fat ones, on whole-wheat bread with a frill of lettuce for an adult touch. Thinking of flowers, of the pink lady's slippers they'd seen along the trail, she asked Libby, "What are you wearing?"

"Mom was afraid I'd wear my ranger uniform, so she picked out the entire outfit." Libby jabbed her bagel-with-hummus-and-sprouts sandwich into the air. "I'll be in a dress the color of this sky. Sleeveless. Brandon will be in *his* uniform, and David in basic navy blue blazer and khakis."

The sky was pale blue, with some fat white clouds bumbling off over the mountains that rose across the soft green bowl of forest below. The view from this summit was to the east. Snowy could always identify Mount Pascataquac because of the fire tower, and she was getting better at guessing which of the others was which from which angle so she didn't have to pester Tom with questions all the time. Eating a carrot stick, she looked at Swiftwater Mountain, whose summit she'd reached on a day hike with Tom and Libby and Ruhamah a week after her first backpack to the pond, keeping going on Libby's gorp. There wasn't much of any place to sit on that summit, so they'd perched crammed together on one uncomfortable rock, bracing themselves to keep from sliding off into the spruces, and then on the way back a rain shower arrived sooner than had been forecast, but drenched Snowy was determined not to show her misery. To her surprise, despite the hardships that hike was fun, particularly in retrospect. Libby made the best gorp ever: walnuts and chocolate chips and dried apricots. This Mount Daybreak hike was shorter, five miles round-trip, and the seating sure was better.

"—honeymoon in Nova Scotia," Libby was saying.

"Nova Scotia," Tom repeated, squashing aluminum foil,

having finished his turkey sandwich. He and Joanne hadn't had a honeymoon.

Snowy said, "That's where Alan and I went on ours," which she hadn't mentioned to Tom before. "Well, it wasn't a real trip, because we didn't have the time or the money; we just took a cruise ship from Portland and spent a day and night in Yarmouth. Then back to Old Eastbourne." She ate a purple grape. When packing her lunch, she plucked grapes off their stems to cut down on any miniscule amount of added weight. Travel was the reason Ruhamah wasn't with them today. Harriet had switched last year's graduation present into an end-of-classes present this year, inviting Ruhamah on a trip to Israel for a vacation before Ruhamah settled down to work in the store this summer. Although Ruhamah had phoned Snowy yesterday, as she did on other trips, Snowy was still much more nervous about Ruhamah's being in Israel than in Cornwall and even more nervous than she was about Christmases in New York City.

Libby munched an apple. "I used to think it'd be neat to do the Appalachian Trail on my honeymoon. Of course there were little problems like finding the right guy and enough time. So I changed to thinking of doing it on my own, but there's still the problem of time."

"The AT?" Tom said, distracted from Joanne and Snowy in Nova Scotia. He ripped open the wrapper of a Snickers. "I never knew you wanted to do that."

"Well," Libby said, "now that everybody else is doing it, I hate to admit to wanting to join the parade."

Tom said, "Why didn't you go after you graduated? That would've been the simplest timing, before taking on a job."

"Money," Libby said. "I want to pay off my student loan."

A loan, Tom thought, which she might not have had to get if I'd stuck to a steady job. He said, "How about doing the AT the sections way? You and I could hike some sections together."

"Cool," said Libby.

Snowy tried to imagine staggering along under a towering

backpack over mountains from Georgia to Maine. She envied Libby such a straightforward ambition. When she was Libby's age, she had still been aiming at joining the company of Emily Dickinson and Edna—

Libby leapt to her feet. "Look out!"

Across the pale blue sky, lightning crackled. Snowy scrambled up and began cramming her lunch bag and water bottle into her pack.

Tom yelled through a thunderclap, "Don't bother with that! Get off the summit! Move!" Half-standing, he fell back onto the ledge. "Shit!"

Libby asked, "Your knee?"

Tom grabbed his walking stick. "Get going! Go!"

But Libby and Snowy helped as he started to haul himself up, Libby with a shoulder under his arm, Snowy throwing her arms around his waist and lifting. The air smelled like ironing. Now the sky held a single black cloud that had materialized right above them, a silly little cloud, Snowy thought wildly, remembering a Johnny Ray song about a cloud crying, as a silly little shower pattered down.

Tom stood upright, took a step, felt his knee buckle again. He shook Snowy and Libby off and dropped onto the ledge. "I'll crawl, I'll be okay! Get the fuck off the summit, *now! Go!*"

Snowy would not. She had left Alan alone and gone to bed, and he had died. She knelt down and began to crawl beside Tom on her hands and knees, seeing as if magnified a million times the glacial striations on the ledges. She could hear a thrumming sound and feel it beneath her fingers.

Then a vivid bolt seemed to blast the rock apart.

Tom shouted, "Libby!"

Snowy lifted her head to see Libby standing there, toppling.

An explosion of thunder sent Snowy sprawling. She sprang up, but Tom was already on his feet, lurching toward his daughter.

The light rain ceased, the black cloud scooted away, and the sky looked just the same as it had a few minutes ago. Libby lay face down. Tom sank beside her and in slow motion reached for her wrist. Snowy thought: She's unconscious, knocked out by the lightning or by hitting her head when she fell.

Very carefully Tom turned Libby over and put two fingers to her throat.

Snowy's heart sounded like the bombardment of the thunderstorm.

Then Tom began to work fast, tipping Libby's head, pinching her nose, breathing into her mouth. When he could speak, pushing her rib cage, he asked Snowy, "Do you know CPR?"

"No. I mean, I've read instructions but I've never taken a class."

"The Jeep keys are in the pocket of my pack. Go down and drive to that house near the trailhead and call the emergency number."

She was running for his pack, unzipping the pocket.

He said, "Leave your pack so you'll be quicker, but don't run. Watch your footing."

II

CHAPTER ONE

SOMETIMES IN THE following days, Snowy began to get them mixed up in her head, her search for Alan that morning three years ago and her descent of Mount Daybreak that June afternoon. She hadn't run, obeying Tom, but she'd gone plunging downhill in a headlong walking pace, her knees as wobbly as the old so-called "jelly legs" symptom of agoraphobia, her heart banging. She had held her breath all the way down those two and a half miles; but no, she couldn't possibly have. Under the spruces and balsams, the shaded trail seemed illuminated, as though lightning bolts from that fleet thunderstorm had floodlit it forever, though when she reached the lower stretch where the trees were mostly beech and birch and the trail should be dappled brightly, it seemed a dark tunnel out of which she would never emerge.

Three years ago, she had been incapable of driving the Subaru fast; from telephone pole to telephone pole she had made her slow way from Hurricane Farm to the store where she'd hoped to find Alan. This time, down at the trailhead she jumped into the Jeep, started it, and then when it stalled she realized she hadn't driven a standard shift in years. The nightmarish darkness closed over her again. Her left foot stamped on the clutch, and she was remembering the driving lessons Tom had given her in high school in the Chevy convertible, and as she lurched and stalled and ground gears, she remembered how patient he'd been, unlike her father, and she almost began laughing when she remembered that Bev's stepfather, trying to teach Bev, used to grit his teeth and say, "Grind me a pound."

A mile or so down the road, she jolted into the driveway of a white Cape. She didn't recognize the maroon Subaru in the driveway—how could she, for as many people in Woodcombe owned Subarus as owned white Capes, and there was a joke about a local woman who'd bought a Volkswagen so she could identify her car amid the others in the village at the store or post office—but she did recognize the woman who opened the door to her banging fist, a year-round customer at the store. Mary and Harold Gorham were summer folk who'd retired here.

"Snowy!" Mary said.

"Please, quick, I need your phone."

Harold came into the kitchen while Snowy was punching the emergency number, and before she finished speaking to the dispatcher, talking slowly though her voice quivered with the effort not to scream, he was yanking his hiking boots out of the coat closet. When she hung up, he said, "I'll go see if I can help. You stay here."

"No," Snowy said. "I'm going back up." If she stayed, the police chief would pull up in his black Jeep Wagoneer and tell her again that somebody was dead.

Mary was getting her own boots out. "Then I'll wait for the EMTs here, to make sure they find the trailhead, and follow. Harold, the first-aid kit?"

Snowy said, "Tom has one in his pack. So does Libby."

But Harold unzipped a backpack, checked, and said to Mary, "Yes." He looked at Snowy. "You told the dispatcher that Tom is hurt too? He might not be able to walk?"

"Not because of the lightning. A football knee." Libby had teased him about it. "He carries an Ace knee brace in his pack."

Mary went into the closet again, this time emerging with a pair of crutches. "From when Harold broke his leg skiing."

Snowy said, "Tom has a walking stick."

But Harold carried the crutches out to the Subaru. In the Jeep,

Snowy followed him back to the trailhead. He shouldered his pack and tucked the crutches under an arm.

At this stage, climbing again the trail she and Tom and Libby had set forth on so blithely this morning, Snowy began to feel extraordinarily clearheaded. The clarity, however, extended only to the climb itself, her second wind, her swift strength, the muscles lifting her up a vertical rise of fifteen hundred feet. Lady's slippers, shy but sexy, still bloomed since this morning. She saw the wild sarsaparilla that Libby had pointed out, and wine-red columbines. In a tasty juicy green glade, there were still nibbled saplings and the moose droppings that looked like those malt balls Puddles used to love.

As Snowy and Harold came out onto the long ledges of the summit, she saw Tom as if she'd never left. He still knelt over Libby, doing CPR.

Harold said, "Let me," set down the crutches, stripped off his pack, and dropped down beside Tom.

But Tom wouldn't relinquish Libby.

Harold said, "You're tired. I'm fresh. The EMTs are on their way."

Tom looked up. "Helicopter?"

Gently Harold nudged him aside and without missing a beat continued the compressions.

Snowy said, "They weren't sure it could land here. They're coming up the trail."

Tom tried to stand, but collapsed with a thud.

Snowy asked, "Crutches? Your walking stick?"

Tom just sat there, watching Harold. Snowy went over to his pack. It was an unstated rule that you didn't delve into somebody's pack unless you were asked to, same as with pocketbooks, but she pawed around in it until she found the knee brace that Libby had insisted he always bring along. He had done so, even though he'd read that such braces weren't much use. Snowy took it over to him, and when he ignored it, she crouched down, untied his left boot, pulled the boot off, and pushed up the left trouser of his khaki hiking pants. He didn't switch to hiking shorts until after Father's Day; the bug season supposedly lasted from Mother's Day to Father's Day. She slid the brace up to his knee, the knee that had got stomped on during a Gunthwaite football game about thirty-five years ago. It had been a minor injury he scarcely noticed at the time. When she'd finished retying the boot she couldn't think what else to do except sit beside him. She reached for his hand. His wonderful capable hands. Then finally she looked at Libby.

She had never seen Alan after he drowned. A friend in the village, Nelson Fletcher, had officially identified the body. Shame at having shirked this duty was part of the cataclysm of emotions that had assailed her then.

Yesterday Ruhamah had timed a phone call from Israel perfectly for Snowy's lunch break. Ruhamah said, "We're sightseeing, and Harriet and Nathan are painting, and Harriet and I have gone to see him play soccer—and Snowy, I planted a tree for Alan today. Harriet told me about this place where you can go choose a little tree and dig a hole and plant it, and so we went there and I did it. I chose an olive tree because Alan liked olives. They gave me a certificate. I cried oceans, but it was great."

At the ceremony at Old Eastbourne, Ruhamah had remained dry-eyed.

Harriet was handed the phone by Ruhamah, and Snowy said, "Thank you."

And when Ruhamah got back on to say good-bye, Snowy managed not to say: Be careful, be careful, come home safe and sound.

Tom jumped up, stumbled, crawled over to Libby, and shoved Harold aside. As he puffed breaths in Libby's mouth, Snowy tried to see a response. Surely the power of his desperation would make Libby start breathing.

She heard footsteps thumping up the trail, and onto the sunny summit burst the EMT crew.

HE WOULD BUILD the coffin himself. That was Tom's one thought when he and Snowy returned from the Gunthwaite hospital that evening, Snowy driving him back in the Jeep.

He almost lost his self-control at the sight of Libby's blue Toyota parked in his driveway, her car out of which she'd bounded this morning after arriving from Plymouth, but leaning on his walking stick he went into the barn, up the staircase to the telephone on the end table beside his armchair in the living room. As Snowy hesitated in the apartment doorway, holding Libby's backpack, he stood for a moment, then lifted the receiver and jabbed Lavender's phone number.

David said, "Hello?"

Tom said, "Something terrible has happened. There was a thunderstorm. Libby, Libby, Libby was hit. She hasn't recovered. She died, David. Would you come get the Jeep right away and drive up to Newburgh?"

A silence. David said, "The Jeep?"

"Or take Libby's car. I'll need your pickup. For the coffin."

"Dad."

"I'll build it tonight."

Another silence. Then: "Let me help."

"No, you go up to Newburgh. I'll be phoning your mother now."

Tom hung up. He felt himself sway. An EMT had strapped his knee; in the hospital, an ER doctor had examined it and talked about shock.

Snowy started toward him, but when he began tapping the numbers for the next phone call she went into his bedroom and shut the door, leaving him alone to tell Joanne.

"Hello?" Joanne's voice was abrupt. He could hear the TV in the background, a sports program, a game. If it was the Red Sox, she'd've let the answering machine take the call. Maybe she had answered, no matter who was playing, because the phone call might be from Victor, if Victor wasn't spending the weekend before the wedding with her.

"Joanne," he said, and couldn't say anything else.

"Tom?"

He tried to remember how he'd told David only a few minutes ago.

Joanne said, "What's wrong? Oh my God, what's wrong?"

"There wasn't any warning in the weather forecast. Not a thing. A clear sunny day."

"What's wrong?"

"Libby."

"She's hurt?"

"A freak thunderstorm. There wasn't anything in the forecast."

"Lightning? Lightning struck her?"

Tom's throat closed up.

"How bad is it? Tom!"

Tom couldn't speak.

Joanne screamed.

Tom said, "David, he's coming to Newburgh tonight. I'll phone Brandon; he can get leave."

"Oh God!"

"Is—someone there with you now? Can you have a friend come over until David gets there? Celeste or Mindy or somebody?"

"*Where is Libby?*"

"The Gunthwaite hospital."

"I'm on my way down right now."

"Joanne, they'll be—they're sending her to the Newburgh funeral home." Both he and Joanne had taught the undertaker's kids; he himself had a business relationship with Russ Hewes, the undertaker. "There's no point in your coming down. It's all in Newburgh, David tonight, Brandon probably tomorrow."

He heard a torrent of sobbing. Joanne said, "Worry, I've worried over all of them all these years—Brandon flying airplanes—Tom, it can't be true! How did it happen? How could it happen? She's a forest ranger! You spend your days in a tower watching for lightning strikes and fire!"

"We were on the summit of Mount Daybreak eating lunch. No warning. The storm was upon us out of nowhere." He should tell her that it was his fault. Finally tears welled up, hot and agonizing. But instead of telling Joanne that he had slowed them down because of his knee, that without him there, Libby would've been off the summit in an instant, and safe, he said, "I'm going to make the—coffin and urn. I'll bring them up tomorrow."

Her voice raw and rasping, Joanne said, "I'll phone Brandon. You'll stay here at the house?"

"If you want me to."

Joanne hung up.

Tom hobbled down the stairs to the workshop. He was choosing the best pieces of stock in the North Country Coffins supply of wide pine boards when David came in. Neither of them spoke.

From the apartment doorway above, Snowy could see that David had been crying. Now he seemed to be mustering every shred of composure. Finally he said, "Lavender is outside. I'll take the Jeep. She'll follow, driving Libby's car home. The keys?"

Snowy said, "I'll get them," and hurried to the kitchen table, where she had set Libby's backpack, and unzipped the pocket in which Libby kept her keys. Then she went into Tom's bedroom, where she'd put Tom's keys on his bureau. Carrying the keys and pack, she ran downstairs.

David was gripping Tom's shoulder.

Tom absently gave the hand a pat.

David said to Snowy, "Thank you," and left, cradling the pack.

"Your knee," Snowy said. "If you can't drive the pickup, I'll drive you."

"Thanks," Tom said from far away, "I'll manage."

Tom knew that Snowy stayed on in the apartment and he supposed she eventually slept in his bed, but he worked through the night on the coffin that would go into the crematory's flames and the little pine box for Libby's ashes.

ON THE FOLLOWING Friday evening, Snowy drove to Gunthwaite to meet Ruhamah's bus at the Trailways stop in front of a Cumberland Farms store. She hadn't told Ruhamah about Libby when Ruhamah phoned yesterday morning from Harriet's Manhattan apartment to report her safe return to JFK airport on schedule; she hadn't phoned Ruhamah in Israel earlier in the week to tell her. It was bad enough having to phone Bev and Puddles, who had never known Libby. Puddles had asked professional questions in a constrained voice. Bev had wept. Snowy had said to Bev, "How can I ever tell Ruhamah?" Bev had said tremulously, "I can't believe I had children so—unthinkingly! I knew better by the time Etta came along, I knew about hostages to fortune, but that pregnancy was a surprise, I'd thought I was through and I forgot the Pill—oh, Snowy! Do you want me to meet Ruhamah with you? What can I do to help?" "I don't know," Snowy said, "I don't know. There's nothing. I've just got to tell her. But when? An eleven-and-a-half hour flight, gaining seven hours—they left Israel at one a.m. yesterday morning and landed in New York at five-thirty a.m., I'll never understand this—but even though she's had a day to recover at Harriet's she is bound to be worn out, with the bus ride and—" Bev said, "Snowy, she's nineteen. Resilient." Then Dudley had phoned, saying, "Snowy, I'm so sorry. I saw it in the newspaper. I haven't phoned or written Tom; should I?" He and Tom had always been uneasy around each other because of their respective relationships with Snowy; neither guy liked the other, which was understandable but regrettable. She had said, "I'll tell him you called, Dudley." If Tom ever returned from Newburgh.

The bus pulled in, and Ruhamah stepped off, wearing jeans and a black T-shirt, her tresses twisted up atop her head. Ruhamah, home safely. Snowy sprang out of the car, ran across the parking lot, hugged her, hugged her.

Ruhamah chortled, "I missed you too!" and gave Snowy a kiss and hug, then pried herself loose to pick up her duffel bag.

As they drove home, Snowy listened to Ruhamah's adventures and suddenly thought that her awful dread was an extreme adult version of what Tom must have been feeling back in 1956 when he'd brought her home from Girls' State, listening to her happy prattle while knowing he was about to give her bad news, to break up with her.

Driving into the village, she thought: I can't do it. She'd had to tell Ruhamah about Alan. That was enough to have to do, ever. Snowy touched the back of her skull as if she could still feel the bump raised there when she'd told Ruhamah that Alan was dead and Ruhamah had shouted, "Goddamn you!" and shoved her against a wall before disappearing into her bedroom. At the time, Snowy hadn't felt it at all.

"Hey," Ruhamah said, interrupting herself. "You just went past the store."

Snowy hadn't realized she intended to or where she was going until she said, "Let's visit the cove."

"Where?"

"You've planted the olive tree for him. We can go to the cove."

"The cove." Then Ruhamah fell silent.

Snowy drove out of the village, past the Roller Coaster Road, along the lake to Tolman Road, onto which she turned. The nighttime sky was a cottony blue, faintly pink. There were lights on in some of the cottages; summer people had arrived, for the weekend or for the summer. She had last driven down this road three years ago, after Alan had died, and here at Murray Cove she had waded into the water the way Alan must have, but instead of continuing beyond ankle depth she had splashed back to shore and driven away to climb Pascataquac to Tom.

Snowy stopped the car. Ruhamah slowly opened the passenger door, and Snowy opened hers. They walked forward on the right-of-way to the rim of a little beach between the wooded lots of a darkened cottage and a cottage aglow, voices murmuring on its porch. Snowy could hear other voices farther away and see a boat tied up at the dock here and dock lights along the cove on either side. When Alan had come to Murray Cove in early May, all the cottages had still been closed, and he had been alone.

Snowy put an arm around Ruhamah.

Ruhamah asked, "You okay?"

"Yes. You?"

"It's taken a while, hasn't it."

They walked back to the car and got in. Snowy said, "Now I have to tell you something."

"Aha." Ruhamah smiled. "Don't worry. You and Tom are getting married? Cool."

"It's not good news. Ruhamah, it's terrible—"

Ruhamah cried out, "Cancer?"

"Libby. There was an accident on Mount Daybreak. Lightning. She and Tom and I were on the summit. She died, Ruhamah."

Ruhamah stared at Snowy, who braced herself. But this time Ruhamah collapsed, sobbing in her arms. Snowy held her tight. Home safely. But never safe, not really.

Eventually Ruhamah sat up and groped in the back seat for the box of Kleenex Snowy kept there. Blowing her nose, Ruhamah said, "Tell me exactly what happened."

Snowy did so. Ruhamah began crying again, yanking Kleenex after Kleenex out of the box like a magician producing a rainbow of scarves from a top hat. Snowy said, "We need tea or something," and started the car and drove back to the village.

David's pickup, in which Tom had driven off to Newburgh with the coffin on Monday, was parked in the barn's driveway. Thank God, Snowy thought, Tom is here. The memorial service is over. But why didn't he return in the Jeep?

She stopped beside the store. Ruhamah stumbled around to the back of the car, hauled out her duffel, and dragged it toward the outside staircase. Snowy, about to follow, paused. A man was walking down the street from the barn. Tom. No, taller. As he neared, she saw by the streetlights that the man was David.

"David," she said, "how are you doing?"

"Okay," he said.

Ruhamah turned. "David."

"It was time to come back," he said. "Get back to work. Both my grandmothers are still up there and so's my grandfather—Mom's father—and some uncles and aunts. Brandon rented a plane and he and I flew over the White Mountains and scattered her ashes, and then Brandon had to leave, and Lavender and I have come back. Lavender's baby is due next week. I'm going over to her place now. I left you a message on your answering machine. Mom got Dad to our doctor, and he said Dad should have a knee operation, arthroscopy, so Dad is staying for that. Other fire towers will cover his area, like they've been doing this week."

"Oh," Snowy said. Then she said, "Um, you aren't returning to Newburgh tomorrow? What about your mother and Victor's wedding tomorrow?"

"Postponed," David said.

"IN LAYPERSONS' TERMS," Puddles said over the phone the next evening, "what they do is scrape the junk out of the knee. That's arthroscopy. He'll be on crutches for a while, but it's no big deal."

"I see," Snowy said. Ruhamah had insisted on working in the store today, but after supper Ruhamah had done some phoning—to various friends, Snowy gathered, ostentatiously not eavesdropping, listening to her Walkman as she futilely wiped at the pine pollen that had suddenly descended everywhere today, like a yellow dust storm—and then Ruhamah had gone to bed and it was Snowy's turn to use the phone. Last night Snowy had looked up "arthroscopy" in her home medical encyclopedia, so she knew what it meant, yet still she felt the need to consult Puddles, always her real medical authority.

Who continued, with her usual lack of a bedside manner, "It's not the operation you should be worrying about, it's having him in Joanne's clutches."

"They're divorced. Joanne is engaged to Victor."

"You said she postponed the wedding."

"Only fitting, during a period of mourning."

"Bullshit," said Puddles.

Snowy gave a little laugh. "Puddles, Joanne couldn't have a wedding right after a funeral. She and Tom...their daughter..."

Puddles said, "I hope you'll be doing something therapeutic tomorrow on your afternoon off."

"I'll probably still be dusting. I'm dusting now."

"Snowy!"

"Not regular housework. Pine pollen is making a mess of everything, the apartment, the store, the car and van."

Puddles had never mentioned to Snowy that for years she had hired a woman to do the housecleaning, and now she changed the subject. "I went with Guy to Hilton Head today. While he played golf with some buddies, I drove around and looked the island over really hard for the first time, but it still seems like a never-never land to me. I got so freaked out I finally grabbed a parking space and walked on the public beach in my bare feet and then I went to a nifty boutique and bought a pink-and-aqua sundress to get my jollies *my* way while Guy was getting his."

"Did you ever consider taking up golf yourself?"

"I tried it once and can't imagine repeating the experience. My father and Guy and all these zillions of men, I cannot fathom how they can become so addicted to riding around in a little cart and hitting a little ball!"

"How about tennis? Bev doesn't have time anymore, but she loved it."

"Cheering was what I loved, though it's supposedly not a sport, and, unlike golf, it's not something you can do until you drop in your tracks. But have you noticed that cheerleading isn't 'out' anymore? Seems like it's beginning to be acceptable again, 'in.'"

"Oh Christ, not really!"

Puddles snapped, "What's wrong with that?"

Oops. Snowy remembered that one of Puddles's twins, Susan, had been a cheerleader. It was okay to laugh fondly at their own cheerleading days, but not okay to imply that Susan too was silly. Snowy said, "Puddles, you ought to coach. You'd be great."

Puddles was silent, struck by the thought. "There's a hell of a lot of gymnastics now."

"You'd've been great at that, if we'd had them then."

"You were the captain."

"God knows why. The token egghead. You were the best on the squad, the best Gunthwaite ever had!"

Always unsettled by compliments, Puddles changed the subject again and prescribed brusquely, "Don't dust tomorrow. Go to a mall!"

"I don't want a mall, I want the old Gunthwaite downtown!"

"Face it, that's over. Bye."

"Bye." When Snowy hung up and picked up her dust rag, those words echoed in her head: Face it, that's over. Then the phone rang, and she grabbed it before the sound could wake Ruhamah. Imploring the gods to let it be Tom, just as if she were back in high school, she gasped, "Hello?"

Dudley said, "Ruhamah phoned D. J. Snowy, we're having our usual Father's Day cookout tomorrow. He invited her out tomorrow night but not exactly to the cookout because he didn't know how she feels about Father's Day, because—because of Alan."

D. J. had graduated from Rumford this month and would be living at home this summer, working at a Gunthwaite law office, before he started Franklin Pierce Law Center in Concord this fall. He was the first of Dudley and Charl's brood to do what Dudley had intended to, go to law school. Did he also have Dudley's old ambition of becoming President of the United States? Snowy said, "We've never made much of a commotion about either Mother's or Father's Day."

"Well, *we* sure do, for obvious reasons: Parenthood has been our main occupation. Why don't you both come? It's a combined bash, with Darl and Bill."

"Did Ruhamah tell D. J. that Tom is having a knee operation up in Newburgh?"

"Arthroscopy."

So Dudley and Charl had pictured Snowy alone again and felt sorry for her. She put her chin up and was about to decline, when Dudley added, "I've been wanting to talk some politics with you. I need your advice."

She looked at the kitchen and living room slick with pollen. A week ago tomorrow, she and Tom and Libby had set forth to climb Mount Daybreak. She said to Dudley, "Ruhamah and I will both be there to wish you happy Father's Day. What time?"

"WE WERE SAILING along," Dudley warbled, "on Moonlight Bay—"

Snowy objected, "We're not sailing. We're paddling."

"We were paddling along," sang Dudley, revising obligingly, "on Belknap River—"

Snowy wasn't too sure how long they would be paddling before they capsized. She had never paddled a canoe before, but after the cookout, to which Snowy and Ruhamah contributed some tortellini salad right out of the store's deli case, and after the Father's Day present-giving, to which Snowy didn't think she and Ruhamah had to contribute anything because Dudley wasn't their father (but would he someday be Ruhamah's father-in-law?), D. J. and Ruhamah had driven off somewhere in D. J.'s old Toyota (why oh why must Ruhamah possess such rectitude, leaving Snowy to worry about whether or not she was still a virgin?), and Charl had shooed Dudley and Snowy away from the teeming multitude, all twelve children and assorted spouses and grandchildren and dogs, plus Darl and Bill and their kids. Dudley and Snowy had strolled down to the dock where she'd mused, "I've looked at this river all my life, but I've never been on it." Dudley asked, "Ever been in a canoe?" She shook her head. He said, "Come on. You're a fast learner." She said, "Eek, what about the waterfall?" "We go in the opposite direction. Get in." So she had obeyed.

Dudley now began singing "Cruising down the River," much more appropriate. In the stern, he was doing most of the paddling, but she imitated him the best she could. They were heading upstream away from that waterfall near the old textile mill that nowadays housed the Gunthwaite Historical Society, and as her nerves abated she could feel the exhilaration of the river alive beneath her, lifting her, holding her, carrying her. It was as though she were riding a horse, something else she'd never done. Or was it like riding a giant snake? Freudian? Whatever it was like, she was riding the river, *her* river. On the glossy green-gold water, they slid past her house on Emery Street. The familiar sights looked different from out here—and somehow British! Why? Oh, *The Wind in the Willows*! She paddled through the old neighborhood seen afresh from this perspective, green trees overhanging the riverbank.

Dudley ceased his song, slowed his paddle, in his mind's eye an image that wasn't British. "This is how the Indians saw the land."

"So many people have docks in their backyards, just like you. In our day, nobody dared go swimming or boating here."

"God, no. If you fell in, the pollution would kill you faster than piranhas. Speaking of Indians, that is, Native Americans: There's a move afoot to change the name of school teams. 'Abnakis' isn't politically correct. Lots of schools are struggling with the problem, including Dartmouth, not to mention the Washington Redskins, the Atlanta Braves, and so forth."

"Oh dear. And the *Smoke Signal*?" This was the name of the school newspaper.

"That got changed some years ago, because any reference to smoke scared the shit out of the administration. They came up with the *GHS Gazette.*"

"How brilliantly original."

"Snowy, there's talk about another change. About how to expand the high school again."

"They've already expanded onto the front lawn and the practice field, isn't that enough?"

"That was years ago, and they need more room. They're thinking this time it might be best to tear down the buildings and start over."

Snowy swung around to stare at him, her paddle caught air, and the canoe tipped.

Dudley kept them upright.

"Sorry," Snowy said.

"That's nothing. When I told Charl, she went ballistic, as our kids would say."

"Is this the politics you mentioned? Not how to beat George Bush in '92?"

"I'm running for a third term on the council again next fall, '91."

"Good, I was hoping you would. And I'm glad Gunthwaite has local elections in the odd-numbered years; it separates them in my mind. Tear down the high school?" Snowy paddled strenuously. "Dudley, will the main plank in your platform be a way to keep the school? You don't want it torn down, do you? I don't know what the architecture is, but it's high-school classic! Can't it be, what's the term, rehabbed? Goddamn it, Dudley, too many fucking things have already been demolished or changed beyond recognition!"

Dudley began to laugh. "Then I don't have to plead for your frank opinion about my dealings with the school and for your support in a potentially unpopular stand?"

"How can I support you if I'm a Woodcombe citizen and can't vote in Gunthwaite?"

"I needed to know if you agreed."

"What you need," Snowy said, "is Alan. The Old Eastbourne expert."

Dudley said slowly, "Now that's a useful idea." After a few moments' silence, he said, "I guess we should start back," and he instructed her through the turning maneuver without dumping them in the water. Heading downstream, he said, "D. J. says Ruhamah had been planning on a history major, like Alan, but then she began considering a forestry major, like Tom's daughter. Now she's back to history."

"Oh," Snowy said. "Forestry is news to me." What else didn't she know?

"D. J. thinks Ruhamah should go for a business degree, an MBA."

"Why on earth?"

"You own a business, Snowy. Look at us, you and me, owning businesses, with not one business course between us."

Alan hadn't had any, either. She said, "The bank owns most of my store."

Dudley said, "But someday the store may become Ruhamah's."

Snowy dug her paddle into the river. Although her vision of Ruhamah's future was vague, it sure the hell didn't include a lifetime of waiting on customers in the Woodcombe General Store. Snowy was resigned to this being her own fate (wasn't she?), but it could not be her daughter's! She said, "After I die, Ruhamah will sell the store."

Dudley said in a rush, "Oh, Snowy, when I read in the paper about that lightning strike on Daybreak—you might have been killed too—" He stopped and switched to a lighter tone. "I would have missed you, pal of my youth."

She said, "Tom. He's wishing he'd died instead. Or with her."

Dudley said simply, "Of course."

The canoe glided back past the big square white house with the black shutters, past the riverbank where she used to sit and daydream, never dreaming that she and Dudley would be canoeing down this river. At age fifty-one!

They rounded a bend and paddled toward the painted-lady house and the party.

Because D. J. would be bringing Ruhamah home, Snowy drove back to Woodcombe alone. Last week at this time, the EMTs were carrying Libby, Libby's body, down Mount Daybreak on a litter, Tom behind them on Harold Gorham's crutches, Snowy behind him. Tom hadn't said a word all the way down.

As she neared the store, she could not quench a surge of hope that Tom had returned. He might have changed his mind and decided to have the arthroscopy done at the Gunthwaite hospital and, if he couldn't drive back to Woodcombe, asked David to come get him. She looked along the street at North Country Coffins. No pickup; David must still be at Lavender's. No Jeep.

After Alan's death, Ruhamah had retreated from her. After Libby's, Tom had.

Then she noticed, parked in front of the store, a make of car rarely seen in this town of Subarus. The year-round and summer people here who could afford really expensive cars bought Range Rovers or Mercedes, and the tourists weren't apt to be the sports-car type. This was a white Jaguar. With New York plates. Even before Snowy recognized the woman sitting on the deacon's bench on the store's porch, a sketchbook on her knees, she thought: Harriet is still dating jocks and still buying white Jaguars.

Harriet!

Snowy jumped out of the Subaru and ran toward her.

CHAPTER TWO

AS THEY HUGGED, Harriet said, "Ruhamah phoned me."

Ruhamah had indeed been busy on the phone last night. Snowy asked, "A bread-and-butter phone call?" She had taught Ruhamah that according to old-fashioned etiquette you were supposed to write your bread-and-butter thank-you note before you took off your hat after you returned from a visit, and even if women no longer wore hats it was still a good rule; Snowy did not approve of substituting a phone call but she bowed to compromise.

Harriet said, "Ruhamah told me what had happened. I'm so sorry."

Ruhamah had told Harriet, Snowy thought, and Harriet, realizing that her dear old roommate had almost been killed so they'd better have a reunion before Death eventually got them both, Harriet had jumped in her Jaguar and driven up here without phoning ahead. Harriet used to accuse Snowy of being compulsive; Harriet herself was impulsive. Snowy drew back and gave Harriet a once-over. The snapshots Ruhamah had taken during New York visits and the trip to Cornwall didn't show the netting of gray filaments in Harriet's short black elegant haircut. But like Bev, Harriet wasn't hiding her gray. And Harriet sure looked like a somebody, even in the outfit she had chosen for this trip to the back of beyond in New Hampshire, faded jeans and a blue sweatshirt with paint splotches. She must have been inspired by memories of what she and Snowy had called their "epithelial tissue," Bennington sweatshirts worn nonchalantly backwards and Levi's, because in Ruhamah's photos she mostly seemed to be wearing basic New York black, quite a change from the California tendencies she'd retained in her dressier clothes at Bennington, a wardrobe too gaudy for Vermont.

"Have you had to wait here long?" Snowy said. "Ruhamah and I were in Gunthwaite—"

"Snowy, this is a beautiful place to wait. Déjà vu hit me. As I started to draw, I remembered doing almost the same scene! We stopped here when you gave me that tour of New Hampshire back when I visited you our freshman year."

"Because I'd heard it was so picturesque. Nary an inkling that someday I'd live here." Then Snowy thought in horror of the apartment upstairs, no guest room to offer except the pull-out sofa. She ran her finger along the porch railing. "Pine-pollen time."

"Is that what it is?" Harriet picked up one of her pastels, a yellow one, and scribbled the words on the sketchbook, where Snowy saw an impression of the village street in a gold haze. "That," Harriet said, "will be what I'll call the painting I'm going to do."

Impressionist. Snowy had fallen in love with Monet when she went to her first museum, the National Gallery of Art, during her Girl Scout trip to Washington. To think that Harriet's progress since the fat women and red circles and such of her Bennington experimental days had led her backward to this kind of landscapes, impressionist! Snowy was overjoyed and respectful. "Do you want to stay down here and work or is it finished? I can bring you something to drink here or we can go up to the apartment, where, incidentally, there's more pine pollen. You can spend the night, can't you? Maybe longer? I've got a pull-out sofa, but if that proves too uncomfortable for you there are a couple of bed-and-breakfasts in town and in Gunthwaite there are inns and motels. Tomorrow, I can leave the store for a while in Ruhamah's and Irene's hands and I'll give you a tour of Woodcombe, though there's not much to see."

Harriet was laughing. She closed the sketchbook, slipped it into her big shoulder bag, lifted a carry-on bag out of the Jaguar, and said, "I'll have to go back Tuesday and tend to business because I've been away, though Kristin has become the best administrative assistant I've ever had. Meanwhile, I want to see everything, starting with the store itself."

So Snowy unlocked the front door, ushered her in, and, embarrassed and shy, showed her the store. Harriet particularly enjoyed the items posted on the bulletin board—Free Manure was her favorite—and the array of workboots dangling from the ceiling, and also, found by Alan in the storeroom, the old wooden cheese box that even had a hole in a corner gnawed by a mouse. "Perfect!" Harriet said. Then she spotted the stack of Woodcombe General Store T-shirts in which Snowy had invested. Harriet wouldn't take one as a gift and insisted on buying it but was gleeful as a kid when Snowy told her to choose whatever she saw in the store that she'd like to eat tonight. Snowy, full of Dudley and Charl's cookout, had planned on a plain vegetable salad for supper, but naturally it was the tortellini salad that Harriet wanted, along with lettuce, tomatoes, a loaf of Italian bread, and a pint of Ben and Jerry's Cherry Garcia, and oh, speaking of cheese, a wedge from that wheel of rat trap cheese and some of those common crackers. Carrying groceries, Snowy led Harriet up the inside staircase into the apartment.

Harriet said, "This is adorable!"

Well, maybe it was, but Snowy said, "Tomorrow I'll show you Hurricane Farm, where we used to live," and then felt ashamed of being ashamed. She set the groceries on the kitchen counter and opened the fridge. "What would you like? There's Diet Pepsi, iced tea, chardonnay, beer. Or I can go back downstairs for anything else."

"I'd love a glass of chardonnay." Harriet walked over to the portrait she'd done of Ruhamah Reed for Snowy and Alan's wedding present. It hung on the living-room wall, between the small windows overlooking the street, and beside it was the pen-and-ink sketch she remembered from the wall over Snowy's desk in their room at school: the Ruhamah Reed House, drawn by Alan, who had minored in art and taken some architecture courses, as the drawing made obvious. Harriet looked again at her own work, the portrait, with an even more critical eye, and then relented, allowing it some merit, and then she wanted to fall down and yowl for that youthful joie de vivre of yore.

Snowy took two wineglasses from a cupboard, her mind racing, trying to remember how to be a hostess, rearranging her work schedule.

Harriet suddenly wondered if Snowy had any idea that the Ruhamah Reed painting would be worth a few bucks nowadays. No, probably Snowy was as clueless as ever. Harriet asked, pointing to the door between the two bedroom doors. "Bathroom?"

"Oh yes, I'm sorry, I'll get your towels—"

"Don't bother now. I'll dry my hands on Kleenex."

Harriet went into the bathroom, and Snowy arranged crackers and cheese on a black platter, part of the set of dishes she'd bought at Bennington Potters with a wedding-present check from Bev's mother. She tried to calm down. How could she? Harriet was *here!*

"Bennington Potters," said Harriet, coming out of the bathroom and seeing the platter. "I still have my coffee mug."

"Some of these dishes got broken, but not bad for twenty-nine years."

Harriet reached into her bag and took out a white box, which she handed to Snowy. "Hostess gift, something I picked up in Israel."

Out of the box Snowy lifted a silk scarf hand-painted with splashes of pink, gold, blue, purple, green, turquoise. The texture was airy, the colors intense. Overcome, she caressed it. "Oh, Harriet, it's *beautiful!* Thank you!"

"I thought it might be a change of pace." Harriet went to one of the windows and looked down over the porch roof at the New England main street.

Snowy poured wine. With Harriet, she had always emphasized or exaggerated her ignorance instead of hiding it, so she joked, "I just discovered chardonnay a year ago, when Bev and Puddles and I went to Camden and Bev selected it for our dinner."

"Could I meet Bev at long last?"

"I'll invite her to dinner tomorrow!"

"I'm planning to take you and Ruhamah *out* to dinner tomorrow. You decide on the place and invite Bev along."

"That would be wonderful." Snowy immediately thought of the nicest place she and Tom had dined at, a recently renovated mansion on the lake. The Gilmore House was worthy of Harriet. Snowy handed her a glass of chardonnay and carried the platter to the living-room area. "Remember when you smuggled tequila into our room in your paint box and introduced me to margaritas?"

Harriet looked at the little pedestal table, a coffee table on which Snowy was setting the hors d'oeuvres. "Remember that coffee table we bought from those sophomores?"

"It was shaped like a boomerang!"

And down Memory Lane they strolled, Harriet curled up on the sofa, Snowy in the Martha Washington chair. Onward down the lane they went as they moved to supper at the kitchen's harvest table. After, they took an actual stroll along Main Street in the dusk, the day draining away, the leafy village a silhouette. Snowy pointed out North Country Coffins, where neither the pickup nor the Jeep was parked.

Harriet said, "Ruhamah seems very fond of Tom. She put a good deal of thought into choosing a souvenir for him, and she settled on a bottle of Sabra. That's a scrumptious Israeli liqueur. Did you like the present she brought you?"

"Um, she hasn't produced any presents."

"Oh yes, I suppose she's forgotten, what with what's happened... Not having children was certainly the right choice for me. I don't know how you can stand the constant worry. I was hoping to meet Tom someday, at long last like Bev. Well, on my next visit."

"Do you want to climb a mountain tomorrow? To see the view from Tom's fire tower? Ruhamah could take you up there. I don't think I'm ready for another mountaintop for a while."

"Maybe Ruhamah wouldn't want to. Let's save that for another visit."

Harriet spoke as if she popped up here regularly, as if it hadn't been decades since her last—and first—visit to New Hampshire in 1957.

"Let's," Snowy said, playing along.

Back at the apartment, Snowy phoned Bev, whose immediate reaction was, "A rich and famous artist! What should I *wear?*"

"Not black," said Snowy, and Bev thought she meant that mourning-wear for Libby wasn't necessary.

THE NEXT MORNING was cloudy, humid, the kind of day that made Snowy remember why she liked winter and wonder why she had yearned for spring and summer. As Ruhamah remarked down in the store, while she and Snowy and Irene took care of the rush of early birds who came in for coffee and muffins and newspapers and odds and ends, "It's the kind of day when even your earrings feel sweaty."

Harriet descended the inside staircase, wearing jeans and the Woodcombe General Store T-shirt. Snowy pointed toward the coffee carafes and an empty little table and brought her a slab of coffee cake. Harriet laughed and said, "Our Coffee Cake Therapy!"

"What's that?" asked the young man at the next table, Jared Smith, one of Woodcombe's many carpenters.

Snowy introduced Harriet, who eyed with interest the big tape measure he wore on his belt, and left her explaining to Jared the importance of coffee cake during their Bennington days: All the students showed up for breakfast on mornings when it was served, and it had become a symbol to Harriet and Snowy of treats necessary for perspective. While Snowy worked, she noticed that Harriet managed to sip and chew during her conversation with him, so apparently Harriet had outgrown her hang-up (a form of agoraphobia?) about eating or drinking in front of a male, a problem that had made her an expert at nursing a beer or toying with a pizza.

Then Patsy Fletcher, one of the customers, said as she paid Snowy for a quart of milk, "Did you hear? Lavender had her baby yesterday."

Snowy said, "Is everything okay? She knew from the ultrasound it's a boy."

"Oh yes, both were fine." Patsy sighed. "And now Lavender has given him up. What a generous soul; I couldn't do it."

"Mmm," Snowy agreed, an idea dawning, like this morning's sunrise skidding pink across the mountains. How about phoning David with an inquiry about Lavender's well-being, and maybe David would mention Tom and—

Ruhamah said, "Snowy, we're under control now. You and Harriet can take off."

As Snowy and Harriet went outdoors, Harriet said, "Instead of a storekeeper, you're more like a hostess at a party!"

Snowy had never thought of it like that. She returned to worrying about being Harriet's hostess, then realized that Jared was following them out.

He said, looking at the Jaguar, "Your car?"

Harriet laughed. "You can tell just by the New York plates?"

"Ever ridden in a pickup with New Hampshire plates?" Jared swung up into his big Dodge 4x4 and quoted the unfortunate New Hampshire state motto on the license plates. "'Live free or die'! I'd be happy to take you for a ride sometime." He roared off.

Harriet said, "There's more than one type of pickup. Isn't he cute?"

"But, alas, so young," Snowy said. "He did some work on the apartment and kept asking me about the 1960s as if it were ancient history."

"Another benefit of not having kids is that I can't say he's young enough to be my son. At least not with any conviction."

Snowy stared at her and made a sudden guess. "Um, how old is Nathan?"

"Ruhamah didn't mention it?"

"Nope."

"Well, let's just say that he's younger than the modern state of Israel."

"Harriet, I don't know that date off the top of my head! Nineteen-forty-something?"

"Do you remember the Six-Day War? He was ten then."

Snowy began walking around the side of the store to the Subaru. "We'd better take my car. Four-wheel drive and back roads. Alan and I were still living in the Ruhamah Reed House apartment when we watched the Six-Day War on television, but what year, let's see, 1967? You mean Nathan was born in 1957? The year we graduated from high school?" Harriet had gone to private school, as a day student. "He's thirty-three? Harriet, he's Coffee Cake Therapy!"

Giggling, they got into the Subaru.

Snowy turned on the air conditioner and drove Harriet and her sketchbook around the village and jouncing out the Roller Coaster Road. Daisies had just begun blooming along the roadside's stone walls. For the first time since she'd sold the place, Snowy pulled into the driveway of Hurricane Farm. Feeling extremely strange, a stranger, she got out of the car and went into the side porch and knocked on the door, while Harriet stood in the yard looking at the house, the barn, the orchard, the woods. Waiting, Snowy allowed herself to look at the herb garden and the vegetable garden. With pangs of jealousy and relief, she saw that Frank was maintaining them, and the flower beds. She knocked again. No answer. She crossed the driveway to the barn and peered in a window. His Subaru was gone. He must already be off doing errands or attending one of his many club meetings.

Harriet said, "What a lovely place."

"Remember when I showed you Bev's mother's place in Gunthwaite? This is different, but the minute the realtor brought Alan and me here, I was reminded of Julia's."

Harriet saw the muscle twitching in Snowy's jaw and didn't take out her sketchbook, much as she wanted to draw Hurricane Farm. During Ruhamah's New York visits and their travels together, she had gradually elicited the details of the situation from Ruhamah, and she had first been furious that Snowy hadn't let her know that she was in trouble, bankrupt, and then she'd been furious at herself for not keeping in touch all those years, and then there was simply an aching regret. Now she felt a prickle of covetousness. If she'd known Snowy was selling this beautiful place…

Snowy pointed. "That's Mount Pascataquac up there. Tom's fire tower." She turned away and said briskly, "Come on, I'll show you a New Hampshire original."

Back in the car, Snowy drove on down the road to the Thornes' farm and parked in the dooryard behind their ancient Ford pickup and Ford sedan. The old Cape's clapboards were so weathered that only patches of flaking white paint remained, under the eaves. Alan used to say that the barn was held upright by the manure shoveled out the stall windows into ever-higher piles along its sides. In a rocky pasture, five Guernseys were chewing cuds. She spotted Cleora hoeing peas in the vegetable garden behind the house, wearing her usual washed-out housedress on her gaunt frame, her motions hobbled by arthritis. Snowy said to Harriet, "We'll go say hello."

"Sure thing."

Snowy remembered, as they walked up the path between the house and the barn, that in many ways Harriet had the ability to adapt, which no doubt made her a great traveler. When Snowy had brought her home to Gunthwaite, Snowy had expected her to behave like Margaret Mead amongst the Arapesh of New Guinea, but Harriet had accepted the Snows' New Hampshire household as natural. Now Harriet advanced casually with Snowy through knee-high grass sticking up around a rusted hayrack, a plow, and unidentifiable parts of implements.

Snowy hailed Cleora. "Good morning! Muggy, isn't it!"

Cleora straightened painfully up amid the pea fences, pulled a man's handkerchief out of a pocket, and mopped her face. "Air's thick enough to cut." She regarded Harriet with unconcealed curiosity.

Snowy said, "Cleora, this is an old friend of mine, Harriet Blumburg. Harriet, Cleora Thorne."

"How do you do," Harriet said.

Cleora nodded to her. "You live around here?"

"New York," Harriet admitted. "I draw some. Would it be okay if I did a quick sketch of this wonderful place of yours?"

To Snowy's astonishment, Cleora looked flattered. "Suit yourself," she said, and in a flash Harriet whipped the sketchbook out of her shoulder bag and began to draw. Cleora asked Snowy, "Ruhamah and Irene minding the store?"

"Yes. I'm showing Harriet the town. How's Isaac?"

"He's as well as he'll ever be."

"And you, how are you doing?"

"I keep going."

Without thinking, Snowy took the hoe and finished the row. She laughed and brought it back.

"I guess you must miss your garden," Cleora said.

Snowy wiped at sweat dripping down her face. Because she used to mulch her garden, she hadn't had to do a lot of hoeing. "I grow some stuff in pots now."

"On your stoop. I've noticed." Then Cleora said, "Isaac and I, we read in the paper about you and Tom on Daybreak. About his daughter. Tell him I told you we're awful sorry."

"I will."

"Done," Harriet said. "I thank you very much, Mrs. Thorne."

As Snowy and Harriet drove away, Harriet said, "A rarity, nowadays?"

"Most definitely."

They went back past Hurricane Farm, Harriet craning her neck, Snowy looking straight ahead. They reached the lake road. She wouldn't show Harriet the cove. Instead, she drove on to the town beach and parked in the parking lot. At one of the pollen-dusted picnic tables, she and Harriet sat down and Harriet sketched the view of lake and mountains, with mothers and children sizzling in the sandy foreground.

Harriet said, "Remember my fat ladies?"

"Yes, indeed. Then spheres and orbs and much experimenting."

"After school, I drifted into a minimalist phase during which my canvases became so spare and empty I'd reduced my subject matter to absolutely nothing at all. In despair, I decided the only way out of that dead end was the opposite direction, and after a flirtation with photo-realism I finally found how to show what I see as the essence. You used to send your poems out to magazines. Do you still?"

"'Little magazines.' I haven't had the time." More than that, she didn't have the confidence.

"You *are* still writing poems?"

"They stopped for a while, but they're back."

"What about readings? Remember when you went to see your first one and returned to our room and told me it was like watching someone masturbate in public?"

Snowy laughed.

Harriet said, "You decided you were the silent-reading school of thought."

"So I've only done one reading in all my career, before agoraphobia."

"But would it help get your name around? You're out of the academic loop, so you have to do *something*. I know, I'm a loner too and I don't want to be in any in-group, but I also run a business and am practical about art."

Harriet? Practical? Like Bev's becoming efficient!

IN THE AFTERNOON, while Ruhamah showed Harriet other sights of Woodcombe, Snowy waited on customers with Irene and mentally went through her closet, trying to decide what to wear with the beautiful new scarf when they went out to dinner. Could she still get into the purple sundress from her pre-agoraphobia days in Pevensay? After work, she tried it on and gave thanks to jogging. Harriet came out of the bathroom wearing black pants with a gorgeous black top of silk-screened blue and purple urns outlined in gold thread, which Snowy assumed had been bought in Israel. When Ruhamah emerged from her bedroom wearing a loose gauzy dress patterned with a Middle Eastern harem-y look and saw Harriet demonstrating how to fling the scarf casually over one's shoulders, she went back into her bedroom for a small package for Snowy who, upon opening it, discovered blue stones on a silver chain.

Ruhamah said, "The storekeeper told me they're blue agate, but whatever, I just liked the necklace and thought it looked Israeli."

"It's absolutely exquisite," Snowy said. "Thank you."

Pleased, Ruhamah fastened it around Snowy's neck.

In the Subaru, Ruhamah chauffeured them out of town and along Lake Winnipesaukee to what had been a private driveway, down through tidy woods to the Gilmore House, white and elaborate, its mansard style sort of Second Empire, or so Snowy had guessed when she came here with Tom, remembering what she'd learned from Alan.

Bev had already arrived and was reading a menu in a gilt chair in the high white-and-gold hall where a staircase curved upward. She got to her feet, and as she stood tall in a linen sheath whose color couldn't be called lime and was definitely chartreuse, Snowy sensed how she was gathering herself for a role for which she didn't yet have a persona. If Snowy ever met Ann Wilmot, Bev's roommate, Snowy knew she would feel the same confusion herself, devoured by curiosity, embarrassed by jealousy, uncertain; Bev, however, would surely rise to this occasion far better than Snowy ever could. *Chartreuse!*

"Bev," Snowy said, "here we are, here's Harriet—" and from the desk in the staircase alcove came the hostess, to whom Harriet said, "Hello, I'm Harriet Blumburg, I made reservations for four."

The hostess picked up four menus and said, "Good evening. This way, please."

So it wasn't until they were settled at a table in the front room, under the ten-foot ceiling of plaster rosettes seemingly squeezed from a giant pastry tube, beside eight-foot windows open onto a terraced garden dropping down to the lake, that Bev and Harriet got a good long look at each other, while Snowy babbled such nonsense as, "Isn't this fantastic, we're finally all together," and Ruhamah, whose travels and freshman year in college had made her less fussy about food, nonetheless studied the menu with her usual wariness.

Then the waitress appeared and inquired about cocktails or wine, and Harriet said to Bev, "Snowy told me how you introduced her to chardonnay last year," and Bev and Harriet laughed and began conferring over the wine list.

Snowy sat back, relieved that her naivete had united them, yet slightly irritated. But as it became obvious that Harriet and Bev were truly hitting it off, she turned her attention to the menu and then gave herself up to the enjoyment of an excellent meal. She chose gazpacho instead of a salad, because she ate so much salad at home, and despite the heat she went wild and ordered the broiled double-thick lamb chops. Harriet chose a seafood sampler, while Ruhamah ordered broiled haddock and Bev decided on Maine crab cakes even though she was in New Hampshire. Listening to Harriet and Bev, Snowy remembered dining here with Tom last month. She could imagine what a feverish daze he must now be in, the same as she had after Alan, worse than any influenza.

The topics Harriet and Bev were discussing ranged from Bev's town in Connecticut, Ninfield, where Harriet had once visited a gallery, to Bev's handwoven silver handbag, one of Mimi's latest creations, which Harriet said she would mention to a friend who owned a Manhattan shop and would love to see Mimi's work

(Snowy suspected that clever Bev had brought the handbag in hopes of such an outcome), but the topic they kept returning to was real estate, which Harriet had never talked much about during Snowy's four years of living with her; but, after all, Harriet had grown up surrounded by the business.

"Patience," Harriet remarked. "That's what my father always said is the main thing you had to have in real estate."

"That's what I've been told," Bev agreed. "I went into real estate because I thought I knew houses. I'd looked at so many with real-estate agents in the years when my husband and I were moving around, and I'd fixed up the ones we bought, and when I finally had some time to do something all my own, well, this was what I knew. How little did I know! But it's a business a woman can make money in, and I can arrange my hours around my daughter's schedule. Snowy, that scarf and necklace are beautiful."

Snowy, jolted out of worries about Tom, said, "Presents from Israel."

"Travel," Bev said dreamily, clasping her wineglass in both hands. "Remember, Snowy, when we were kids and we'd go to the library and sit on the floor in the stacks in the travel section and look in the books and talk about safaris and gondolas and the Orient Express?"

Harriet asked Bev, "Where would you want to go now?"

"The prize for selling the most in our company this year is a trip to Key West. I went there once with my mother, but I'd be happy to go again."

"And you?" Harriet asked Snowy.

"I'm living in the prettiest village in New Hampshire, what more could I want? Except dessert." Yet, as Snowy ordered the strawberry-kiwi mousse, she suddenly thought: Scotland. That's where she and Alan had planned to go someday; back before her agoraphobia and his quitting Old Eastbourne had altered all plans, they had talked of how they'd seen the basics in England and next they would visit Alan's roots. Ruhamah's roots, albeit attenuated by another generation. Tom's roots were also there.

Harriet said, "Strawberry-kiwi mousse? Feh!"

Snowy hadn't heard that "feh" noise, like sneezing while starting to say "feather," since Harriet had last made it on some rare occasion in their college days, and she started laughing. To Bev she explained, "It's an advanced and impassioned 'ughy-pew.'"

Bev begged Harriet, "Say it again!"

So during dessert and coffee, Harriet taught and Bev learned "Feh!" while Snowy giggled and Ruhamah looked indulgent.

When Snowy and Ruhamah and Harriet returned home, Snowy found a message on the answering machine. Oh, let it be from Tom!

It was from David, sounding jubilant, the opposite extreme of what he'd been Friday night. "Did you hear? Lavender had the baby! Now we're planning the wedding." Laughter in the background. "We're getting married next Saturday evening at Lavender's house—" Over his shoulder, "Okay, okay, it'll be *our* house." To Snowy, "And you're invited, you and Ruhamah and the entire town!"

And, Snowy realized, Tom and Joanne of course. Together here, parents of the groom. She shouldn't go. It would be too awkward. David, in his enthusiasm, hadn't taken that into consideration, and Lavender probably hadn't given it a thought.

Ruhamah said, "Won't this wedding be a hoot!" Then she looked at Snowy in consternation. "Why's he doing it so soon after—Libby? He told us his mother had postponed hers."

Harriet asked, "Who was that on the machine?"

"Tom's younger son," Snowy said. "I guess he has decided that life goes on."

After Ruhamah and Harriet were asleep, Snowy dragged a carton out from under her bed, opened it, and much as she'd sat on the floor of the library stacks, she sat looking through her accumulation of magazines, the ones in which her poems had been published. Which magazines were still in existence? What new ones had sprung up? Did the village library have a copy of *Literary Market Place* or any little-magazine directories? She lacked the confidence, yes, but she recognized the desperation.

The next morning, when Harriet and Snowy were saying goodbye beside the Jaguar, Jared Smith came out of the store and asked Harriet, "Leaving so soon?"

"Oh, I'll be back."

"That offer of a ride in my pickup still stands."

"I'll trade you a ride in this car. You show me yours, I'll show you mine."

Snowy exclaimed, fanning herself, "None of this steamy stuff in front of my store!"

Harriet gave her a hug, waggled fingers at Jared, got in the Jaguar and drove off.

"Cool," said Jared.

SATURDAY WAS RAINY, yet that evening when Snowy parked her car behind others lining Crescent Road and she and Ruhamah joined other townspeople hurrying toward the white Cape, she knew that spirits were not at all dampened, and when she saw the Jeep parked in the driveway, hers leapt. Tom! He had come in his own vehicle, not Joanne's! She restrained herself from bowling people over in a mad rush forward; decorously she followed the flow entering by the front door, which at Lavender's, as elsewhere, no doubt was only used for formal events.

Although this wasn't formal, it certainly was an event, reminding Snowy of Mimi's reception at Hurricane Farm, when, however, the weather had been sunny. Because of today's rain, indoor improvisation was necessary, and in the low-ceilinged crooked-floored living room, food intended for an outdoor buffet had overflowed from the dining room and sat ready on every flat surface, including an ironing board inadequately hidden under a bedsheet. Fresh flowers in mason-jar bouquets and tangled in wreaths added their moistness to the rainbow of slickers and umbrellas in the hall.

Snowy was wearing a brand-new pink sleeveless dress. She had taken time off from work Wednesday to go shopping in Gunthwaite for an outfit that would wow Joanne, and this was the best she could find. From Gunthwaite she'd driven on to Mimi's Weaverbird to buy a wedding present for Lavender and David. All day today she'd debated whether or not to wear the bloodstone necklace Tom had given her or the Israeli necklace, and at the last minute she'd put on the bloodstone.

The ceremony began without much ado right after she and Ruhamah squeezed into the crush, Snowy swiveling her head but not seeing Tom. Or Joanne. A local woman who was a justice of the peace stood in front of the woodstove piped into the fireplace and introduced Lavender and David to the room, as if everybody didn't already know them. Then Lavender read the wedding vows she'd written. She was wearing a white-and-lavender waistless jumper that rather resembled a maternity dress, and she went on at some length about love and the harmony of souls. Snowy expected that David, standing opposite her in the khakis and navy blazer Libby had said he'd be wearing to Joanne's wedding, would start cringing in embarrassment, but he just beamed. When his turn came, he glanced over to his left and said, "I had some help from an English teacher," and as he read Robert Frost's short poem about cleaning a pasture spring, which could be considered a great love poem, Snowy rose on tiptoe, high as she could, and between the backs of people's heads she saw Tom sitting on a sofa, his walking stick leaning against the cushions. Beside him sat Joanne.

Snowy's heart broke. For them.

They both looked lost. Tom looked old, and Joanne's cheekbones looked painful, her skin stretched so taut it outlined a death's-head.

Now Snowy knew nothing mattered at all. She touched the bloodstone. Her appearance, her dress, were utterly inconsequential. She felt faint with grief.

On the other side of the fireplace sat Lavender's parents, Violet and Rick Hyland, who were, Snowy recalled, divorced. Violet was blotting her eyes with a Kleenex. Joanne wasn't crying. Nor was Tom. The justice of the peace pronounced David and Lavender husband and wife, cheers rang out, Violet flung herself on her daughter and new son-in-law, and Joanne got up, saying something to Tom. Although Snowy couldn't hear her, Snowy guessed she was telling him to stay seated and rest his knee.

The party began. The crowd struggled toward food, talking about gypsy moths and septic systems, and Snowy turned to Ruhamah to suggest they leave, but Ruhamah said, "I'll get us something to eat," and dived into the fray. Snowy realized she was starving; they hadn't had a chance for a sustaining snack between closing the store and coming to the wedding.

"Snowy."

Joanne stood there.

Snowy said, "I'm so terribly sorry."

Joanne said, "Thank you for everything you did. Going for the EMTs."

The last time they had exchanged words, Snowy thought, had been on the Gunthwaite High School football field, September 1956, just before Snowy's senior year began. Joanne, who was about to depart for her freshman year at Rumford Teachers' College, who indeed was getting a ride to Rumford with fellow freshman Tom, had come to watch the new Varsity cheerleading squad practice. Joanne had wept then, tears of nostalgia for her high-school cheerleading days. She'd asked if Snowy wanted her to talk to Tom about his breakup with Snowy. Declining the offer, Snowy had wanted to say: Tell him I'll love him forever and ever. Instead she had said, "Tell him I said good-bye." All these years later, she could only repeat, "I'm so sorry, so sorry."

Joanne said, "I've never had a chance to say I'm so sorry about your husband."

Snowy nodded, now beyond speech.

They stood looking at each other, both thinking how implacable, how unmerciful life could be.

Then Joanne said, "I'm glad David and Lavender decided to go ahead. Lavender showed me the place mats you gave them. Very nice. She said a friend of yours wove them?"

"Bev's daughter Mimi."

Daughters, they thought.

Joanne said, "Tom is doing things faster than his doctor advised. The surgery was Tuesday, and he was off crutches by Thursday and driving again yesterday. Make sure he doesn't really overdo."

What? What was Joanne saying? Was Joanne putting the care of Tom into Snowy's hands? And, even amid her confusion, Snowy wondered if Joanne intended a double entendre about overworking Tom's knees.

Joanne continued, "He and David are swapping jobs for a while until Tom's knee mends. David will be tending that tower, and Tom will be running the factory."

Needing to be absolutely clear, Snowy asked, "Tom is returning to Woodcombe?"

"He says he lives here." Joanne looked past Snowy, her eyes filled, and she stepped away into the crowd.

Behind Snowy, Ruhamah said, "I didn't mean to interrupt."

"It's all right, my baby."

Ruhamah gave her a paper plate, which was almost buckling under mounds of macaroni salad, potato salad, and a heap of cold cuts. "Oops, I forgot napkins." She vanished again.

Snowy looked up from the plate and saw Tom in front of her.

He asked, "After Alan died, did you ever feel like saying to him, 'Okay, we've been through that; you can come back now'?"

Snowy replied, "Yes."

He said, "It's what I want to say to Libby."

SNOWY AND TOM left the party. She drove to Main Street with Tom in his Jeep, helped him up the stairs to his apartment, and spent the night in his bed, holding him.

He said, "Everything seems cold. Empty. Like when you have to get up in the morning too early and the room is dark and cold. Or like going into a camp that's been closed up all winter. Or like a beer joint in the morning, the atmosphere all wrong."

Lightly she said, "Beer in the morning?"

"Not since my college days. My flaming youth. Don't worry about that. I can't describe it right, cold, stark, but lights pulsing."

"Like a kind of fever," she said, her hand on the forehead she remembered smooth, now seamed.

"Like that thunderstorm," he said, "except with lightning flashes in a dark and cold place, not on a warm sunny day."

Throughout the summer she watched over him, and as he settled back into a routine, first in the workshop and in August up at the tower, she saw him recreate the easygoing surface he presented to the world and knew that the core within was now more than reserved; it was chill, despairing.

Then one evening in August in Snowy's apartment, where Tom was making one of his microwave suppers for them, Ruhamah switched on the television news and they learned that U.S. troops were being ordered to protect Saudi Arabia from Iraq, which had invaded Kuwait a few days ago. Desert Shield, the operation was called, which struck Snowy as hilarious. "Dress shield?" she remarked.

Tom said, "Shit!" and left the Lean Cuisine revolving in the microwave and headed back to his apartment.

Brandon. Oh God, Snowy thought. She rescued the meal and went over to see if Tom was okay. He said, "I couldn't get Brandon at the BOQ. Joanne is going to keep trying."

Brandon, thirty years old, an Army pilot, was a child in danger.

The next day Brandon phoned Joanne, who phoned Tom. Brandon hadn't been sent off to save America's oil supplies, at least not yet.

All summer, Snowy heard no mention that Joanne's wedding plans had been resumed.

A little magazine accepted a poem Snowy had sent in. Her payment would be two free issues, just like when she was beginning, decades ago. She didn't tell anybody, but she sent out more.

Cedric Barlow, the father of Frank Barlow, died in his sleep. Snowy missed his impatient errands in the store, his grumpy voice, his peremptory demands. Dealing with Cedric had been a major hurdle she'd overcome when emerging from agoraphobia. She wrote Frank a sympathy note. In the store, when Frank thanked her he said, "I'll only sell Dad's house to a keen gardener," and people talked about Cedric's generous bequest to the garden club.

When Ruhamah returned to UNH that fall, she drove herself in the secondhand Honda Civic Tom had helped her choose.

Another little magazine took one of Snowy's poems.

The day after Thanksgiving, Puddles phoned, wailing, "Guy and I had a showdown at the OK Corral last night when we got home from Susan's dinner. He's decided he definitely wants to retire next year. He'll only be sixty-one; why can't he at least wait until sixty-two or sixty-five like everybody else? He says he's pooped. He says he's kept going as long as he can. He says he wants to have some fun before it's too late. Okay, but to him golf is fun! I talked with his doctor after his annual physical, and aside from his hearing there's nothing wrong with him except boredom, and for that he's going to uproot us and drag me away from the work I've devoted my life to! Away from Susan and Little Guy! My parents and my brothers! He's going house-hunting in Hilton Head this weekend and I can come along or not, take it or leave it, the goddamn fucking sonofabitch!"

"Oh, Puddles," Snowy said. "I'm sorry. Hey, look at it this way: Maybe Guy has regretted enticing your family to Helmsdale and wants you to himself now, away from them and the kids, for a second honeymoon in his retirement."

Puddles paused, considering the notion, which had never occurred to her. "Nope. He just wants Hilton Head golf courses.

I reminded him how my folks aren't getting any younger, and my mother's arthritis is getting worse, but he only said that *he* isn't getting any younger." She paused again, thinking of her own arthritis, which she was sure she'd managed to hide from Snowy and Bev in Camden. They would have attributed any grunts and groans to her weight. Of course the weight didn't help; she ought to get the lard off before she upped her medication. Nurse practitioner, heal thyself.

Snowy asked, "So Guy won the gunfight?"

"I can't divorce him. I was ready to when I fell for Calvin. I haven't got the energy anymore."

"Do you still love Guy?"

"For God's sake, Snowy, there's not mad passion, but what's there supposed to be after all these years? You may have loved Tom forever, but you haven't had to *live* with him day in, day out!"

"True," said Snowy.

As Christmas neared, Jared Smith overheard Snowy and Irene talking about Ruhamah's upcoming visit at Harriet's, and he gave Snowy a big envelope for Ruhamah to take to her. When Ruhamah returned from New York, she reported, "It was one of those 'Brake for Moose' bumper stickers. Harriet figures he's daring her to put it on her Jag," and they laughed.

Desert Storm. The name was even more disconcerting than Desert Shield, sounding like a Valentino movie or a romance novel, but Snowy didn't do any ridiculing because war began in January and Tom, on the phone to Brandon, learned that Brandon was in charge of flying a group of nine planes to Saudi Arabia. "Mohawks," Tom explained to Snowy, "small fixed-wing intelligence-gathering planes, not long-distance planes, so they have to stop and refuel on their way over." They went via Scotland, from which Brandon phoned Tom to joke about not having time to buy a Forbes kilt.

Bev phoned Snowy and rejoiced, "I didn't win the trip to Key West, but I came in second!"

"Congratulations!"

"Second to that top-producer Lorraine Fitch, who's been in real estate for eons, knows everybody, and has connections everywhere. A distant second, but still second!" Bev added, "For what I suppose is a consolation prize, Geoff Plumley is taking me to a play in Boston."

Geoff, thought Snowy; not Geoffrey anymore. "A date?" she asked.

"Well," Bev said, "kind of. But we'll talk business; that's all we talk about."

Joanne phoned Tom, so distraught with worry about Brandon that Tom said to Snowy, "I've got to go up there," without explaining the old guilt of the rape now mixed up with his new guilt. He tossed a duffel in the Jeep and took off, leaving North Country Coffins once more to David, spending the war in Newburgh with his ex-wife.

January. February.

Three more of Snowy's poems were accepted, and now that she knew the two acceptances weren't a fluke she wanted to tell Tom, but he wasn't here. Up in Newburgh, was he sleeping on the sofa? Or in a guest room? Oh God! If he and Joanne *were* sleeping together, who was the mistress, Joanne or Snowy? Neither, because he was single? Tom, the tomcat. Terrified by her imaginings about how he occupied his nights, she tried to concentrate on picturing his days doing handyman-husbandly chores around the house while Joanne was at work. He would be reading all the war news in the papers. Tom and Joanne must sit together watching the evening news.

Please, prayed pagan Snowy, keep Brandon safe. She thought of what she called her Left-Field Theory, her old term for troubles-don't-come-singly. While she was worrying about Tom and Joanne and Brandon, what would happen that she hadn't expected?

Tom didn't phone. She told herself this was a good thing. If he phoned, it would mean that something had happened to Brandon. But still, wouldn't he like just to—to chat? Didn't he yearn to hear her voice, as she did his? She saw David's pickup at the workshop during the day, and David or Lavender occasionally stopped at the store for groceries, but David maddeningly never volunteered anything. The topic of Lavender's conversation was her latest pregnancy; she had hardly given her uterus time to cool off before starting Tom and Joanne's first grandchild and the first baby she would keep. So Snowy forced herself to be casual with David and Lavender.

On February 27, Bush ordered a cease-fire. On March 3, Iraq agreed to abide by the United Nations resolutions.

March 4, a Monday, was a horrible sleety day. Snowy phoned Irene and told her not to bother coming in. There were scarcely any customers. Then at noon, who should breeze in on a blast of icy air but Tom, *Tom,* and she provided entertainment for the two carpenters killing time drinking coffee as she dropped a ledger onto the counter with a crash, tripped over a case of antifreeze, and fell into Tom's arms.

"Brandon?" she asked.

"He's okay. A quick war. He joked about how the units were moving so fast it was hard for the planes to keep up."

But it hadn't seemed quick to Snowy, and she knew it hadn't to Tom and Joanne.

CHAPTER THREE

AND SO SNOWY and Tom's life together resumed. She tried to convince herself it didn't matter what she was, mistress or whatever, because he had come back. But would he return to Newburgh again? She wished Victor would reappear like a cartoon caveman and drag Joanne off by her beautiful hair, but from what she remembered of Victor in high school, this didn't seem likely.

Tom said, "That's good about the poems. Really good. Am I allowed to read them?"

"Okay," she said. Having told him, she told Bev, who said, "Someday there's going to be a statue of you in Gunthwaite!" When Ruhamah came home for spring recess, Snowy casually mentioned the poems, adding, "It was Harriet's prodding that got me sending them out," and when Harriet phoned to ask if Ruhamah would like to go along with her to Italy this June, Snowy thanked her for both suggestions.

At the end of her sophomore year, Ruhamah announced that she'd decided to major in business administration. Even though Snowy was prepared for this, even though she was relieved by Ruhamah's practicality, Snowy first felt horrified that a daughter of hers wouldn't devote her life to the arts and then guilty over the situation that had determined Ruhamah's choice.

The anniversary of Libby's death approached. If, Snowy thought, Tom decided he had to spend the day in Newburgh, she would understand, she *would.*

But this year June 10 would be a Monday and one of his days at the tower. He ought to stay in Woodcombe.

Finally Tom said tersely, "I've arranged to have the other fire wardens cover my area Monday. I've got to go up to Newburgh. David and Lavender are going too."

"Oh," Snowy said.

"Joanne isn't particularly religious. But she's a great one for parties; well, you know what I mean. Ceremonies. She wants to do some sort of remembrance or something."

"Oh."

"Will you be all right?"

"Yes. Will you?"

He didn't answer.

Snowy spent that Monday working. But after she closed up the store she couldn't face the claustrophobic apartment, so she started walking down Main Street, in the opposite direction from North Country Coffins. The village was quiet; people were indoors, making or eating dinner. The purple lilacs in front yards on both sides of the street were beginning to turn brown, petals dropping, but still she was caught in a heavy cross fire of lilac perfume. White Lilac, her high-school cologne, sold in those big bottles…

A flatbed truck rumbled toward her up the street. As it neared, she saw lettered beautifully on its door: Washburn's Custom Signs.

Dudley braked and leaned out the window. "Snowy, get in."

She clambered up into the passenger seat.

He asked, "Ruhamah is in Italy?"

"Mainly Tuscany."

"Is Tom in Newburgh?"

She nodded.

Dudley said, "I'll never say anything against your Tom Forbes, but sometimes he makes me wonder."

"He's not 'mine.'"

"Does he think you're 'his' Snowy?"

She didn't answer that. She said, "When it comes to their children, he's Joanne's. Which is as it should be."

Dudley reached over and kneaded her shoulder.

The little massage felt heavenly. There was no reason for Bev or Puddles to have remembered the exact day of the Mount Daybreak tragedy, but Dudley had, and he was the one who was checking to see if she was okay. Dear Dudley.

He said, "On these days the only thing to do is keep moving." He drove to the store. "Run up and put on your bathing suit. I've got mine on, and I promise you that a city councilor doesn't wear a Speedo so you won't have to avert your gaze. I brought towels."

"I do not want to go swimming."

"We're going to go play. At the boardwalk. Where there's a water slide we might want to try."

"A water slide? I've never been on one."

"And I've never been on one without a kid in tow."

"Aren't water slides awfully germy?"

"Who are you, Howard Hughes?" Dudley gave her a push. "Run on up."

So she stopped arguing, stopped thinking, and did so. In her bedroom, she found her old one-piece blue bathing suit in the bottom drawer of her bureau, shucked her T-shirt and jeans and underwear, pulled it on, put on the jeans and T-shirt again, grabbed her shoulder bag, and dashed back downstairs.

"Let's play!" she said.

Dudley drove to Lake Winnipesaukee, snared a parking space near the boardwalk, and they fortified themselves with hot dogs at a stand, then bought a box of Karamel Korn to share as they strolled along in the early-summer crowd, Snowy remembering how she and the girls in the Gang used to come here to "broad around," seeking boys, romance. She and Dudley got silly, bowling and playing miniature golf with much badinage, and finally, egging each other on, they went back to his truck, took off their clothes (Dudley sang, "Seems like old times!"), locked her shoulder bag and their wristwatches and his wallet in the cab after Dudley had removed enough money for the water slide, and in their bathing suits they hurried over to that water slide, which had a Jack-and-the-Beanstalk theme.

As they joined the queue climbing up the beanstalk to the giant's castle, Snowy felt young eyes looking askance at them and said, "Dudley, we're too old. We should've brought some of your grandchildren with us, for camouflage."

Dudley roared, "Fee fi fo fum!" and if that didn't startle everyone around them enough, he began declaiming:

> "'Age cannot wither her, nor custom stale
> Her infinite variety; other women cloy
> The appetite they feed, but she makes hungry
> Where most she satisfies—'"

Laughing, imploring, "Shush, shush," Snowy was so distracted that she didn't have a chance to be frightened as at the top she sat on the edge, slid forward, and then shot down the chute through warm and extremely chlorinated water.

Not bothering to change back into dry clothes, they rode home singing their favorite novelty songs from their youth. Snowy was proud of her almost total recall of "Open the Door, Richard," but Dudley excelled with his rendition of "I Never See Maggie Alone." For "Pistol-Packing Mama," he was Bing Crosby and she the Andrew Sisters, and she was being Patti Page and he the overdub of "How Much Is That Doggie in the Window?" when he pulled up in front of the store.

"Thank you," she said. "This was even more fun than our sandbox." She hesitated, thinking that she should invite him up to the apartment for a drink—no, he was driving—for a cup of coffee, but she just wanted to hit the sack, she could sleep now, and anyway, he should be getting home to Charl.

"And I thank you," he said. "For more than tonight. Thanks to your suggestion, I got preservationists interested and we came up with a plan to rehab the high school instead of build a new one. The city council and the school board are working things out at last, and we're all going to recommend the plan. The voters are bound to go for it; the cost is less."

"Oh, Dudley, that's wonderful! And you'll surely be reelected!"

"Thanks to you," he repeated, leaning forward.

They exchanged a best-of-friends hug. She quickly gathered up her clothes and shoulder bag, opened the truck door, and jumped down. He drove off.

Up in the apartment, she found no message on the answering machine; nothing from Tom.

BUT THE NEXT afternoon, Tom came into the store. He looked different. As he invited her to his place for a barbecue supper, Snowy tried to figure out what the difference was, yet not until that evening, when she walked down the street and around the barn to the backyard and saw him sitting at the picnic table, did she realize that he looked the way Bev had hoped she would after cosmetic surgery: rested.

Standing up, he poured her a glass of chardonnay and said, "When Ruhamah gets home and you can take a day and night off, want to go on a backpack?"

They hadn't gone on a day hike, much less a backpack, in the past year.

"Sure," she said.

He handed her a box of Triscuits. "Yesterday I was walking in the woods behind the house, the first hike Libby and I ever did together, me carrying her most of the way, and all of a sudden I was pretending I was walking on the Appalachian Trail." He opened the lid of the little Weber grill that sat on the end of the picnic table and, with tongs, deftly turned over the boneless skinless chicken breasts ruddy with the Kansas City barbecue sauce he doused turkey burgers and chicken in. He said, "Ten more minutes." He claimed that his grilling always took twenty minutes, total, be it salmon or zucchini, anything.

Sinking onto the picnic-table bench, Snowy knew what was coming before he said the words.

"So," he said, "that's when the idea hit me. I'll hike the AT."

She said, "It's too late, isn't it?"

He chose her surface meaning and replied, "Yes, this year. April is the month to start. So I'll get in shape this year and go to Georgia next April. And start hiking to Maine."

"What about the fire tower?"

"I'll give it up. Maybe I can get the job back the year after." He fiddled with a plate of sliced tomatoes.

"Your knee."

"It's fine now."

"Fine for climbing up Pascataquac, but for hiking with a heavy backpack a zillion miles up and down mountains for months?" Then Snowy told herself: Stop it. Be positive. She looked at Tom's rested face. His decision had brought some peace. "It's a great idea, Tom. Don't hikers on the AT have somebody sending them supplies along the way? Can I do that?"

He kissed her and said, "Not a zillion miles. About 2,150."

The next night, Puddles phoned. "There's good news and bad news and they're jumbled up. Susan just told us that she's pregnant again."

Snowy said, "I assume that's the good news?"

"Well, of course, but I want to be here in Helmsdale through the pregnancy, but last weekend we were finally shown a house on Hilton Head that meets all Guy's criteria. These months we've been looking, he kept changing his mind from condos to townhouses, a fancy name for duplexes, and finally he decided he needed to have a whole house with its own lawn, and I was beginning to hope everything was too expensive or he was so fussy about a house built by someone other than himself that he'd end up deciding to build, which would give me more time here. But now we've seen this house and he wants to make an offer immediately."

Instead of sympathy, Snowy felt exasperation and envy. Everybody had plans and projects. Her big goal was to succeed with her new experiment, a video-rental shelf. But she said, "I'm sorry, Puddles. What do you think of the house?"

Puddles said reluctantly, "It's nice. On a little curvy street with lots of trees. The same size as this house, three bedrooms. It's got a good feel. *Except,*" she continued fiercely, "for the pink wall-to-wall carpeting. Pink! Reminds me of those underpants in Woolworth's, remember? I told Guy I couldn't possibly live in a house with pink wall-to-wall."

Snowy laughed. "Isn't that rather easily remedied?"

"That's what Guy said. I'd hoped the extra expense of new carpeting would slow him down, but nope. Well, I'm going to take my time about finding a new clinic. Like until the baby is born."

When Puddles hung up, Snowy went to her desk in her bedroom. No, her big goal was the same as it had always been. She just kept losing sight of it.

Thus, when Patsy Fletcher came into the store one midsummer morning in her role as the latest president of the Friends of the Library instead of just as a customer and asked if Snowy would do a reading of some of her poems at the library, Snowy gulped and agreed. Ruhamah acted so indifferent when Snowy mentioned it to her that Snowy suspected Ruhamah had suggested this to Patsy, at Harriet's instigation. Decades ago, Snowy had done her one and only reading, in the Pevensay library. Back then she hadn't yet become an agoraphobic basket case, but the wear and tear on her nerves had been formidable. This time, would doing the reading bring back agoraphobia? Worry, worry, dread, dread. In the following days, when Snowy wasn't worrying about agoraphobia, she worried over the selection of poems, she worried about what to wear, and she told Ruhamah and Tom she would kill them if they attended.

The dreaded evening came. The Woodcombe library's little meeting room was packed with polite and kindly townsfolk and summer people. Although Snowy knew them, they seemed to be an expanse of alien staring eyes as she stood at the podium sweating, heart hammering. This, she tried to reassure herself, was normal: Almost everybody panicked over public speaking. This was not the onset of a fatal panic attack. She gripped the podium, and she and the room held steady. The floor didn't begin to undulate in waves, the walls to pulse. The faces grew familiar. She did the reading, and afterwards during the coffee and cookies she chatted as if at the store. Tom showed up to walk her home, and she told him, "I didn't do it well, but I did it."

He said, "I'll be happy if I can say that at the end of the AT."

Tom was preoccupied by the Appalachian Trail. Throughout the summer and fall he hiked on his days off, Snowy going along whenever she could. He was relieved when Lavender and David's baby, a little girl, was born safely and easily in October, and he was moved that they named her Elizabeth after Libby, but more real to him were the maps he pored over and thumbtacked to the walls of his apartment, the AT books he read, the gear catalogues he studied, the lists he made. He kept track of Snowy's gossip, he knew that Puddles and Guy had bought a house on Hilton Head but Puddles was living alone with her cat in the Helmsdale house, which hadn't sold yet, he listened to Snowy's rejoicing when Dudley Washburn was reelected to the Gunthwaite city council that November, and in December he celebrated with her when a magazine accepted another of her poems, but his mind was on the trail. Could he do it? He would be fifty-four years old. People much older had hiked the AT, he kept reassuring himself, and so had people with more problems than an unreliable knee.

Snowy phoned Bev and said, "Ruhamah is going to Harriet's as usual for Christmas and Hanukkah."

"Lucky Ruhamah," said Bev absently. In her bedroom, she was

doing paperwork at the antique slant-top desk she had recently bought.

"Um, I just learned Tom and I won't be going to the Alpine Avens Inn on Christmas Eve this year because he has to stay in Woodcombe on Christmas Day because Lavender and David are having a big family feast for the baby's first Christmas, which strikes me as ridiculous because what the hell does it mean to a three-month-old, but Brandon is coming, he has never visited Tom here before, has spent his leaves in Newburgh if in New Hampshire at all, and Joanne, Joanne the new grandmother, she's going to be here—"

Bev heard Snowy give a little squeal, as if swallowing a sob. Bev said, "How domestic!" and wanted to throttle Tom. But who was she to judge, keeping Roger around as she did, while dating Geoff? But she and Roger weren't divorced, only somewhat separated. And they hadn't suffered a tragedy, knock on wood, *knock on wood.*

Snowy said, "He's even taking time out from his AT planning to carve a mobile for the baby. Bev, how can I be jealous of a baby and a grandmother!"

"Come to my house Christmas Eve and stay over and go with Roger and me and the kids to Mimi's for Christmas dinner. You know she'd love to have you."

"Maybe the dinner. Thank you. Tom will come here Christmas Eve. That'll be okay, but I didn't realize the inn had become a tradition I'd miss." Snowy told herself: Stop whining! She asked Bev, "How are things with Geoff?"

"Still more business than pleasure. We talk shop all the time. I guess that *is* our pleasure! We're so businesslike that I'm sure nobody in the office, not even Lorraine Fitch the Bitch, has the least suspicion."

"That soulful widow's peak of his. But you've been dating almost a year. Doesn't being businesslike mean exercising a hell of a lot of self-control?"

Bev removed her reading glasses, rubbed her eyes, and decided it would be a relief to 'fess up. "When we lose control, it's so unromantic, I've been ashamed to tell you. We have sex in a businesslike fashion."

Stunned silence from Snowy.

"See?" Bev cried. "It sounds so sordid! Every two weeks we go to a motel near Manchester and take care of those urges. Very efficient."

Snowy found her voice. She laughed and said, "And liberated!"

"It's a nice motel. It could almost be romantic. Sometimes I wonder if it sort of is, for Geoff." Bev began to laugh, too. "At first, I'd be enjoying the newness of sleeping with someone other than Roger, and it *is* fun, and then I'd wonder, why am I doing these contortions with this stranger, how ludicrous and embarrassing! I don't suppose you ever felt that way with Tom, after Alan."

"Well, no, not really. He wasn't a stranger. But it had been thirty years, so it was a little surprising."

"That man Puddles had her fling with in his mattress factory... Needless to say, let's keep my fling a secret from our dearest friend the blabbermouth."

Snowy asked, "What will happen with Geoff when Roger is here at Christmastime?"

"Oh, nothing. Business as usual. People are up here for the holidays, thinking maybe of a condo for ski weekends. Geoff sells. And I'm trying. Then after Christmas, no doubt we'll be back to the Manchester routine. I do like him a lot, Snowy." Bev suddenly remembered something she *had* intended to tell Snowy. "I think Etta may be following in your footsteps. Not poetry, but she's been writing little pieces about horses and finally she sent one to a horsey newsletter and the other day she learned that it's been accepted."

"Bev, that's wonderful! And so sensible, nonfiction. Give her my congratulations and a hug."

"I will, and you can do it in person at Mimi's on Christmas."

"See you there."

But as it turned out, Ruhamah developed a cold and decided

against going to New York, a very convenient cold, Snowy thought, for a daughter worried about a mother spending Christmas Day alone, even alone amongst old friends. Yet the cold soon became convincing. Snowy supplied Ruhamah with aspirin, throat lozenges, aloe-treated tissues, and fretted that it might be the flu. When Tom came over on Christmas Eve, he and Snowy had an eggnog in front of the TV while Ruhamah snuffled and sneezed in her bedroom; the Alpine Avens with its Yule log, this was not.

Snowy and Ruhamah didn't go to Mimi's on Christmas Day. They stayed home, Ruhamah in her pajamas and bathrobe. The sun stabbed icy-bright into the apartment, dazzling Snowy with memories of so many other Christmases. Awkward ones with Mother and Daddy; happy with Alan and Ruhamah. After she and Ruhamah opened presents, Snowy kept busy with the preparation of the smallest turkey she'd had in the store, but this didn't help, and after dinner the early dusk of late afternoon brought no reprieve, only memories more subtle, nuances. She and Ruhamah were reading in the living room, the dishwasher chugging, when she heard boots on the outside staircase. Then Tom's tap on the door.

Snowy sprang up. She called, "Come in!"

In Tom came, with a taller man behind him, and the apartment seemed filled with glacial air, males, parkas looming. Then Snowy saw the resemblance, and Tom was introducing this man, who held a Saran-Wrapped paper plate of Christmas cookies. "Snowy and Ruhamah," Tom said, "this is Brandon. Brandon, Henrietta and Ruhamah Sutherland."

Ruhamah sneezed and gurgled and groped in her bathrobe pocket for a soggy Puff tissue.

Snowy said, "Hello, Brandon." An only child, mother of an only child, Snowy was always fascinated by siblings' similarities and differences, and of course she was avidly interested in what the combination of Tom's and Joanne's genes had produced. Captain Brandon Forbes had inherited Joanne's cheekbones but not, as David had, her beauty. With Tom and

Joanne for parents, however, he could hardly help being good-looking, and so he was in Tom's straightforward way, with a dollop of this and that added from both sides of his family. Although Tom had mentioned a couple of jokes Brandon had made, Snowy expected the military son to be a stolid and solemn type or at least as quiet and reserved as David had been before Lavender, but then Brandon smiled at Snowy, and the smile was pure Tom. Snowy's heart melted.

"Snowy," he said. "I'm glad to meet you. And Ruhamah." He held out the plate to Snowy. "Lavender sent these and hopes Ruhamah is feeling better."

Snowy could hear Bev's mother's long-ago remark about Tom: "I always liked Tom; he's a charmer." Snowy took the plate and said, "Thank you." She looked at Tom. "A drink?"

Ruhamah went into a sneezing fit and bolted into her bedroom.

"On the other hand," Snowy said, "you might want to flee the plague."

Tom had chanced it last evening, but now he said, "Maybe we'd better. What about you, Snowy?"

She said, "I don't have time to catch it. Back to work tomorrow." She didn't add that Puddles had insisted she boost her immune system with some stuff made out of coneflowers, Echinacea, from a whole-foods store. The Helmsdale house had sold but Puddles still hadn't moved to Hilton Head; she and Reese the cat had moved in with Susan, Dean, and Little Guy. There, Puddles seemed to be educating herself about Susan's rebellious use of so-called alternative medicine, which previously had provoked scathing comments. Snowy realized that Brandon was observing her and Tom with interest.

Tom asked, "You're okay?"

"Yes."

He and Brandon left then, with Brandon saying an insouciant "Merry Christmas and Happy New Year," as they went.

Ruhamah's door opened. She'd changed into jeans and an

Italian sweater, brushed her hair, dimmed her reddened nose with makeup, and applied lipstick. "Oh," she said. "He's gone—they're gone?"

Shit, Snowy thought. Shit, shit, shit.

ON NEW YEAR'S Day, Puddles phoned and announced jubilantly, "Susan's little girl arrived at 12:01 this morning and won a prize, First Baby Born in Helmsdale in 1992!"

"What a great way to start life. Everything okay? Have Susan and Dean finally decided on a name for her?"

"Everything's fine. But," Puddles said, her voice turning diffident, "come to find out, they'd decided on a name all along and wanted to surprise me. They're naming the poor little thing after me."

"Jean! I was hoping they would. After all, they named Little Guy after Guy."

"But a Guy has been in Guy's family every generation; they *had* to. It never crossed my mind they'd use Jean. Poor kid, winning a prize and then getting a booby prize."

"Jean is a lovely name. Come on, Jean Pond Cram, you're tickled."

Puddles gave a giggle.

The next Sunday afternoon, Snowy and Bev went shopping together for a present in the baby-boutique section of a children's store in the Gunthwaite Mall.

"Ruffles!" Bev said. "Thank heavens. Little boys' clothes are so boring. I did my best to have fun with Dick's and Leon's, but it was still a yawn. I hope Mimi has a girl."

Snowy concentrated on a pink burp bib.

Bev said flatly, "She isn't going to have any children at all, is she."

Mimi had asked Snowy not to tell, but that was five years ago. Snowy said, "Some couples are complete in themselves, Bev. Alan and I very nearly decided against an intrusion."

"Hell and damn."

"Zero population growth," Snowy began, then remembered that Bev would be in favor of a growing population to sell houses to. "Um, what about Dick and his latest girlfriend? You've got three other kids; don't worry, you'll be a grandmother sooner or later."

Bev rallied and made her "oh, horrors!" face. "Not by Etta, not for years and years, I hope, and sometimes I wonder if maybe I already am one thanks to Leon!"

But not thanks to Leon and Ruhamah, Snowy thought. She asked, "The Plumley Awards banquet must be coming up soon?"

"Next Saturday."

"You'll win that trip to San Francisco!"

The next Sunday morning, Bev phoned and said forlornly, "I lost again, and this year I came in third. I've been working harder than ever, I'm getting better than ever, but this wasn't enough. I even dropped behind my last year's sales."

"It's just luck, Bev. Everything is luck."

"Lorraine Fitch has all the luck in the world."

Later that week, Puddles phoned and said, "Mother and baby doing fine. Also Dean and Little Guy. My usefulness is over here, so I've accepted the best offer from the Hilton Head medical centers. I'm a new member of Palmetto Family Medicine, and I'm leaving the Helmsdale Clinic as of today."

"Really?" Snowy said, thinking Palmetto Family Medicine would never know what hit it. "You've finally made the decision? Your Helmsdale patients are going to miss you."

Puddles admitted, "There was a big party at the clinic this afternoon, my patients as well as my colleagues. They gave me new socks for my new stirrups and lots of beefcake posters to update my Burt Reynolds on the ceiling." Her voice quavered. "And they gave me a watch that knows more than I did when I graduated from Mass. General."

While Puddles mopped her eyes and blew her nose, Snowy tried to think what it would feel like, after all this angst and dawdling, to go ahead at last and leave a place where you'd worked and lived for thirty years. Scary but exciting. Snowy asked, "So when are you off to Hilton Head?"

"Tomorrow. I'll be back under the same roof with Guy after all these months. I sure can see why you and Bev are living separately from Roger and Tom."

"Did Guy have new carpeting installed?"

"I picked it out," Puddles said. "Pale gold. I had dark blue here, so it'll be a change. Change!" Then she added, "Do you want to hear the latest cute thing Little Guy said? Of course you do. He asked me, 'Are you taking your living room with you?' He can't fathom that our house is sold and the new house will be different. I'll send you and Bev the most recent photos of him and Jean—also photos of that house."

TOM'S PREPARATIONS FOR the Appalachian Trail dominated the winter. By the time April approached, Snowy felt prepared to hike the damn thing herself and she actually *wanted* to, not only for the purpose of being with him and sharing the hazards instead of blindly worrying in Woodcombe, but also for the changes of scenery and the tests of her own abilities. Yet instead she must be Penelope to his Odysseus or the damsel to the crusader or any little woman staying behind to keep the home fires burning.

Studying the AT map, she said, "The trail goes right through Hanover. I could leave Ruhamah minding the store and meet you there, bringing the next mail-drop package instead of mailing it. That'll be the Glencliff post office mail-drop, with your cold-weather gear." He had explained that probably in Virginia he wouldn't need his heaviest clothes anymore, so he'd mail them to her, and then when he neared New Hampshire she should send them to Glencliff for his trek through the White Mountains on to Maine. She added, "We could have lunch."

He thought for a while. "I'll be too grungy to go in any place decent."

"The restaurant doesn't have to be a fancy one. You'll be treating yourself to a pizza whenever you come out of the woods to get supplies; I'll bet we can find a pizza joint in a college town."

"No, we'd better not meet."

"I could hike along with you for a bit," she persisted, although she knew that David had asked to hike some of the trail with him through the White Mountains when he got this far, and Tom had said no. He wanted to do it alone. Brandon would see him off at the start of the trail, and David would come collect him at its end, but in between, no.

Tom said, "Better not. If we met, I'd just start missing you all over again."

So she would have to exist without him for six whole months. She would run the store and mail him supplies and follow his progress on her copy of the long narrow map pinned to her bedroom wall.

On Wednesday, April 1 ("I'm an April Fool," said Tom, kissing Snowy good-bye), David drove Tom to Boston, and from Logan Tom flew to Atlanta, where Brandon picked him up, having arranged a couple of free days for this momentous send-off at the other end of the state from Fort Stewart. The next morning, Brandon phoned Snowy, as arranged, and said, "He's off! He at least allowed me to hike up Springer Mountain with him to the start of the trail and I got some pictures of him there. I'll send you one."

Breathlessly, Snowy asked, "How is he, is he okay?"

"He was all psyched up and raring to go. Incidentally, he mentioned that Ruhamah is coming home this weekend for her birthday. Wish her happy birthday for me, would you?"

Snowy hauled her thoughts back from Tom alone on an unfamiliar trail. She said with emphasis, "It's her twenty-first birthday." And you, charming Brandon Forbes, are or will be thirty-two this year.

Sounding unabashed, he said, "That's an important birthday."

As Snowy hung up, she suddenly wondered if Ruhamah's silence about any boyfriends at UNH meant there were no *young* men in her life. What with Ruhamah's penchant for older men and their interest in her, was she dating professors? Or, as Ruhamah had always sort of implied, was she really too busy with studies for any social life, the exception being D. J.?

When Ruhamah came home Saturday, Snowy intended to mention only that Brandon had seen Tom off, but then she relented and relayed his birthday wishes. Ruhamah's expression was impassive and she didn't reply to that; she asked when Tom would be phoning Snowy himself, and she asked about the partial inventory computerization that she'd set up during spring recess, to Snowy's consternation.

On the fifth day of his hike, Tom phoned from Neels Gap, Georgia. Sounding euphoric, he said, "I'm at the Walasi-Yi Center, which the trail actually goes *through,* under a sort of breezeway. Luxuries—bunkroom and a shower, and a Laundromat where I've got a wash going right now."

She wanted to inquire about his knee. She asked, "How's the weather been?" although she was keeping track on the national weather map on TV.

"Okay. The hardest thing to get used to is that this is what I'm doing now, this is the job I start working at when I get up in the morning: I walk. Up and down mountains, rain or shine. That's all I'm supposed to be doing. Everything okay there?"

"Fine," she said, feeling dull and tired and chained to the Woodcombe General Store.

At work the next morning, the work she went to every morning, she looked around the store and tried to take some pride in what she'd accomplished, she and Ruhamah. They were supplying a need and making a living, however precarious, unlike three other New Hampshire general stores she'd heard about who'd closed in the past three years.

And she was supplying Tom. To North Carolina and Tennessee post offices she began mailing the cartons he'd addressed and numbered, these mail-drops of Pop Tarts, Kraft Macaroni and Cheese, tuna in oil (not in water, the oil calories necessary), Snickers bars, toilet paper, moleskin, batteries, film, extra socks, to Tom Forbes, c/o General Delivery, Hold for AT Hiker.

Whenever he phoned her, she tried to divine his true state as he joked about craving ice cream, how he'd eaten a whole half gallon right outside a grocery store, or told her about the birds and flowers he'd seen and the increase in miles he was averaging, eight miles a day, eleven, fifteen. He hadn't hooked up with any other "thru-hikers," as people hiking the entire AT were called; he hiked alone. He hadn't even chosen a trail nickname, the way most thru-hikers did, like a CB handle. She worried herself sick about his knee, about injuries in general, about hypothermia, treacherous terrain, getting lost, rattlesnakes, bears. About lightning. God, she *was* like her mother, a born worrier!

Tom hadn't mentioned the AT to townsfolk, but David and Lavender did, and his adventure seized the imagination of the town. In the store, so many people asked Snowy for details and updates that she brought the map down from her bedroom and posted it beside the bulletin board, marking his progress in red like a fund-drive thermometer.

This May, at the end of Ruhamah's junior year, Harriet invited Ruhamah on a trip to Provence.

"Wow, France," Snowy said to Ruhamah. "And maybe next year it'll be Scotland."

"Why Scotland?" Ruhamah said.

"Some of your roots."

Ruhamah said abstractedly, "Harriet picks places for her own reasons." Then she said, "Snowy, between now and then I have to decide about the MBA. To do it full-time in two years, part-time in three and a third years, or not to do it at all."

A master's degree from UNH's Whittemore School of Business and Economics did not seem essential for work at a general store, but Snowy hoped Ruhamah's goals were now higher. Snowy said, "Full-time."

"But that's two more years of you on your own here during the school year, with just Irene. And two more years of tuition."

"No arguing. Decision made."

Snowy sent off to Damascus, Virginia, the mail-drop package containing Tom's summer-wear, the nylon running shorts and cotton-polyester T-shirts he'd decided on instead of his regular hiking clothes because they were lightweight and dried fast. When he sent the package of his cold-weather clothes, he included a few rolls of film for her to have developed. She rushed with the film to a Gunthwaite photo shop and paid extra for one-hour developing, but the pictures were a great disappointment, showing only scenic vistas and wildflowers and such. *Why* couldn't he have handed his camera to somebody at some shelter and posed for a snapshot even if he felt like a damn fool? Thus, instead of the photos, she cherished the slightly moldy wool sweater, knitted cap, gloves, and the Laundromat-fresh (thoughtful Tom) thermal underwear.

In Virginia, Tom's elation ebbed. On the phone he joked about the monotony of ramen noodles and about crowded shelters, and beneath his light tone she heard the letdown. She wanted to tell him it was okay to give up, but he said, "Tell me what flavors of Ben & Jerry's you've got in the store's freezer case right now," and she recited them, and he sighed, "Ah, that's sexy," and they laughed. He said, "The halfway point is coming up, West Virginia."

When he reached West Virginia and the Appalachian Trail Conference headquarters in Harpers Ferry, his spirits seemed to lift. She sent off the next package to Pennsylvania.

On the map in the store, the red line kept edging north. Pennsylvania went on forever. New Jersey. New York. Connecticut. Massachusetts.

Ruhamah finished computerizing the store's inventory system, tackled the bookkeeping, and tried to be patient while teaching Snowy the new organization.

Snowy's poems were appearing regularly in magazines. She was asked to do another reading at the village library, and then came a phone-call request from the president of the Friends of the Gunthwaite Public Library—the Gunthwaite library, the imposing stone edifice which she'd first entered as a trembling child, too small to see over the massive golden oak checkout desk! Snowy babbled to Bev, "I was so surprised, my mind went blank and I couldn't think of an excuse. What do I wear? In Woodcombe, I've just been country-casual at the podium. Maybe people don't care what poets wear? Edna St. Vincent Millay though, I gather she was as great as you on stage and she wowed them with her gowns as well as her delivery." Bev said, "I think it's time I took you to the Mall of New Hampshire." So Snowy gave herself an afternoon off, and they drove to Manchester. The huge mall almost induced an all-stations-alert panic attack, but Snowy stuck close to Bev, who led her into Filene's and decided on a pale pink linen blazer, a white silk shell, and white slacks more elegant than Snowy's old white pants, which Snowy still considered her summer best. Bev said, forging onward into the shoe department to find dressy sandals, "It's worth the expense, Snowy. This outfit will give you presence and confidence." It did. The Gunthwaite library meeting room was packed with an audience that included a certain Gunthwaite city councilor, his wife, and all of their kids that they could round up. Although as usual Snowy went sweaty and dizzy at first, she calmed down enough by the end of the reading to enjoy the question-and-answer session, even Dudley's straight-faced query, "Henrietta, where do you get your ideas?"

One evening in early August, when she was unloading the

dishwasher, Tom phoned and said, "I'm in Bennington. I made a side trip. The town sure has grown since I was here in 1957."

Back then, he had driven over from Rumford to see the college, in hopes of glimpsing her walking around the campus. She hadn't known this until thirty years later. She said, "Have you been to the school?"

"There's some summer stuff going on. Now I'm at a motel, and I've experienced this miracle called a hot shower, and Snowy—"

She interrupted, "What motel?" Was the Sleepytime Motor Lodge, where she and Alan used to shack up, still in existence? Then she remembered that the Sleepytime wasn't in Bennington; it was just over the New York line, this nearby state line having been a popular destination because you could drink at eighteen in the Empire State.

"The Knotty Pine," Tom replied. "Have I mentioned that in motels I start out luxuriating in the bed but pretty soon I can't stand it and I spend the rest of the night sleeping on the floor? Um, Snowy, I've been wondering if, when I get to New Hampshire, you might like to hike a piece of the trail with me after all. I've been looking at the map, and you know where the trail comes down Mount Moosilauke to Kinsman Notch? We could meet there, and you could go on with me up to Gordon Pond, a little over three miles. It'd be like our first backpack. We could camp there overnight and then you'd go back down to the notch and I'd go on to Mount Wolf and Kinsman Mountain and on. And on."

She grabbed the rooster memo pad. "When do you figure you'll reach the trailhead?"

"I'll call you from Hanover with a better estimate, but probably two weeks."

"Oh, Tom, I can't wait!"

"Neither," he said, "can I."

When they'd hung up, she stood beaming at the phone, basking in happiness. What had changed his mind? Seeing the college and thinking of the years without each other?

She waited anxiously for him to cross into New Hampshire. She would be able to worry about him more clearly on home ground, what a relief! Over the years, Tom had done lots of pieces of the AT in New Hampshire, so he knew what to expect and he would be safer. Theoretically.

One afternoon he phoned her at the store to say he'd reached Hanover.

FOUR DAYS LATER at noontime, she was unchained from the store and driving up I-93 into the White Mountains. The weather had been sunny for Tom's arrival in New Hampshire, and warm, in what weather reports had begun calling the coldest summer on record. Today was hot, the three horrible h's, hazy hot humid. She'd be pouring with sweat once she began hiking. Since his call from Bennington, she'd done her homework and read up on this little piece of the AT, learning that the Kinsman Ridge Trail didn't fool around and started out straight up. Eek. She wasn't in hiking shape, not having hiked at all this summer, with Tom gone. She would have to make do using her jogging shape. No matter, she'd be with Tom at last!

She got off the interstate in Lincoln and drove Route 112 into Kinsman Notch, a narrow forbidding cleft.

She was early, but when she turned left off the road into a parking area, she saw him sitting on the ground, leaning against his backpack, writing in a notebook. He glanced up.

"Tom!" she cried, leaping out of the car. God, God, how she'd missed him.

He rose to his feet. He had lost weight, and he looked much younger. Despite his white curls and beard, which he'd kept trimmed, despite his gold-rimmed trifocals, he almost looked like a little boy, in his navy blue running shorts, gray T-shirt, and a baseball cap.

Suddenly shy, Snowy stopped stock-still. "I thought for sure I'd get here before you."

Tom saw the telltale muscle jumping in her jaw. He said, "Guess I've mentioned I couldn't wait to see you."

"Oh, Tom." Snowy ran to him.

He said, "But I'd better stay downwind of you."

"Fuck that," said Snowy, and hugged him.

He put his arms around her, his face in her hair. Christ, how he'd missed her.

When they eventually separated, she said, "First things first." She opened the trunk of her Subaru to show him a cooler, then lifted the cooler's lid to display the four pints of ice cream within, a spoon on top. "An assortment of flavors," she explained, handing him the spoon.

"What a welcome sight, you and Ben & Jerry."

She thought he'd been exaggerating about the hunger for fat, but in the time it took her to remove the supper supplies from the cooler—a bottle of chardonnay, Ziploc bags of Swiss chard, cucumbers, lettuce, stir-fry chicken cubes—and load them into her pack, he had polished off New York Super Fudge Chunk and Chocolate Chip Cookie Dough. As she changed out of her shoes and socks into hiking socks and boots, he finished Cherry Garcia and Chunky Monkey. In her heyday she had been famous for her appetite; she shuddered to think what her capacity would be if she were a thru-hiker. Imagine, though, being able to eat all you wanted and lose weight!

Tom looked back toward the Beaver Brook Trail section of the AT he'd come down. Something nagged at him, something seemed to be dogging him, but what? In his hurry to see Snowy, had he forgotten anything back at last night's shelter?

She asked, "How was Mount Moosilauke?"

"Hazy, but I'm not complaining. The times I used to climb it in my Newburgh years, I even got into snow on the summit in summer." He investigated the mail-drop carton of cold-weather clothes she'd brought instead of mailed. "Well, I'm definitely going to be needing all these." He stowed them in his pack and looked at her, at her breasts in the wicking T-shirt, at the dark green hiking shorts, and he heard his voice go hoarse as he asked, "Ready?"

"Yes."

Snowy locked the car. They shouldered their packs, picked up their walking sticks, crossed the road, and began climbing the vertical trail. She sweated and panted, feeling like a wimp; Tom had already done about eight miles today, from the Jeffers Brook Shelter up over Moosilauke, elevation 4,802 feet, down the steep Beaver Brook Trail. He'd always been an easy striding hiker, but he went up this side of Kinsman Notch at a new slow steady pace. She labored after him, fearing her pack would topple her backward to plummet straight down into Route 112. When the trail leveled and they stopped for a swig out of their water bottles, she knew from her homework that this was only a temporary reprieve and more tests of her endurance lay ahead, and so it proved, the trail twisting up and down over knoll after knoll. As she mentally cursed the hike, suddenly she realized she was smiling. They were placing their feet carefully on ledges cushioned with emerald-green moss; they were passing yet another boulder draped in dreamy moss and squelching through sphagnum moss as airy as green sea foam. She was with Tom amid all this green.

When they stopped again for a drink, she asked hesitantly, not wanting to pry into his grief about Libby, "What do you think about as you hike mile after mile, day after day? Besides food?"

He almost replied: Susan Hayward. That was one of the strange memories that had drifted into his mind as he walked along: his forgotten infatuation in elementary school with this redheaded movie star. Had Susan Hayward led to his falling for Bev in high school? He said, "I think about the trail, where

I've been and where I'm going. Where I'll sleep." As he hiked day after day, he often hankered for beds and thick mattresses, even though he couldn't sleep on them when he got to hostels or motels; as he hiked, he would remember the first bed he'd been on with Snowy, at a party at Victor Andrews's grandfather's camp on the lake; and he would think of how, since Libby died, Joanne had been sleeping in the spool bed in Libby's bedroom. At first he had reacted with distaste to Joanne's sleeping where Libby used to sleep, finding it macabre, but then as he spent his nights in Newburgh alone in David's old bedroom, he began somehow to equate it with Joanne and Libby's having shared the same body for nine months. He said to Snowy, "But mostly I do think about food."

"As I told you on the phone, I'm making supper tonight. Fresh everything."

"What a treat that'll be."

They hiked onward. At last Tom turned off the main trail and they descended to the pond. Because of its proximity to the AT, Snowy had resigned herself to finding a horde of thru-hikers here, but at least for now she and Tom had it to themselves, and it seemed secret and remote, a wilderness pond tucked under the hump of green Mount Wolf ahead.

They lowered their packs and turned to each other, and then they were kissing, and after five months apart they couldn't wait a moment longer. She wanted to embrace, engulf, and surround him at the same time she wanted to disappear into his embracing arms. On the pond floated green lily pads with yellow blooms.

When they'd scrambled back into their clothes, laughing, Tom lugged his pack away from the shore into the woods to look for a spot for his tent farther back amongst the firs, and she knelt and unzipped her pack to take out a dry T-shirt, digging under the other presents she had brought him, blueberry muffins she'd made last night with blueberries David and Lavender had picked on Pascataquac, tomatoes from her tub of tomato plants, a hunk of Fay's truffle cake. Hearing footsteps, she said, "Lavender sent the latest photo of the baby," and looked up and saw not Tom but a stranger. Her first reaction was: the Ancient Mariner.

He wasn't old, and his beard wasn't long or gray, like the Ancient Mariner's, just an unkempt black bristly brush. His eyes, however, did glitter.

Still crouching, she carefully said, "Hello."

This tall gaunt man must be a thru-hiker. His big backpack rode high above his head, his greasy hair was pulled into a tangled ponytail, his shirt and shorts were filthy, and she could smell him.

He asked, "Where are you from?"

"Here. New Hampshire."

He nodded. "I saw your license plates."

My God, had he seen her and Tom in the parking area and followed them? Had he witnessed their reunion on the shore of Gordon Pond? She blushed, embarrassed and outraged. Well, that meant he knew she wasn't a woman hiking alone. He must know Tom was nearby. Where *was* Tom? Snowy's heart began to hammer. Had this guy followed him into the woods and stabbed him or—no, she would have heard any commotion. But, her heart louder and louder in her ears, as she crouched there she slid her hand back into her pack, and as she groped for her Ziploc of emergency equipment that contained a little jackknife, she longed for the Mace gun she always jogged with in her pocket, bucolic though the village of Woodcombe might be. It hadn't ever occurred to her to put the Mace gun in her pack.

The guy confided, "I'm from New Hampshire too."

She couldn't breathe or speak. She cleared her throat and said conversationally, "Are you hiking the AT?" The emergency bag *would* be at the very bottom of the pack, and she was still easing her hand downward, past her Goretex rain jacket.

"Only," he said, "as far as Cannon Mountain. I'm going to take the Old Man of the Mountain hostage."

She stared at him. She almost laughed. The Great Stone Face, the famous fluke of rocks that formed a beaky profile high up Cannon Mountain, had long been New Hampshire's symbol, emblem, pride and joy. This guy *was* crazy. "Oh?" she said.

He reached up and patted his pack. "If they don't do what I want, I'll blow it up. I've got the stuff in here."

Over the years, the Old Man had needed various face-lifts, by surgeons performing death-defying feats on ropes, using fiberglass, cement, pins, cables, turnbuckles, and whatever else was necessary to keep New Hampshire's symbol held together. The guy was a wacko, but he knew the importance and vulnerability of the Old Man. She swallowed and asked, "What is it you want?"

He launched into a speech. Snowy realized he probably hadn't done much of any talking all along the AT. "Isn't it plain?" he said. "They've got to stop this first-in-the-nation crap. They've got to give up the primary! Look what we've got running for president this year thanks to New Hampshire, an Arkansas governor, Bill Clinton! I've seen the country now, I've been thinking about it all the way from Georgia, and it's plain as day that New Hampshire should get the hell out! Stop hanging onto the primary! Stop being responsible for electing these assholes! New Hampshire's in it for the money and the power of the primary, but look at this white-bread conservative state, no state income tax, no sales tax, no blacks—*we're* the first in the nation?"

As he ranted, her hand touched the Ziploc at the bottom of her pack. It was, of course, sealed. One-handed, she tried to peel it open, wondering how Dudley would argue with this madman. The trouble was, she tended to agree with the guy. She said soothingly, "Granted, New Hampshire isn't representative enough, but—"

"You agree! Now, you come along with me. You're from New Hampshire. You want to put this right, same as me. Get up. Come on. Come *on!*"

Everything seemed to stop. The hot thick air went as solid as aspic. The lily pads and waxy blossoms were rooted immobile to the bottom of the still pond. Motionless, she couldn't hear a single bird, a single insect.

The man said, "That thru-hiker. Did he just hump you and keep going on ahead?"

Snowy got to her feet, trembling, her left hand lifting her pack, futile protection, a useless shield, her right hand scrabbling inside again amid the presents, the food, the wine. The wine.

The man stepped toward her.

She dropped the pack and swung the bottle of chardonnay, and the man's face exploded while the bottle remained intact. Out of the woods charged Tom, knocking him backward into the pond.

Now it seemed to her that everything in the world was moving, jittering up and down, jittery like a caffeine high. She stared at the man floating unconscious in the water, blood swirling from his face. Then his pack rolled him over facedown.

She cried, "He'll drown!"

"Let him," Tom said, but he waded in, and together they hauled the man out onto the bank.

Snowy said, "Maybe he's already dead, maybe I killed him!"

Tom found his pulse. "He's alive."

They both thought of the other time he'd sought a pulse.

Snowy said, "Did you hear him about the Old Man? Should we look in his pack for explosives? Dynamite? A bomb?"

"Can you hold him upright?" Tom unbuckled the man's pack and slid it off his shoulders. Gingerly, he opened the top compartment. "Holy shit. It *is* dynamite."

"Really? He really meant it? What do we do?"

Tom said, "We're going to tie him up," and ran into the woods.

Snowy hurried to her pack for her first-aid kit, but its Band-aids seemed inadequate. Blood was pouring out the man's smashed nose, out of the cuts on his cheekbones.

Tom loped back carrying his pack. "Christ, I'm sorry, Snowy. I kept looking for a more and more private place to camp in case other hikers arrived, and there you were alone—" He yanked his clothesline out of the pack. "When I started back and saw him, heard him, I guessed you were going after something in your pack."

Now at last she got out her jackknife. She cut the clothesline into lengths.

Tom tied the man's wrists and ankles, then pulled a bandanna from a pocket and wiped at the blood. "I thought so. I've seen him at shelters occasionally on the way. Somebody asked me where I was from, and when he heard New Hampshire, he buttonholed me, wanting to talk about New Hampshire. A weirdo, so I avoided him. I haven't seen him in a while, but something kept bothering me today. Snowy, we've got to get the cops as well as the EMTs. Can you go back down to the car and find a phone? Your best bet is that Lost River tourist place. I'll stay here and make sure he does too."

They both thought of the other time she'd had to go down a mountain to find a phone.

She asked, "Will you be okay?"

"I'll try not to kill him. The goddamn bastard—he saw you, he saw us—"

She put her arms around Tom. "We won't let him ruin any of it, the pond or the AT."

"Right. Except, will the cops want me to stick around instead of returning to the AT? And there could be all sorts of legal ramifications. The guy could maybe sue *us*."

"Oh no."

"Well, we can't do anything except what we should. 'Our duty.' Can you follow the trail? The white blazes—the AT blaze is always white."

"I'll leave my pack here." She took out her wallet and car keys. "I'll get back as soon as I can."

He kissed her.

Up and down the trail twisted again and again over those endless knolls. She moved fast, without the weight of her pack, but the pace felt slow and her mind was burdened by the image of Tom up there thinking of Mount Daybreak and Libby. She was so relieved to reach the final precipitous pitch to Route 112 that she didn't pause even a second to gather up courage but went right down like a mountain goat.

SNOWY WORRIED ABOUT the effect on Tom of the EMTs' arrival in the woods, but this wasn't the same as Libby. This person was alive. And once the EMTs had patched the man up, he was voluble again. Escorted by police and EMTs down the trail, with Snowy and Tom bringing up the rear, the man was eager to tell everybody all about himself and his plans to hold the Old Man hostage. His name was Kenneth Collins, he was thirty-six years old, and he was a road construction worker from Manchester, where he'd lived until last March, when he started hiking the AT, and upon reaching New Hampshire he had stolen the dynamite from a construction site.

The police took Tom and Snowy's statements and asked them to attend the arraignment the next morning. Then, the police said, Tom would be given permission to continue on the AT, after providing them with an itinerary and a schedule of phone calls he would make to Snowy so she could keep him apprised of any developments that would necessitate his return.

In this height of the tourist season, she and Tom doubted they'd find a vacancy at a nearby motel or campground so late in the evening, but they drove around, Snowy doing the driving because Tom hadn't been behind a wheel in months, and at last they managed to snag one in a shabby motel that reminded

Snowy of the Sleepytime Motor Lodge, and there they collapsed on the bed with a six-pack of beer and a take-out pizza, Snowy's Ziploc of chicken having been deposited in a trash bin. They clicked on the TV but didn't watch it. They talked and talked away the shock, Snowy saying the encounter was less frightening than a poetry reading, and they got laughing over the damn New Hampshire primary, and then they rolled into each other's arms to try to obliterate the image of the voyeur. Tom didn't unpack his air mattress; he spent the entire night in bed.

The next morning they drove on through Kinsman Notch into the Connecticut River valley to North Haverhill, the Grafton County seat, and pulled off the road at a sign for the Grafton County Courthouse and Administrative Offices. School architecture, Tom called the 1970s brick building designed with peaks and angles and lots of big windows that had had to be retrofitted, probably during the first energy crisis, to save heat, just as the windows of the much older Gunthwaite High School had been. The courtroom's blond wood surprised her; she had imagined all courtrooms must be done up in ponderous dark wood. During the arraignment they learned that Kenneth Collins was, as a policeman put it, a loner with a long history of mental illness. Kenneth Collins seemed pleased by the proceedings and smiled often at Snowy as she shakily recounted what had happened; he seemed flattered that she'd bashed him with the chardonnay. Did he think he was a ship she had christened? He ignored Tom.

Afterward, an excited local reporter asked them questions, and then Snowy drove Tom back to the parking area where they'd met yesterday.

They got out of the car. Tom said ruefully, "Now you're really going to worry."

"No," she lied. "No more than before."

He kissed her, shouldered his pack, and walked across the road.

Driving back to Woodcombe, she finally cried. But as the reaction set in, she felt first horror that she'd actually hit someone, then pride that she could if need be.

When she arrived home, she found people in the store reading the Manchester *Union Leader.* Other reporters had got hold of the story, and a frightened Ruhamah and a harried Irene had lists of messages of phone calls to the store's phone from the *Union Leader* as well as the *Gunthwaite Herald* and the *Concord Monitor*—and even the *Boston Globe*!—along with those from Bev, Dudley, Alan's mother, and David. And Joanne. Ruhamah told Snowy, "I took that one a few minutes ago, and Joanne said she'd been leaving messages on our home machine but when you didn't phone back she called the store, and she's not the only one, the answering machine upstairs is full. Joanne sounded like she's coming unglued." So Snowy went upstairs, Ruhamah on her heels, and phoned Joanne immediately after hugging Ruhamah again.

"Tom's okay," she told Joanne. "He's a hero. And, needless to say, he's obstinate. He's back on the trail."

"I knew it!" Joanne cried. "I can't take this, I can't take this!"

"The wacko was an exception, Joanne. The AT is usually safe to hike."

Weeping, Joanne hung up. Snowy looked at Ruhamah. "You talked with David?"

"He phoned this morning. He'd heard it on the radio."

"Had he phoned Joanne?"

"I think he was avoiding that."

"Could you give him a call and ask him to call her? Tell him Tom and I are fine and Tom is continuing." While Ruhamah did, Snowy changed into clean jeans, and, with some forethought, a Woodcombe General Store T-shirt. She and Ruhamah went back downstairs to the store.

The phone commenced to ring again, and soon Snowy was giving interviews into the receiver cradled in her neck as she waited on customers, cut and weighed cheese, scooped ice cream. She wasn't sure she wanted to answer questions about foiling the madman's plot, but as Tom had said at the courthouse, they had to so reporters wouldn't get inaccurate information elsewhere.

One of the reporters, a woman from the *Gunthwaite Herald,* had attended her reading at the Gunthwaite library; she asked if Snowy would be writing a poem about what had happened. Taken aback, Snowy blurted, "Probably, eventually."

A crew arrived from Channel 9, New Hampshire's main commercial TV station, along with newspaper photographers. Posing behind the counter and on the front porch, Snowy smiled bravely and answered more questions and thought: Do it, do it, good publicity for Woodcombe General Store.

As Snowy was closing up, she saw Bev's car stop outside. An elegant secondhand Mercedes had recently replaced Bev's station wagon. Bev rushed into the store, redheaded Etta behind her carrying a big paper bag and looking like Bev at seventeen but lacking the glamour Bev had possessed even in her teens. Bev hugged Snowy and said, "You're going to be on TV! At the office, I saw Channel 9 announcing you'll be on the evening news! We've brought Chinese food and we'll all watch!"

If Snowy had had any say in the matter, Snowy wouldn't have watched, but a fearful fascination did begin to grip her in the apartment while she and Bev and Etta and Ruhamah filled their plates and sat down in front of the TV. She nearly did a spit-take of General Gau's Chicken when she saw herself on the screen and realized for the first time that she resembled her mother, in face if not in figure, Mother not having been a jogger. And listening to herself, she knew that Bev would have done a much better job of telling the story as well as being a heroine.

Bev thought so too, but said loyally, "You were wonderful!"

The next day, Snowy and Kenneth Collins were pictured on front pages, along with a photo of Tom that must have been dug up from an article about fire towers that the *Union Leader* had done a few years ago. All the newspapers except the *Gunthwaite Herald* identified Snowy as a "storekeeper" or "store-owner." The Gunthwaite paper called her a "poet-storekeeper," which must have struck readers as pretty peculiar, but it caught the attention of those reporters from the other papers, who phoned back with questions about a poem, so in the subsequent diminishing follow-up stories she was called a "poet-storekeeper" everywhere.

Bev phoned Puddles, who phoned Snowy and cheered, "Our quiet little Snowy, clobbering a terrorist! I didn't know you had it in you!"

"Neither did I," Snowy said.

Then Puddles's voice went brusque. "I had to have Reese put down yesterday."

"Who?"

"You know, our cat. The damn thing was nineteen years old. Even older than Guy, in cat years!" Puddles burst into tears.

Harriet phoned, having spotted an item about Snowy and Tom and Kenneth Collins in the *New York Times,* and advised, "Capitalize on the publicity for yourself, not just the store. Goose your muse and get a poem out of this as soon as you can. Pretend you're a poet laureate having to produce for an occasion."

Snowy said, "I'll try."

A week later Tom phoned from a motel in Gorham, New Hampshire. "Are you okay?"

"Did you see the newspapers?"

"Not until today."

"The furor is dying down now. Are *you* okay?"

"Yes," he said, "no trouble, no publicity. If the cops didn't want to keep track of me, I would have taken the precaution of finally using a trail name at shelters and huts in case Tom Forbes was in the headlines, but I haven't had any reaction. Thru-hikers don't pay much attention to the news. Guess what trail name I would have chosen?"

"I can't."

"The Snowman. People would think it was a reference to white hair or to drugs in my past or something."

Snowy was so flattered she was rendered speechless.

Tom said, "I got the package you sent here. Only three maildrops to go!"

And on he went into Maine.

Thanks to the publicity, Snowy received invitations to do readings at other libraries around the state, but she could accept only those fairly close because she feared falling asleep during a long drive after a day's work in the store, which was even busier than usual, thanks also to the publicity. On nights at home, she obeyed Harriet and worked on the poem.

Up toward the top of the AT map crept Snowy's red marker. In mid-September, Tom phoned from a legendary stop on the AT, Shaw's Boarding House in Monson, Maine, and said, "Tell David he can pick me up twelve days from now, September 26, if he doesn't hear otherwise from me."

"The last leg," she said. At last.

September 26 was a Saturday, and leaf peepers crowded the store. Snowy wondered if anticipation could kill you. Anxiety tightened as she sold camera film and postcards and Pepsis, tightened and tightened as she sold potato chips and T-shirts while he climbed Mount Katahdin to the end of the Appalachian Trail.

That evening he phoned. "The Snowman made it!"

"Oh, Tom! Congratulations, congratulations!"

"David and I are at a motel in Millinocket now. Be back tomorrow."

Ruhamah was hovering. When Snowy hung up and hugged her, Ruhamah said, "We'll have a welcome-home party."

"Tom isn't much of a one for parties."

"The village will want a big blast. Blame it on me, and leave it to me."

After work Sunday afternoon, Snowy took a shower and changed into her best jeans and an aqua Lands' End sweater, and she was putting on fresh makeup when she heard a car door slam. She ran into the living room and looked out a window into the street.

Not Tom. Brandon. Brandon, who, as far as Snowy knew, was down in Georgia. He had got out of a car and was standing there.

Ruhamah was tying white balloons (white to match the AT blazes) onto the porch railings, and she laughed and said, "Good timing," and gave one to Brandon, who held onto her hand. Ruhamah laughed again, said, "Work!" and pointed at a stepladder. Brandon climbed up and tethered the balloon to the store's sign.

CHAPTER FOUR

TIPPED OFF BY Bev, the *Gunthwaite Herald* reporter came to the party and scored a scoop, an interview with Tom that revived the media's interest in the Old Man Bomber, as Kenneth Collins had been dubbed.

Thus, two days later, Snowy and Tom found themselves driving down to Manchester and locating Channel 9 in one of the old brick mills, which, strung along the Merrimack River, still seemed to epitomize the Industrial Revolution despite modern occupants. They sat in a studio, blinded by brilliant lights as the live interview began, feeling ridiculous with the show-and-tell props they'd been asked to bring (Tom's backpack, Snowy's daypack, and a bottle of chardonnay of the same size and brand as the one she had wielded), and then relaxing a bit, Tom because the young woman interviewing them turned out to be a hiker and knew about the AT, Snowy because Tom was there and doing most of the talking. She realized this must be his teaching voice, lightly commanding attention; he was performing for the TV audience instead of a classroom.

Then came the moment that was the reason they had agreed to do the interview.

The interviewer turned to Snowy, and everything went blurry again with fear. Snowy fought to recapture some composure as from far far away the interviewer made a little joke, saying, "I understand that you're a poet—and I hope I can understand the poem you've written about what happened."

Snowy replied, "I've been called 'accessible,'" caught Tom suppressing a sudden grin, and amended hastily, "My work has been called 'accessible.'" She stopped herself from adding that this adjective could be the kiss of death, and said, "The title of this poem is 'Tapestry Granite.' That's New Hampshire's variegated granite, gray and pink and black." She began to read from her typed pages, although she was able to recite the sonnet sequence from memory.

When she finished, the interviewer didn't speak.

Sheer angry embarrassment washed over Snowy. What in God's name was she doing here? She put her chin up.

"Cool," said the interviewer, and then recovered herself and continued smoothly, "That was very illuminating, and we're honored that you read it here first. Thank you both for coming here. I'm proud to have met you."

Driving home, Snowy and Tom stopped for supper at the Miss Leicester Diner where Snowy decided on the old-fashioned hamburger and French fries, to celebrate surviving the interview. Tom said apologetically, "According to what I've read and what people say, I'm going to keep on eating as if I'm still on the trail for a couple of weeks," and ordered two cheeseburgers for himself, French fries, and a chocolate frappe.

"Sleeping outdoors, too?" Snowy had spent last night with him and he'd remained indoors in his bed, but the night of the party Brandon had stayed in David's old room in Tom's apartment and the next morning when Brandon came into the store to say goodbye before driving back to Logan, he joked about discovering that despite a drizzle, Tom had taken his tent and air mattress out to the backyard instead of sleeping on the Sealy Posturepedic in his bedroom. Thinking of Brandon, she decided it was high time she and Tom discussed his number one son.

Tom said, "Well, until it gets colder. Then I'll be tucked up snug in bed. I'm supposed to go through a period of depression—" He saw the awful look on Snowy's face. "No, Snowy, no, not *clinical* depression, don't worry a minute about that! It's all a matter of adjusting to civilization. I've adjusted fast to plumbing." He smiled at her.

Snowy smiled back tremulously. The waitress brought Tom's frappe and the coffee she'd ordered. Snowy took a scalding sip. "Ruhamah said Brandon told her he's going to be made a major."

"Yup. Moving up."

"After he gets a leaf or something pinned on, there'll be a party at the officers' club. He invited Ruhamah."

Tom absolutely goggled at her, and this time Snowy really did smile, he looked so stupefied. Men.

The waitress brought their meals.

Tom said distractedly to the waitress, "Thank you," and asked Snowy, "How old is Ruhamah? Twenty-one?"

"Yes. What's Brandon's love life been like up to now?"

"Damned if I know." Tom began devouring French fries. "He brought girls—young women—home more than David did, and I guess some lasted longer than others."

"What on earth made him decide on a military career?"

"For one thing, it helped pay college costs. For another, he gets along with my brothers, saw their lives in the Army. Maybe he saw how messy my life was by comparison, how pissed off I was at public education, then my venture with the coffins, so he went for an organized life. Hell, I don't know. Once he was in, he got hooked on flying."

"Ruhamah is talking of cutting a few classes and going, maybe taking a side trip to visit Puddles. If I'll okay the expense. I gather Brandon wanted to pay for the flight and everything, but she isn't having any of that."

"So. So Brandon has fallen for Ruhamah. Well," Tom said gallantly, "who can blame him, she's your daughter."

"I don't suppose there's anything for us to do except sit back and wait."

"Same as with the trial of the Old Man Bomber."

ON THE RAINY morning of Wednesday, November 4, Dudley phoned Snowy in the store, not in her apartment, something he'd never done. "Got a minute between customers?" he asked. "I just wanted to gloat with you!"

She said, "Clinton won! A Democrat in the White House after all these years!"

"Isn't it incredible?"

Snowy looked at the headlines on the newspapers stacked near the cash register, on the newspapers being read by people having coffee. "But our generation was skipped over. From George Bush to Bill Clinton. We're missing in between; we're 'the disappeared' again." Immediately she regretted the observation. If Dudley had fulfilled his youthful ambition, he would have been the United States president to represent their generation.

Dudley quoted Wordsworth. "'Where is it now, the glory and the dream?'" Then he said, "But we keep on in our way, don't we."

Desperate with remorse, she said, "Let's not allow us to get skipped over in Gunthwaite. Why don't you run for mayor next year?"

"Does my political advisor know that Gunthwaite hasn't had a Democratic mayor in sixteen years?"

"All the more reason. But Dudley, would you still be able to handle your painting business if you won?"

"Oh sure. Mayors of Gunthwaite have regular jobs. Mostly lawyers. Being mayor doesn't pay much. As for the time involved, well, since I became councilor, more and more of the business is being handled by Johnny and Arlene"—two of Dudley and Charl's children, Johnny's father having been Jack O'Brien—"so, well, hmm," he mused. "There's general goodwill toward this Democratic member of the Silent Generation, thanks to you and the high-school rehabbing. But..."

"We've got to keep trying." Lowering her voice, she told him what she hadn't told anybody else, not even Tom. "I've put together a collection with that Old Man sequence for the grabber, and I've sent it to a New York publisher first, a big place that still publishes some poetry, and then I'll try it at the small presses."

"Good for you! Okay. Nothing ventured, nothing gained. D. J. is itching to run another campaign. I'll tell him what I'm considering. How's Ruhamah?"

"Busy at school. Sorry, I've got a customer, gotta go. Give Charl my love." Snowy hung up and rang up Arthur Bronson's purchases, making conversation with this landlord of Tom's while wishing that Ruhamah had been as forthcoming about her visit to Fort Stewart, Georgia, as she had been about her side trip to Hilton Head Island. The island, Ruhamah said, did have a rarefied atmosphere, and Puddles's house really was beautiful. Both of Puddles's twins had made the effort (probably browbeaten by Puddles) to drive there to meet Ruhamah over dinner. Ruhamah had taken many photos of the occasion, and Puddles had sent some more, which supplemented those Puddles had already sent of the house, so this part of Ruhamah's trip was well-described and well-documented but all Ruhamah said about the rest was that seeing a military base was enlightening; she hadn't taken any pictures. "And," Snowy had told Tom, "after the officers'-club party, Ruhamah supposedly stayed at a motel where Brandon had reserved a room for her, and that's all I know." Snowy and Tom had then attempted not to envision what they themselves would've got up to. Tom didn't mention that David had told him Joanne had not been happy to learn from guileless Lavender that Brandon had invited Snowy's daughter, of all people.

As Christmas approached, Snowy phoned Bev and said, "Hooray, hooray, Tom and I are staying at the Alpine Avens this Christmas Eve. Evidently Lavender and David have calmed down about the wonders of baby Elizabeth, so Tom doesn't feel obliged to go to their house for Christmas. Joanne will, I suppose."

"And Brandon?" Bev asked, fascinated by this development between Snowy's and Tom's offspring. Brandon was a handsome pilot; how could Ruhamah resist?

"Tom hasn't heard that he's coming. Ruhamah is going to Harriet's as usual. Is Roger due?"

"I can't wait to see him! Isn't that funny?"

The day after Christmas, Tom remarked to Snowy, "David says Brandon didn't come to their Christmas. Says he's in New York for a few days. Then he's leaving Fort Stewart. Going to Korea. They use those planes a lot there, for localized spying."

Snowy and Tom looked at each other.

Snowy said, "Couldn't he have chosen somewhere less dangerous?"

"He's in the Army. Maybe he didn't have much of a choice. It's only for a year."

When Ruhamah returned from Harriet's, she made no mention of having seen Brandon in the city. She talked of business trends and sight-seeing and showed Snowy a new outfit she'd bought. While they were watching the evening news, Snowy commented, "Tom has heard that Brandon will be off to Korea."

"A career move," Ruhamah said.

Snowy said, "His poor mother."

Ruhamah went into her bedroom to catch up on her studying.

Puddles phoned and said, "Guy gave me a kitten for Christmas. Isn't that just like a man? He didn't consult me, he didn't ask if I wanted to take on another goddamn cat, because of course I'll be the one dealing with cat food and kitty litter; he just went out and got it and put a fucking red ribbon on it."

"What have you named it?"

"It's a she. Well, she's ginger with these black paws that look like pom-poms, so what could I do but name her Pom-Pom?"

Later, after the holidays when Ruhamah was back at UNH, Harriet phoned Snowy and said, "I hope I didn't neglect Ruhamah too much during this visit. Nathan was here from Israel, and we were hanging his latest show at the gallery, but she seemed to keep herself busy with shopping and sight-seeing."

"She had a great time, as always. Thank you, Harriet."

"Do you have an up-to-date passport?"

"Me? God, no, it must've expired decades ago."

"Renew it."

"Why?"

"You'll see. Don't mention this to Ruhamah."

Dying of curiosity, imagining possibilities, Snowy went to the post office for an application.

Bev phoned the next Sunday morning and yowled, "Runner-up! I'm a pathetic runner-up, I came in second!"

"Oh hell," Snowy said. This year the Plumley Salesperson of the Year prize was a trip to New Orleans. "But that's better than last year's third place."

"Feh!"

"Did Lorraine Fitch win again?"

"Yes. Snowy, I keep telling myself over and over that this is like high school and stupid! I've got very good at selling in these past five years, I'm earning a nice living, and that should be enough, but I want the damn award!"

"I wish Geoffrey Plumley could be less honorable and let you know ahead of time so you're not left in suspense until the banquet. Why don't you ban those Manchester trysts unless he tells you when he's got the final figures?"

"Damnit, maybe I just will! But it doesn't sound very liberated. It sounds like time-honored feminine wiles. And it's not businesslike. I have to be businesslike with Geoff. It's wonderful how he's not jealous of my work, the way Roger is. Geoff would be crazy if he were jealous; my work makes him money. And if I keep it businesslike, I'm still sort of being faithful to Roger. What was that poem about 'faithful in my fashion'?"

"By Ernest Dowson," said Snowy the scholar, "it's the poem that 'gone with the wind' comes from," and Snowy the best friend said, "You'll win next year."

Bev said gloomily, "Not unless Lorraine Fitch drops dead."

"You will win."

"Do I even want a trip? If I went anywhere, I might miss a customer, a listing, a sale. I'm addicted, Snowy. Oh—I forgot the other news. Leon has moved out. At age twenty-seven, he's decided it's time to leave home, and he's moved in with the latest girlfriend. She lives in that housing development that went in where the sandpit used to be."

The sandpit, Snowy thought.

"So," Bev said, "after Etta leaves for college next fall, my nest will be empty. I've joined you and Puddles."

Snowy didn't point out that Leon seemed the type who'd keep returning to the nest.

Late in January her new passport arrived, but in the same mail there was a letter that made her completely forget Harriet's mystery. She usually opened her personal mail during the few minutes she spent in the apartment for lunch, a hasty procedure of slitting envelopes while she ate, and this day she was in enough of a rush that she didn't notice the return address, so the letter, when she unfolded it, struck without warning.

Wingfield Press, in New York, wanted to publish her *Tapestry Granite* collection. A Wingfield editor, Kara Prescott, wrote that they were very excited about it and were offering an advance on royalties of three thousand dollars. Kara looked forward to hearing from her.

Snowy collapsed.

Why was she sobbing her eyes out over such happy news? Why was she suddenly tired, so tired, as if she had been quarrying and lugging blocks of that granite for years and years and years?

"HYPE," SHE SAID to Tom, after she'd dried her eyes and rushed to the barn only to start crying all over again as he danced her around the workshop floor. "I sent copies of the most lurid newspaper stories along with the poems. Anything to get their attention! Did they decide because of the poems' merit or because of my notoriety?"

"Notoriety isn't the right word," he said. "You're a heroine! And who cares why they bought the book? In this case, the end justifies the means."

"I won't believe it's true until I see the contract. We won't tell anybody until the contract arrives, *if* it does. I've got to get back to the store so Irene can go to lunch."

"How about dinner at the Gilmore House tonight?"

"Let's wait until I have a contract to sign."

Tom said, "Um, with your contracts for your other books, did you have a lawyer look them over?"

She said slowly, "No. I knew Commonwealth Publishing so well, because I'd worked there summers and Bennington's Non-Resident Terms. I'd typed some of their contracts myself. I didn't use an agent or a lawyer."

"Maybe it's something to think about."

That evening, Snowy wrote back to Kara Prescott, trying not to be effusive and overly grateful (though Kara must know that Snowy would give Wingfield Press her firstborn in gratitude), aiming for a tone that was professional and dignified, yet enthusiastic. After many drafts, she still feared the letter sounded gauche, from a New Hampshire hick, but finally, exhausted, she gave up and mailed it the next morning without rewriting it one more time.

In the days that followed, the world seemed to be flickering like an old television screen and she couldn't catch her breath. Had she gone mad and imagined the letter from Wingfield Press? Occasionally she dashed from the store up to the apartment to take it out of her desk drawer and reread it. The letter was real. The words had made the same sense to Tom as they had to her. She wanted to show it to Alan, who had been with her when she received the letter saying her first collection had been accepted by Commonwealth. She had dedicated all her previous books to Alan; *Tapestry Granite* was dedicated to their daughter.

A week later, Tom and Snowy were notified that Kenneth Collins was pleading not guilty by reason of insanity to the variety of charges. The trial, a bench trial with only a judge, no jury, would start on March 15. Snowy said with relief, "Before the season begins," having feared she'd be obliged to leave Ruhamah and Irene to cope with summer people and tourists. Tom said, "Before the fire-tower work starts." He had been able to get the Pascataquac job back, because one season of fire-warden duty was more than enough for the guy who'd taken the job last year.

In the next day's mail came a fat envelope from Wingfield Press. It contained a letter from Kara saying how much she looked forward to working with Snowy, and two copies of the contract.

Tom said, "I'll make reservations at the Gilmore House!"

"No," Snowy said, trying to breathe, "no, I don't dare. We'll wait until I get my copy back with their signatures. *If* I do. But before I return them—I've been thinking over what you said, and I guess I'll ask Jason Ellsworth to check the contracts."

She phoned the law firm's receptionist and arranged an appointment for the next afternoon, when she left Irene in charge of the store and drove to Gunthwaite to her old house, the present premises of Hayes, Smith, & Ellsworth. The first time she'd come here, after Alan's death, she'd been confused by the redesign of the interior, but when she had entered Jason's office she'd got her bearings, realizing it occupied what had once been the kitchen, her mother's kitchen of white-painted wooden cupboards, dark-red linoleum, white-and-red dotted Swiss curtains, and the rooster collection. Now, while Jason went over the contracts, she sat on the other side of his impressive desk and thought of how upstairs, in her old bedroom, she had written her first poems.

After Jason okayed the contracts, she drove home composing the letter to Kara that would accompany them when she mailed them back. It was a bit easier to write than the previous one.

But then the days of waiting stretched the elastic band of tension until Snowy thought she'd snap and ricochet around the store.

Tom was afraid she would have a stroke. Trying to divert her, he insisted she go snowshoeing with him; he asked her to show him how to roast a chicken; he told her that according to David, who had heard it from Joanne, Brandon was now in Korea; he made love to her; and he even gave her his AT journal to read, something he'd never intended to do.

Reading the notebook, Snowy found a meticulous record of his daily mileage, lists of flora and fauna, notes about amusing comments he'd read in the logbooks of shelters, cryptic notes over which she puzzled ("spark-plug gaps"; "band saw"; "Susan Hayward"—*Susan Hayward?* As far as she ever knew, Kim Novak had been his favorite actress), and she thought there was nothing about Libby, until she came to a page on which Tom had jotted down from memory a poem, Snowy's first poem, written at age sixteen. He was an English teacher and could have remembered many famous lines on the subject, but he had written down this:

Death:
Save it will wait
Until this life
That moves so fast
Gives time
For dreams to last
And least of all
Be something more
Than merely dreams
Dreamed before.

Snowy's contract was returned, signed. As she ran from the store to Tom's barn this lunchtime, she gulped great lungfuls of the wintry air and everything shifted into focus, steady. But the weight of granite remained, through another barn dance with him, through phone calls to Ruhamah, Bev, Harriet, Dudley, and to Puddles, who said, "How can you sound so calm, cool, and collected? You should be turning cartwheels!"

THERE HAD BEEN another snowstorm on March 13, with two feet of new snow drifting to four in places, so on the sunny fifteenth, when Tom and Snowy drove up to North Haverhill, Tom at the wheel of Snowy's car, the trip on old highways seemed like a sleigh ride. Fresh snow undulated over the swells of fields and lapped around tree trunks in the woods. Paths shoveled out one more goddamn time were tunnels to the doors of houses. A plastic laundry basket, a sudden red in all the white, made Snowy think of blood, murder. Last summer's incident at Gordon Pond could have had a very different outcome. She dreaded this trial, but she should rejoice that she and Tom were alive to attend it. She reached over and rested her hand on Tom's thigh, and he linked fingers and gave her hand a squeeze.

In North Haverhill, they parked at the courthouse. Outside in the cold and inside in the lobby, reporters and TV cameras were waiting. It was like the "hot oven," that playground torture of her childhood when you had to run the gauntlet between two lines of kids hitting at you. Tom put an arm around her, guiding her forward through the crowd as he said in his teacher's voice to the reporters, "We'll talk with you afterward."

They went into the blond courtroom. Snowy had watched so many lawyer shows on TV, ever since *Perry Mason,* that the reality looked like a performance by amateurs. Lawyers said, "Uh" and "You know" too often and shuffled papers as if searching for their lines, which maybe they were. Chairs scraped. No jury, and no whodunit, for Kenneth Collins had confessed and everyone had agreed that he was the culprit and nutty as a fruitcake. Bev, Snowy knew, would have many scathing comments about the lack of drama were she here.

Kenneth Collins smiled conspiratorially at Snowy throughout the proceedings and again ignored Tom. Snowy tried not to look at Collins, but she tried to feel compassion, pity. This creature, she thought, had jump-started her so-called career.

After the judge committed Collins to New Hampshire Hospital for treatment, Tom kept his promise to the reporters and he and Snowy held a little press conference in the lobby, which with its blond walls, big windows, and teal-cushioned chairs reminded Snowy of some libraries more modern than Carnegies in which she'd done readings. "Yes," Tom said, "we're relieved at the outcome and hope Collins receives the help he needs."

A reporter asked, "Ms. Sutherland, what do you think about the possibility of parole after four years?"

Snowy hemmed and hawed, wishing she were Bev. The New Hampshire Hospital was located in Concord, and back when she was young, if you heard that anybody was "in Concord," you knew the phrase meant the insane asylum. It didn't sound remote or secure enough to her now. Finally she answered, "In my heart I want him to be released if he's really well enough someday, but in my head I want him locked up forever, with the key thrown off the Old Man of the Mountain."

Mirth and scribbling. A reporter asked, "Will you be writing a poem about the trial?"

"Well, probably, someday, one way or another. We poets, writers, we use everything, one way or another." But not Alan's death.

During their drive home, Tom said, "Okay, now we can turn our attention to your birthday Friday. Fancy dinner or fish fry?"

Age fifty-four! She wasn't a Comeback Kid, she was a Comeback Grandma Moses. If she'd come back at all. That Friday night after work, she and Tom went to the Friday fish fry at Peggy Ann's Place on the road to Gunthwaite, and in a cozy booth they pigged out on as big a treat as a Gilmore House gourmet meal, fried haddock and French fries and coleslaw. For the first time Snowy described to Tom eating fish-and-chips out of newspaper-wrappings in English fish-and-chip shops with Alan. Then, over servings of chocolate-pudding cake, she said, "Could you help me decide what to do with his things? It'll be six years in May. I finally should—his clothes—maybe Ruhamah will want to help with those now. But other things such as his toolbox, which tools should I keep for my own use, well, *your* use when you fix stuff at my place, and his skis and snowshoes and... Don't if it's hurtful to you, if Libby—"

Tom said, "Sure, I'll help."

When they returned to her apartment, he produced a birthday present, a laser-carved granite paperweight for her desk in her bedroom. Granite.

That Sunday afternoon, Snowy and Bev made a birthday trip to the Mall of New Hampshire, where Bev decreed, "*Not* matronly," and they scoured Filene's for a dress for Snowy to wear to Ruhamah's UNH graduation and one for Bev to wear to Etta's high-school graduation. Successful in this mission, they then stopped at Filene's Chanel counter, because one of Bev's wealthy customers, a woman from Boston whose purchase of an estate on Lake Winnipesaukee just might win Bev this year's Plumley Salesperson of the Year Award, had remarked to Bev that Chanel was the only makeup to use. When Snowy learned the prices, she nearly had a heart attack, but she deserted Revlon as fast as Bev for Chanel's Teint Naturel.

Returning home from this satisfying expedition, Snowy found two phone messages on her machine. D. J.'s voice said, "Hi, Snowy, I'm in Gunthwaite for the day and wondered if Ruhamah is home this weekend. We've been pounding the books so much this year we can't seem to meet up. Well, I hope she'll have time to work on Dad's campaign with me this summer."

Hmm. A while ago, Snowy had asked Ruhamah about D. J.'s plans after he finished law school this spring and passed his bar exam, and Ruhamah had replied, "He's already decided on a job offer from a Concord law firm." So Ruhamah and D. J. were sort of keeping in touch. Despite Brandon.

The next message was from Harriet: "Sorry I missed your birthday. I'm just back; had to go to Brazil. Give me a call when you come in."

So Snowy phoned her and said, "Brazil?"

"Buying for the gallery and doing some painting. Now, Snowy, about Ruhamah's graduation present. Let me do this. I want to. You and Ruhamah are going to Scotland. I know you both can't be away in June, so I'll come up and stay in your apartment and help Irene handle things and paint your village some more, while you and Ruhamah check out Sutherland and Edinburgh for a week. You ought to have more time there, but you'll fret if you're away longer.

When your tickets and itinerary arrive, don't tear them up. You and Ruhamah are flying from Boston to Glasgow. I'll phone her now and tell her. Good-bye!"

"Wait!" Snowy cried, but Harriet had hung up.

What the fuck was Harriet talking about? I can't go, Snowy thought, I can't accept such extravagant generosity. Presents of trips are okay for Ruhamah, but not Ruhamah and me. Besides, I'm necessary here in June, I'm indispensable, I can't go. Then she thought: Ruhamah's roots. And some of my own, for all I know.

Snowy's parents had never been interested in their ancestors, and their indifference should have induced an opposite reaction in her, but instead she'd spent her genealogical curiosity and research on Old Eastbourne families and houses when she'd worked there with Alan, and before that she'd devoted all her zeal to Ruhamah Reed's background and its influence on Ruhamah Reed's poetry. Now Snowy thought: My mother's maiden name was Chapman, my grandmother was a Wainwright, and wasn't my great-grandfather's name Boyd—hey, come to think of it, isn't that maybe a Scottish name? My father's mother's maiden name was Higgins, that's Irish, but what about his grandmother, and all the other branches on both sides of the family?

She rushed to her bedroom desk, grabbed a piece of paper, and attempted to sketch her family tree, suddenly ashamed at just how sketchy it was. She must phone Alan's parents to find out more about the Sutherland family tree. Excitement ignited within her. Then the prospect of getting into an airplane damped it down to dread. And driving on the left! She and Alan had shared the driving during their trip to England, but now she was still not casual about driving on the right here at home. Ruhamah had done some driving in Cornwall, but—

Snowy crumpled up the paper. Damn Harriet!

"THE TEN-THIRTY to Edinburgh," Ruhamah said, reading a sign in the Inverness railroad station. "Sounds like the title of one of your Agatha Christies."

"Platform Three," Snowy read, and she and Ruhamah walked along the platform to Coach B, found their seats, stowed their luggage, and sat down, Snowy insisting Ruhamah have the window seat. They waited to be transported to the last destination of their trip, their first ride in Scotland not in their rented Ford Escort.

A half hour ago they had left that car at the car rental garage, Harriet's travel agent having decided it would be easier to drop it off in Inverness and take a train to Edinburgh. As the train pulled out, Snowy opened a map of Scotland and marveled at all the territory that that Ford had covered since Ruhamah had driven it out of the Glasgow airport and headed north, unbelievably only last Monday. Today was Friday, and they would be flying back Sunday. She had not had a panic attack on the flight from Boston to Glasgow Sunday night; she had even dozed through a movie, while Ruhamah slept like a seasoned traveler. Nevertheless the flight home was a worry to be kept at bay, along with really ridiculous worries about Tom's missing her the way he had during Girls' State and thus breaking up with her. Of course she missed him awfully, though it was only a week, not six months on the AT. She worried about Joanne. She worried about the store, although it was in the capable hands of Irene—and of Harriet, who, after all, was a glorified storekeeper as well as an artist.

The morning was what was called "bright" here. She would remember better the mist.

Out the train windows were suburbs, then sheep and heather, then mountains and hikers. Even when the scene was empty of people or animals, it seemed overpopulated compared with the Sutherland area, where the worst of the Highland Clearances had happened, fifteen thousand people evicted so that the land could be used for the more profitable sheep.

A man maneuvered a refreshment trolley clanking down the aisle.

Ruhamah asked Snowy, "Cokes?"

"Fine," Snowy said, noting the trolley's menu of tea, coffee, whisky, shortbread, tuna mayonnaise sandwiches, cheese-and-onion sandwiches, packets of crisps. But their breakfast in their swanky hotel this morning had been of the thorough Scottish variety, in which oatmeal ("porridge"!) was just the overture to a magnificent symphony, so she reluctantly declined the opportunity to sample railroad-trolley food and bought two Diet Cokes with the money that had changed to decimal since she and Alan were in Britain and thus was easier to understand, but she longed for shillings and crowns and guineas.

Roofless houses. That would be the main image she retained of the trip so far, the small old stone houses bare of thatch, bleak and cold and abandoned in misty glens.

Ruhamah nudged Snowy and discreetly pointed at the woman in the seat in front of them and another woman across the aisle. Both were reading a pulpy type of women's magazines, and Snowy could see the titles of the engrossing articles: "Getting Older Doesn't Bother Me" and "My Doctor Groped Me."

Their first day in Scotland, on the left Ruhamah had driven the narrow roads past long lakes and stark mountains, on up through the scary mountain pass of Glencoe, scene of a massacre of Macdonalds by Campbells in 1692, according to Snowy's guidebook, until they reached a Victorian mansion near Fort William at which Harriet's travel agent had made reservations. Snowy had been prepared enough by Ruhamah's travels with Harriet to know that Harriet liked her creature comforts on the road, but this was the lap of luxury! The next day, up the Caledonian Canal Ruhamah drove, passing Loch Ness where they looked in vain for Nessie, bypassing Inverness, heading farther and farther north to Dornoch. Here, the travel agent had booked them into a fifteenth-century castle! That night they dined on salmon and Aberdeen Angus beef, and the next day they drove little roads into the Sutherland glens that Alan's father's family had been forced to leave about a hundred and fifty years ago.

Snowy had taken over some of the driving by the time they came to John o' Groats at the top of the map, a name with romantic wanderlust connotations—"from Land's End to John o' Groats," and Ruhamah had been to Land's End in Cornwall so now she'd seen both tips of Britain—but in actuality it was a drab place, a tourist trap, and they'd not lingered. In Bettyhill they stopped at the Strath Naver Museum for additional information about the Sutherland evictions and spent the night at an early nineteenth-century inn, talking of the burning of crofts, of deaths from exposure, of emigration.

Yesterday they explored their way south toward Inverness, toured the Culloden battlefield where Bonnie Prince Charlie was defeated in 1746, and located their next hotel, a mansion called the Culloden House Hotel, once a castle. After registering, Snowy read up on the details of this place and was flabbergasted to see the name "Forbes." The Forbeses, she read, had been prominent in Inverness and had bought this estate in 1626. They were not Jacobites; during Bonnie Prince Charlie's attempt to regain the British throne, they were on England's side. The prince had requisitioned Culloden House for his headquarters before the battle. Bonnie Prince Charlie had slept here!

The train zoomed onward past sheep and meticulously cultivated fields. Maybe someday, she thought, when Tom and I are as old as all the retired folks sightseeing here, we can come to Scotland and search out his Forbes background—and my Boyd. They would not, however, be staying in the caliber of place that Harriet could afford. Bed-and-breakfasts, the way she and Alan had done in England. Or maybe she and Tom could backpack here in their dotage. Stay in hostels. Elderhostels? She wouldn't have to pack dressy clothes and shoes for dinner, though it was fun to doll up with Ruhamah and be pampered beyond her wildest dreams. The train passed a firth. Swans!

The women with the magazines were now reading "The Secret of Beautiful Hair" and a summer fashions article.

Would she and Tom ever be able to retire from groceries and coffins?

The train ran alongside an auto-wrecking establishment, backs of an old housing estate, some semidetached stone houses. The city was beginning, but there were still fields, and a firth. Wait, was this *the* firth? She checked her map.

"Ruhamah," she said, "the Firth of Forth!"

"Almost there," Ruhamah said.

Housing estates; a shipyard. And then they were on the railroad bridge over the firth. Snowy looked at the regular bridge that seemed to span an impossible length. Eek!

The train crossed the firth safely and finished the journey at Waverley Station. Waverley. Like Sir Walter Scott's Waverley novels. She and Ruhamah were in Edinburgh.

In a black taxi, they craned their necks—Snowy exclaimed, "That *must* be the Scott Monument!"—as they sped to their last hotel, a short trip to a Georgian townhouse. While they unpacked, Ruhamah made tea with the electric kettle on a stand beside a bureau, and then they sat in green velvet armchairs at the window beyond the twin beds and ate the provided shortbread, and Snowy asked, "How do we Americans live without teatime?"

"We eat a Snickers midafternoon."

They laughed.

Ruhamah said, "Things always feel weird toward the end of a trip. Tired?"

"Nope," Snowy said, trying not to be annoyed by the youthful solicitude Ruhamah had displayed on this trip for her ancient mother. "Raring to go. Only one more day."

Ruhamah opened a map of Edinburgh. "There's not enough time left today to do justice to the castle. Let's walk back to Princes Street and gawk."

"Okay." Snowy got to her feet and picked up a list of suggested restaurants, thinking always of food. "And have dinner somewhere."

On the famous Princes Street of shops, more famous back when the shops were not chain stores, the hazy sun was in their eyes as they walked past Burberry's and Marks and Spencer and Edinburgh

Wool. When they crossed to the Scott Monument, a huge Gothic tower, they saw tour buses waiting.

"Hey," Ruhamah said, "want to take a tour? Get our bearings?"

This was something they hadn't done before, so Snowy said, "Sure," and they hopped on the nearest one, paid, and climbed up to the open top.

The tour wasn't exactly a success, because the commentary was recorded on a speaker, and although resourceful Ruhamah turned up the sound, it was still mostly drowned out by traffic noise. Nonetheless, for fifty minutes they saw some sights, Ruhamah took some photographs, and Snowy acquired a general feel for the geography and the contrasts, the Pizza Huts and Edinburgh Castle. Despite the many pictures Snowy had seen of the castle, it didn't look at all the way she'd imagined; instead of being high and aloof on its rock, it was crammed smack-dab in the middle of the city, the part of Edinburgh called the "old city," which was so gray and so—*old.*

Back at the Scott Monument, they consulted the restaurant list and went scouting down streets until hunger forced a decision, and in a small dining room decorated with a frieze of a poem about whisky, Ruhamah had lamb cutlets and Snowy salmon in a tarragon-dill sauce.

The guidebooks said that Edinburgh was a safe city, but Snowy was relieved when their evening stroll back to their hotel was over and she and Ruhamah were locked in their lovely room, drinking tea and watching TV. At last she admitted to herself that she was weary, that her constant vigilance about safety and her wariness about agoraphobia had just about reached its limit.

After breakfast, which included potato scones, Snowy and Ruhamah walked to the castle. They were fairly early, but already tour groups were milling around from various buses. Snowy wasn't quite sure why she wanted to go into the castle. Because it's there? You couldn't visit Edinburgh and not visit the castle. She and Ruhamah got in one of the lines for the tickets, paid, and went in. Snowy spotted a gift shop and laughed. Ambience! But then, realizing she hadn't done enough homework about the castle because she'd concentrated on Sutherland, she popped into the shop and bought a castle guidebook to supplement her *Fodor's,* along with more postcards to add to those she'd accumulated on the trip.

"Gatehouse," she said to Ruhamah, putting on her reading glasses. "Portcullis gate."

Ruhamah giggled and snapped another photo of Snowy as Tourist.

Up the stairs they climbed, looked at gun batteries, which induced melancholy rather than admiration, then went into the castle to the room where Mary, Queen of Scots, gave birth to the baby who became two kings, King James VI of Scotland and James I of England.

Ruhamah said, "It's a wonder every woman didn't die in childbirth back then, in a castle or on a croft. The hygiene, the damp cold, these stone buildings. Let's go see the Great Hall."

This hall was full of armor and weapons.

"Birth and death," said Ruhamah. "Had enough?"

"Yes. Let's walk the Royal Mile."

On this street that ran from the castle to Holyrood, there were tartan souvenirs, woolens, and shortbread everywhere. As Snowy had noticed previously on the trip, whenever you went into such shops, the immediate impression was of red, because of the Walker shortbread tins and a predominant color in the tartans. She window-shopped, tempted. Harriet was paying for all the big stuff, the plane and car and room and board, but Snowy was on a budget for the remainder and so far hadn't splurged except to buy a soft wool scarf for Irene, a Celtic brooch for Bev, and for fussy-eater Puddles a joke, a small tin of haggis. She *should* buy Tom a gift, and this was the last day. She went into a shop and bought a wool tam in the Forbes tartan.

While Snowy was making the purchase, Ruhamah studied the guidebook. "Did you know there's something along here called the Writer's Museum?"

"I saw it mentioned," Snowy said.

Ruhamah asked, "Don't you want to go there?"

The Writer's Museum, Snowy thought, was obviously a place to be avoided because it would make her work seem so paltry. But hell, hadn't she been looking at the grandiose Scott Monument, not that you could miss it? She asked Ruhamah, "Where is the museum from here?"

"On a side street back a ways. Lady Stair's Close."

They walked back toward the castle and spotted a tiny opening into some sort of enclosed courtyard, and there it was, the Writer's Museum, formerly Lady Stair's House, an old mansion whose turrets and chimney pots contributed to a very imaginative effect, appropriate to the present purpose. Hesitantly, Snowy followed Ruhamah inside. She walked through the Sir Walter Scott exhibit in the main room. She read how he had worked himself to death, writing to pay off the debt of his publisher. Robert Burns, a sign said, was upstairs, and with fear she climbed those stairs to face the emotions that seeing his work exhibited would churn up. But as she looked and read, what she felt was sick-at-heart pity when she learned that he had blithely sold the copyrights to his poems for next to nothing. Writers and money.

Ruhamah said, "They've got Robert Louis Stevenson in the downstairs room."

"Let's have a look and then go get some lunch."

"Remember how you read *A Child's Garden of Verses* to me over and over?"

And here, to Snowy's surprise, was the exhibit that most moved her, the Robert Louis Stevenson exhibit, of all things, here tears welled up, and suddenly she felt the strangest sensation of weight rising off her, a loosening, an exultation. For the first time, she thought of the upcoming publication of her *Tapestry Granite* collection with pure joy.

CHAPTER FIVE

"IT'S BEEN FUN," Harriet said early Tuesday morning. She'd deemed Snowy un-jet-lagged enough to resume work at the store, so she was heading back to New York and now stood on the stoop for a last chat with Snowy. Ruhamah was already down in the store.

Snowy asked, "Really? You've heard us rattle on about everything we did last week, but what about you? Did you really get all the painting done you wanted or did the store interfere?"

"I had plenty of time for everything. Even, as I told you, dinner with Bev at that Gilmore House. Oh—she taught me 'Vaa' in exchange for 'Feh.' How come you never said 'Vaa' to me?"

"You never deserved scolding," Snowy said. "And besides, you couldn't understand my New Hampshire accent, remember? What if I'd started throwing in French-Canadian noises?" She realized Harriet wasn't listening to her reply. Harriet was looking past Snowy's hanging basket of red impatiens, looking up the street, and looking anxious.

Harriet said, "Remember how Jared Smith invited me for a ride in his pickup? I took him up on it this time."

"You did?"

"He let me drive his truck, and I let him drive my car. Would you believe he has a hot tub out at that little cabin of his he built in the woods? It was heaven."

Snowy started laughing.

Harriet's expression changed to relief. The Dodge 4x4 was

speeding up the street. She gazed out at the village. "This is one of the most beautiful parts of the world," she said, and started down the stairs with her suitcase.

Snowy followed, saying, "I still can't even begin to thank you for the chance to see another beautiful part," although she and Ruhamah had been trying ever since their return Sunday night.

"Believe me," Harriet said, "it's my pleasure."

At the foot of the stairs, as Jared jumped out of the pickup, Snowy gave Harriet a hug, left them to their farewells, and went in to work.

Tom had hiked down from the fire tower and driven to the store last evening, when Snowy, up and about after sleeping all day, was going over with Ruhamah and Harriet the postcards and brochures and guidebooks that had to serve to illustrate their adventures until Ruhamah's photographs were developed. A quick kiss; no privacy. After work today, Snowy drove to the parking area at the Pascataquac trailhead, shouldered her pack, and climbed quickly, almost running up the trail past the overgrown cellar hole that didn't seem so old as it had before the trip to Scotland. But this farm like many others had been abandoned as had the crofts. Alan's ancestors had been driven out by sheep; these farmers or their children had left because of granite. Go west, young man! They'd gone, leaving New Hampshire's rocky soil for dreams of rich deep farmland. Breathless, she emerged on the bare summit and ran to the log cabin.

Tom opened the door and stepped onto the porch. He'd been watching for her.

With Alan, love at first sight. When she met Tom, she was a high-school freshman and he was dating Bev, and it had been "Wow!" at first sight on her part, while of course he hardly noticed Bev's little best friend. Now, a zillion years later, she still thought: Wow!

"Hi," she said.

He put his arms around her, backpack and all, and they just stood hugging tight.

Then he said, "Welcome home."

She shrugged the backpack off and flopped down in one of the two white plastic lawn chairs he'd carried up here to furnish the porch.

"Cold drinks," he said, and went into the cabin.

She sat, catching her breath. He had been building this porch when they had met up here. For the project, he'd used the old service road, which in earlier days of the fire tower the fire wardens had driven up in a Jeep, instead of packing supplies up on their backs. Then the tower had been closed many years, and during this time the road had become a forgotten overgrown path. Tom had driven his Jeep and a rented trailer partway up it, as far as he could get, unloaded the logs and lumber, and over a period of time lugged them the rest of the way to the summit. Once, when she and Tom were leaving the cabin together, he'd shown her the road and they had bushwhacked down, a fast direct route, no switchbacks to ease hikers' knees. If only, she thought, the cabin could have running water and the service road were still open and he could drive up in his Jeep all the way, bringing a toilet and plumbing supplies! To her, the outhouse was the cabin's drawback, that and sometimes too many hikers around.

She looked at the metal staircase zigzagging up the legs of the tower to the cab on top. Six years ago after Alan died, desperation and need had got her up those stairs to Tom, scary stairs she otherwise could never have climbed. Nowadays she went up them without dizziness just to see the view.

Tom came back out with two gin-and-tonics and a bag of Pepperidge Farm Goldfish Crackers, which he placed on the little white plastic table between the chairs. Sitting down, he said, "Hot dogs are on the menu tonight."

She said demurely, "Indeed."

He grinned. "I thought you should have an All-American meal."

Out of her pack she took the present she'd wrapped in tissue paper. "A souvenir."

Slowly he unwrapped it

"A tam for Tom," she explained. "The Forbes tartan."

He smoothed the fabric and tugged the tam onto his head at a rakish angle. "Thank you, Snowy."

"It looks perfect." It did.

"How was work today? Are you going to have an itchy foot, like me after the AT?"

"It's difficult settling back into a routine, isn't it?"

"Well, I sure the hell realized I'd better keep having this change of scenery, up on a mountain half the year. When I started the coffin factory, I thought it'd be so much better than teaching, where I was just going through the motions. But with this kind of woodworking, once you've got things jigged you do the same operations over and over. No wonder people cut off fingers. Snowy, don't look like that, David and I are *careful.* I just meant I realized I'm very lucky to have the fire-tower job." He sipped his drink. "Is your change of scenery at your desk?"

"I suppose." She tried to think how to tell him what had happened at the Writer's Museum, but instead she said, "You have a low boredom threshold."

"Not," he said, "with you." He grinned again. "Want to postpone supper?"

"Yes! Will you keep the tam on?"

THAT FALL, RUHAMAH returned to UNH to start her master's and share an off-campus apartment with a friend instead of continuing with dorm life, after a summer during which she worked with D. J. planning Dudley's campaign for mayor, received letters from Korea and wrote replies, and talked Snowy into adding submarine sandwiches to the store's menu.

"Subs," Snowy had complained to Bev over the phone. "Grinders. I'm making sandwiches now on top of doing everything else. I've already made all the sandwiches I ever want to make, in private life."

Bev asked, "Are they selling?"

"Are they ever! Ruhamah was right, damn her."

Despite this griping, Snowy didn't really begrudge the extra work. The weight that had lifted in the Writer's Museum was still suspended, and although she knew that as the publication of *Tapestry Granite* approached next year, she would be worrying about reviews (hell, she'd be writing the worst reviews herself, in her mind), she now felt that for the first time in years she was holding her head up, standing straight. Poet-storekeeper. When she'd eventually explained it to Tom, she said, "The inner voice, the critic, the worrier, has shut up, at least for the moment." "Like on the AT," he said.

And that fall Etta left for college, Mount Holyoke, which was Bev's mother's alma mater. Snowy remembered discovering Julia's Mount Holyoke yearbook in the living-room bookshelves at Bev's house one morning in seventh grade; she had sat on the floor studying it and had resolved that she too would go to college. Etta's horse, Prancer, also went off to college, to be boarded at Mount Holyoke's Equestrian Center.

Bev phoned and said, "The nest is empty. Well, nothing to be done about it except throw myself into my work absolutely completely. The Plumley awards, it's going to be an even bigger deal than ever before. Instead of just the awards banquet, Geoff has arranged for a two-day conference in mid-January at a Holiday Inn on the ocean, in Eastbourne. There'll be seminars and discussion groups and, don't laugh, inspirational speakers. And the awards."

Snowy said, "That mansion on the lake you sold, the condos, everything, you've got the best chance yet, with four months left in the year. Is the first prize still a trip?"

"To Telluride."

"Where's that?"

Bev sighed at Snowy's ignorance. "It's a famous skiing town in Colorado."

"Oh." Snowy recalled how she and Bev had hated skiing and had given it up in relief after junior high. "Remember how we used to say the only fun part of skiing was the cocoa at the snack bar?"

"This is *glamorous* skiing, with movie stars."

"Oh," Snowy said again, and added, "You'll win!"

Bev said, "I think I forgot to tell you that back when I started working at Plumley's and went to my first sales meeting, Lorraine Fitch the Bitch commented on how I was one of only two New Hampshire natives there. It was not a compliment. The implication was that we natives could never be moneymakers because we aren't real hustlers. Geoff came to my defense, or so he thought, by saying I'd lived away for thirty years. But Lorraine could be right. I'm never going to win."

"You are!"

"Let's pin our hopes on Dudley's winning in November."

In the primary, Dudley had easily won the Democratic nomination, because no other Democrat had bothered to make a try at unseating John Watson, Gunthwaite's four-term Republican mayor, who had been preceded by two other Republicans in Gunthwaite's recent history. Snowy said, "Well, to call Dudley an underdog is putting it mildly. God, how I wish I could vote in Gunthwaite!"

"You're doing better than that, giving him the endorsement of a genuine Gunthwaite-born heroine."

Snowy laughed. Ruhamah and D. J. had proposed this endorsement idea to her in a hesitant but determined fashion, figuring she'd need a lot of convincing before she would use her notoriety—heroism—for political ends. She, of course, had leapt at the chance to help Dudley.

Bev said, "I wish Mother could've been with me, helping Etta move into her room. She would have been so tickled."

"Yes," Snowy said.

Bev hung up and had a good cry.

As Dudley's campaign continued, in addition to writing and taping more endorsements, Snowy attended what Dudley called a "charrette," one of the meetings he had instigated as a councilor at which citizens discussed various community problems. The topic of this charrette was the future of Main Street, and at Dudley's suggestion she read her first published poem, "Sweetland," and then talked a little about how she and her best friend, Bev Colby Lambert, now a well-known real-estate agent, had worked as waitresses at the old Sweetland restaurant that had been razed and replaced by the Gunthwaite Savings Bank's drive-up window. She spoke of the yearning she felt for the Main Street of her youth, where you could buy just about everything you needed and see everybody you wanted to see—and some folks you didn't. (Amusement in the audience.) The next day, to unwind from all that, she got silly and wrote a campaign song by putting rousing new words to the Gunthwaite High School song. She sent it to Dudley as a joke, but Dudley and Charl's chorus of kids began singing it at every opportunity.

When Snowy and Tom went hiking the Sunday afternoons he wasn't at the tower, this year she learned to see autumn colors up close. Instead of enjoying only the vast vistas of foliage, she stood absorbing the brilliant red of blueberry bushes against delicate green lichens.

During the final week before the Gunthwaite elections, Ruhamah cut classes and came home to spend most of her time at Dudley's house (the painted lady having become campaign headquarters), working with D. J. who was playing hooky from his law office. The night before the election, Snowy phoned Dudley and said, "I know you're madly busy, but I just want to wish you good luck."

"I was going to phone you," he said, sounding uncharacteristically tense. "No matter what the outcome, I want to thank you. You made the difference. You made me see the possibilities of preservation, and that led to the focus groups and charrettes that have led to my 'livable communities' and 'smart growth' campaign."

"I didn't do anything except be a curmudgeon!"

"Yeah, sure."

"Good luck. Puddles says to tell you if she were in Gunthwaite tomorrow, she'd vote early and vote often."

This got a laugh out of him, and Snowy said good-bye, but as she was hanging up she heard him say in a low voice, "I love you."

She stared at the phone. Preelection nerves. She would pretend she hadn't heard. And what if she had? She loved him too. Old pals.

But she decided not to go to the painted lady after Gunthwaite's polls closed at seven the next evening. She tried to keep busy working on the store's accounts on the damned computer in Ruhamah's bedroom, but she was too distracted to be accurate and gave up. In her Martha Washington chair she hid in a murder mystery, an old favorite for comfort, Ngaio Marsh's *Death of a Peer,* staying up later and later, way past her bedtime.

The phone rang, and she raced to the kitchen.

Ruhamah yelled, "He won!"

THEN THE FIRE-TOWER season was over, and Tom was again down the street all the time. Snowy and Tom, each living alone, in separate households, though spending most nights together in one apartment or the other. Was this, Snowy asked herself, an intelligent arrangement, or foolish, or just lazy? She didn't ask Tom. As she left his bed one morning for her run through the village, she guessed what his reply would be: If it works, don't fix it. A pale full moon was fading behind the last rust-colored leaves and the airy bare branches.

For Thanksgiving, David and Lavender decided to take Elizabeth to Florida to meet her great-grandmother, Tom's mother, and they invited Tom. He had been feeling guilty about not seeing his mother since Libby's memorial service, so he flew down with them. He returned with the news that Lavender and David had announced that their second child was due in April. Snowy told him that during Thanksgiving at Alan's parents' house, she'd learned from Phyllis that Bob had lung cancer.

"Advanced," Snowy said. "Bob isn't discussing it. He's behaving the way my father did."

Tom asked, "How long has he got?"

"I phoned Puddles, who didn't sugarcoat anything, as usual, and her guess is he won't see 1994."

Tom pulled Snowy to him.

Alan's father died on Christmas Eve. Snowy found the message from Alan's sister on her answering machine when she and Tom got back from the Alpine Avens Inn on Christmas, a cold sunny Saturday. Margaret wept to the machine, "Mom is holding up so far. She's been prepared; not like with Alan. The service is Wednesday."

Tom asked Snowy, "How old was Bob?"

"Seventy-eight."

"My father was sixty-seven. That's beginning to seem very young."

"I'll have to call Ruhamah at Harriet's. I'll have to call Phyllis."

After Ruhamah came home and they'd gone to Eastbourne for the memorial service, Ruhamah proposed another change for the store, one that was more drastic than subs.

"Oh my God," Snowy told Tom in his apartment, "expansion. Ruhamah has decided we should remodel the store office to make room for more tables. 'A gathering place.' She wants to expand the idea of a general store as a gathering place. A coffeehouse can be one, and a diner, and she wants to combine them all. We'll do the office stuff upstairs, which we're mostly doing nowadays there anyway, on her—our—computer. Computers! She thinks we should have a computer in the tables area for people to play with, and she says we have to buy a fax machine for our own use and offer the service to customers. Me, using a fax machine!"

Tom said soothingly, "They're like a phone. You'll get the hang of it. You've already learned more about computers than I ever will." Then he asked, "Who'll you hire for the remodeling work?"

"Ruhamah talked with Jared about starting after New Year's, during the slow season. I have the final say about the whole idea, she claims, but what do I know? She's the one with the business courses. All I know is that Alan got too deep into debt. I won't do any more than we can pay for."

"Then that's okay. And Jared is okay, but I'll keep an eye on the carpentry."

"I won't add any more gathering-place features than we can handle. I won't hire more help. Ruhamah has told Irene about the plans, and Irene isn't thrilled, but she didn't up and quit."

Tom changed the subject. "David says Brandon phoned Joanne at Christmas."

"All the way from Korea?"

"You—Ruhamah—didn't get a call from Korea?"

"Ruhamah usually answers the phone when she's home, not me. I didn't overhear anything."

"Brandon is coming home, David says, to work in the assignment branch at the Pentagon."

"The Pentagon? Good heavens!"

"Well, a major is just a peon in the Pentagon."

But, they thought, Washington, D.C., was much closer to New Hampshire than Korea, or Fort Stewart, Georgia.

Tom changed the subject again. "My New Year's resolution is to restore the Chevy. I've begun phoning around to try to find parts for it."

The cream-colored convertible. Snowy said delightedly, "An antique, like us!"

1994. THE YEAR that *Tapestry Granite* would be published. One Sunday evening in January, Snowy was working at her bedroom desk on a list of people to whom Wingfield Press could send review copies, when the phone rang. She went into the kitchen and answered it, and Bev said, "I'm back from the conference."

Slow on the uptake, Snowy asked, "What conference?"

Bev said, enunciating, "The Plumley Real Estate Awards Conference this weekend."

"Oh yes," Snowy began babbling, "it was this weekend, I'm sorry, my days are all mixed up thanks to the carpenters and—" She fell silent and waited.

Bev drew out the dramatic pause, the suspense.

Then Bev screamed, "I won!"

"Congratulations, congratulations!"

"Lorraine almost won again, but I edged her out by a million! I'm the top producer for 1993!"

"Million?" Snowy asked.

"I won! Me, a New Hampshire native!"

Snowy realized that because of natural reticence about money, she'd never asked Bev for actual figures. "Um, how many million are we talking about?"

"I generated sales of eleven million. Poor Lorraine, she only had a measly ten."

"Generated?"

"That's how they calculate these things, adding up our 'sales activity.'"

"Everything you sold added up to eleven million dollars? Holy shit, Bev!"

"And next month I'm off to Telluride. I'll rent skis and boots out there, but I'm going to have fun *buying* my ski clothes and après-ski outfits."

"Mmm," Snowy said, racking her brains for any commission-percentage figure Bev might have mentioned.

Bev added, "I'm going to be accompanied by a traveling companion. Geoff."

"That's great, Bev. Everything's great. Congratulations!"

"I'm phoning Puddles next. Then Roger—I can't resist gloating. But I won't tell either of them about Geoff."

After Bev hung up, Snowy went to her bedroom doorway and looked at the review list on her desk. Pathetic. She felt the weight hovering above her.

When she judged that enough time had elapsed for Bev to have phoned Puddles, Snowy herself phoned Puddles, who said, "I'm hoping Bev'll win a trip to Hilton Head next, and you'll come with her."

"Um, do you know what a real-estate commission amounts to?"

"I wasn't sure about New Hampshire, so I asked her, and it's around six percent. But there are lots of variables, depending on whether or not you list *and* sell a place, or just sell it or just list it, et cetera, et cetera. The real-estate company gets half the loot. But still, if Roger wasn't already paying for Etta's college, I bet Bev could all by herself."

After they said good-bye, Snowy went down the inside staircase into the store and gazed at the gap where the office wall had been removed. Gone too was Alan's rolltop desk; Ruhamah had directed Jared and his crew to move it up to her bedroom, leaving hardly enough space in that bedroom to swing a cat. Looking at the changes being made, the disruption of the precarious security she'd achieved, Snowy felt fear.

UNTIL THIS YEAR, the cream-colored convertible had been stored under drop cloths in the back of Tom's workshop. Now it was bared, and in the evenings and on weekends Tom kept his New Year's resolution. His plan, he told himself, was to retain or restore as much of the original as possible, but not to the point of being stupid. He detached the engine, and a wrecker came from a Gunthwaite garage that rebuilt engines and picked it up to do a complete overhaul. Meanwhile, he bought a new clutch, spark-plug wires, coil and condenser, alternator, and new hoses, and took the radiator to a radiator shop for reconditioning. Only the dark red leather front seat, not the back, needed recovering; he had never been a backseat guy. The convertible top was shot to hell, cracked and disintegrating, so he had a new one made. He pulled the door panels off and replaced the window seals, he worked on the frame, he took off the fenders for repair and priming and then put them back with new beading, and after the engine was returned and reinstalled and the car was reassembled and registered, he drove it to a local body shop for rust work, new rocker panels, and a paint job. When the publication date of *Tapestry Granite* finally arrived on April 20, he had cleaned the interior and polished the chrome, and he drove Snowy to a celebration dinner at the Gilmore House with the top down.

As they raised their wineglasses to toast the book, he thought that he was more happy about *Tapestry Granite*'s publication than Snowy. That inner peace she'd found during her trip to Scotland had been disrupted. Her worrying was back; she'd fretted over the cost and consequences of the store's renovations this winter and lately she was braced for bad reviews, even though the prepublication ones had welcomed her return, calling the book a "comeback volume." Hell, he thought, what did anything matter except that at last she was in print again, her new collection published? He was so proud of her!

"To *Tapestry Granite,*" he said.

She echoed, "To *Tapestry Granite,*" and after they'd sipped, she laughed. "We should toast Kenneth Collins. If I hadn't clobbered him, if you and I hadn't saved the Old Man, *Tapestry Granite* would be gathering dust, in manuscript."

"The hell with Kenneth Collins."

"Well, interviewers will mention him in any interview I do. I ought to give him credit."

"Collins didn't write the poems, Snowy. And I'm not being naïve about the publishing game."

He watched her small hands smooth the tablecloth and touch the vase of daffodils.

She said, "When my first book was accepted, I thought it was because I had an incurable disease. I thought Alan had been told by my doctor that I had cancer, and he and Mr. Palmquist, the editor I'd worked for at Commonwealth Publishing, had arranged this pretense so I would die with a smile on my face." She raised her glass again. "To the insecurities of artists!"

After Lavender and David's new daughter was born two days later, Joanne came down from Newburgh that weekend to see the baby, who had been named Lilac. (Tom remarked to Snowy, "Thank God it wasn't a boy; they might've named him Pansy." Snowy scolded, "Tom!") Tom was off-duty from the fire tower, but he had already paid a call on his latest granddaughter to give her the mobile he'd carved, so he figured he could lie low until Joanne was gone, and therefore he was in his backyard raking the blackened wet leaves out from under the old apple tree when he sensed movement and looked up to see Joanne walking around and round the Chevy in the driveway, surveying it.

"Well," she said. "This sure brings back memories."

She was wearing jeans, a sweater, a Polartec vest. Many a time, he thought, she'd been naked on the front seat or at the very least had the damn layers of petticoats up under her chin.

Joanne remembered how they'd brought Brandon home from the hospital in this car. Their first son. Now she was down here alone to visit their second granddaughter. She said, "Lilac looks like my mother, doesn't she. More than Elizabeth does."

"You know I can't tell at this stage when babies are just blobs."

"Blobs!" She laughed. "So this is the new location of North Country Coffins. May I see inside?"

He leaned the rake against the tree and escorted her indoors on a tour of the workshop, knowing she didn't give a shit about it but was dying of curiosity about the apartment upstairs, which he didn't offer to show her. He said, "How are you doing?"

"I've had a good group of kids this year, but I'll be glad as usual when June is here."

She hadn't answered his real question. She glanced at the staircase, and then she walked out of the barn, past his Jeep in the driveway, to circle the Chevy again.

She said, "David told me Brandon will be coming up from Washington to see the baby. Do you think he'll also be seeing—that funny name, I can never remember it—Snowy's daughter?"

"I don't know. Ruhamah is at UNH until the end of the semester."

"She is? Lavender mentioned she'd graduated."

"She's getting her MBA."

"Oh."

They thought of their own struggles to get their master's degrees, the juggling of work and school and parenthood.

Joanne caressed a creamy fender. "Want to take me for a spin?"

A vision of all the possibilities flooded him, of a return to the beginning and this time doing right by her. But it was as much of a fantasy as was his swift practical calculation of where in the woods they could go parking without risking the Chevy's muffler system. He said, "That wouldn't be too smart, would it."

"No, I don't suppose so."

He wanted to ask: Do you ever date Victor or anybody? He wanted to ask: Are you still sleeping in Libby's bed?

And she answered one of the unasked questions. "I'm using Libby's room for my home office now," she said. "Just for that." She walked off down the driveway to her Toyota parked on the street.

When Brandon came to see the baby the next weekend, he arrived with Ruhamah in her Honda. She had picked him up at

Logan, and after the visit they drove off to UNH so that, they said virtuously, Brandon could spend the rest of the weekend exploring the changes at his alma mater. Tom listened to Snowy wonder how often Brandon might already have been able to explore UNH since his return to the United States, without Ruhamah's ever having said anything, and he wished he could go back to his good old days of vagueness about Brandon's females. Were Brandon and Ruhamah doing this just for the hell of it, to rattle him and Snowy? Brandon wouldn't, would he, knowing it was bound to upset Joanne? Was it true love?

For an end-of-classes present this year, Harriet took Ruhamah with her to Portugal.

Through the spring and summer, when Tom's schedule at the fire tower permitted, he and Snowy went for drives in the Chevy. He drove Snowy to her readings and book signings at libraries and bookstores all over the state, making himself scarce while she performed. He joined her for another live interview on Channel 9, but she did the newspaper interviews alone. She was busting her ass publicizing the book. Overcompensating for the years of agoraphobia?

During the summer, Joanne came to Woodcombe often to visit her granddaughters. Tom avoided her, but he was happy that he saw more of Brandon than he had in ages, thanks to Ruhamah. Brandon stayed at Tom's barn, sleeping in David's old bedroom, and thus Joanne finally got a look at Tom's apartment one Saturday. Tom was working up at the tower and learned later that Brandon had invited Joanne to lunch in the apartment, a peace-and-quiet respite for Grandma. None too pleased, Tom derived some satisfaction from replying, when Brandon asked if he could borrow the Chevy to take Ruhamah for a ride, "Remember when you called it 'that old clunker'? Not on your life!" Then he felt mean-spirited, yet he did not hand over the keys.

Harriet returned to Woodcombe, and instead of staying with Snowy and Ruhamah during her week's visit, she moved into Jared Smith's cabin in the woods. Tom decided that Harriet was worthy of the Chevy, and he took her with Snowy for a drive around Lake Winnipesaukee, the top down, Harriet reminiscing about her California youth.

While he was restoring the car this winter, Snowy had once inquired if he intended to show it off at antique-car shows and he'd said, "Good God, no!" But one evening on their way back from a library reading, they happened to pass a dairy bar whose parking lot was full of old cars. Cruise Night, said the sign outside.

Snowy exclaimed, "Could you turn back? Do you hear that music? It's Elvis!"

Tom had never understood the appeal of Elvis, and he'd been relieved that Snowy was only half a fan, finding Elvis's music but not his looks sexy. To Tom, the best singer of the 1950s and ever after was Tony Bennett. Yet he obediently made a U-turn and drove back to the dairy bar, where loudspeakers were thumping out "Blue Suede Shoes." His horrified eyes fell on senior citizens jitterbugging in the parking lot under the floodlights.

Snowy asked, "What's a Cruise Night?"

"I think it refers to the cruising that kids did in cars, like in that movie, *American Graffiti,* or like Harriet was talking about." He parked at the edge of the car jam, beside a Ford with fins. "We Gunthwaite kids, we never cruised, particularly."

"We just went parking." Snowy jumped out of the Chevy. "Tom, there's a Model T over there and a Volkswagen over there and a Mustang, but most of the other cars are cars of our teens—with 'Antique' license plates! I was making a joke when I called the Chevy an antique, but these owners are serious. Isn't it unnerving!"

Tom hadn't bothered with special plates. But as he too got out and gazed around, he was assailed by a strange sensation he'd never felt this winter working on the Chevy. He was part of history, for God's sake. And he really *was* getting old. For the first time he understood Somerset Maugham's comment about the infirmities of age being nothing compared with the burden of memories.

Nearby, a car door slammed shut, and Snowy said, "Listen to that! It sounds like a vault! Eek, the size and weight of these vehicles we learned to drive in, this Chevy, my folks' Ford—we were driving tanks!"

The cream-colored convertible had now been noticed. As Elvis sang "Heartbreak Hotel," people came wandering over, and Tom found himself explaining that he had owned the '49 Chevy since 1954, when he'd bought it the moment he turned sixteen and got his driver's license. He heard himself describing every step of his restoration work. As the atmosphere became too reverent, he was tempted to tell his audience that in high school this girl-magnet convertible had been called by the guys "the Cunt-Wagon," but he refrained, even when Snowy went off to the dairy bar's counter, out of earshot. He had never told her this, certainly not in her girlhood and not later, though he knew she wouldn't be shocked now and would find it funny.

She returned with two big drink containers, out of which poked straws. "Frappes," she said, "of course. Yours is chocolate; mine, strawberry. They aren't charging fifties prices. Almost three bucks now for a frappe, and it used to be thirty cents at Hooper's and Sweetland."

Tom said, "I remember when the price went up to thirty-five cents. Inflation."

"The music is getting to me even more than the cars. Do any places closer to Woodcombe have Cruise Nights? Does Gunthwaite? Would we want to go to another?"

"I think once is enough, don't you?"

Snowy nodded, but she hummed along with Elvis, "Don't be cruel, to a heart that's true."

IN OCTOBER, SNOWY came home from a hike up Pascataquac where she'd spent this Sunday afternoon in the fire tower with on-duty Tom and saw that her answering machine had two messages on it. She hit the Play button. Irene's voice, usually matter-of-fact, sounded almost hysterical: "Snowy, I won't be in tomorrow. Sorry."

Snowy felt a chill. Irene might get short-tempered during busy spells, but she never became hysterical.

The next message was from Bev. "Give me a call when you have a chance."

Ever since Snowy had learned this winter what Bev was earning, Snowy had tried not to behave differently toward her, but she couldn't help seething with envy. She hated herself for not minding Bev's money when Roger was doing the earning and Bev was simply spending. She lifted the receiver and tapped the number of Irene's little gray-shingled Cape on Center Road. No answer. Then she phoned Bev.

"Guess what," Bev said. "The nest isn't empty anymore. Leon has moved back. He and his girlfriend broke up."

Snowy said, "In one of Sarah Orne Jewett's stories she has a mother say sadly, about a son who's leaving the farm, that he was the one she'd thought would stay at home. Maybe that's what Leon is, a son who stays at home. On a farm, he'd be useful muscle."

"Leon could be useful here, if I didn't have to nag. Why can't males realize that chores must be repeated and you can't take out the trash once or unload the dishwasher once and that's it forever? But actually, Snowy, Leon *will* be useful. Ever since Telluride, Geoff has been getting more and more serious about us. More romance, less business. He's in love, and he's adorable, and now he's acting as if he's about to pop the question. He won't if he thinks marriage will include my son underfoot."

"You don't want to get married?"

"Do you?"

Snowy hesitated, reluctant to tell Bev that Tom had never asked or hinted. And what would Snowy answer if he ever did? Should she propose to *him?* Did she want to?

Bev said, "We're fifties girls. We're supposed to be married. And anyway, I am married, to Roger. That's useful, too. But it's getting so I have more in common with Geoff than Roger. Do I love him?"

"Bev, you know how I mentioned that Joanne was in town a lot this summer, seeing her granddaughters? I thought that would end when school started and she had to go back to work, but she came down this weekend to baby-sit. I can't help it, I don't like it."

"Joanne is invading your territory. Your turf."

"Well, I suppose I've got to share it now that her son and daughter-in-law and grandchildren are living here."

"And her ex-husband. Whatever happened with Victor?"

"I don't know. Maybe she associates him and the wedding plans with what happened to Libby."

"Did she see Tom this weekend?"

"He's up at the tower. She hasn't yet climbed Pascataquac to get at him. At least as far as I know."

"You can't talk to him about it? Tell him it bothers you?"

"I feel so ridiculous! Petty! He and I—we're us and always have been."

"You trust him?"

"Yes..."

"Yes, but he's a man!"

"That's just it."

Working alone the next day at fever pitch, waiting on leaf peepers as well as the regulars, Snowy felt doubt and suspicion curdling inside her. When at last six o'clock came, she locked up and dragged herself up the stairs to her apartment and looked at the phone. She should call Tom at the cabin and ask him what his intentions were.

The phone rang. Suddenly she was too tired to talk to any more people, Tom included. She let the machine take it.

A woman's voice said, "Snowy, this is Gert."

Irene's sister, mother of Irene's nephew who used to help out at the store. Snowy grabbed the phone. "I'm here. I just came upstairs."

"Irene found a lump yesterday. She went to the doctor today, and she's in the hospital now."

"Oh no," Snowy said. "Oh no."

"She's having a mastectomy tomorrow. The whole works; she isn't messing around."

A radical mastectomy. Not a lumpectomy. That was Irene.

Gert said, "She's worrying about leaving you in the lurch. We're trying to think who you could get to help you. If only my Darren hadn't lit out for Alaska!"

"Do not worry about the store, either of you. Gert—"

"Like I told her, it's not a death sentence anymore."

When Dudley phoned a month later for some political talk, he said, "Jesus, Snowy, you sound exhausted. Haven't things calmed down at the store until the holidays?"

"Not really." She explained about Irene's mastectomy. "Irene wanted to come back to work afterward, but she's finding she is too tired from chemo. These general stores need at least three people to handle things, but I'm still working alone. The one person who answered my ad was a sixteen-year-old girl who hadn't read it correctly, thought the job was just for after school, and wore a button saying, 'Please Do Not Disturb. I'm Having a Sexual Fantasy.' I gotta admit I rather admired that."

Dudley laughed, then said, "Hmm. I have an idea. What do you pay?"

"Six bucks an hour."

"I'll check with Charl. Maybe we can be of help to you, for a change."

"Many many thanks," she said, and when they hung up she wondered if one of his kids might be available full-time.

During the late morning rush the next day, as Snowy was ringing up purchases and taking orders for organic turkeys for Thanksgiving and exchanging gossip, she noticed a woman sitting at one of the tables, watching the scene.

Rita Beaupre!

Vivid Rita, wearing jeans and a red turtleneck, a red parka draped over her chair. Hair even blacker than in high school, rosy lipstick and blush and purply eye shadow, wow! But saucy titsy Rita, athletic Rita, the only one on their cheerleading squad who could do a split, had thickened so much that her waistline must measure almost the same as her once-famous bustline, and Snowy eagerly anticipated phoning Bev tonight to report that Rita's bras nowadays must need a block and tackle.

Snowy gave Rita a little wave, and when all the customers had been waited on, Snowy came out from behind the cash-register counter and walked over to Rita's table. In high school, after Tom had dumped Rita for Snowy, Rita had loathed her. Snowy said too enthusiastically, "Hi, Rita! Great to see you!" They had, after all, been JV and Varsity cheerleaders together; indeed, until Rita, a class ahead (Tom's class), had graduated, they were partners on the squad because they were the same height. Snowy sat down in the empty chair at the table. "How have you been?"

Rita asked, "Do you work your ass off like this all day?"

"The busiest times are early-morning coffee, then now, when the mail goes up at the post office, and then five to six o'clock, when people stop in on their way home from work."

"I saw Charl the other day. I took my grandchildren to the studio for a picture for Christmas cards."

"She must be terrific at that job."

"I told her how Mallory, one of my grandkids, is living with me now, so instead of waitressing at night I'd like to work during the day, only weekdays, not weekends."

Snowy, in her hurry to justify not having recognized Rita as a waitress, didn't catch Rita's implication and said, "Waitressing at the Parmigiano? I saw you there years ago, but it's awfully dark in there and I didn't realize until after." A lame excuse for not recognizing your cheerleading partner, even thirty-odd years later.

Rita said, "I recognized you. And Tom."

Snowy didn't know what to reply.

"So anyway," Rita continued, "last night Charl calls and mentions you're advertising for help."

Snowy stared at her.

Rita said, "I could give you a hand from, say, eight to two. Weekdays."

Rita Beaupre working here? Snowy did *not* want that! Then suddenly she could hear the imitation Bev used to do of Rita coming through the tunnel between the high-school buildings, greeting everyone with her shrill "Hi's" that rose to a smoke-alarm pitch when Rita reached Tom at his traffic post at the head of the tunnel. Involuntarily, Snowy giggled.

Pissed off, Rita jumped up from her chair. "I can make a lot more waitressing than you pay here."

Snowy said hastily, "I was remembering our cheerleading days. Didn't we have fun? I talk with Puddles on the phone now and then and we laugh and laugh about cheering." Which wasn't true, and too late she remembered that Rita and Puddles hadn't exactly got along. Snowy stood up, remembering how Puddles had told Rita that the squad would be better off if Rita pulled her megaphone over her head so the rest of them could be heard through her screeching. Snowy almost started giggling again, and gulped.

"Puddles?" Rita said, interested in spite of herself. "Where's she living?"

"In South Carolina. Rita, why don't you change your waitressing hours and waitress during the day?"

Rita's expression became uncertain. Under her brave makeup, she suddenly looked worn out. Careworn. She blurted, "I'm sick of trying to keep up with these goddamn young kids slinging hash. I was thinking that clerking in a little store would be easier. Allison, she's my youngest, she's Malloy's mother, she's getting child support and sending it to me for Mallory, so I can manage without the waitressing tips, and I figured..."

A customer was standing in front of the meat counter reading the list of sandwiches. Snowy moved toward him and, still trying to wriggle out of the situation, said, "It's probably only temporary until Irene Mason is well enough to return."

Rita said, "That gives me a chance to give it a try and see if it's the kind of job that would suit me in some other store."

"Um," Snowy said, "okay, then." She realized she'd better phone Charl and Dudley to find out what the hell had been going on in Rita's life since high school. Snowy didn't even know what her last name had become.

"Start tomorrow?" Rita said.

Snowy said weakly, "Great."

Rita put on her red parka. "I read in the paper about the lightning. Tom and Joanne's daughter. Awful."

"Yes."

"I read about him and you with that Old Man weirdo."

"Mmm."

"North Country Coffins down the street, that's Tom's place?"

The customer made his decision and said, "An Italian sub, the works," and Snowy nodded to Rita, who left. As Snowy sliced open the sub loaf, she wondered to what degree Tom's nearby presence had influenced Rita's decision to apply for a job at the Woodcombe General Store. Joanne, and now Rita. Christ almighty! She glanced out the window and saw Rita driving away in a red convertible that was not an antique.

During supper at Tom's, she told Tom about Rita, and lo and behold, Tom knew some of the details of Rita's past, thanks to a visit to his tower by Adele and Sam Page a few summers ago. Tom didn't say so, but Snowy guessed Adele had been trying to fix him up with Rita. The nerve! Later, while Tom was watching TV, she phoned the Washburn house and got Charl, who filled in the blanks: "Rita kept her ex-husband's name, Henderson. She's had plenty of boyfriends, Snowy, but she never remarried, Dudley says probably because the guys were mostly already married, like Paul Henderson was when she met him. She supported her three kids—two girls and a boy—by waitressing, and now finally the kids have jobs and are married and settled so Rita could kind of relax and maybe move out of that duplex she's been renting on Junction Street all these years, maybe rent a nice condo, and maybe have a permanent relationship with some decent *single* guy, but what happens? Allison gets divorced and takes off with a new boyfriend for a new job in Atlanta, and neither Allison's boyfriend or Allison's ex wants little Mallory, so Allison asks Rita to look after her. Naturally, Rita had to say yes. Mallory is six and cute and the best-behaved of those grandchildren of hers Rita brought into the studio, but still, imagine having a six-year-old to take care of again!"

Snowy next phoned Bev, who said, "Rita Beaupre? Feh!" and then added gleefully, "I'll bet her bras have flying buttresses!"

Jealous and flat-chested in high school, Snowy and Bev might have had to bide their time like the Count of Monte-Cristo to get revenge, yet it was worth it.

Snowy phoned Puddles, who sputtered, "Have you gone cuckoo? Well, you sure are a glutton for punishment, letting yourself in for all that yakking all day long." Then Puddles went on to report about her doctor daughter, "Amy's taste in men keeps becoming more interesting. She met the latest at a supermarket. He has a shopping-cart care business; he goes around cleaning and repairing shopping carts. She stopped to tell him what a great service this is and how we all hate carts with thumpy broken wheels, and they got talking, and violins!"

When Ruhamah came home for Thanksgiving vacation, upon meeting Rita she was at a loss and somewhat stunned by her makeup and chatter, until Dudley and Charl were mentioned and Rita remarked that her son had been in D. J.'s class in high school. Then Ruhamah pigeonholed her as one more parent from Snowy's bunch of old GHS friends, and after that she only felt relief that Snowy had a capable helper again at the store.

Alan's mother and sister had decided not to cook this year, so instead of going to Alan's parents' house, with Bob now missing from the dinner table as well as Alan, Snowy and Ruhamah met Phyllis and Margaret and Howard at an Eastbourne restaurant.

Snowy figured Rita wouldn't be able to work during holidays, with her granddaughter out of school, but during Thanksgiving vacation and also Christmas vacation, while Ruhamah was making her Christmas visit to Harriet's in New York, Rita parked Mallory at a day-care center and pitched in. Of course, working meant Rita got to see Tom, whose most ordinary comment she seemed to interpret as flirtation from the Fabulous Fifties. Snowy was amused. Mostly. Tom thought: One thing's still the same; Rita still talks a blue streak.

Irene, who came in to shop and chat, was delighted not to have to worry anymore about Snowy's working alone and at last told her, "I think I'm done work for good. Time to stop and smell the roses."

So what could Snowy do? She consulted Ruhamah, who said, "Rita works hard and she's reliable. And you and she have an excellent rapport."

Snowy gaped. Rapport? It was a matter of manners on her part and tenacity on Rita's.

Ruhamah said, "Let's hope she wants to make it permanent."

The next morning, during a lull, Snowy asked Rita, "Would you like to work here permanently?"

Rita took her sweet time replying. She refilled a coffee urn; she reorganized the muffins on the plate under the glass dome. Then she shrugged, heaving her massive bosom, and said, "Okay."

"LORRAINE WON," BEV said over the phone one Sunday night in January. "I lost. I came in second."

"Oh damn, Bev," Snowy said, "I'm so sorry," and as she spoke she did a quick search of her soul and found that she really meant it. The Plumley Real Estate Awards Conference had been this weekend.

But then Bev's tone changed from discouragement to ebullience. "Can you run away and play tomorrow?"

"God, how I would like to. Joanne was here this weekend. I am getting so sick of this. I should have thought David and Lavender would have had enough of her at Christmas."

"A free baby-sitter is always welcome, I guess. Let's run away."

"I don't think I can leave Rita handling the store alone."

"She may have to do it sometime, Snowy, in an emergency or whatever. It'll be a rehearsal for her. I'm checking a property up your way tomorrow morning, and then I'll stop at the store and buy a couple of your subs to take out and we'll go have a picnic. I've got something to show you."

"What is it?"

"You'll have to come along to find out."

"Rita leaves at two."

"I'll return you by then. Please, Snowy!"

"What kind of sub do you want? On the house."

Monday was a cold biting day under a lid of gray sky. Customers only came in for vital necessities, so Snowy grew less anxious about leaving Rita alone. Rita, it was obvious, was looking forward to ruling the roost—and to seeing Bev, who made an entrance worthy of the occasion, striding tall into the store wearing an outfit of long leather coat and high-heeled suede boots that cut Rita and Snowy down to pygmies.

"Rita!" Bev exclaimed, and enveloped her in a hug.

Jack O'Brien, thought Snowy, reaching into the deli case for the paper bag containing their picnic. That's what Bev and Rita had in common, dating big fullback Jack before he ended up marrying Charl.

Rita said, "So you're selling real estate these days. I've been paying rent most of my life, but I've gone out with a couple of realtors and I know it takes a lot of work but now and then you strike it rich." She glanced out the window at the Mercedes. "Looks like you're doing okay."

"It's secondhand," Bev said.

Rita said, "So's my Chrysler convertible. I've bought convertibles ever since they started making them again. Back when we used to ride around in a convertible in high school"—sidelong glance at Snowy—"we didn't even have seat belts, and now here I am with children's seats in the back for my grandkids! I asked Snowy, and she said you don't have grandchildren?"

"Not that I know of," Bev said, and she and Snowy fled outdoors to the Mercedes. Snowy put the paper bag in the trunk. Bev flung her latest big leather shoulder bag into the back, started the car, and said, "Do you suppose one of the realtors Rita has dated is Geoff? I doubt if she would appeal to him, at least these days, but you never know."

"Geoff isn't married. Remember, Charl says she tends toward married men."

The interior of the Mercedes felt like an office, with papers and pamphlets on the backseat. As they drove out of town, Snowy pretended she was going shopping for a house, a whole house to live in again, a dream house. But she'd already had those, the remodeled fish house in Pevensay and then Hurricane Farm. When Ruhamah finished her master's this spring and came home, would she want to keep on sharing the apartment over the store? Would Ruhamah want an apartment of her own?

Out on the main road, Bev turned off onto a road to Lake Winnipesaukee and confided, "Roger has finally got around to acquiring a girlfriend. I'm sure of it. At Christmas he produced condoms, for the first time since I got a diaphragm for our honeymoon. Geoff and I use condoms, but I haven't with Roger. I told Roger that I was unlikely at my age to add a fifth child to our brood. He said something convoluted about our long-distance relationship and being adult about safe sex. He had some new variations in bed, and I don't suppose he'd been reading a manual."

"Are you upset?"

"In fact," said Bev, "it's titillating. Does that make me kinky?"

Snowy thought that in her own case, if Tom started fucking someone else, she would die.

Nearing the lake, Bev took Lakeside Road, and they drove through a winter ghost town of closed cottages, new ones with snow-heaped decks, old ones with porches. Then as they neared East Bay, the lots grew larger; more woods remained, pine boughs beckoning in the wind.

Bev turned carefully onto a narrow drive, and the Mercedes proceeded in a stately fashion down between snowbanks to a circular driveway.

Bev said, "Not quite a painted lady."

The big old summer cottage—camp, Snowy reminded herself, we used to call them camps—had shingles stained dark brown, its shutters and trim dark green. Understated elegance; subtle opulence. Despite its size, even in the winter with the white lawn in front and the white lake behind, it didn't stick out, proclaiming showplace, and in the summer, she knew, it would blend into breezy shadows.

Snowy asked, "This is the surprise?"

Bev picked up her shoulder bag and got out of the car. Snowy opened the passenger door and heard the trees lamenting overhead. Bev went around to the trunk, took out the paper bag, and walked to the screened porch that embraced the house. Ever so gracefully she climbed the broad front stairs. On the top step she turned to Snowy and posed.

Bev said, "This is Waterlight, and I'm going to buy it."

And Snowy saw the place as the correct setting, the perfect stage set for Bev, which the Blue Road ranch house certainly wasn't; this was even better than the Connecticut colonial she'd seen in photographs. Involuntarily, she exclaimed, "It must cost a fortune!"

"I can afford it. I've got an inside track here; Betsy and Kent Potter are getting a complicated divorce and have to unload. They live in New York, and they're skiers, so they didn't just use this as a summer place. It's winterized. I'll live here year-round. Leon too, until he decides to leave the nest again. Keeping this place up will keep him occupied. There are six bedrooms and four bathrooms.

In one wing there's a suite. Would you like to rent it? With kitchen privileges!"

"Huh?"

"You need a change, Snowy, as much as I do." Bev pointed to a sign over the porch door. It said: Welcome to the Lake.

III

CHAPTER ONE

INSTANTLY, SNOWY DISMISSED the idea. She turned it into a joke, and wasn't Bev's offer really almost a joke, some sort of token gesture Bev felt obliged to make, to lessen the difference between this beautiful house and the apartment over the store?

"Sure," Snowy said. "Invite Puddles too, and we'll be the Golden Girls."

Bev opened the porch's screen door, crossed the porch, and unlocked the front door. "Come in and explore. I won't do a sales tour; I'll use my subtle approach. Explore on your own and get the feel of the place."

With considerable reluctance, Snowy went up the steps onto the porch. Piazza, she thought. Years ago, it would have been called a piazza. The ceiling of narrow boards was painted sky-blue, a sort of tradition in some old porches. She walked slowly along the porch around to the back, where the house seemed to rise higher as the snowdrifts sloped steeply down to the shore—and a boathouse, brown shingles, green trim. Of course Waterlight would have a boathouse. What type of boat or boats were in it? Open water surrounded the dock, churned by one of those agitator gizmos. She looked farther out at the wide view of the bay, at the snowmobile tracks looping the bob houses on the snow-covered ice. Who the hell would want to live on a lake nowadays, with snowmobiles roaring past in the winter and those awful new jet-ski boats in the summer? You might as well live on a NASCAR racetrack.

She continued along the porch to the other side of the house, the ground rising to the level of the porch again, and on a flat stretch of snow she spotted a high rectangular enclosure of wire mesh. Holy shit. Making a full circle, she reached the front door, peered into a big hallway where Bev was turning up a thermostat, and asked, "Is that a tennis court out on the side lawn?"

"Won't it be fun? I'll teach you. Come on in. The kitchen is down this wing, and I'll be there when you're ready for lunch. Your suite is downstairs in the other wing. Incidentally, most of the furniture in this place is being sold with the property. Explore, explore!"

As Bev headed off down a hall to the right, Snowy forbore making another obvious joke, one about having to leave a bread-crumbs trail to keep from getting lost. She entered the house and closed the front door, a solid sound. For a moment she stood very still in the hallway, wanting to be back at the store, in the apartment, imprisoned, without choices. Then she tiptoed over to a tall water-worn buoy that was bolted to a wall. It meant depth, deep water. How could Bev dare to suggest she live on a lake, even Lake Winnipesaukee, the lake of her childhood?

Hung on another wall were some fish embalmed by a taxidermist and also some outlines of fish drawn on slabs of wood and pieces of darkening paper. Unzipping her parka, she read a few of the notations: "Bass, 18 inches, 3 lbs., Caught by Wilbur, 7/5/36," "Bass, 14 inches, 1 1/2 lbs., Caught by Joe, 7/21/65," "Pickerel, 18 inches, caught by Kate, age 6, 8/10/93." The other walls displayed framed photos of generations of people fishing and water-skiing and clowning and gazing soulfully at sunsets.

Suddenly she heard her mother describing a favorite bathing suit; Mother had bought it in her teens with the money she earned helping Grandma cook and clean for the roomers: two-piece, powder blue, wool.

A dramatic staircase, perfect for Bev, rose out of the hallway. Snowy crept past it, through an arched doorway into a living room bigger than her apartment and two stories high, with a three-sided second-floor balcony. Oh Christ, a moose! On a huge fieldstone fireplace, the great-antlered head of a bull moose thrust itself out. Quickly she looked away, remembering the moose in the spring dawn at Swiftwater Pond. After the moose, what struck you next about the room was the light, for even on a dreary winter's day an airy luminousness came from the white lake through the back wall of French windows, suffusing everything, the clusters of cushioned wicker armchairs and upholstered sofas on the various oriental rugs and braided rugs and hemp rugs on the wide-board floor, the bookcases of paperbacks and Book-of-the-Month Club selections and *National Geographic*s and bird books and wildflower books, the side tables cluttered with binoculars, birds' nests, interesting rocks and pebbles, the lake light finding all the nooks and crannies and, in the corners, window seats inside which, she knew, were stored Monopoly and checkers and jigsaw puzzles.

Retreating to the hallway, she tiptoed down the left corridor, past a smaller room with a squashy sofa, a recliner, and assorted chairs all aimed at a console television set, into the wing. Her suite. A sort of anteroom, the size of her apartment's living-room area, contained that type of desk called a secretary. She peeked through the glass doors of the bookcase on top and read the spines of paperbacks. Three Agatha Christies! Was this a sign? No, you idiot, she told herself. Every summer cottage in the world must have at least one Agatha. In the room there were also a slipper chair upholstered in green-and-white stripes and a rattan daybed with green cushions. Green and white, the Gunthwaite school colors. Could this be a sign? *No.*

She ventured into the bedroom. Unfair, unfair, it held that light from the white lake. In the summer, light from lambent water would be diffused through the shade of trees. On a winter's eve, there could be firelight flickering in the relatively small fireplace (no moose here, thank God), and you could curl up in that crewel-covered wing chair or the plump little loveseat upholstered in a blue floral print or on the blue padded window seat. The dressing table and two bureaus were old, the king-size bed newish. She suspected the bedding came from Garnet Hill, whose catalogues she had drooled over. She sat down on the bed and bounced. A firm mattress; extra-firm? She thought of how she and Tom had joked about his mattress. Tom, here in this room? Tom not right down the street but how many miles away? Fifteen? She smoothed a quilt folded across an old steamer trunk.

A door opened into a bathroom. A claw-footed bathtub, a shower stall. A wooden medicine cabinet over an old white basin. Photographs of sailboats on the walls.

Back in the bedroom, she opened a door beside the television set. The walk-in closet was the size of her apartment bedroom. On several hangers hung summer-people clothes, female and male. Talbot's. Orvis. On the shelves, a ski sweater and a wide-brimmed straw hat.

Enough! She ran back to the entrance hallway and down the right-hand hall, then stopped at the doorway to the dining room. In summer, you could hop up from the long table, go out through the French windows to the porch, and cross the side lawn to the tennis court and work off some calories. She remembered a conversation with Bev, back in Bev's Connecticut days, when Bev admitted she didn't know how many cute little tennis outfits she owned.

She found Bev where Bev had said she'd be, in the kitchen. Snowy blinked. Somebody had gone crazy with colors here, and in a wooden chair painted hot pink, her coat thrown off to reveal her outfit of a cable sweater the auburn that her hair had once been and a tweed skirt, Bev sat writing in a notebook at a bright red table surrounded by five other straight-backed chairs in dazzling shades of green, yellow, blue, orange, and purple. Other furniture, vintage cottage and new versions, a hutch, a rocker, a bench, some bar stools, sizzled in similar hues. The walls were dandelion yellow, while the plank floor was striped in sherbet colors. The cupboards had been painted blue, but this was just background for the wild variety of dishes on the shelves behind the glass doors. The white of the stove, dishwasher, and fridge could only be glimpsed under the bright magnetized potholders and dishtowels, children's drawings, snapshots, clippings. The toaster was scarlet, the coffeemaker emerald, and the blender tangerine.

Bev looked up over her glasses and saw Snowy standing mesmerized. "Oops, I forgot to warn you to shade your eyes before entering."

"And you forgot to warn me about the moose."

"Oh goodness, yes, you met Teddy!"

"You mean he isn't named Bullwinkle?"

"He's older than that. He's even older than we are! According to Kent Potter, after an ancestor of Kent's shot him ages ago the poor creature got nicknamed Teddy. Roosevelt. The Bull Moose Party, which I had to look up to refresh my memory. I'd like to get rid of Teddy, but I don't think I will, he seems such a part of the house. Mimi says she'll weave him a scarf. What do you think?"

Snowy took off her parka. "I think I'm ready for lunch."

Bev stood up and began to bustle around the kitchen in a proprietorial way. "I saw that you brought Diet Pepsis, but would you rather have a cup of tea now that you know I can provide one?" At the sink, she filled a brilliant blue teakettle; she set it on the stove, turned on a gas burner, and opened a cupboard door and mused, "Which color mugs for our picnic?"

"What *is* it with the frenzy of color here?"

"Betsy redid the kitchen last summer. She'd just found out about the women in Kent's life in New York, and her first reaction was to pick up a paintbrush. By the time she'd finished redecorating, he was involved with a woman on the lake, and Betsy learned there'd been other summer flings, and she came to her senses, packed up the kids, and went home to a lawyer. Oh, let's just match our eyes," Bev said, and lifted down a blue mug and a green mug. From a red-and-gold chinoiserie tea caddy, she took two tea bags, realizing that Snowy was following her motions as if she were performing some unknown ritual.

Kitchen privileges, Snowy thought. Not my own kitchen. She asked, "Neither of them wants to keep the cottage?"

"Betsy loathes it now. Kent can't afford it, because of the divorce." The kettle whistled. Bev poured. "Awfully sad, but I'm being ruthless and taking advantage of the situation, with advice from Geoff, who also happens to have a buyer for my ghastly ranch house."

"That 'suite.' Was it where they slept?"

"I guess Kent did, toward the end, but it was Kent's parents' before they died, and then for guests. I'll take over Betsy and Kent's bedroom upstairs, and Leon has hoseyed the back bedroom down here, which has its own outside door. Etta can have her choice of all the others." Bev set the mugs on the table and gestured at the blue chair. "That chair will be yours!"

Hesitantly, Snowy sat down. "Bev, thank you for the offer, but I've already got a place to live."

Bev went to the fridge for the paper bag. "Did you see the dining room? We can have dinner parties, with Geoff and Tom and the twins and Dudley and Bill and everybody, and it'll be such fun!"

"I can't commute from here to the store. I have to be available, on the spot."

"You commuted from Hurricane Farm."

"That was closer, in Woodcombe!"

Bev set out the subs Snowy had wrapped in butcher's paper, the bag of low-fat potato chips, two packets of Snackwell fat-free cookies, and two napkins. "Has Ruhamah said anything about spreading her wings after graduation?"

"No."

"Then," Bev said, sitting down, "she'll be back in the apartment for good this spring. If nothing develops with the delectable Brandon. She'll be there on the scene to take care of the store."

Snowy bit into her tuna sub, chewed, and swallowed. Food

seemed to kick her brain into functioning again. "I've been wondering if she might want an apartment of her own now. Maybe she'd like to rent your suite-with-kitchen-privileges."

"I haven't offered it to her. I'm offering it to you. Snowy, you need a change. And imagine, living on Winnipesaukee! The lake has always been for *them,* the summer people, not for us. Remember that lake view from afar I grew up with at my folks' house? I am finally going to live on the lake, go swimming whenever I want, I'm going to water-ski again—"

"You said that's excruciatingly boring."

"Well, after forty years it'll be exciting again. I can at least give it a try again. Think of the quiet times, Snowy, just taking a cup of coffee down to the dock first thing in the morning and seeing a loon."

Snowy pointed with a potato chip out a window. "The lake isn't quiet. Hear those snowmobiles? Speedboats in the summer—"

"There's a nice quiet sailboat in the boathouse. There are canoes." Bev sipped tea. "You're thinking about Tom, about not living next door to him."

"And are you thinking that because of the Joanne problem, I should play hard to get?"

"Is that such a bad strategy?"

"In any case, I can't afford to pay rent. I'm already paying a mortgage for the roof over my head, so it would be wasteful to pay twice."

"I was only suggesting rent because of your pride. You could be my houseguest. But if you insist on paying—remember, you won't be paying for Ruhamah's apartment anymore, not to mention her tuition, so you *can* afford it." Bev's mug clattered onto the red table. "Snowy, look at the size of this place. It's wasteful not to share it with my best friend." Bev got down to the nitty-gritty. "And your presence, along with Leon's, will keep me independent. Geoff and I have been talking of this place as an investment I shouldn't pass up, but it's more than that. His condo is the way he likes things, compact and convenient. This place is me, mine.

But I'm afraid if I'm alone in it, or have just Leon around in these wide open spaces, Geoff will think I want him to move in, and come summer, with lovely weather, he'll want to himself."

"Alan," Snowy said, pushing back from the table, jumping to her feet. "Ruhamah and I went to Murray Cove once. But to live on a lake? I couldn't. I still can't go swimming. I couldn't live here and look at a lake, day in, day out."

Bev stood up and put her arms around Snowy. "My father and the other Marines killed in the third wave of the attack on Iwo Jima—when I was growing up, I pictured it as a big ocean wave drowning him. Those summers working at Camden, seeing the ocean every day, going swimming and sailing, that helped as much as reading about what happened at Iwo Jima and talking with Mother."

"Oh, Bev."

"It has also occurred to me that you and I are going to die too. We're turning fifty-six this year. Before we know it, we'll be sixty! I don't know what I expected I'd be doing at sixty, but I think I sort of assumed I would die young, tragically, like my father. Here I am doddering along selling real estate. In five years it'll be the millennium! Remember when we were kids and would figure out that we'd be sixty-one in the year two thousand? Remember how ancient that seemed?"

Snowy said, "I insist on paying rent. And I'll have to discuss things with Ruhamah."

"COOL," SAID RUHAMAH over the phone from her Dover apartment. "What furniture will you be taking?"

"I haven't thought that far. I just wanted to get your reaction. Heavens, Bev hasn't officially bought the place yet. If things do go ahead, I wouldn't move until you're back here after graduation and whatever trip Harriet is planning for a present."

Ruhamah persisted, "Are you taking your desk?"

Snowy thought of the fancy secretary in the suite and of her beloved old mahogany veneer desk. "Yes."

"Then I'll move the rolltop and the computer desk in there and turn your bedroom into our office."

Snowy wanted to say: Hey, wait a minute. She said, "I'll let you know if the sale goes through."

And she waited to broach the subject to Tom. Maybe she could wait right until spring. Swear Bev and Ruhamah to secrecy and not tell Tom until she had to. How was he going to react? Would he even give a damn if she no longer lived down the road?

A week later, Bev phoned her in her apartment before supper and rejoiced, "The closing went smoothly! I am now the owner of Waterlight! I'll be moving in with my pine cupboards and loon collection next week. Now I can tell Roger about this fait accompli, but first I'll call Puddles."

"Give her my love. Congratulations, Bev." Snowy hung up and turned to Tom, who was at the stove stirring one of his skillet can-opener concoctions, tonight's mostly black beans, corn, and tomatoes. "Bev has bought a new house."

"She must run across bargains." Tom reached for the TV remote and raised the volume of the TV, lowered for the phone call. They usually watched the local news while making supper.

Tearing lettuce into the salad bowl, Snowy hugged their domestic little scene tight around her. So what if she and Tom were as set in their ways as an old married couple? She loved this, didn't she? Why the hell had she let Bev convince her to disrupt her life? Then she thought of Joanne's probable arrival at David and Lavender's this weekend. She could drift along, or she could do something.

The newscaster was reporting an accident on a lake downstate. An ice fisherman riding a snowmobile had gone through the ice, but he saved himself, until rescue came, by hanging onto his beer cooler.

Tom began to laugh, glanced at Snowy, stopped.

Snowy laughed.

Tom said, "They should quote A. E. Housman about malt's justifying God's ways to man."

Snowy put the salad in the fridge and heard her voice say, "Speaking of lakes, Bev's new house is on Winnipesaukee, and it's one of those glorious big old camps. It's so big, in fact, she thinks she'll rattle around in it, even though Leon will be living with her. She has offered to rent part of it to me."

Tom's attention was back on his skillet and the TV news. "Hmm?"

Snowy remembered Puddles's comment about how most deaf husbands weren't really deaf. Tom wasn't a husband, her husband or Joanne's anymore, but she restated fortissimo, "Bev thinks it'd be fun if I rented a suite in one of the wings and moved there. A pied-à-terre. That way, Ruhamah can have this apartment to herself."

Tom reached for the remote again and clicked the TV off. He looked at her.

She said, "Maybe this Sunday afternoon you and I could drive over and see the place. It's called Waterlight, and it's winterized so Bev will be moving in next week, but—"

"Waterlight? Big brown-shingled camp?"

"You know it?"

"Saw it once from the water. Rent a suite?"

"You were in a boat?"

He switched off the burner under the skillet. Slowly he said, "Back in high school, a bunch of us were helping Victor get his grandparents' camp ready for that party after the junior prom, putting out the raft and stuff. The rowboat was going to Victor's house to be painted, but before we loaded it into a pickup, some of us went for a row. One of the places we saw along the shore was the brown camp, and Victor said it was called Waterlight. The name stuck in my mind."

"Are you ready to dish up? I'll toss the salad."

"Are you going to leave?"

After that party, Tom had abandoned his fancy-free life and given her his little gold football and his letter sweater. At last they were going steady. Snowy said, "Remember how at that party, Puddles got drunk and—"

Tom yelled, "What the fuck are you up to?"

She recoiled. He had never ever shouted at her before, and it was as if he'd slapped her across the face. Her skin stung, flaming.

"Huh?" he yelled. "You're planning to up and leave without discussing it with me?"

Slap, slap, slap! *Nobody* had ever shouted at her like this.

"Are you? Answer me! Come on, come on, what the fuck are you up to?"

Shocked, shaking, on the brink of tears, she said, low and reasonable, the rational person in a sudden madhouse, "Tom, you're jumping to conclusions. Bev suggested the idea, but she hadn't formally bought the place until today, so there hasn't been anything to discuss. Let's have supper and talk about it."

Yet his over-reaction intensified. "Why would you even consider it, for Christ's sake? Why? I moved an entire business to Woodcombe to live with you!"

She wanted to roll up in a ball to protect herself. She did not point out that he had first come to Woodcombe on his own, to work at the fire tower, nor that they weren't actually living together. Forcing back the tears, she smiled brightly and said, "Well, Winnipesaukee in the summer is tempting, isn't it, just for a temporary stay, a change of scenery."

This stopped him. He asked, "Temporary?"

"Like a vacation at the lake, but I'd still be working. What's that saying, 'a change is as good as a rest'?"

The phone rang.

Moving to answer it, Snowy gave Tom a wide berth, as though he had actually hit her and might do so again.

He said, "The way you put it at first, it didn't sound temporary."

Should she let the machine answer, so she could keep talking to Tom, keep revising and mollifying? She lifted the receiver. "Hello?"

Puddles said, "Wow, what news! Bev has promised to send photos of the place. Wish I could come be the third Golden Girl! Good for you, Snowy! This'll teach Tom not to take you for granted. In my opinion, he's been having his cake and eating it too, so to speak." Puddles laughed uproariously.

Tom had lifted a bottle of merlot out of a cupboard and was pouring some into the two wineglasses Snowy had put out when she set the table maybe fifteen minutes ago instead of the infinity it seemed. He gave a glass to her and carried his to the sofa and clicked the TV on.

If only, Snowy thought, Nurse Puddles were here to take care of her, to bandage her wounds and soothe and comfort. I am *not* hurt, she told herself. And if she told Puddles what had happened, instead of providing comfort Puddles would be ordering her to yell back.

Puddles was saying, "I would've bet you'd never budge one single mile away from Tom!"

Snowy said quietly, "Anybody would think the place is on the far side of the moon. It's only a few miles away. Nothing will change."

"Sure it will. Why don't you move there now, instead of waiting for summer?"

"I can't leave the store until Ruhamah is here."

"You left it overnight when you were living at Hurricane Farm. Most people don't live in their stores, Snowy."

"Well, maybe it'll be temporary, a summer stay. Waterlight is a very big place, and in the winter if Bev can close off the section I'd be living in during the summer, along with other empty rooms, she'd save money on heat."

Sidetracked, Puddles confessed, "God, I'm spoiled; I can't

imagine spending a winter up there ever again. I've got a little arthritis, and my bones ache just thinking of your weather."

Snowy looked at the back of Tom's head. *Her* bones were aching.

As Puddles began talking about her job and her grandchildren, Snowy tucked the receiver against her ear, turned the burner back on under the skillet, and dressed the salad with vinaigrette. She might not be physically hurt, but oh, she felt as if she'd been worked over with a tire iron. All her worrying about telling Tom hadn't prepared her for this. What *had* she expected? What had she hoped? That Tom would ask her to move in with *him?* That he'd ask her to go steady? Why had he gone berserk?

Snowy said, "I've got to bid you fond adieu, Puddles. Supper is ready."

"Don't let Bev forget to send photos!"

Snowy spooned Tom's creation onto plates, added some salad, scooped up the silverware she'd set on the table, and carried everything to the living-room area. Wordlessly, she handed him a plate, fork, knife, spoon, and sat down in the Martha Washington chair. They ate supper, watching the evening news, not talking. Her heart was aching, too.

HE DIDN'T APOLOGIZE. She didn't understand this as much as she didn't understand why he had flown off the handle that way. Maybe he really had gone temporarily insane.

After supper, he put the dishes in the dishwasher, said, "See you tomorrow," and left. Finally she had an opportunity to let loose the held-back tears, but she found she was so stunned that she couldn't cry. Her parents had not yelled; Alan hadn't. Of course there had been moments of rage, but nothing like this. She took a long shower in the apartment's shower stall, thinking of how healing it would feel to soak in that old bathtub at Waterlight. Wearing a flannel nightgown and bathrobe but shivering, she sat at her desk in her bedroom and told herself to walk in his moccasins, see it from his point of view. Why had he become so angry at the suggestion of a change in their way of life, their habits, their unspoken arrangement? She refused to use the popular phrase, "fear of commitment," but in some way was this the cause? Was he afraid of being forced to take action? Could this fear spark such an explosion?

The next day, she phoned Ruhamah. "It's official; Bev has bought the place. So after you've returned from—has Harriet said where you're going on your trip?"

"I've been talking with her, and we decided that for the grand finale we'll travel in the States, not overseas. Maryland, Virginia, Washington."

"Washington, D.C.?"

"Yes, Snowy, the Washington you visited on your Girl Scout trip. Finally, I'll get to go."

Washington. Where Brandon worked and lived.

Knowing what she was thinking, Ruhamah said, "Brandon is arranging his leave to do some sight-seeing with us."

"Oh. That's nice."

Ruhamah continued, "I'll only be gone a week. When I get back, why don't you take a week off for a vacation yourself, to relax after moving to Bev's."

"I may not be moving for good. It may just be a summer stay. I'm just going to see how it works out."

There was a silence. Then Ruhamah asked, "But you're taking your desk?"

"Yes, you can turn my bedroom into an office, even if it's only temporary."

Tom never did apologize. He acted as if they'd had an ordinary discussion about Bev's house. Before they drove over to see it that Sunday afternoon, Snowy phoned Bev and said, "Tom got kind of upset by the idea of my moving in for good, so I've let him think it's only a summer vacation. That'll be our story, okay? And maybe it *will* be just the summer, depending. Is it all right with you if I'm indefinite?"

"You're being flexible," Bev said. "For our Snowy, the born long-range planner, that's quite an accomplishment. Is Joanne in town this weekend?"

"She came into the store this morning for the first time."

"Now she's invading your turf in earnest!"

"Rita was there, just by chance because she doesn't work weekends but she'd forgotten something-or-other so she and Mallory stopped in, and in came Joanne, and they had a little Class of '56 reunion right on the spot."

At Waterlight, Bev gave Tom the real-estate tour and picked his brain for advice about various repairs for Leon to tackle. Snowy trailed along behind, wanting to move in this very moment and do nothing but work at her dear old desk in these new surroundings, and she wished the cottage were truly far away from Woodcombe. Upstairs, bedrooms opened off the balcony hall and looked out over the porch roof at the weekend activity in the colony of bob houses. The sound of snowmobiles was like steady traffic on a highway. When Tom told Bev about the snowmobiler who had hung onto a beer cooler, Snowy was surprised that he could speak of that evening or even remember the news item.

As the winter of 1995 wore on, the daily routine seemed less constricting than during other winters. Business was up at the store, and her new poems were being published in magazines, some even winning prizes, but the main reason, she sensed, was the prospect of change, which continued alternately exciting her and terrifying her. Even if, after all, she only spent the summer at Waterlight, even if she pretended this would be a lengthier version of the overnights at Bev's of their schooldays, it was upheaval.

The winter doldrums were also enlivened by a weekend visit from Harriet, who stayed at Jared's place and drove around with him in his pickup to sketch some winter scenes, but who was having tea in the store and talking with Snowy late that Saturday afternoon when Joanne came in, with three-year-old Elizabeth in tow.

Snowy hissed to Harriet, "Tom's ex," and stepped to the counter. "Hi, Joanne. Hi there, Elizabeth."

Elizabeth said anxiously, "Swiss Miss."

Joanne said, "An emergency! I just discovered that Lavender is out of cocoa. Where would I find some?"

"I'll get it," Snowy said, heading down an aisle. "Oh, Joanne, this is my roommate, Harriet Blumburg, up from New York for the weekend."

Joanne went over to the little table where Harriet sat. "I'm an old friend of Snowy's. And Tom, you know Tom Forbes? I'm Joanne Forbes. He and I used to be roommates, that's what we called it, because we got married in college and lived in the married students' housing."

"Swiss Miss!" squealed Elizabeth, as Snowy hurried back with a box.

Harriet said to Joanne, "And this is your granddaughter?"

"Yes. Elizabeth, say hello to Harriet." But Elizabeth was intent on the purchase, and, not insisting on manners, Joanne let herself be tugged by Elizabeth to the cash register, where as she paid, she asked Snowy, "So what's the latest about Rita's romance?"

"Rita's what?"

"The time I ran into her here, she told me she's got a new guy."

Feeling completely stupid, Snowy said, "She hasn't mentioned him to me."

"Oh," Joanne said, and hoisted Elizabeth up into her arms. They left, Elizabeth clutching the cocoa.

Harriet came over. "Has that woman seen a shrink?"

"I don't know. I don't think so."

"It's not something you folks in New Hampshire do?"

"Well—Ruhamah did."

"Oh shit, Snowy, I'm sorry. Didn't mean to be a wiseass. But that Joanne Forbes looks like she needs help."

"I'm afraid she thinks she needs Tom."

"Her roommate. Does she visit him when she's here?"

"I don't know. He hasn't mentioned it."

Harriet said exasperatedly, "You reticent Yankees!" Then, as a customer approached with a half gallon of milk, she whispered, "I'm off, back to Jared's. He *isn't* reticent."

Next Saturday, March 11, Snowy thought, would be the fortieth anniversary of her first date with Tom. Naturally, Tom wouldn't remember. Should she remind him, making a joke about the milestone? In winter the Gilmore House was open on weekends so they could go there and have a big-deal meal, to celebrate. For that matter, they could recreate the first-date evening and go to the movies in Gunthwaite and to Hooper's Dairy Bar. And go parking? Let's not get absurd.

She found she couldn't summon the energy to tell him or even experience the emotions herself. She would ignore the occasion and let him remain ignorant. That Saturday night, in his apartment, while he made a pancakes supper, he told her about seeing a chipmunk emerge up through the snow near the back stairs this morning, take a tentative step, then scurry madly around in a circle, obviously thinking, "Holy shit, cold, cold, *cold!"*, and dive back down the hole in the snow, not to be seen again. Tom said, "The males start courting in March, but ten-degree weather was too much for this little fellow's libido." Even with such an opening, she couldn't bring herself to tell him. After supper, they watched a video of *Howards End.*

Rita didn't mention any boyfriend, but as Snowy observed her more closely with customers, it began to dawn on Snowy that Frank Barlow, the owner of Hurricane Farm, was lingering longer than usual in the store, listening to Rita's chatter, and looking at her amplitude with appreciation.

Snowy finally told Bev about this, when she phoned Bev on April 18 to wish her happy birthday before Bev went out to a birthday dinner with Geoff. Bev said, "Frank Barlow; he's divorced and hasn't remarried, right? A single guy? Rita has reformed."

"Today after she was through work, she didn't drive off in the direction of Gunthwaite. She went the opposite way, back toward the lake, toward the Roller Coaster Road." Snowy did not have to add: Is she going to *my* house, Hurricane Farm?

Bev said, "Maybe she was going to the beach." For an April swim?

"Maybe I'm imagining things," Snowy said, imagining Rita picking a bouquet from the golden masses of daffodils Snowy had planted.

"Maybe she did date Geoff. You know what, I think I'll be brash and ask Geoff outright. What's the use of being our age if we can't ask what we want to know?"

"Puddles always has," said Snowy.

The next day, Bev reported, "Geoff didn't have the faintest idea who Rita is. Did you ask her about that Frank?"

"No," Snowy admitted. "I'll wait and see."

Bev changed the subject. "Next Sunday afternoon, let's go to Filene's and find you something to wear to Ruhamah's graduation."

Ruhamah had been saying that Snowy shouldn't bother attending another damn graduation, and Snowy knew what she meant but kept thinking of Alan, feeling she should be there to represent the proud parents of a new MBA recipient. Bev's suggestion gave her the perfect reply to Ruhamah, so she phoned Ruhamah and said, "I *am* coming to your commencement. It's an excuse to buy a new outfit."

Ruhamah said, knowing there was no argument for this, "Well..."

Snowy said, "Shall I invite Tom too?"

"Okay. Can he get David's pickup and we'll move my stuff back the same day?" Ruhamah added, "D. J. will help. He's coming to the graduation."

Ruhamah had invited D. J. to her graduation? Ruhamah would be seeing Brandon on her graduation-present trip? Snowy gave up and phoned Tom and invited him.

"Sure," Tom said. "Have you heard the latest doings at David and Lavender's? They've acquired a puppy from the Gunthwaite humane society and Elizabeth named her Swiss Miss."

Tom and Joanne, with two granddaughters and a grand-puppy.

Snowy decided to concentrate on clothes.

At Filene's, in a dressing-room mirror Snowy and Bev studied Snowy wearing a honey-colored linen-rayon sleeveless sheath, with a matching short-sleeved jacket. Snowy asked, "Are you sure this is the best? It reminds me of that dress I made in junior high, in home-ec, except that had a white bolero, piqué, remember?"

Bev said, "Remember the circle skirt I made? Polished cotton. And remember how we wore our cinch belts backward, the buckles in the back, for a smoother effect?"

"I wish sacque dresses would get a retro revival. Remember those chemises in college, circa 1958? They were wonderful; you didn't have to worry about sucking your stomach in. Not that we had much to worry about then. Here I am nowadays working out with that *Abs of Steel* video—oh, I never thought, the TV in my suite doesn't have a VCR, does it? I'll bring the one in the apartment. Ruhamah can replace it with her own."

"Sacque dresses!" Bev adjusted Snowy's little jacket. "I guess the important thing is, no matter how embarrassing it is to think what we used to look like, at each stage we did look right for our time."

Snowy stared at her reflection and realized that now, in her fifties, she had gone from being cute to, at last, settling into herself. Did she look more like a Henrietta now than a Snowy? Her editor at Wingfield Press called her Henrietta.

On the day of Ruhamah's graduation, Snowy and Tom drove to Durham in David's pickup, whose cab Tom had cleaned meticulously for Snowy's new outfit, and after the commencement ceremony, Snowy and Tom and Ruhamah and D. J. had dinner at the New England Center, and then, in Dover, at Ruhamah's apartment they changed out of their formal clothes into jeans and T-shirts and loaded Ruhamah's possessions into the pickup, which Tom and Snowy drove back to Woodcombe, while Ruhamah drove her car and D. J. his. That evening, after everything had been carried up the outside staircase to the apartment, they all collapsed around the dining table, drinking beers and toying with deli salads Snowy had brought up from the store. D. J. was drinking a non-alcoholic O'Doul's because he'd be doing some more driving, to Dudley and Charl's to spend the night. Ruhamah kept glancing at the dozen pink roses that Snowy had arranged in a vase when the florist delivered them yesterday. The accompanying card said, "Congratulations and love, Brandon."

Ruhamah was back under this roof, not just for the summer but for good—or for as long as she wanted to. Wasn't it time, Snowy thought in sudden exasperation, to scrap any remaining hypocrisy about sleeping arrangements? Ruhamah was twenty-four years old. When Snowy was her age, Snowy had been married two years. Ruhamah was a grown woman, who had been living in her own apartment. And obviously Ruhamah and D. J. should have a chance to be alone together.

Feeling as brave as Puddles, Snowy jumped to her feet and said, "Well, Tom, shall we call it a day? I'll be at Tom's tonight, Ruhamah."

Tom grinned, said, "Goodnight, all," and followed her out the door.

They heard a startled silence, then Ruhamah's chortle and D. J.'s laugh.

The next day, Ruhamah unpacked from the move home and packed a duffel for her trip. The next morning, after Rita arrived for work, Snowy drove Ruhamah to the Manchester Airport and tried to hide an attack of nerves as she saw her onto a flight to Washington, where Ruhamah would meet Harriet. And Brandon. In 1955, the Girl Scout troop had taken a chartered bus to Washington and sung so many verses of so many sing-along songs on the way that it was a wonder their troop leaders hadn't leapt out of the bus and thrown themselves under its wheels.

That evening, Snowy began her own packing. Tom had assembled an array of Staples boxes for her, and into them she put the contents of her desk, essential files from her filing cabinet, and books she couldn't live without, even if it was just for a summer; these included, of course, some Agatha Christies. Into her suitcases went the clothes that wouldn't wrinkle; she would pack the others at the last minute. She was reminded more of packing for college than of the packing she'd done for other moves.

The day before Ruhamah was due to arrive back in Manchester, Tom and David carried Snowy's desk down to David's pickup and helped her lug the boxes and suitcases, and in her car she followed them to Waterlight for the unloading, in which they were assisted by Leon, pressed into service by Bev, who invited David to bring Lavender and the children for a swim anytime. During all the commotion and talk, Snowy looked at Tom and saw him as the still eye of a hurricane.

Snowy wasn't leaving forever, and she'd be back to spend nights in Tom's apartment again and no doubt he would be staying over in her suite; nevertheless there was a desperation in the passion in her bed that last night in her apartment.

And the next morning she was still so hoarse from that farewell that she had to tell Rita she must have caught a cold. Ker-choo.

"YES," SNOWY REPLIED to Geoff Plumley seated beside her at the big wicker table on the porch, laughing animatedly because what else could she do, since she was supposedly sort of his dinner partner and she'd been yakking about computers too long with Bill LeHoullier on her other side, "yes, my daughter's latest idea is to buy another general store, one that needs to be rescued to be restored as 'the heart of the community,' but that's *just* an idea, for the future."

"Well," Geoff said, his gray eyes on Bev down the length of the candlelit table, his widow's peak precise in contrast to his graying tousled hair, his burgundy polo shirt and wrinkled khakis managing to look tweedy, "when Bev mentioned it, I thought we could begin to keep it in mind. You never know."

"How true," Snowy said. "At the moment, though, I'm still trying to recover from buying a new car; well, a secondhand one."

"Let me guess. Woodcombe. Therefore, a Subaru?"

She laughed again. This Subaru was a blue station wagon; she'd traded in both the old Subaru and the van. "Would you like some more salad? Wine?"

By August, Snowy and Bev had got their hostess-with-the-mostest routines down pat for the dinner parties Bev had envisioned, some of which were elaborate affairs in the dining room, while more were casual on the porch off the kitchen, but they had been uncertain about this Saturday night's party because it was in honor of Harriet, so should it be California laid-back or New York formal, should it feature New England cooking or more general cuisine? Harriet had asked to meet Dudley and the twins, which also meant Darl's husband, Bill, and of course there would be Jared, with whom Harriet was again staying on this latest visit to New Hampshire, and Geoff; Tom couldn't come because he was on duty at the fire tower. Bev and Snowy eventually decided to do one of their lobster dinners, the serving of which Bev had mastered in her Camden-waitressing summers and Snowy had learned in her Eastbourne-Pevensay years. They would buy some intriguing breads and a couple of blueberry pies from Indulgences. Snowy would bring potato salad from the store; she always left early on dinner-party nights, feeling both guilty and devil-may-care. Although Snowy explained to Bev that Harriet adapted easily to her surroundings and had loved Snowy's mother's chicken and dumplings, both she and Bev continued to worry over what they'd be presenting to a cosmopolitan world-traveler, but these concerns paled when Roger phoned Bev from his car this afternoon to say he finally had got a free weekend and was on his way to Gunthwaite to see Waterlight at last. Bev immediately phoned Snowy at the store and shrieked, "Snowy, Roger is arriving out of the blue, but Geoff is already invited!" Snowy thought fast, asking, "Doesn't Roger still think Geoff is simply the owner of your real-estate office? Inviting Geoff would be a business obligation?" Bev said, collecting her wits, "I'll tell Geoff to play it cool, and I'll tell Roger I've invited Geoff in hopes one of us can interest Harriet in some lakefront. And because Tom won't be here, you can give the impression that Geoff is yours." "Hold on," Snowy said, "you're the actor, not me." Suddenly Bev had an awful thought and said, "Do you think Roger isn't coming here just to see Waterlight and the children and show me his new tricks in bed? Do you think he is going to ask for a divorce?" Ignoring this hypothetical problem in this emergency, Snowy said, "Send Leon or Etta to the fish market to buy another lobster, and I'll bring extra potato salad."

Out through the screens, past hydrangea bushes with blossoms like creamy pom-poms, past the lawn dropping down to the shore, a jet-ski boat zipped across the lake, and beneath that noise and the voices at the table Snowy was sure she could hear the wake's waves slapping and lapping. An evening in summer at the lake. Her hostess outfit tonight consisted of a lake-blue short-sleeved cotton sweater and white drawstring pants, while Bev, after some last-minute vacillation caused by Roger's presence, had settled on a weskit top she'd bought in sage green, with a green-print wraparound skirt. Snowy repeated to Geoff, "More salad? Wine?"

Geoff transferred his gaze from Bev, who was talking to Harriet on her right, to Roger, who had been seated between the twins to keep him confused and was happily protesting as they reminisced about his basketball feats. "What?" Geoff said. "Oh, no thanks. Is he staying here?"

"Um, I don't really know," Snowy said, trying to catch Bev's eye. Scarlet carcasses lay cracked open, emptied, and people were sitting back, buttery and and replete. Time for dessert.

Bev nodded at Snowy, and together they shushed offers to help as they began clearing the table. As usual, Leon had been hired for busboy-and-dishwashing duties, but earlier, after he had loaded the gazpacho bowls into the dishwasher, he had wandered off, also as usual, so now Bev found him watching TV in his room and herded him back to work.

"Is Geoff okay?" Bev whispered to Snowy.

Snowy lifted dessert plates out of a cupboard. "He is pining. And wondering where Roger is spending the night." Snowy herself wondered what it must be like to be seated at a table with two men you were sleeping with.

"I hope you were vague?"

"Yes."

Bev set off the coffeemaker. "Harriet is going to Mimi's shop again tomorrow on her way home. Isn't her Jared the rugged-individual type!"

"I saw you twinkling at him."

"In a maternal fashion."

Giggling, they carried dessert out to the porch. Their guests had started to shift around, and by the time the pies and the coffeepot and liqueurs and After Eight mints were on the table and Snowy and Bev were serving, Snowy found that—eek—Geoff was sitting across the table talking to Darl, one person away from Roger.

Dudley had taken Geoff's chair, and as Snowy passed him a plate, Dudley said, "Another splendid feast made by your own fair hands."

Snowy laughed. "By Fay's hands and others'."

"Your magic touch makes it splendid," he insisted. He and the twins and Bill had been to several Waterlight parties this summer, but always before Tom had been here. Watching her tonight, without Tom, Dudley thought it was a great pity that she had met Tom Forbes after her husband's death and had immediately taken up with him again. Was this summer an attempt to recapture single life in college? He added, "But I'll have to run twice as far tomorrow to work the feast off."

Dudley had begun jogging when he became mayor, and Snowy wondered if while he ran he pretended he was the president in a pack of jogging Secret Service guards. She'd adjusted to jogging here on Lakeside Road, which she had to herself at five a.m., the summer people and their dogs still asleep; she was reminded of running the Pevensay Point Road, but instead of the ocean she now had views of the glossy early-morning lake, and the summer air smelled like fresh dill, and occasionally she heard the prehistoric yodel of a loon. Bev had been right about the benefits of getting familiar with a lake; however, Snowy still hadn't gone swimming. Or water-skiing, or sailing, or canoeing. She hadn't even had a tennis lesson from Bev. Too busy. She worked at the store during the day, she worked at her desk in the evenings or drove someplace to do a reading, and aside from these parties, her playtime consisted of Saturday nights with Tom here or at his apartment and hikes with him on Sunday afternoons if he wasn't on duty. If he was, she climbed Pascataquac to see him and sometimes spent the night in his cabin. Could Bev be right again? They were kind of dating, instead of behaving like an old married couple. When he stopped in at the store, Snowy feared she was flirting like Rita. Unseemly! She felt very discombobulated. She asked Dudley, "How's the campaign going?"

As he told her the latest about his bid for a second term, she saw Harriet switch chairs to talk with Charl and Darl. Jared poured himself some Drambuie and moved to shoot the shit with Bill about the Internet. The volume of voices grew higher than ever, but it was dominated by Roger's (like Dudley he had been a champion debater), and heaven help us, Roger was discussing real-estate laws with Geoff, and both men in this musical-chairs game now got up and sat down on either side of Bev, without a break in their discussion. Bev made her femme-fatale face at Snowy. Bev was actually relishing the situation!

Snowy realized Dudley had gone quiet. He was watching Roger. When Bev had greeted Dudley and steered him over to Roger as a distraction, she'd reminded them that they'd had mutual interests in high school though they'd been two classes apart and that they'd met at her fiftieth birthday party when Dudley was a city councilor, and she had concluded with, "Nowadays Dudley is our illustrious mayor!" Roger had said, "There's a thankless task." Dudley had rejoined, "But somebody has to do it." Roger had laughed and said, "If I move back to Gunthwaite, you've got my vote," and Bev had stared at him.

Dudley said to Snowy, "Let's go for a walk now, to get rid of a few calories."

Snowy glanced at Bev, who was listening to Roger and Geoff and looking like a leading lady if ever there was one. Snowy said, "Okay," and because all the guests were engrossed in their various conversations, she didn't bother drawing attention by excusing herself.

Lights from the porch and house blotched the lawn. In the dark beyond, little spiral-shaped lights lined the path to the shore. As she and Dudley walked down the slope, Dudley said, "What would you say if I told you that my total concentration isn't on this campaign?"

Snowy stopped. "Is something wrong, Dudley? Are you okay, and Charl—and the kids?"

He laughed. "Oh my God, have we reached this stage, when concerns about health pop first to mind?"

"Whew." Snowy resumed walking. "So, what else are you concentrating on?"

"Not exactly concentrating. Just pondering. The House."

"Your painted lady?"

"The House of Representatives."

Snowy stopped again. "New Hampshire's?" she asked, certain it wasn't.

"The U.S. Not next year, but in 1998."

Her first reaction was: Dudley, you can't raise the money for that! But she said, "At last, at last I'll be able to vote for you!" Then came her next reactions in a rush: Dudley, you're a Democrat in New Hampshire! It's such a long shot! And if by some miracle you should win, Charl would not want to live in Washington.

And he said, "I'm daydreaming, is what I'm doing. I couldn't ask Charl to leave Gunthwaite and Darl. The last of the kids will be out of high school by then, so I wouldn't be uprooting them, but—oh, who am I kidding? A sign-painter without a college degree, I'm lucky I ever got elected mayor of a small city. Probably I'll get voted out this November."

"Ruhamah says D. J. is predicting a landslide. Other mayors are making pilgrimages to you to find out how you resuscitated Gunthwaite."

"'Revitalized,'" Dudley corrected, resuming the walk. "That's the word they use. Ah, Snowy, the scaling down of ambition. I thought I'd succeeded in doing that, and it is something I should definitely come to terms with at my age, along with those health concerns. Why do the goddamn youthful visions get more vivid? Why can't they fade the fuck away?"

She remembered her yearnings on the riverbank. Then the years during which she felt aimed like an arrow at a future of success, when the poems would be as near to perfection as possible, her name a household word—well, in literary households, at least. She gave a whimper.

Dudley said hastily, "I'm not depressed, Snowy. I'm just angry."

They had reached the beach. She said, "Let's go for a swim," and kicked off her sandals, shucked her sweater and pants, and in her underwear she ran splashing into the water.

SITE FIDELITY, TOM thought, as he emerged from the outhouse, swept his eyes across Pascataquac's summit swarming with Labor Day weekend hikers this sunny Sunday afternoon, and went up the cabin's porch steps and across the porch and unlocked the door. Transition months, autumn and spring; he'd read somewhere that these were the busiest times for shrinks. Taking a can of Diet Pepsi out of the refrigerator, he felt besieged by the need to cut and run. Where to? Why? Could you have a third midlife crisis? He was fifty-seven, so that wasn't exactly midlife anymore, unless he lived to be a centenarian. He remembered his mental picture of what the teaching life would be like; God knows he'd had no illusions, but he had hoped it would be simple, allowing some measure of satisfaction and contentment. Deadly boring, is what it was. To make life become alive, he had started a coffin business! Deadly again, pun intended. The point of fire towers was to save lives, forests, and that had appealed, but so had what he'd imagined would be solitude, yet up in the tower too often he was playing host to deadly dull tourists and whole damn Boy Scout troops, as he had been this weekend, and by this summer's end it was driving him bananas.

The cabin interior was tidier than during the week, because Snowy would be arriving, and although the place was definitely still rudimentary, with its log walls, pine shelves, a hot plate, a wooden-slab table, a fieldstone fireplace, an old sofa, and in the bedroom bunk beds (into one of which they squeezed when she slept here), he had over the years gussied it up with various civilized comforts for her, such as the scatter rugs and the electric kettle he'd lugged up the trail and the clothes rod he'd installed. Snowy would be spending tonight here, and he was sure they'd be discussing the borrowing of David's pickup to bring her stuff home from that lair of hers in Bev's mansion. Now that the summer was over, he was glad she'd had her change of scenery, though he still considered it a crazy notion to live in somebody else's house when you owned your own. But the nagging thought that he and Snowy ought to be sharing a place together made him jumpy. What if tonight he blurted out a suggestion that she move in with him, into his apartment, so Ruhamah could continue to have that apartment over the store to herself? Shit! Site fidelity. Or cut and run. Opening the door, about to start back to the tower, he almost bumped into Joanne.

"Oh," Joanne said.

"Hi, Tom," said Lavender beside her, carrying Lilac, and behind them was David, looking wary, wearing a rucksack, with the puppy on a leash, and Elizabeth rushed for Tom's arms.

Swiss Miss barked and wagged.

God, Tom thought. He set down the Pepsi on the porch table and swung Elizabeth up. David and Lavender had climbed Pascataquac a few times previously with the kids, but never had Joanne accompanied them.

Lavender said, "Thought we'd check here before we went up the tower."

"Um," Tom said. "Pepsi?"

"Yes!" exclaimed Elizabeth.

David said to Elizabeth, "Well, why don't we go look for some blueberries first. And remember the reindeer moss, and the time we saw the boreal chickadee?" With his free hand he peeled Elizabeth off Tom like Velcro. He carried her toward the low-bush blueberries, tugging Swiss Miss along, while Lavender followed with Lilac.

Tom tried to think of a lighthearted comment to make to Joanne but could only come up with, "All set for school on Tuesday?", which was an idiotic question because Joanne was always ready for the start of school and actually looked forward to it, even to the deadly *deadly* DEADLY teachers' meetings. Then he realized Joanne wasn't listening. She was intent on the view.

She asked, "Which one is Mount Daybreak?"

After a moment, he put his hands on her shoulders and turned her toward the west. "The one with the long bare ledges."

She pointed. "That one?"

"Yes." Under his touch, she felt so different from Snowy, taller, shoulders sloping, not square. What courage, he thought, for her to come up here to look at the Daybreak summit.

She asked, "Have you ever been back there?"

"No."

"I suppose you have binoculars here?"

"A pair in the cabin, but the really powerful binoculars are in the tower."

She said, "Then let's go up the tower."

At that moment, he saw Snowy emerge from the woods in her hiking shorts and shirt, her green rucksack on her back, in her fists the two trekking poles he had bought her when he bought himself a pair, easier on the knees than walking sticks. She was bringing a library book for him in that pack, as well as something for supper.

In the same instant, he knew she had seen him and Joanne standing like this together on the cabin porch.

Once when he was hiking, he and a bear had surprised each other across a swamp. As he'd stood rooted, the bear had changed directions so fast it seemed to spin around inside its skin. That's what Snowy did, running back down the trail.

BRAKING TO A STOP in the circular driveway, Snowy realized she couldn't remember any of the drive from the Pascataquac trailhead parking area, through the holiday traffic, to Waterlight. She hadn't pulled that sort of scary amnesia since the days when driving was second nature to her, pre-agoraphobia, when her mind would be elsewhere while her body was behind the wheel.

Hers was the only vehicle here. Bev's Mercedes was gone; she was showing a house this afternoon. Leon was off somewhere in his pickup, and Etta was at Springmeadow Farm readying Prancer for their return to Mount Holyoke. So, Snowy thought, going indoors, she didn't need to hide, and she had time to repair her wet face and prepare some explanation for Bev about why she wasn't on Pascataquac.

As she started down the hall to her suite, she heard the phone on her desk ringing. Tom? Goddamn him to fucking hell. She would not answer.

But then as she entered the anteroom that had become her office and living room, Puddles said to the answering machine, "Shoe hickeys!"

This startled Snowy so much that she grabbed the receiver and asked, "*What* did you say?"

Puddles carried her telephone and a glass of iced tea across the living room's pale gold carpet to the shadowy porch under the southern type of pines she'd never quite got used to; not the Christmasy pines of New England, these had very tall bare trunks with a little pine froufrou at the top. Around this house were some young oaks, too, and the camellia trees she loved, which bloomed in the fall, pink and white. She said, "I didn't want to tell you unless I got over the first hurdle," and sat down in a wicker armchair painted the black-green called Charleston green. "I'd been thinking about what you suggested, coaching, and this summer I began checking around, and last month I found that a Varsity coach at the high school in Broughton, on the mainland, she needed help because her assistant coach suddenly had to move when her husband got transferred; the assistant coach's husband, I mean. So this desperate head coach took me on as a temp, and I rearranged my schedule. Snowy, I was scared shitless! There are *twenty* cheerleaders on the squad, not eight like ours, and the cheering is *nothing* like what we did;

it's even changed some more since Susan was cheering. These girls are real athletes, they do tumbling, gymnastics, stunts, and dances, and I'm not a gymnast, not a choreographer, I'm just an old ex-cheerleader. But you know what saved me? I pretended I was Gilly and Jonesy. Some aspects of coaching have not changed."

Miss Gilson and Miss Jones had been Gunthwaite High School's women gym teachers who coached cheerleading, Varsity and JV, respectively. Gilly had been a holy terror; Jonesy, nice. Snowy could guess from which coach Puddles was drawing the most inspiration. Snowy said weakly, "Puddles, this is wonderful."

"Let me tell you, it's a hell of a lot more work than we ever had to do. The girls who are the bases, the ones who lift the flyers, they go home after practice with shoe hickeys on their shoulders."

Snowy wouldn't have believed a few minutes ago that she could be laughing. "Oh, Puddles."

"The first football game was Friday night. Sheesh, I was more of a nervous wreck than when we cheered at our first football game."

"You weren't nervous then. You were in your element, and I bet you were Friday."

Puddles giggled. "They did pretty well and they looked okay. Their uniforms are great, little pleated skirts, not plain pleats like our green jumpers had but with white inserts—the school colors are orange and white. The tops are V-neck jerseys, a lot more titsy than our white blouses."

"You really would've wowed the Gunthwaite crowds in that," Snowy said. Of their triumvirate, Puddles was the one who'd developed attention-getting boobs.

"Well, I couldn't squeeze into a uniform nowadays. Everything costs a lot more nowadays, too, uniforms, bus trips; the girls are planning their fund-raising, and I can already see I'm going to be pressuring my colleagues at the clinic to buy candy. At

Gunthwaite, we didn't have to shell out for anything except our blouses and socks and saddle shoes and sneakers, did we?"

"And our green Lollipop underpants. Remember how it was decreed that we had to wear two pairs? At least they weren't so bad as our gym-suit bloomers."

Puddles laughed and sipped her iced tea. "There. That's my news." She didn't want to tell Snowy the other news: She'd lost some weight and was doing some way-out New-Age nonsense. Snowy jogged, Bev used a treadmill; that was normal. Now here she was taking tai-chi classes, for God's sake. But she had to admit Susan was right, it helped the arthritis.

Snowy said, "Congratulations, coach!"

"No, I won't deserve congratulations unless I'm good enough to be made the permanent assistant coach, but I haven't got a snowball's chance in hell of that; they're bound to find a real coach sooner or later to replace me. What's your news? What's up with Bev and Roger since he came to that dinner party?"

Reminding herself that Bev hadn't ever told Puddles that Geoff was more than her boss, Snowy said, "Roger has returned for a couple of weekends. Waterlight has changed his mind about Gunthwaite, and he's talking about semiretiring to Gunthwaite in a few years and moving in here." Far from asking for a divorce, Roger seemed to be looking forward to a resumption of married life.

"How does Bev feel about that after being on her own for—what is it, eight years?"

"Like Scarlett O'Hara. She'll think about it tomorrow."

"Oh, I do wish you and she would take a trip south! I know, I know, you're too busy. Okay, have you decided to stay or move back to Woodcombe?"

Snowy had decided to return. Roger's visits in addition to Geoff's visits made her feel underfoot, though Bev pleaded that Snowy's presence was more necessary than ever, as a buffer. Snowy knew she would be underfoot in the store's apartment, now that Ruhamah was used to having it to herself, but damnit, the place was her home. She had considered renting some other apartment in Woodcombe, but that seemed an unjustifiable expense. She had pushed away the memory of Hurricane Farm and the luxury of her own house. And she had tried to erase the worry that she was deciding to move back because she didn't want to provoke another of those temporary-insanity rages of Tom's. She truly missed living down the street from him. She missed his closeness. She would go home and resume her old life, which would be spiced up by this summer.

Now she said to Puddles, "I'm staying on here."

CHAPTER TWO

"IN NOVEMBER," RUHAMAH said, locking the door after the last customer of the day had left, "you have to think British to survive; you have to get out the Earl Grey and crumpets and pull the curtains against the rain and stir up the fire. Think snug. I'm working my way through all the Miss Read books in the library. That's the atmosphere we want to project, to attract more out-of-town customers this month than just hunters buying six-packs."

Snowy said wearily, "I remember in one Miss Read book, some woman says that when life gets drab and discouraging, she opens a new cake of soap. Hunters. Guns and beer, such a sensible combination. Ruhamah, we're a general store, not a 'destination.'"

Ruhamah sighed and checked the woodstove. Her mother was acting more obstinate or timid than usual, ever since something had happened between her and Tom, which Snowy wouldn't discuss. After Labor Day, Snowy had announced that she was staying at Waterlight. Snowy had begun disappearing into the cellar-storeroom whenever Tom came into the store, and soon he started buying his groceries elsewhere. Rita had asked Snowy, "Did you and Tom break up?" Snowy had said, "This isn't high school, Rita." Perturbed, Ruhamah suspected that Joanne's frequent visits to Woodcombe were at the root of the trouble, but what could be done about that? As Brandon said, you couldn't control a grandmother.

Ruhamah said to Snowy, "We're a general store in Woodcombe,

the prettiest town in New Hampshire. This makes us a destination, and let's stretch it to twelve months of the year. There are three of us working here in the winter now; I don't want to lay Rita off, do you?"

"No," Snowy said, hoping she sounded convincing.

"Granted, snug is easier in December, thanks to the holiday spirit, than in bleak November, at least until Thanksgivingtime. Let's buy new tablecloths, warm and cheery. They'll be comparatively inexpensive but make a big difference. And we can add crumpets to the menu."

"Crumpets have to be toasted—"

"Scones, then."

"Oh, what the hell, both." Snowy put on her jacket and picked up her shoulder bag and gave Ruhamah a hug. "See you tomorrow."

She looked so tired that Ruhamah said, "Why don't you spend the night here instead of driving to Waterlight in this dark and rain?" Making the suggestion embarrassed Ruhamah, because when Snowy had decided to stay on at Bev's, Ruhamah had completely turned Snowy's bedroom into an office, storing Snowy's bed and bureau in the shed, so if Snowy stayed over she would be sleeping on the pull-out sofa.

"It's good of you to offer," Snowy said, "but getting away from the store is one of the main points of Waterlight, isn't it."

"Well, frankly, I'm confused about the whole situation."

"I'm not too clear myself," said Snowy, unlocking the door and stepping onto the porch.

Ruhamah called after her, "Put out a new cake of soap!" and locked up again.

Walking toward her car, Snowy looked past the post office at the fluorescent glow in the windows of North Country Coffins. She could keep on walking, to that barn and Tom. She was the one who had changed everything, who had shaken up their status quo last summer, who had not marched resolutely across the summit of Pascataquac to Tom and Joanne and made civilized conversation until Joanne left, and she was the one who wouldn't let life return to normal afterward. She hadn't spoken to Tom since that Labor Day weekend. She was the one who should apologize.

Bev, when Snowy told her everything, had said, "Tom isn't being fair, either to you or Joanne. He's being a damn man, so drastic measures are necessary, but you ought to consider keeping a line of communication open. Through Ruhamah and Brandon?"

Snowy had replied, "I can't live without him. But I'm so petty, I can't share him. I'm a mess. And I'm too worn out to play games."

Bev had reflected a while and then said, "I'm good at romance. I'm no good at the long haul."

"I was thinking that the romance *was* the long haul."

That conversation had occurred when the foliage season was beginning, with leaf peepers converging on Woodcombe, so Snowy had been worn out physically as well as in her spirit. Now here it was November, with all the leaves gone except some rust-brown oak, and Ruhamah was worrying about the off-season, but still Snowy felt like a candidate for one of those coffins being built in that barn up ahead.

Down in the dumps, her mother would say. I'm feeling down in the dumps.

Depression?

Heavyhearted, Snowy got into her car and drove out of the village, headlights probing the early darkness, wet and shiny.

After their impromptu swim this summer, Dudley had taken to stopping by the cottage on Sunday afternoons, to give her and Bev canoe lessons; however, because Bev was often away showing a place then, Snowy received most of the teaching. Uncharacteristically, Dudley didn't talk much, but she figured theirs was the easy silence between old friends while they paddled across the cove. Yet back at the cottage he would linger so long in a porch chair that she began to worry about his motives, as the ice melted in his iced tea and the glass beaded. What a relief when the mayoral campaign began this fall and Dudley became too busy to hang around Waterlight! What joy when Dudley won reelection earlier this month!

There *was* happiness in her new life. Tonight at Waterlight, for supper she and Bev sautéed chicken breasts with green peppers and garlic, a la Craig Claiborne. Then she carried a mug of coffee to her suite, where at her desk she began working on the new poem, entering the trance. Wonder of wonders, now that Tom wasn't around, she was writing about Alan, Alan's death, and even more wondrous, despite the agony of the effort, when she finished each night's work she felt happy.

But later, lying in bed, without Alan, having chosen to be without Tom, she thought of time running out, and distraught, she punched on a bedtime murder mystery in her Walkman, yet the words of a Keats sonnet paced through her mind:

> When I have fears that I may cease to be
> Before my pen has glean'd my teeming brain,
> Before high-pilèd books, in charact'ry,
> Hold like rich garners the full-ripened grain...
> And when I feel, fair creature of an hour!
> That I shall never look upon thee more,
> Never have relish in the faery power
> Of unreflecting love;—then on the shore
>   Of the wide world I stand alone, and think,
>   Till Love and Fame to nothingness do sink.

No phone call came from Tom inviting her to the Alpine Avens for Christmas Eve. Snowy helped Bev decorate Waterlight within an inch of its life, and she joined in Bev's family Christmas, feeling like a maiden aunt. Ruhamah was in New York at Harriet's. When Lavender came into the store a couple of days after Christmas, Lavender talked about how Brandon had gone to Newburgh to visit Joanne and both he and Joanne had come down to Woodcombe for the day, and amid other details Snowy learned that Tom had flown down to Florida to spend the holidays with his mother.

In January, Bev returned beaming to Waterlight from the Plumley Real Estate Awards Conference weekend. "I won! I'm in first place again!"

"Oh, Bev, hooray!" Snowy said, hastily recalling that the prize trip was to Montreal. "Is Geoff going to Montreal with you?"

"Well, the more I thought about it, the more I thought I'd like to go with Roger. His family was from there originally, remember, and his mother moved back after his father died. Roger and I and the children visited her there several times before she died, but I don't think Leon absorbed much. Now that he's older he ought to see it again and, well, I told Geoff that my companion on this trip would be Leon. Of course Geoff wouldn't want to go if Leon was along. I didn't mention I'm planning to invite Roger. Will you be okay in this house all by yourself?"

"I'll be fine."

"Maybe you could give Tom a call."

Bev and Leon and Roger left for a week in February. On Wednesday evening, Snowy stopped staring at the telephone, grabbed the receiver, and tapped Tom's number fast. She got his answering machine. What to say? She hadn't planned anything to say to him, or to a machine. She hung up, energy ebbing to lassitude again.

The next day at the store, Rita said, "Adele phoned me last night. Joanne's father died yesterday, a heart attack. Joanne was too shook up to drive down from Newburgh, and Adele was going to go get her, but Joanne had phoned Tom and he went."

In the afternoon, the *Gunthwaite Herald* was delivered as a snowstorm began. Snowy opened a copy to the obituaries and saw that Joanne's father's name was David. Snowy hadn't known that Joanne had named her younger son after her father. Now Joanne, the only daughter, would probably be spending more of her spare time in Gunthwaite than in Woodcombe, to help her mother. But even though Joanne had brothers, probably she would be asking Tom's help with the manly chores.

Were Joanne and Tom sleeping together?

Probably. In feverish images, Snowy saw them.

She felt as if she were going to faint, to keel right over into the display of Valentine candy.

Ruhamah said, "Snowy? Are you all right? Why don't you stay here tonight instead of driving to Waterlight in this snowstorm. We can go over my idea for a back porch."

"Yes," Snowy said, "I think maybe I'd better."

SO FOR THE first time since last June, Snowy ate supper up in the apartment. In the office, her old bedroom, she tried not to be frightened by Ruhamah's proposed plan to redesign the loading dock out back and build a back porch for more tables and chairs. She slept on the pull-out sofa, wearing a pair of Ruhamah's pajamas.

The next morning revealed only about four inches of snow, enough to be a bother but not backbreaking. After her shower she borrowed underwear and a chamois shirt from Ruhamah, put on yesterday's jeans because Ruhamah's were too long, and after their breakfast, while Ruhamah was shoveling the front walk and the sidewalk in front of the store, Snowy hoisted their second shovel and waded through the snow toward North Country Coffins. In years past, Tom would drive over to the store in his Jeep to plow the parking area, but this winter Ruhamah had hired somebody. Snowy thought that Tom might have spent the night at Joanne's in Gunthwaite, and David would be busy clearing snow at his own house before he got to the workshop, so she would make this gesture, shovel a path down the driveway to the barn.

But there the Jeep was, a snow-covered hulk parked off the street at the start of the driveway. Tom emerged from the barn, looking so exhausted she felt afraid. Men were always dropping dead shoveling snow. But he hadn't yet done any shoveling or plowing this morning.

He saw her and stopped. They stood separated by twenty feet of snow-drifted driveway.

She held up the shovel and called, "Can I help?"

He didn't answer. He started moving again, toward her or toward the Jeep, which was it?

A car came down the street. A Subaru, of course. Frank Barlow parked beside the store's sidewalk, jumped out, and scurried around to open the passenger door. Men still did this? Women still let them? Rita emerged, regally. Mallory, Rita's granddaughter, was strapped in back, and Rita opened the back door, leaned in, spoke to her, and kissed her. Then Rita stood and waved as Frank drove off toward Gunthwaite, presumably taking Mallory to her elementary school.

Snowy didn't wait any longer to find out what Tom would do. She dropped the shovel, stomped through the snow to him, looked up at him, and said, "Life is too short for this."

"I love you," he said. "Always have, always will. Can you leave the store today? Let's get the hell away from here."

She threw herself into his arms, in front of Rita and Ruhamah and the whole village. He was cold and warm, cautious, impetuous, aging, strong. He was Tom.

THEY TOOK HER car, Tom driving. He asked, "Where should we go?"

"Anywhere. Where would you like?"

"I've wanted to see where you lived in Pevensay. If that isn't an intrusion."

"I'm curious about your Newburgh house, myself."

They began to laugh.

Tom said, "We'll do a tour, from the sea to the mountains!"

And so they did. Down in Pevensay, the snow was sloppy, the ocean an icy gray that matched the gray shingles of the remodeled fish houses boarded up across the road from the white-foaming waves slamming and thundering over the rocks of the sea wall. Her house at the end of the road, opposite the jetty, was closed, too; summer people now owned it. Tom parked in the road, and as they stepped out of the car into slush, zipping up their parkas, bracing themselves against the salty wind, the spindrift soaring, Snowy inhaled a deep breath of the ocean air.

She said, "When I first met Alan, when he was showing me the Ruhamah Reed House for my thesis, I asked him if he got so used to the ocean smell he didn't notice it, and he guessed he did, but I said if I lived on the ocean I never would, and I didn't."

"You must have had a hard time leaving this."

Seagulls were cruising overhead, mewing. She said, "I would have had a worse time if we hadn't found Hurricane Farm. The minute I saw it, I was reminded of Julia's house; you know, Bev's folks' house. Kismet, I thought." She added, "Have you heard that Rita is going out with Frank Barlow?"

He looked blank.

So, Snowy speculated, Joanne hadn't mentioned this gossip to him? More likely, he hadn't paid attention. Snowy began telling him about buying the falling-down fish house and all the work she and Alan had done to fix it up.

"Young-marrieds," she said. "Typical. Probably you and Joanne were doing the same."

"Oh yes."

On the jetty, strands of seaweed were waving like cheerleading streamers. "I'm sorry about her father."

"He was an okay guy."

"Is she staying in Gunthwaite?"

"She's taken some personal days off from school." He looked at the house. "To think I met Alan those times I went into the store and I never knew it was your husband I was talking to."

"To think he told me about the new fire warden coming in to buy groceries to lug up Pascataquac and I didn't know it was you. He liked you."

"I liked him."

Snowy's eyes were teary, but this was caused by the wind. She said, "Brr, I'm cold and hungry," and got back into the car and directed Tom to Pevensay's one restaurant that stayed open year-round.

After lunch, sustained by fish chowder and lobster rolls, they drove west to I-93 and headed north, being passed by cars and trucks towing snowmobile trailers, the drivers frantic for fresh snow to ruin. She and Tom reminisced about what a challenge it had been to go parking in a snowstorm in the cream-colored convertible, with no snow tires. Tom reminisced, swearing, about putting on chains. In the White Mountains, she and Tom pointed out to each other the mountains they'd climbed, together or Tom alone. As they passed the Old Man of the Mountain, which they had saved, they talked of Kenneth Collins doing time in the booby hatch.

Snowy said, "What happens when they let him out?"

"God knows," Tom said.

She shivered. "Creepy."

He turned up the car heater.

Then they were off the turnpike and driving west into a river valley. Snowy and Alan, during one of their White Mountain sightseeing trips, had detoured to see Newburgh, because she had read about the town's logging history. She had not had an inkling that Tom Forbes lived here.

He slowed, with seeming reluctance. "The school is up on that hill."

She leaned forward and peered up at the Victorian high school she remembered, a great concoction of turrets and gables marred by an ugly cinderblock addition that had offended Alan considerably. Another addition had been wrapped around one side. "I don't remember that piece on that end when Alan and I came through here."

"New gymnasium," Tom said impassively. "The older addition is the elementary school, which used to be in the main building, which is now all junior high and high school. My classroom windows were those on the first floor, left."

He drove on.

The quiet little Main Street didn't seem to have changed much since she'd come here before, hoping to see vestiges of saloons and dance halls. The liveliest place today was the Sit 'n' Snack Luncheonette, where many pickups with plows were parked.

Tom slowed again, at a building beside a lumber mill. "This was the old coffin factory I bought."

"You sold it to the lumber mill, didn't you, when you moved operations to Woodcombe?"

"They've expanded into it."

"Ruhamah is planning to expand onto a back porch."

"Really? Who'll do the work? Jared?"

"She's discussing it with him."

"Sounds like a good idea."

"I always worry she's overreaching."

He accelerated past some factory housing and said, "David used to rent an apartment in that old mill house," and turned off onto a side road and drove past some mobile homes. "This used to be all woods."

There were still woods, and a field, and soon on a knoll she saw a white farmhouse with a gray barn. She recognized it less from Tom's brief description than from a feeling of familiarity because of having imagined it so often, Tom and Joanne in this house. The long driveway had been plowed.

Tom explained, "A neighbor keeps Joanne plowed out," and drove up to the house and stopped, but then he just sat, the car idling. He said uncertainly, "It's her house. We hide—she hides a spare key on the back porch, but—"

"No," Snowy said. "We shouldn't go in. I mean, you can, but I shouldn't. I'm glad enough to see the outside. You must have done an awful lot of work."

As they sat looking at Joanne's house, Tom asked, "Would you want to move into my apartment?"

If Snowy had been standing, her knees would have buckled. Stunned, she thought: This is where he is making the suggestion, here in the driveway of the house where he lived so many years with Joanne. Men!

Tom pointed toward a downstairs window and spoke rapidly. "That was Libby's room. After she died, Joanne slept there. Finally she moved back to our—the 'master' bedroom. Whenever I've been here, I've stayed in David's old bedroom. If that's of any consequence."

She should dismiss the rush of relief that swept over her. Tom and Joanne could've made love a million places other than in their bedroom (she and Alan certainly had!). But Snowy knew that Tom was telling her that he had been faithful. It *was* of consequence, yet even if he hadn't been, her answer would be the same.

Tom had turned to her, his expression quizzical but his blue eyes behind his glasses scared. The car's heater wasn't turned high enough to have caused the sheen of sweat on his face.

Suddenly laughing, delirious, she said, "David's other old bedroom, the one in your apartment. Could that be my office, for writing?"

He grabbed her, hugging her across the console. "We'll go get your desk tomorrow. Come home with me tonight."

BEV WAS MAGNANIMOUS when she discovered, upon her return from Montreal, that Snowy had moved out, leaving a note of explanation, and over the phone that evening Bev insisted on reimbursing Snowy for the rest of the month's rent. "Use it to buy yourself a present; this deserves a present, but what kind? It's not quite a housewarming occasion or an engagement or whatever. You're living in sin, isn't that thrilling? The next generations think nothing about it, but Snowy, it's a milestone for us!" Bev knew that she herself could carry off living in sin with much more pizzazz than Snowy could. "Anyway, we're too young to be Golden Girls. But it was fun, wasn't it? The dinner parties? The moths you'd capture and set free far out of my vicinity?" Bev had always been afraid of moths. "The time this fall when we saw the loons running on the water, practicing for migration? Our being roommates, almost? Wasn't it fun?"

And Snowy remembered the morning lake, calm and limpid. "It certainly was."

Then Bev proceeded to report on her trip, while Snowy carried the receiver around this love nest over a coffin factory. The apartment had become very familiar these past nine years, yet now it was all different, because she hadn't only moved her office furniture here, she had also brought treasures she'd left last summer at the store's apartment, from the pewter salt shaker and pepper mill to the Ruhamah Reed portrait. Even her mother's rooster collection. If she was going to do this, she would do it completely. Poor Tom! In the evenings after work, he was building more bookcases for his living room (*their* living room), but he seemed to relish the project. She could hear him down in the workshop right now. She looked at her left hand. The day she had moved in here, she'd taken off her engagement and wedding rings and put them away in her jewelry box. If Tom noticed, he didn't say anything.

After Bev's call, Snowy phoned Puddles and said, "I'm calling from Tom's apartment, which is now our apartment."

"No shit!" Puddles said. "You're shacking up?"

"That's what we're doing."

"Did you two discuss marriage?"

"This is much less complicated."

Puddles interpreted Snowy's answer as a no. "What does Ruhamah think of Mom's cohabiting?"

"Ruhamah's comment was, 'It's about time.'"

"Time," Puddles repeated. "It *is* about time, isn't it, about the lack of time."

"Ruhamah is too young to grasp that part, how it speeds up faster than you're told it will."

"Makes me want to strangle my cheerleaders, the time they waste. Well," Puddles said, deciding that she approved, "good for you! Does Joanne know?"

"She must. David might be circumspect, but Lavender is sure to have blabbed it."

"Who else knows?"

"Heavens, everybody. The whole village."

"The twins? Dudley?"

"Um, no. I haven't sent out announcements, Puddles. Some people will learn in due course. It's not exactly an earth-shattering event." But Snowy thought it might be to Dudley, and she dreaded Dudley's having to make a polite pretense at felicitations.

Puddles's interest was unrelenting. "What about Alan's mother?"

"She doesn't come to Woodcombe, so there's no need for her to know. I don't suppose Tom has told his mother. She's eighty-something, she might have a seizure. Age—God, Puddles, there's something so unseemly, so *comic,* about Tom and me living together at our age, but nobody has laughed at us, at least to our faces. Maybe people are finding us *cute,* and that's worse!"

"What about Rita?"

Snowy didn't want to think about Rita.

Puddles said gleefully, "I bet Rita is pea green with envy!"

"Not exactly." The day after Snowy moved into Tom's apartment, Rita had appeared for work wearing a large diamond ring. "Rita," Snowy said to Puddles, "is engaged."

"Huh? No kidding? Who's the damn fool?"

"The man who bought my place. Hurricane Farm."

"Snowy, you mean Rita Beaupre will be—oh Jesus H. Christ, she'll be living in your beautiful house?"

"She already is, at least sometimes. I'm very happy for her."

"Bullshit! What does Ruhamah think about Rita in your house?"

"Ruhamah? Philosophical."

"Yeah."

Snowy said, "Rita has had a hard life, but she has finally landed on her feet."

"It's only an engagement. She could blow it. So to speak."

Snowy forced a laugh.

Puddles asked, "How was Bev's trip?"

"They visited Roger's roots, and therefore Leon's, besides the usual sight-seeing."

"If Roger retires to Bev's house, they won't be shacking up. What a riot, Bev and Roger are still married."

After Puddles said good-bye, Snowy told herself to get it the hell over with and picked up the phone again, punching Charl and Dudley's number. To her relief, Charl answered. Snowy said, "Hi, this is Snowy, and I thought you and Darl and Dudley and Bill would get a kick out my news. Tom and I are living together; I've moved into his apartment."

Charl cried, "We know! I've been meaning to call you, but things have been busy. D. J. told us!"

Ruhamah, Snowy thought.

"I'm so happy for you," Charl said with much more sincerity than Snowy had put into a similar phrase a few minutes ago. "Isn't it funny, here I've been hoping that D. J. and Ruhamah would finally make a decision—to get married, but I know how young people are these days so I was ready for some other arrangement—and you and Tom make the decision first! Dudley," she called, "Dudley, it's Snowy, come wish her the best. Dudley?"

Snowy said, "There's no need—"

Charl said, "He didn't hear me. But we all wish you and Tom the best. It's so romantic, Snowy."

"Love to you and Darl and all. Bye."

Snowy roamed the little apartment, touching everything Tom had made, from the kitchen table to the carving of her Shetland collie, and she listened to the sound of his sander downstairs. Contentment? Yes, but mixed with a young-marrieds enchantment. Next Sunday afternoon, she thought, we should go shopping for new curtains. That's what she would spend the reimbursement from Bev on.

SNOWY FULLY EXPECTED Joanne to ignore the changed situation and recruit Tom to do chores at her mother's house anyway. When this didn't happen, she wondered if Tom had refused and not mentioned it to Snowy. Then all became clear a couple of weeks later; during a slow afternoon at the store, Rita was babbling on to Snowy about her guest list for the wedding to be held in the village church, not at one of Gunthwaite's two Catholic churches, and Snowy was actually listening when Rita said, "Joanne asked me to add Victor. You know, Victor Andrews. Adele sent him a copy of Joanne's dad's obituary—Adele and Sam are organizing our class reunion again this year, the *fortieth,* I can't believe it, so Adele has everybody's address—and Victor wrote Joanne a letter. Remember, they almost got married years and years ago—"

"Six years," Snowy said. In June, Libby would be dead six years.

"—and he hasn't married anybody else since then. Joanne wrote back, and he phoned her, and da-dum, he came up to Gunthwaite from Nashua last weekend and met Joanne at her mother's house and helped out, isn't that great?"

"Yes!" said Snowy fervently.

In April Tom returned to the fire-tower job, so there were series of days and nights when Snowy was alone in the apartment. Maybe this was the best of both worlds, she thought, and maybe he thought so too. During the spring, she and Ruhamah had to cope with the chaos caused by the construction of the back porch, so Snowy welcomed the solitude in the evenings in which she could concentrate on the new collection scheduled to be published next February. She and Kara, her editor, had settled on which would be the title poem: "Widow's Walk." Because of the title, people would expect her to dedicate this collection to Alan. But she was dedicating it to Tom.

Without the Old Man Bomber publicity, would the book be noticed at all? Had the good sales of *Tapestry Granite* been a complete fluke? Wingfield Press wouldn't publish a third collection if *Widow's Walk* didn't sell well, and her comeback would be as ephemeral as she had always feared.

Puddles phoned one evening and said, "We just had the cheerleading tryouts, and I don't know what to do. The judges were wrong."

"Huh? Didn't you and the coach judge the tryouts?"

"They don't do it the way our tryouts were done, with Gilly and Jonesy and the girls already on Varsity doing the judging. They get in three coaches from other schools, so the judging will be unbiased, supposedly."

"For heaven's sake."

"Lots of schools do this nowadays."

Contemplating the concept, Snowy carried the phone to the kitchen, where she'd been rinsing her lone supper plate and silverware, Tom being at the fire tower. On the beech tree outside the sink window, a few remaining pale dead leaves were the color of thin lemonade, and below, snow still covered the ground, but everywhere were the pink tints of spring. Although spring was just beginning, she wanted to jump on the brake and yell, Stop, stop, it'll be over too soon and I can't wait again until next year! She had already seen three robins. A phoebe had returned to its nest under an eave of the barn and was calling its name over and over from dawn to daylight-saving dusk.

Puddles said, "So the judges don't know what the girls are like, only how they perform. There's a checklist of criteria. When we were on Varsity and judging the tryouts, remember, we just took notes and then we voted, but Gilly and Jonesy had the final say."

"It definitely wasn't a democracy."

"Well, this system is supposed to be fair, but I think it's a lot worse than what we had. Isn't it better to have judges who know the JVs that are trying out for Varsity and who have seen all the girls learning the routines before the tryouts, so you know who's a natural, who's a hard worker, who pisses people off? With other sports, coaches pick the team, and doesn't that make sense with cheerleading too? But then there are those who still say cheerleading isn't a sport. Or if it is, they're handling it as if they're judges at the Olympics, for Christ's sake!"

Oh, how many directions this debate could shoot off into! Snowy cradled the receiver in her neck and put her plate in the dishwasher. During Tom's fire-warden months, maybe they could do a load of dishes only once a week, saving electricity and water. "But the judges aren't unbiased?"

"They were inconsistent. They let some girls get away with screw-ups while others who did great didn't make it."

"Can't your head coach complain?"

"Ashley? She's the don't-make-waves type when it comes to the school administration."

"And you can't complain?"

"Me? A temp, hoping to be made permanent? Maybe if we'd qualified for Nationals they wouldn't still be looking for an assistant coach with the right credentials. I can't make waves either. I keep hoping the judges' decisions were a fluke. Maybe it won't happen like this next year."

Snowy could remember with stark clarity her first tryouts her freshman year, and she could still feel the shock, the sickness, the hot face and icy hands, of the moment she saw the semifinals list of the chosen girls posted on the gym-office door and her name wasn't on it. She would have given up then, but Puddles had cajoled her into trying out for JVs, reminding her that freshmen hardly ever made Varsity. But the list was an indication of which freshmen had the best chance of making JVs. She remembered standing on the auditorium stage in her gym suit (little green skirt, those awful bloomers beneath), looking out at Gilly and Jonesy and the Varsity cheerleaders before she and Puddles launched into their routine. Puddles was very good. She herself was borderline—and yet she *had* made JVs and then Varsity and then Gilly had named her the Varsity captain, and all this nonsense had helped shape the person she'd become, God help her. When Tom first asked her out, he been only vaguely aware that she was a JV cheerleader (Rita had his full attention), but would he have been interested in her at all if her sole claim to fame was getting good marks? Vehemently she said to Puddles, "Tryouts! What a nightmare!"

"And I'm just going to have to shut up about those judges."

"I'm sorry," Snowy said, knowing that shutting up would damn near kill Puddles.

After they said good-bye, Snowy went to her office and looked at the row of books by Henrietta Snow on a bookshelf, at the manuscript on her teenage desk, and she was struck by the horrible realization that she was still trying out.

Rita was a June bride. Lavender ran the store that Saturday afternoon so Snowy and Ruhamah could attend the wedding. Tom had to be on duty at the tower, to his vast relief.

"White?" howled Puddles, phoning Snowy in the evening. "Rita wore white?"

Snowy said, "Yards and yards of white satin."

Bev shrieked at the receiver, "But acres of bosom displayed!" Rita had surprised Bev by inviting her to the wedding. After the reception, Bev had stopped at Snowy and Tom's apartment for coffee to try to offset the champagne.

Snowy said, "The village church survived the ceremony, and Mallory was an adorable flower girl, and then we all hastened to Hurricane Farm for the reception—"

Puddles said, "At Hurricane Farm? Jesus, Snowy!"

Far too brightly, Snowy said, "Imagine Mimi's reception you went to there, only with Rita's kids and grandchildren—and her sister and brothers, they were behind us in high school so I didn't remember them. No family for Frank, his parents are dead and he and his wife didn't have kids, but he invited friends in town. And Rita invited ex-cheerleaders from the Class of 1956, Joanne—she was there with Victor, I'd never have recognized him, bald—and Adele and even Nutty, remember Nutty?"

"That brownnoser! What's she been doing all these years? Wasn't she supposedly going to be a gym teacher—isn't that what she used to tell Gilly and Jonesy to butter them up?"

"She told me she started Springfield College but then she dropped out to get married and had a bunch of sons, so they were her gym classes. She's been living down in Massachusetts. She was very interested in your coaching."

Puddles said gruffly, “I hope you didn’t tell her I’m only a temp.”

“It didn’t cross my mind.”

“Will Rita quit work at the store, now she has married her sugar daddy?”

“No, she says she likes the people. After she and Frank get back from their honeymoon—they’re taking Mallory to Disney World—she’ll keep on working. Frank is busy with all his organizations and projects that she doesn’t seem particularly interested in. They don’t seem to have much in common.”

“Sex,” Puddles said. “Fun in the sack. I’ve forgotten what that is.”

Snowy said, “Well, I confess I’m really relieved she’s staying and we don’t have to try to find somebody new for the store.”

Bev grabbed the phone. “Snowy hasn’t told you the best part. Guess who caught Rita’s bouquet?”

Puddles said, “I hope to God it was Joanne.”

“Ruhamah did!”

The bouquet seemed to have no significance to Ruhamah, and Snowy concluded that the catch was an automatic reflex left over from her baseball days. Throughout this first year after she got her master’s, Ruhamah’s life seemed to revolve around her work, the store. (At that age, Snowy thought, mine revolved around the poetry and Alan; my career as a general factotum at Old Eastbourne had come in third and then disappeared entirely when I was thirty-two and Ruhamah was born.) Both Brandon and D. J. were still on the scene, but Ruhamah remained casual and noncommittal about them. During Brandon’s visits to Woodcombe now, he stayed with Ruhamah in the store’s apartment, and when Ruhamah went down to visit him, she stayed at his. Sometimes it was D. J. who was Ruhamah’s guest; sometimes Ruhamah went to Concord, to D. J.’s condo. Like Bev, Ruhamah was keeping two guys on a string.

Once after Ruhamah returned from Washington, Snowy pried, saying, “I hope you aren’t feeling trapped here, if you want to move down there. Please don’t feel you have to stick around because of me and the store. Things can be worked out.”

Ruhamah gave her a withering look. "Snowy, can you picture me as a military wife?"

"You like to travel."

Ruhamah said, "If Brandon decides to leave the Army after twenty years, he'll be out in 2002."

The distant future, Snowy thought.

But Ruhamah said, "That's just six years away," and Snowy realized Ruhamah would be only thirty-one then. Brandon, forty-two.

Snowy asked, "What would he do after the Army?"

"Oh, something or other with planes."

"You don't want to move to Concord, either? Get involved in a business there?"

"My challenge," Ruhamah said firmly, "is right here."

Later, repeating the conversation to Tom, Snowy said, "I got the strong impression that her dear old mum is included in the challenge. Computers, expansion, crumpets."

Tom said, "David is beginning to think that North Country Coffins should have a Web site. Jesus!"

"Your problem with computers is that you want to understand them completely, the way you do a piece of machinery. Be like me and just follow little mole tunnels to the stuff you need."

Tom grumbled, "Coffins in cyberspace."

Joanne hadn't caught Rita's bouquet, but she and Victor didn't waste much time after the six-year delay. They were married in July by a justice of the peace in Newburgh, with Joanne's mother and Brandon, David, Lavender, the granddaughters, and Victor's children attending, and then they went off to Nova Scotia before they settled into Victor's condo in Nashua, where Joanne had easily found a teaching job. The swift collapse of Snowy's worries reminded her of the Berlin Wall coming down.

Snowy asked Tom, "You okay about all this?"

"Funny to think of the Newburgh place as a summer home. That old dilapidated wreck of a farm."

Snowy asked Bev, "Can I can dust my hands of Joanne? I've

lived with that awful jealousy and angst for so long, I can't believe it's over. Is she as much out of our lives as she'll ever be?"

"I hope so, but remember, her son and grandchildren are in Woodcombe. Did you find out if she wore the wedding dress she'd bought six years ago?"

"I got Ruhamah to quiz Brandon, and he said she wore a suit, some kind of pink."

Bev said, "Sometimes in a store I see a dress and think it'd be just right for marrying Geoff in. Is that as good a reason as any for getting married?"

Snowy laughed.

When the fire-tower season ended in November and she and Tom were together every day again, she didn't miss the solitude, as she'd feared. This idyll continued; the young-marrieds rapture didn't slacken, but intensified. Were they making up for lost time?

At Thanksgiving, Snowy and Ruhamah went out to dinner in Eastbourne as usual with Alan's mother and sister and brother-in-law and did not mention Snowy's living with another man. But some of the recent Christmas traditions changed. Ruhamah and Harriet had a chat on the phone that resulted in Ruhamah's planning to stay home so that Brandon could spend his leave with her after a visit to Joanne and Victor's, while Jared would be the one spending the holidays with Harriet in New York.

Tom said, "So Ruhamah will be around to look after the store. You've never been to Florida. Would you want to go this Christmas?"

Snowy stared at him. After Grandpa died, Grandma had sold their Gunthwaite house and had moved to St. Petersburg, to live near Mother's brother, Uncle Charlie, and his wife, Aunt Mildred, and Snowy used to hope she and her parents would visit them. But her father always said, "A trip like that costs too much. Besides, I've heard enough to last me a lifetime about the weather down there and how you can pick oranges in your yard; I don't have to go there and see it for myself." On rare occasions, her uncle and aunt and grandmother had driven up to New Hampshire to visit, but never did she and her parents go to Florida. Looking at Tom, for a split second she felt that she would be disloyal to her father and his stubborn stance if she went. She asked, "Do you mean we'd visit your mother?"

"I did last Christmas."

Snowy knew.

"Doug and Wendy were there too, as usual, but they could do with a break, and now that their first grandchild has arrived, they want to have Christmas with him."

"Grandchild?"

"I guess I forgot to mention it."

Tom's little brother, Doug, a baby boomer born a year after their father returned from the War, Doug, the little boy she and Tom used to baby-sit for, Doug was a grandfather!

Tom said diffidently, "Just an idea. Flying is a hell of a hassle during the holidays."

Snowy said, "Julia, Bev's mother, lived in Port Salerno. On the Atlantic side."

"Would you want to see that? We could drive over."

Snowy steeled herself and asked outright, feeling like Puddles, "Would your mother want to see *me?*"

"She liked you, back in high school; she thought an A student would be a good influence on her lazy middle son."

Snowy remembered that dinner at Tom's house and how his mother's no-nonsense manner had unnerved her. The thought of meeting Mrs. Forbes again made her feel sixteen and terrified again.

Snowy asked, "What does she know about—us? Does she think I'm 'the other woman'?"

Looking a bit uncomfortable, Tom said, "I haven't phoned her about Christmas. I wanted to get your reaction first. If it's yes, then I'll phone her and out and out tell her we're living together. After I moved to Woodcombe, when I moved the business here, and the divorce and everything, nobody told her you lived here in town, but after the Old Man Bomber made even the national news, and all her old friends in Gunthwaite sent her clippings about you and me being together at Gordon Pond and you clobbering the Bomber, well, I explained about us. She said you sounded resourceful."

Snowy gave a slightly hysterical giggle.

Tom said, "Now Joanne has remarried, Mom must've stopped hoping that she and I might get back together. Mom will be glad to see you."

Maybe.

But Snowy had no family left except for Ruhamah. Everyone had died, her parents, her grandparents, Uncle Charlie, Aunt Mildred, and her real aunts on her father's side. Tom did have family. Bravely Snowy said, "It's a great idea. I'd love to go."

Thus, Snowy found herself on December twenty-third in Logan Airport, part of the hordes she'd always smugly considered complete idiots when she saw them in TV news reports about the travails of holiday travel. During the flight she opened the same old Agatha Christie she'd brought along on the flight to Glasgow to hide in for comfort, and she sat jammed in the window seat tight beside Tom, his presence reassuring. They changed planes in Atlanta and landed safely in Sarasota.

Warmth! Sunshine! The temperature in Woodcombe this morning had been twenty-eight; yesterday, eighteen. Yesterday she had been wearing a thermal undershirt beneath a flannel shirt. Today she and Tom were dressed as lightly as possible in preparation for the weather change, but she couldn't believe it when they stepped off the plane. How could this climate exist on the same continent as New Hampshire's?

"It isn't natural!" she said. "This is December!"

Tom laughed, and in the rental car he turned on the air conditioner. "Remember," he said as they drove off, "my folks' dream house is only a bungalow."

Snowy began singing, "We'll Build a Bungalow Big Enough for Two," and then realized she could recall all the words because she and Dudley had sung it on their drive home from their evening playing games at the boardwalk. She hadn't seen or talked with Dudley since she moved to Tom's. She fell silent, gazing out the window at Florida.

Tom said, "Actually, the bungalow is big enough for company.

Dad built an addition. I expect we'll be sleeping separately in the two guest rooms."

"We can tiptoe to and fro."

"I wouldn't put it past Mom to sprinkle flour on the hall floor, and there would be our telltale tracks."

On an inlet from the Gulf, in a compound of other bungalows, the Forbes bungalow was set on a lot that was smaller than the one on Gunthwaite's Morning Street where the Forbeses' old narrow white clapboard house with dark green shutters and a side porch had stood under a tall old elm. As Tom parked in the little driveway behind a Ford in the carport, Snowy pointed at the tree in the yard. Hanging amid its shiny green foilage were— "Oranges?" she asked.

"Yup."

Tom hoisted their two suitcases, and Snowy followed him, quaking, up the seashell-lined walk.

A short chunky white-haired woman opened the front door directly into the living room. "Tom. Snowy. Come right in. How was your flight?"

Mrs. Forbes had shrunk and spread, and now she too wore glasses, but her eyes were still very blue, and her demeanor was still as brisk as Snowy remembered. Mrs. Forbes gave Tom a thorough hug and commanded, "Put those suitcases in the right-hand room," and turned to Snowy, who was expecting a handshake at the most. Mrs. Forbes embraced her. Over Mrs. Forbes's shoulder, Snowy saw Tom standing dumbstruck and then she registered that Tom's mother was assigning them to the same bedroom.

Mrs. Forbes said, "Welcome to Florida, dear."

In the picture window, a silvery artificial Christmas tree had been set up, decorated with seashells. Snowy loved it. She would not be dreaming of a white Christmas.

CHAPTER THREE

"I'VE SLIPPED IN the standings," Bev said over the phone, "right out of sight. I didn't win anything at all!"

"Damn," Snowy said, getting nervous because that's how Bev sounded, not mad or frustrated but strung out. Snowy carried the phone receiver away from the living room, where Tom was watching *Nostromo* on *Masterpiece Theatre,* into her office.

Bev jittered, "I knew I'd sold fewer places than Lorraine, but I hoped I would come in second. I didn't even place third."

If Bev's sales were down, was she having trouble meeting the mortgage payments, which must be huge? Snowy's palms began to sweat. Then she remembered that Bev could always turn to Roger for help. But would she?

"That's the bad news," Bev said. "Now for the worse news. Who was it who said, 'Behind every cloud there's another cloud'?"

"Judy Garland, I think. Bev, what's happened?"

"Leon is moving in with his latest girlfriend, Elisa, the one who works in that brokerage firm, who's divorced and has a house on Taylor Avenue, plus a small son and large cup size, though not in Rita's league but let's hope she will be thirty years from now."

Snowy said disbelievingly, "Leon is leaving Waterlight?" She had always figured he'd never give up such luxurious digs, no matter what attractions any of his girlfriends possessed.

"So there goes my Geoff deterrent. Here comes a marriage proposal, I just know it. Geoff will be suggesting we live in his condo in the winter and Waterlight in the summer. Oh, Snowy, what should I do?"

"Live in sin, like me."

"It wouldn't be good for business. And what about Roger and his ideas about semiretirement??"

"Are you in love with both of them?"

"Yes!"

And probably Ruhamah was in love with both Brandon and D. J. Snowy didn't know how Bev or Ruhamah remained sane. One man, namely Tom, was plenty. But then suddenly she thought: What would have happened to *my* emotions if Tom had reappeared on the scene while I was dating Alan? Or after I'd married Alan?

She looked out through the doorway at Tom sipping from a mug of decaf.

Bev said, "I love them both, but I want to be independent of them. I want to live here in my own little castle." She suddenly wailed, "I wish Mother were living here with me. Ever since you told me about Port Salerno, I've been missing her."

As Tom had promised, he and Snowy had driven across Florida, and following Bev's directions they'd located the bungalow to which Julia and Fred had moved from Gunthwaite. Snowy had never been able to fathom Julia's completely uprooting herself from the farm that had seemed so much a part of her; okay, Julia had gone to Florida because of Fred's arthritis, but after Fred died Snowy had hoped that Julia would return to New Hampshire. Julia, however, had stayed on, laughing ruefully about having been seduced by easy living. Snowy now could sort of understand, though she and Tom had agreed that they were perverse enough to prefer coping with northern weather. After the Port Salerno trip, they had also made a pilgrimage to St. Petersburg, but condos now covered the area where Snowy's grandmother and aunt and uncle had lived.

Snowy said, "Ah, Bev."

Bev said, "God, I'm such a mess. I'll buck up. Leon is still going to take care of Waterlight, so I don't have to look for another handyman. What I've got to concentrate on is *selling.*"

After they said good-bye, Snowy's phone rang again. It was Irene, who had been feeling so fit lately that she'd begun making fudge again for Snowy to sell, just as she always used to, but who otherwise continued in her retirement from work at the store. "I know it's late," Irene said, because people in Woodcombe didn't phone each other after nine o'clock unless it was an emergency, "but I just heard and I figured you'd want to know. Isaac Thorne died this evening. He lasted a lot longer than anybody expected, didn't he, but now he's finally gone."

Snowy thought of all the times she had passed Isaac in his barnyard during her morning jogs up the Roller Coaster Road from Hurricane Farm. She would give him a wave and he would give her a remote nod that, she suspected, hid his amusement about people who had to seek out exercise. She asked Irene, "How is Cleora?"

"Well, it's not as if it's a surprise. I suppose their kids will be coming back for the funeral. He's been taken to the Higley Funeral Home."

Which was the place in Gunthwaite that had handled Snowy's parents' cremations twenty years ago. Cleora wouldn't be buying a coffin wholesale from Tom.

Irene said, "I wonder if she'll get rid of the cows, after all."

The next morning, Snowy left Ruhamah and Rita at the store and drove along the main road, under iced and powdered trees, to the Roller Coaster Road. Winter conditions always added to the thrills of its dips and jolts.

Rita and Frank were people who left up Christmas wreaths. In Snowy's opinion, Twelfth Night was the limit, but a big wreath with pine cones and Christmas ornaments and plastic fruit and a fat red ribbon still hung on the front door of Hurricane Farm.

At the Thornes' farm, Snowy pulled into the dooryard, where only the Thornes' old car and pickup were parked; none of the kids had yet arrived, and no friends were yet visiting. She looked at the stark cold scene, the weather-beaten farmhouse with its barn sagging against piles of manure. Cleora would have done the chores already this morning, the milking, the chickens. Smoke dribbling from the farmhouse's center chimney only made the place look colder.

On the morning of Alan's death, the town police chief had recruited Cleora to stay with her, and Cleora had sat in the kitchen of Hurricane Farm, answering the phone.

Snowy got out of the car and lifted out a Saran-Wrapped platter of cold cuts and cheeses. As she went up a shoveled path to the side door, Cleora opened it into the kitchen.

"Come in," Cleora said.

On the old gray linoleum was a scuffed trail of the newspapers Cleora put down to sop up snow and manure tracked in. The heat of the woodstove heightened the smell of manure, which mingled with the fragrance of baking and of coffee brewing in a new-looking Mr. Coffee on the counter, perhaps a Christmas present from one of the absent children. Corn muffins were cooling on a rack.

Snowy said, "I'm so sorry about Isaac."

"I'm getting rid of them cows. I always said I would if it was up to me."

Snowy offered the platter. "Ruhamah assembled this. We weren't sure what might come in handy for you. She sends her sympathy."

"She's a good girl. Guess I'll stick it in the icebox." Cleora found room for the platter in the old yellowed refrigerator amid bowls containing eggs and great lumps of butter, and then she checked the woodstove's oven, in which Snowy glimpsed two pies.

Snowy asked, "How are you doing?"

"We were married sixty-six years. I was sixteen, he was nineteen." Cleora poured coffee into two big thick off-white cups that Snowy recognized from the Woolworth's of her youth. One said MOM and the other said POP, in maroon, and both were chipped, as were their saucers. Cleora said, "I remember you take black," and handed her the POP.

Unzipping her parka, Snowy said faintly, "Thank you."

"Have a seat." Cleora gestured toward one of the rusty chrome chairs at the Formica table. This kitchen set might have been new when Snowy was in high school; the tabletop had once been aqua, a favorite fifties color, now blurry. The chair seats were patched with layers of duct tape, and a pillow was squashed into the broken wicker seat of the rocking chair beside the woodstove.

Snowy sat down at the table, shrugging off her parka, and tried to think if Cleora would want to talk about Isaac's death, or about the funeral plans, or about her own plans.

But Cleora, setting a plate of corn muffins and a bowl of butter with a knife in it on the table, wanted to gossip. "Drat these legs," she said, easing herself into the rocker. "Well, I hear they've got themselves one of them hot tubs at your old place."

Rita had jabbered about this and Snowy had tried not to listen. "Yes, I guess there are some changes."

"Help yourself, help yourself. They've got a satellite dish."

"Thank you." Snowy broke open a muffin. "No cable company wants to come to Woodcombe, which may be a good thing." She spread the fresh butter, remembering how her mother used to say that you could always tell what kind of a housekeeper a woman was by looking at her butter dish. Cleora still milked cows and *made* her own butter, despite arthritis. Well, that would be over when the cows were sold. Snowy thought of Puddles's mentioning her arthritis too casually and of Bev's stepfather's arthritis causing Julia to move to Florida. She asked, "Will you be staying on here? Are you thinking of a warmer climate?" Stupid! How could Cleora afford to move if she wanted to, unless those kids paid?

Cleora snorted. "I intend to die in my own house in my own bed, same as Isaac."

And Snowy thought of the husband and wife who had died in the house that Mimi had bought. Would she and Tom be dying in the apartment over North Country Coffins? What a convenient location!

Cleora hauled herself to her feet and picked up two crocheted pot holders. Opening the door of the woodstove, she asked, "How's that New York friend of yours?"

"Harriet's fine. She'll be up for a visit next month."

"I hear she's got a boyfriend in town." Cleora took out the two pies, custard, freckled with nutmeg.

"Yes, Jared Smith." Who also has a hot tub.

Cleora made the comment she'd been leading up to. "And I hear you and your boyfriend got back together."

"Tom. Remember when you first met him? Your cows had broken down a fence and Tom and I rounded them up. Or at least traipsed after them when they decided to return."

"He fixed the fence, too."

"Cleora, is there anything we can do to help?"

"Don't you worry."

Out the window, Snowy saw some sort of large American car jounce into the driveway. She stood up. "Pennsylvania license plates," she told Cleora.

"Bert," she said. "He lives nearest."

Not having met any of the Thornes' kids, Snowy had automatically thought of them still as children, but the man getting stiffly out of the car had to be a candidate for social security. Then another car pulled in behind his, Irene's Subaru, and Irene and her sister, Gert, began extricating themselves and loading up with Corningware. Reinforcements had arrived, family, neighbors bearing casseroles.

"IT'S ALWAYS A crapshoot," said Jane Hammond, owner of All Booked Up, the bookstore in Gunthwaite's Abnaki Mall. "You never can judge how many people will show up."

"Never," agreed Harriet, who had insisted on driving Snowy to this first book signing for *Widow's Walk.* Tom wanted to, but he and David had got a big order and were working through the weekend. "I've found with my gallery that you can't predict turnout by publicity or weather or other events occurring on the same day, or anything. It sure is a gamble."

Snowy, settling into the author's chair behind the table near the entrance, knew from experience that Jane and Harriet were right. With *Tapestry Granite* she had sat like a wallflower in bookstores on rainy days when people should be flocking into malls; she had done a land-office business on sunny days when they should be at the beach; on other bad-weather days the books had sold like hotcakes, and on other fair-weather days she had kept the same forced smile on her face that she had during the selection of the Junior Prom Queen and Court, when she hadn't been chosen. This Saturday afternoon at the end of February was rainy; the weather felt as weird lately as the news earlier this week that the Scots had cloned a sheep. Maybe not one person at all would show up.

She was wearing a book-signing outfit that she'd bought in Gunthwaite's Pendleton shop without Bev's supervision because Bev was so busy lately: a black watch plaid blazer, black slacks, and Gunthwaite-green sweater. With Tom's bloodstone necklace. Out of her briefcase she took her book-signing supplies and arranged them beside the pile of copies of *Widow's Walk*: two pens, a Flair and a ballpoint, in case one didn't work; a notebook in which to write the customer's name before she inscribed a book, so she could double-check the spelling with the customer (even simple John could be Jon); a square of blotting paper because she was an old-fashioned girl, so old that she'd been taught to use a pen nib dipped into the inkwell in her grammar-school desk; and a terry cloth guest towel because her hands inevitably started sweating. Why the fuck did she put herself through this? Out of her shoulder bag she took her glasses. She was ready. Jane had readied the bait, the posters on the glass wall of the store and on the book-signing table, the urn of coffee and plates of cookies on another table nearby.

Snowy said, "Everything looks lovely, Jane. Your ad in the *Gunthwaite Herald* was great."

Jane laughed. "And so was their article about the new book by the woman who saved the Old Man. We've done all we can. It's in the hands of fate."

Snowy looked at the stack of books. Had she herself done all she could with *Widow's Walk*? The advance reviews were okay. But were the poems really any good? She realized that for the first time in her life she could answer that inner critic with a Yes, goddamnit, yes! She glanced at the door. She only had to sit here and survive for two hours. She could do it. Amongst all the articles of advice about book signings she'd read, the one piece of advice she couldn't follow was to get out from behind a table, to greet customers at the door and embarrass them into looking at her wares. *That* she could not do.

Through the doorway rushed Charl and Darl, a wonderful sight.

They chorused, "Snowy! Harriet! Oh, isn't the book beautiful!" and then while Darl and Harriet talked, Charl sat down at the table in the extra chair for customers and grew quiet, holding a copy and gazing at the cover, an abstract that a Wingfield Press cover artist had designed from pictures Snowy had sent of Old Eastbourne's roofs and widow's walks.

Snowy said gently, "It's not all sad. Some of the poems are funny."

Charl raised tear-filled eyes. "Even after these thirty-six years, on a very cold night I think about Jack falling asleep in the snow." She yanked a Kleenex out of her shoulder bag and dabbed at her face. "But aren't we lucky, though, to have Dudley and Tom." She opened the book. "It's dedicated to Tom!"

Snowy hadn't told Tom ahead of time, guessing that he would try to talk her out of it, and when he'd opened her advance copy and seen "To Thomas Forbes," he'd briefly lost the power of speech but then said just what she'd expected, "You shouldn't waste a dedication on me." She knew he meant that their love didn't need declaring. She had told him, "There's a poem in here you haven't seen. About the AT, another kind of 'walk' but for a similar purpose."

Charl said, "Tom must be tickled!"

"I think so," Snowy said.

"Could you sign this for me and Dudley, and another for Darl and Bill?"

Snowy knew how to spell their names, but what should she say in the inscriptions, especially the one that included Dudley? Three potential customers were sidling up to the table. She couldn't think. In desperation she just scribbled, "Love, Snowy." Another customer poured herself a cup of coffee and came over to the table. Charl said, "Darl, we're hogging things," and Darl said to Harriet, "These cookies look yummy but let's get out of Snowy's way and go to Indulgences." As the twins hurried off to the cash register with their books, Harriet told Snowy, "I'll do some sight-seeing after and be back at four," and then went with them down the mall's corridor to Fay's bakery, where Fay, perhaps inspired by Snowy's success with a coffee shop, had installed a few little tables.

More people gathered to look through *Widow's Walk* and to chat. Snowy began to feel, as she always did when things got busy at a signing, that she was the hostess of a party, but at this party she had to write in books while making small talk, an art she hadn't mastered as she had weighing steaks and ringing up purchases while making chitchat in her store. And here at a hometown signing, there was the added challenge of recognizing people from your past. She wiped her hands on the guest towel.

Then came a lull. Snowy leaned back in her chair.

Dudley paused in the doorway of the store.

It had been over a year since she had seen or talked with him. Snowy leapt up. She wasn't following that advice about collaring customers, but she was running to the door and she was saying, "Dudley, Dudley, it's been forever."

He said lightly, "And you're my vice president. We should be getting together to plan the reunion. Frankie lives in Santa Fe and Shirley is in Fort Worth, so we're the only two class officers still in the area."

Although she had been vice president of their class their senior year, while he as usual had been the president, she had never helped him plan a reunion nor had she ever been to one.

"Okay," she said, surprising both of them.

He moved forward, toward the stack on the table. "Congratulations on the new book."

"Don't buy a copy. Charl has been in; she already has."

He picked up a copy and opened it, turning to the dedication page. "Congratulations on the new life."

"Not so new."

He glanced around. "The dedicatee isn't here?"

"He had to work."

There was a silence, which seemed to Snowy to reverberate with Dudley's disapproval, his disappointment in her.

He said, "You don't really have to help with the reunion. Over the years, Charl and Darl have done most of the organizing, and now Darl has got the info on her computer, addresses and everything, so the great event is under control."

"Oh. Well, then."

They stood there, not looking at each other. No, Snowy thought, Dudley cannot make me feel guilty about living with Tom. But she did feel guilty about avoiding reunions, and she no longer had the excuse of agoraphobia. And she felt awful about the loss of Dudley's friendship. Why the hell had this been caused by moving a couple of doors down the street to live with Tom? If her stay at Waterlight had made Dudley think she was available, didn't he understand that she'd never be available to him, even if he wasn't married, because they had learned long ago, after she'd dated him on the rebound from Tom, that *friends* were what they truly were, ever since their sandbox days?

Dudley held the book. He found he was reading her name on

the cover over and over. Henrietta Snow. She had once explained to him that she hadn't used her husband's last name in her writing life because she'd had poems published in her maiden name before she met Alan Sutherland, and she wanted to avoid confusion, but she'd also done so for feminist reasons. That was, she'd admitted, a fairly fuzzy decision made in pre-women's-lib days. Henrietta Snow, Henrietta Snow was the person he'd known all his life. But now she was almost married to Tom Forbes.

Dudley said, "I saw in the paper about the Old Man Bomber."

"Yes, I guess the article about the new collection had to mention him."

"No, before that article. The item about his getting out of New Hampshire Hospital."

"*What?*"

"You didn't see it in the *Union Leader?* Snowy, you really should read a statewide newspaper."

And you, Snowy thought, should have phoned and told me. "Kenneth Collins is loose now?"

"No, not until June. Then he'll be going to one of those intermediate treatment centers."

"What does that mean?"

"A community halfway-house type of place."

"Shit, shit, shit!"

Luckily, the person who walked up to the table as Snowy spoke was Bev, who didn't have to come to the book signing to buy a copy because Snowy had as usual given her one and sent one to Puddles, but Bev had promised she would drop by for moral support. Bev was looking very much the successful real-estate salesperson, wearing a long red wool-cashmere coat and smooth black boots. She said, "Are you doing a reading? 'Shit, shit, shit'? I don't remember that immortal line in your book. Hello, Dudley. What was your favorite line back in English lit, Wordsworth—"

Snowy said, "It was a toss-up between 'The sea that bares her bosom to the moon' and—"

Dudley supplied, "'A Pagan suckled in a creed outworn.' Bev, Snowy and I have been talking about the reunion."

Bev clutched her throat and crossed her eyes. "Our fortieth!"

Dudley didn't grin. "Instead of the country club as usual, it's going to be held at Trask's."

Snowy squeaked, "Trask's?" The factory where her father had worked.

But Bev said, "Oh, the new convention center," and Snowy remembered that this had been one of mayor Dudley's accomplishments, getting the Trask building rescued.

Dudley said, "We want to help publicize and support the center. The reunion will be the first Saturday in August. Surely you two could deign to grace it with your presence." He stalked out the door.

Bev said, "What's wrong with him? That's not the most enticing or courteous invitation I've ever had."

Snowy realigned some copies.

Bev asked, "Do you think we should finally break down and attend a reunion of the Class of '57?"

Bev always used to say that the very thought of a reunion made her gorge rise. But five years ago, Snowy sensed she was tempted to attend their thirty-fifth, to strut her stuff and show off her independence.

Snowy said, "Maybe we should."

"It might be useful, for business. I like your outfit; I always forget how much I like black watch." Bev sank into the extra chair. "How's *your* business doing this afternoon?"

Snowy sat down again. "It got pretty lively for a while."

"Mine isn't." Bev unbuttoned her coat, then pulled it close around her as if she were still cold. "Everything's quiet. Geoff and I haven't even made one of our business trips to the Manchester motel. I haven't had to fend off any kind of proposal from him."

"Do you suppose Puddles would come to the reunion? Oh, she says hi, she phoned last night. Her cheerleading squad was eliminated in the preliminary round at Nationals, but she's still elated they got that far. Speak of the devil—isn't that Geoff out there?"

Bev turned and looked out the glass wall into the corridor. Wearing the handsome parka he'd bought for their trip to Telluride, Geoff was striding along talking to the short young woman trotting at his side.

"That's Caitlin Perry," Bev said. "She's the new salesperson. I didn't know we had anything listed in this mall." She started to stand up. "Maybe Caitlin got a listing today. She won the Most Promising Newcomer award last month." Bev sat back down and hugged her coat. "She looks like a munchkin, doesn't she?"

"Hi, Snowy. Hi, Bev." A pretty gray-haired woman, vaguely familiar, approached the table.

Snowy blinked and groped for her name.

"I'm Diane, remember me? I live in California, but I came back to see my sister, she's been in the hospital, and I saw in the paper about this and I just had to stop by! A few years ago my sister sent me a clipping about you and Tom and some crazy guy in the mountains. Did you really hit him with a bottle of wine?"

It was Diane Morrissette, another classmate, another cheerleader—and another of Dudley's former girlfriends. Jumping up to greet her, Snowy thought that a book signing could be quite enough of a reunion, thank you. "Yes," she said, "a California chardonnay, as a matter of fact."

ON AN APRIL Monday, climbing the stairs to the apartment after work, Snowy heard the phone ringing. Tom was already up here, setting the table, and he answered it, saying, "Sure, Puddles, she's just coming in, hang on." He handed the receiver to Snowy and raised his eyebrows.

Puddles cried, "We're getting sued!"

"You and Guy?" Snowy asked, immediately picturing one of Guy's houses collapsing. "Guy's business? Did I hear you right? The connection sounds bad."

"I'm on my cell phone."

Impressed, sidetracked, Snowy said, "You have a cell phone?" Then she added, "Puddles, I hope you're not using it while you're driving!"

"I'm stopped." Puddles looked out her car window at the Exxon gas station she'd pulled into. Nearby, a roadside stand was selling Vidalias and pecans. "I was on my way back to Hilton Head from Broughton, but I couldn't wait to call and ask you what to do. Snowy, four of the girls who tried out for the squad earlier this month and didn't make it, they're suing the school!"

"Really?" Carrying the phone into her office, Snowy tried to imagine such a thing happening in Gunthwaite in the 1950s. "They're suing the whole school system? You yourself aren't being sued?"

"No, no, I'm safe, I'm only remotely part of the school system, but Snowy, I saw the same thing I saw last year at the tryouts. I think the girls are right and the judges were wrong!"

Snowy heard the rumble of TV news from the living room and the clank of pots from the kitchen. She asked, "The supposedly fair system failed again?"

"The judges can't help being subjective, no matter how much they claim to be objective. Same as last year, so it wasn't a fluke, so I protested to Ashley, the head coach. She was upset, but she still didn't want to take on the school administration. So I shut up again, but there were all these poor girls who didn't make it crying their heads off and I knew that at least a couple of them definitely should have."

Back in their own high-school years, if Puddles hadn't been chosen, Puddles's folks should have sued. But that was undreamed-of then.

Puddles continued, "Aside from the emotional part, lots of

girls and their parents nowadays have a financial investment in it. Girls take gymnastics and dance and stuff for years, instead of just learning on the spot the way we did. So the parents of four of them got themselves a lawyer, who has filed a lawsuit. What should I do? Keep my mouth shut?"

"Puddles, I don't know."

"I've been hoping and praying the school will let me be the official assistant coach now that we got to Nationals this year. Ashley and I have learned so much, I'm hoping we'll get there again next year, maybe into the finals. If I say I agree with the girls, I've had it."

"Conscience or career?"

"Is there a way I don't have to choose?"

"You could work from within to change the system. What's the term, 'bore from within'? You wouldn't be able do that if you speak up and they fire you." Snowy smelled spaghetti sauce; Tom was heating Ragu. She said, "Bev and I have definitely decided to go to the reunion. Tom even said he'd go, be my escort, though he looked long-suffering. Have you decided if you're coming?"

"I can't decide anything!" For the first time, Puddles noticed a dead armadillo on the side of the road. It seemed so sad, so sad.

Snowy said, "Last Friday night, Bev's birthday, she and I went to the movies, to one of that bunch of cinemas in the old movie theater. It was really strange; I'd never been in there since they chopped it up. The cinema we were in was upstairs, in the old balcony!" What was even weirder was that Bev didn't have anything more exciting to do on her fifty-eighth birthday. Bev hadn't thrown herself a party at Waterlight, as she had last year, or gone out with Geoff, as she had other years. Mimi, who had thrown that big bash for Bev's fiftieth, was probably saving up for her sixtieth. Bev had phoned Snowy and suggested the movies. "After, we went to Hooper's and had hot fudge sundaes."

Puddles wasn't listening. She said, "Well, good-bye," and jabbed the cell phone off.

Feeling that she had failed Puddles, Snowy joined Tom in the kitchen. Making the salad, she asked during a commercial, "Are you glad you played football in high school? Was it useful?"

"It was fucking stupid," he said.

Oh God, she thought, his football knee, which he probably still blamed for Libby's death. And a football game had caused the death of her freshman-year boyfriend, Ed Cormier, breaking his back and his spirit.

Then Tom laughed. "But it was crazy. Do you remember the time—hmm, my sophomore year—when Butch was out deep to receive a kickoff, with the sun in his eyes, and the football hit him square on the head? He was so mortified it's a wonder he didn't quit the team, but we kidded him out of it."

Snowy didn't remember. She would have been a freshman, sitting with the Gang in the bleachers. "He was wearing a helmet, I assume?"

"Leather. We'd gone back to wearing leather helmets after we switched to plastic. But that's another story."

"Tell me."

So during supper at the trestle table, Tom told her about how the old leather helmets had been replaced by the latest plastic type, but there were a frightening number of concussions, one nearly fatal—"It was at an away game, Rochester, and Sam got knocked out, but instead of taking him to the hospital there, the coach brought him home on the floor of the bus. Stupid bastard! Good thing Sam had a thick skull." Tom twirled spaghetti round and round his fork. "But after that, the coach dug out the old leather helmets. The guys were not pleased. They loved the new ones because they thought plastic looked more professional. The problem was, the lining wasn't thick enough to absorb a hit, and the plastic was too hard. With the old helmets, the leather itself absorbed a good deal of the force." Tom chewed and swallowed, remembering. "Later, we used newer plastic ones that were better."

"I can't imagine going out on a field knowing you're going to be knocked around."

"You hope you're going to do most of the knocking around yourself."

Snowy thought of men wielding clubs, swords, bows and arrows, men on battlefields, men storming over the top out of trenches into no-man's-land, men fighting door-to-door, hand-to-hand.

Tom said, "Fucking stupid."

To amuse him, Snowy told Tom about the cheerleading lawsuit.

After supper, the phone rang again. Snowy grabbed the receiver, hoping Puddles had had a brainstorm and reached a solution.

Bev exclaimed, "Etta just phoned. She's made her decision and she's staying in New England! She's going to take the job on the editorial staff of that horse magazine down in Amherst!"

Amherst, Massachusetts. Home of Emily Dickinson. Snowy said, "You must be so relieved." Etta, graduating this spring, had been considering magazines in Virginia, Kentucky, Colorado, as well as New England. Snowy thought of Ruhamah's decision: Woodcombe General Store. And she thought of her own: Marrying Alan and working at Old Eastbourne instead of becoming an editor at Commonwealth Publishing, which was her ambition when she'd worked there during her Non-Resident Terms and summers.

Bev said, "Oh, it's such a relief. Who knows, she'll probably eventually move around, farther away, but at least at the beginning she'll still be in a next-door state. She's calling Roger now."

"He'll be proud and happy."

"He'll tease her about the time Prancer fell in the swimming pool." Then Bev said, "I thought the card might've got delayed, but there wasn't one in today's mail."

"Card?"

"Roger always sends a birthday card, ever since I moved up here. He has never forgotten or sent a belated one." Bev had sped home from the office, certain there would be a nice big sentimental card in the mailbox at the head of Waterlight's driveway. It would bring solace, after these increasingly awkward days at Plumley Real Estate. But there had been only junk mail and bills. Crestfallen, she had driven slowly down to her dream house, where the ice on the lake was melting, showing gray tracings of snowmobile tracks like those childhood magic slates.

Snowy said, "He just must have forgotten. Maybe he's got some important case or something."

In a small voice, Bev said, "Geoff forgot my birthday, too."

"Oh, Bev."

Bev's tone turned caustic. "I'm now fifty-eight. Caitlin Perry is twenty. We can only speculate about the age of Roger's little friend down in Ninfield, but I would bet, wouldn't you, that she isn't almost sixty?"

"Um."

"I keep thinking I should move on from Plumley Real Estate and affiliate myself with another real-estate firm. But I stand a better chance of selling if I stick with the situation I know. I hold my head high. If any of the salespeople who suspected that Geoff and I were having an affair, if any of them are pitying me or gloating, they aren't showing it. Not even Lorraine. I'm beginning to realize that she and Geoff had probably had some business meetings in the Manchester motel before I arrived on the scene. Snowy, how could I have been so dense?"

"Um."

"I've been remembering how I realized, after Roger and I broke up in high school, that he wasn't just my boyfriend, he was my *friend.* Sometime during the marriage and the kids, that friendship got lost again. His arrogance about my exam results! Oh hell and damn. Maybe I'll invite Roger to be my escort to the reunion."

The next evening Snowy phoned Puddles and got Guy, who said in his South Carolina accent, drawing the words out, "She's at a meeting about the cheerleading lawsuit. Tempest in a teapot, if y'all ask me."

"I'll give her a call tomorrow night."

"I'll tell her. Bye." His "bye" sounded like "baa."

"Thanks. Bye." Hanging up, Snowy considered calling Bev to see how she was doing. But she didn't know what to say, so she didn't.

Puddles phoned the following evening before Snowy had a chance. "The shit," Puddles announced, "is hitting the fan."

"There was a meeting?"

"A big powwow, the school administration and the school board, all shaking in their boots. A rumor went around school yesterday that the principal was going to avoid going to court by capitulating, letting the four girls be on the squad, so lots of the other parents of girls who didn't make it, the ones not suing, showed up to yell that that's not fair. Meanwhile, yesterday the girls who'd been at the tryouts got up a petition saying that Ashley and guess who, yours truly, should be the judges! So these girls were there too, with this petition. What a brawl!" said Puddles with relish.

"Were you asked your opinion?"

"The petition gave Ashley the backbone to speak her mind, and I was right there beside her while she told our bosses that cheerleading should be handled the same as the other school sports, with the school's own coaches making the selection. So I piped up and added that they could either let the lawsuit go ahead or see if the plaintiffs would agree to new tryouts, with Ashley and me judging. I sounded really restrained and reasonable, if I do say so myself."

"Good for you!"

"Well, Ashley and I got applause from the parents and the girls, but the powers-that-be were looking so flustered I couldn't tell what they thought, if anything. They adjourned and scurried away, hiding from the rabble. Ashley phoned me at the clinic this afternoon and said that rumors were still flying but she trusts her source who told her that the school honchos and their lawyer were meeting with the girls' lawyer sometime today. Does that bode good or ill?"

"Damned if I know."

"I'll phone you the minute I hear."

Snowy reported Puddles's news to Tom, who predicted, "The school board will cave," adding, "God, am I glad I am out of public education."

The next day the store's phone rang as Snowy was tidying tables after the morning-coffee rush, while Ruhamah was unpacking their new supply of T-shirts, so Rita at the cash register answered it. "Yes," she said, "this is Rita. Who? *Puddles?*"

Snowy hurried to the counter, thinking that Rita and Puddles hadn't talked since Rita graduated from high school, and that was probably a very good thing. But Rita seemed to be settling down for a friendly chat. "Yes, I'm Rita Barlow now, it was a beautiful wedding, and Frank is a wonderful husband, just great with my grandkids, and the house—do you know the house? I'm adding my touches—oh sure, Snowy is right here."

Snowy took the receiver. "Hi, Puddles."

Puddles was jubilant and impatient to impart her news, but she took time to remark, "She's still a bitch, isn't she."

"Er, well, not really. Tell me, tell me, what's happened?"

"They worked out an agreement that sounds like gobbledygook, but it boils down to what I suggested. New tryouts, with Ashley and me judging!"

"Hooray!"

"And Snowy, to make me official, they've offered me a contract. I'm the assistant coach, no longer a temp!"

"Oh, this is terrific!"

As Puddles talked on about the awful responsibility of judging and about the problems that lay ahead, the problems inherent in all tryouts, now complicated by this controversy, Snowy thought of how sometimes success came at you sideways. No matter how hard you worked, you needed luck. A threatened lawsuit had given Puddles the job she wanted. Kenneth Collins had got *Tapestry Granite* and thus *Widow's Walk* published.

Puddles said, "But now that I'm a real coach, I sure as hell have to be here in August when practice starts for the football season, so

I won't be coming to the reunion. You'll have to tell me everything. What Linda looks like, what she wears, and you tell *her* about my daughter the doctor. I wonder if Norm will be there."

"Norm?" Snowy asked in surprise. Although Norm Noyes had been Puddles's faithful suitor, Puddles had scorned him.

"Well, I can't help being curious about everyone, including Norm."

As they said good-bye, Snowy suddenly thought: Would I have agreed to go to this reunion if I hadn't had two collections recently published?

WHEN SNOWY HAD repeated to Tom what Dudley had told her about Kenneth Collins, Tom had got on the phone to D. J. at his Concord law firm. D. J. made inquiries and confirmed that instead of full release from New Hampshire Hospital, Collins would be going to an intermediate treatment center in Concord in June.

Tom had asked, "But he won't be locked up while he's there?"

D. J. had said, "It's a community halfway house. He'll still be in treatment, but the idea is to ease him back into the outside world."

Tom had found himself glancing toward the bedroom closet, in which he stored the .22 rifle he hadn't used since shooting a woodchuck the last summer he gardened in Newburgh.

Now it was June, and Snowy, who had taken Dudley's advice and been reading the *Union Leader* or the *Concord Monitor* daily during slow moments at the store, spotted the story even though she only glanced at the paper today, there being few slow moments because bridesmaid Ruhamah was at her roommate's home in Wilton for Lauren's wedding on Saturday. Why the hell did the news of Kenneth Collins's move to the halfway house make her palms sweat, her heart race? She was back at Gordon Pond, facing those glittering eyes.

After work, she phoned Tom, up on Pascataquac for a three-day shift. "It's in the paper. The Old Man Bomber is out of the loony bin."

Tom said, "The guy is just a sad sack. Nothing to worry about."

"I know."

He wanted to say: Make sure you lock up tonight. He didn't say it.

But Snowy went downstairs into the workshop and checked the locks. Returning to the apartment, she locked the door behind her. Throughout the evening, friends and acquaintances phoned, having seen the news in newspapers or on TV or heard it on the radio.

Bev had caught it on New Hampshire Public Radio as she drove tiredly home after a wasted day showing houses to a couple who had seemed serious but had turned out to be, in real-estate jargon, tire-kickers. She dragged herself into Waterlight, down the hall to her kitchen, whose bright colors that had been so amusing made her want to scream. She tried to phone Snowy, but the line was busy and Snowy didn't have call-waiting. Snowy scrimped and saved on stuff like this, and Tom didn't splurge either. But Bev had observed that North Country Coffins appeared to be a thriving little business. And Snowy's little store hadn't gone under, knock on wood, so why the hell couldn't Snowy at least get call-waiting? Bev dialed again, and this time Snowy answered.

Bev asked, "You've heard about Kenneth Collins?"

"Yes. Nothing to worry about. They wouldn't be letting him out of the hospital if they didn't think he was ready to start getting back into real life."

Snowy sounded too glib, as if reciting something she'd been saying over and over.

So Bev agreed, "No, they wouldn't." But she couldn't help asking, "Is Tom up at the fire tower?"

"For a couple more days."

"Are you nervous there alone? Do you want to come spend the nights here?"

"Thanks, but I'm fine." Snowy suddenly wondered if Bev had become nervous about being alone in the big house. "How are things with you?"

"There's good news: I've lost those five pounds of winter weight, so we can start searching in earnest for what to wear to the reunion. Let's go to the Manchester mall Sunday afternoon."

"Have you decided if you'll ask Roger to come to the reunion, be your escort?"

Bev had hoped Snowy would have forgotten this dumb idea that had occurred to Bev when she was feeling unbearably abandoned, but of course Snowy remembered. Bev confessed, "As a matter of fact, I gave him a call. He said he was afraid he'd be tied up. Isn't it useful to know so far in advance that you're going to be tied up?"

"Did you ask him if he was into bondage?"

Bev began to laugh too hard. "Oh, how I wish I'd thought of that! I was so humiliated I couldn't think of anything except to pretend I'd really called just to talk about the children. Something has certainly happened with that woman of his; she must be putting the pressure on. Or has he got *another* new woman, and it's serious?" The kitchen's colors, painted in a frenzy by a betrayed wife, capered and jeered. "He didn't bring up the subject of retiring to Gunthwaite; that idea seems to have died. But he still didn't bring up the subject of a divorce, either."

"You can go to the reunion as an independent woman. Isn't that the image you wanted?" Then a lightbulb blazed in Snowy's head. "Hey, Tom loathes reunions, he's never been to any of his high-school reunions, and he's only going to this one to be a nice guy. So why don't I let him off the hook, and you and I can go alone together? Independent women."

Bev gasped with relief, "Sunday, we'll find just the right outfits for the image."

So after work on Sunday, Snowy drove to Bev's house, and in Bev's car they drove to the Mall of New Hampshire. Snowy imagined all the girls—women—in the GHS Class of 1957 setting forth on this life-or-death mission, all the women everywhere who had ever gathered up the courage to attend a class reunion. Talk about stress! After a few forays into boutiques, she and Bev attacked Filene's.

Bev had decided to go for a tailored look, and she carried armload after armload of blazer-skirt combos and suits into a dressing room, but she was dissatisfied with all of them, and when she returned to the racks yet again to continue the search, she found herself being drawn over to dresses. Flipping through hangers, she came upon The Dress. She could even get married in this one. No. Yes, try it on, for a reunion, not for a wedding. She fumbled, fearing they didn't have it in a size 10. They did! She grabbed it and rushed to the dressing rooms. "Snowy?"

"I'm in here."

Bev took the dressing room next door and stripped off her shirt and jeans. The sleeveless pale green dress floated down over her, its flickering tints diaphanous, reminding her of Waterlight in a misty springtime dawn. And glory be, the décolletage amazingly flattered her boobs, disguising the lack thereof! This was one of those rare moments in clothes-shopping when you knew immediately you'd found the treasure. But the dress didn't project the right image. She called to Snowy, "Come see!" and then said uncertainly, "It's too romantic, isn't it?"

For once, Snowy made Bev's decision. "It's perfect. Buy it."

And for once, Snowy had already made her own final choice. Tall Bev was standing there in a long dress; short Snowy wore a miniskirt outfit. A silky flouncy little skirt and a matching short-sleeved peplum top. Snowy didn't like the new versions of miniskirts, which seemed too tight and crotchy, but this reminded her of some she'd had in the 1960s and '70s. The color was good old Fabulous Fifties aqua, with a print of blue blossoms the shade of Tom's eyes. How could she resist, though it cost more than she'd planned to spend? Even when Bev laughed and said, "You're cute as a button in that," she didn't change her mind. She said, "Mission accomplished!"

"Shoes," Bev reminded her, "and new underwear. Lingerie, pantyhose. And elegant small purses. I've got the right jewelry for this dress." The emeralds Roger had given her for their twentieth anniversary. "Your Israeli necklace would look lovely with your outfit, and your blue dangly earrings, so we're all set on that front."

"God," Snowy said, "this is as complicated as getting ready for a prom."

"No, it isn't. Remember our layers of crinolines over our hoops? Strapless bras? Falsies? Garter belts—and sanitary belts and Kotex if we got unlucky with the timing? Compared to the fifties, this is a piece of cake."

Snowy suspected that Bev was whistling in the dark.

AUGUST 2, 1997, 6:30 p.m. On State Avenue, near the high school from which they had graduated in June forty years ago, Bev steered her Mercedes down the driveway of Trask's to the parking lot behind the big brick factory. The reunion's cocktail hour had started at six, and there were plenty of cars already parked here. Bev had wanted to be fashionably late, which made punctual Snowy antsy.

Bev and Snowy got carefully out of the car.

Bev thought: My audience awaits.

My father, Snowy thought, worked here forty-five years. In her youth she had been vague about the place, grasping only that it made the machines that made something else and Daddy was the foreman of the lathe department. As she grew up, she paid attention enough to know that Trask's manufactured gear cutters. This place had put food on the table and clothes on her back, but she had never been inside it. Maybe if her mother had been able to have more children, maybe if Snowy had had a brother, her father would have taken a boy to see his place of work, *the* place where most of Gunthwaite's workforce toiled. Although Bev's stepfather had worked at the bank and Puddles's father had worked at the shoe factory, Trask's employed the fathers of almost everyone else she knew, including Tom—and Dudley.

Now, thanks to Dudley's efforts, the nearly derelict factory had become the Gunthwaite Conference and Convention Center, its exterior spiffed up with white trim, dark green awnings over all the windows on the three floors, and under every window a green window box bursting with red impatiens.

Bev said, "Which of us talked the other into doing this?"

"Want to go home?"

Snowy and Bev looked at the green porte-cochere awning, on which hung a white banner with green lettering that said: Welcome GHS Class of '57. Green and white balloons bounced lazily.

Bev said, "Puddles would kill us after we got her all excited and then we didn't go. I can just hear her accusing us of pulling out. Anyway, it would be a shame to waste these outfits."

A car came down the driveway, followed by another. Snowy said, "We'd better scoot indoors so we don't have to meet people before they've got name tags."

She and Bev scooted up the walk, around the building to the front door, high heels clattering on the pavement like the sound effects in old radio mystery shows. Margo Lane in *The Shadow.* Snowy hadn't worn high heels in years, so she'd practiced after work with Tom laughing at her and making remarks about vanity. But tonight when he'd seen her for the first time in the new outfit, the miniskirt, he didn't find her silly. His eyes bugged out, he gulped, and he said, "You sure you don't want me to take you?" It was very satisfying.

Yet during the drive to Gunthwaite, Snowy's confidence had ebbed, and now as she and Bev went into the building, she sensed Bev readying herself for an entrance, and as always Snowy envied Bev's stage presence. In the hallway, a sign on an easel welcomed them again in green and white and told them to go to the Trask Room. This name, a last remnant of the building's past, both pleased Snowy and made her want to weep. She looked around, trying to imagine her father working here, day after day, week after week, year after year.

He wouldn't have heard sounds of revelry coming from a door to the left. Voices, laughter, and the Chordettes singing "Mr. Sandman."

Bev's hip-swinging walk had been famous in high school. She had toned it down afterward, but now as she headed toward that door, the long pale green dress swayed like a pendulum. Snowy looked down at herself and promptly forgot the ego-boosting expression on Tom's face. Was she fifty-eight-year-old mutton dressed as lamb? Oh, fuck it, she thought, I won't let this be a competition about looks and weight and clothes and accomplishments; I just want to talk and laugh with some old friends. But she felt as faint as she did before a reading.

Bev made her entrance. Here comes the star of the Gunthwaite High School stage and the Queen of the Junior Prom, white hair and all!

Snowy followed her into the noise. Agoraphobia loved to hit you in big rooms, of course, and Snowy saw that this was very big, decorated with green-and-white pennants, streamers, and bunting. People were standing around talking at the top of their lungs in the front half of the room near the bar, and beyond them stretched an area of round tables draped in white tablecloths perked up by green napkins. As the walls began to pulse, terror struck her. The monster had returned, the floor would begin to dip up and down in waves, and she would scream or have a heart attack. After all these years of freeing herself, after years of dealing with people at the store, after climbing mountains, after the readings and the book signings, it was coming back. Oh God, oh God—

Then Dudley was beside her, taking her arm and Bev's and escorting them to a long table, garlanded in green and white, beside the door. Charl and Darl were jumping up from their chairs behind it, squealing with delight as Dudley proclaimed, "Look what I found!"

The twins wore identical shocking-pink pantsuits. Charl said, "We were getting worried," and leaned across the table to hug Snowy and Bev, while Darl handed them their name tags, which were actually stickers, not tags, with—eek!—their yearbook pictures, hazy gray photocopies but unmistakably their eighteen-year-old selves, alongside their computer-printed names. After the first instant of shock, Snowy was grateful for these aids to classmates' names; she hadn't had time to do her homework and delve into her yearbook to refresh her memory.

Darl said, "If we made the lettering large enough so us old folks could read it without our glasses, the tags would have to be *huge*. You two look gorgeous!"

Snowy said truthfully, "So do you two."

Darl said, "I think we all look pretty good, considering. The turnout is pretty good, too. Out of our class of one hundred fifty-two, we had almost a hundred responses, sixty-three acceptances. Counting spouses, we've got ninety-five people here. I'm sorry Tom couldn't come." Darl remembered that Tom wasn't a spouse. She sipped from her glass of zinfandel. "You know what I mean." She glanced over her shoulder at Bill, her husband, who was tending to the tape deck, and added, "Oh, how we all loved Tom! He ought to be at any reunion of ours!"

Bev and Charl giggled, Dudley cleared his throat but didn't say anything, and Snowy, affixing the sticker to her top like a brooch, realized the room's din had lowered. She turned, and the room steadied. The faces of the people staring at them were the faces of strangers. Who, she thought, *were* these old folks? Then a tanned balding man, wearing a sports jacket with stitching on it that reminded Snowy of Roy Rogers's shirts, walked in a trance toward Bev.

Bev laughed and said, "Frankie! I'm Bev," as if he didn't know, and gave him a hug.

He came into focus for Snowy then. Frankie Richardson, class treasurer and Bev's boyfriend in eighth grade. He had been captain of the football team their senior year, and after Tom had broken up with her the previous summer, Snowy had dated him occasionally.

Two couples strolled into the room, the people who'd arrived in the parking lot after she and Bev had.

Dudley had been greeting everyone, but he left the newcomers to the twins and put his hand on Snowy's shoulder, guiding her away toward the bar, seeing the muscle twitching in her jawline. Had he pressured her into doing something more than she was capable of? He knew that for over a year now he had behaved like an asshole. "Snowy, are you all right?"

The din rose again.

Snowy said, "I'm fine. Didn't you say that Frankie was in Santa Fe? Does he usually come all this way for reunions?"

"Not since our twentieth, but he sent his e-mail address along with his bio when he sent back the reunion form saying he wouldn't be attending, and after we learned that you and Bev were coming, Darl sent out some e-mails with the news in hopes of attracting people who'd declined, and Frankie changed his mind in a flash, by e-mail reply. Let's get you a glass of wine. Chardonnay, I presume?"

"I'll never live that down, will I." At the bar, Snowy opened her new little blue shoulder bag that could only hold her reading glasses, lipstick, and some money, but Dudley said, "This is a present from the president for the vice president." As he paid, Snowy watched Bev mingling in grand style, Frankie at her side. Within two minutes of her arrival, Bev had a male in tow. Bev hadn't bothered putting on her name tag; she didn't need one. "Thank you," Snowy said, taking the glass, which hardly jiggled in her hand. "Is Frankie married?"

"His wife died a few years ago. Breast cancer."

"Hell."

"That's part of the statistics Darl didn't get into." To change the subject, Dudley said, "I'd hate to see what you've got in your attic."

She stared at him, then looked down again at her outfit, fears confirmed. Her once-dear Dudley was being cruelly sarcastic. She said, "This is new retro, not out of a trunk. Anyway, I don't have an attic per se anymore; I'm living in one." She put her chin up.

His heart nearly broke. He said hastily, "A reference to Dorian Grey's attic. You look so young, a person who didn't know would think you'd come to the wrong reunion. You should be at your fifth."

She gave a relieved laugh and he tried to think what he really wanted to say but he, Dudley Washburn of all people, was at a loss for words.

Two women rushed up. Snowy couldn't see their name-tag photos before the women were hugging her and saying, "I'm Carol Tucker, I'm Dotty Mooney!" Carol had been a cheerleader, and like Snowy and a lot of other women here, she was still miraculously a blonde; heftier now, she wore a sprightly blazer over slacks. Dotty's brown hair was graying, and although she must have put thought and effort into the choice of a long flowery dress, it still had the haphazard look of her high-school clothes. Snowy was overcome with great affection for both women, members of the Gang. Dotty said, "We read about you and Tom in the paper, capturing the Old Man Bomber!"

Dudley checked his watch. "Time for the class picture." He took a spoon from the bartender's array of utensils and tapped ringingly on a glass. In the voice of the class president and city mayor, he announced, "Members of the Class of '57, let's go out to the lawn for the photograph that will commemorate this great occasion. Spouses and others, you can stay here and keep drinking!"

Charl ran over to him and clutched his arm. "But Linda isn't here yet, and she always comes."

Dudley said, "Sorry, love, we must stay on schedule, for the caterers."

He and the twins had to act like border collies with a flock of recalcitrant sheep to get the Class of '57 herded out to a front lawn that hadn't been here in the old days of Trask's, a slope of lush green grass where the photographer for whom Charl worked was waiting to take the picture. As Snowy moved along in the crowd, her heels stabbing the turf, she talked with Carol and Dotty, answering their questions about Puddles, learning that Carol lived in Leicester and used to do some volunteer coaching for the Leicester squad—"coaching our rivals!"—and that Dotty lived in Milford and had four children and eight grandchildren. Suddenly Snowy realized she was enjoying herself.

Bev angled toward her, accompanied now by *two* men, Frankie and a dapper guy with crisp dark hair and a glint of irony in his eyes, who said to Snowy, "Remember me?"

Snowy tried to sneak a peek at the name-tag picture on his navy blazer.

He gave her a hint. "Remember Blue Island?"

"Joe!" Snowy cried. Joe Spencer, a boyfriend in junior high. She'd gone out with him her senior year, too. She saw that Frankie was wearing cowboy boots, shiny and supple.

Frankie said, "Let's sit together at dinner and tell Joe's wife about Blue Island."

Charl called, "Snowy! Frankie! Stand in the front row! Isn't it wonderful, we've got three of our class officers here this year!" Then she whirled around. "Linda!"

Linda Littlefield had arrived, more fashionably late than Bev. As Snowy watched Linda walk across the lawn and Dudley hurry to greet her, Linda was only slightly out of focus so Snowy guessed she would probably have recognized Linda elsewhere, away from this context. In high school, Linda's prettiness had been demure, her smile dimpled, her pale blond hair flirty in a short ponytail, but her voice always made Snowy think of crushed ice. Now the sweet-cold elements had combined into a lovely poised woman, wearing a beautiful pale yellow pantsuit that must be made of silk crepe. Her hair was—another miracle!—the pale blond of forty years ago, now worn in a smooth shoulder-length sweep tucked behind her ears.

"Sorry," Linda said in that very same voice. "There was an accident on I–93 that held us up."

"Oh, how awful," Charl said, "but how lucky your husband's a doctor. Did he help?"

Linda said, "Just a fender bender at a tollbooth."

In the row behind Snowy, Bev whispered, "And no malpractice-Good-Samaritan conflict. Do you think she's had a facelift?"

But Snowy was thinking about her own high-school ponytail and the bobby pins she had worn while cheering to keep her nape hairs neat. During the Varsity tryouts, some had fallen out onto the auditorium stage. When Linda's turn had come to do a cartwheel, her hand had skidded on the floor and she had fallen. And when the results of the tryouts were announced, Linda was the only girl on their JV squad not to make Varsity. All her life Snowy had wondered if Linda had slipped on the bobby pins, if in the horror of the moment Linda had realized she had touched bobby pins and later brooded over to whom they belonged amongst the girls who used bobby pins, and if the fall had been the reason Linda didn't make Varsity. Linda had done plenty of cartwheels at JV games, had already done one during these tryouts, so the judges knew she could do them. But had Snowy unintentionally raised doubts in the judges' minds? At the time, Snowy felt fear, not guilt. She was afraid it would be found out that her bobby pins had caused the accident. Otherwise, she had been ruthless, not caring about anything except having made Varsity herself. Then with the years, guilt grew. Add it to the burden! Linda was right there in the accumulated guilt of a lifetime, the worries, remembered gaffes, faux pas, failures.

The photographer yelled, "Settle down! The sooner we get this done, the sooner you can get back to the bar!"

Darl called, "Married classmates, stand together!"

Dudley dashed over to stand between Snowy and Charl. On Snowy's other side stood Frankie Richardson with his new cowboy aura.

"Ready?" yelled the photographer. "Say cheese!"

Snowy had read in a Nancy Mitford novel that saying "brush" produced a winning smile.

Dudley said, "Camembert," and Charl giggled, "Oh, Dudley."

The photographer yelled, "One more!"

Snowy remembered wearing a cap and gown for the last such photograph.

"That's it!" said the photographer, and the pose of the Class of '57 disintegrated. Dudley and Charl went over to thank him for his time and patience.

People began heading back into the building to the booze without any urging from Dudley and the twins, but Snowy said to Bev, "Let's say hi to Linda first," and they worked their way sideways through the crowd across the lawn and found Linda talking with—Snowy squinted at the picture on the name tag. Nancy Gordon! Another member of the Gang, Nancy had made JVs the year after Snowy and Puddles and the twins and Linda, and she'd stayed there. Linda had quit cheerleading rather than remain on JVs.

"Snowy! Bev!" Nancy exclaimed, and squashed them in hugs.

Nancy had gone to the same grammar school as Snowy, and now that Nancy was in focus Snowy saw her as she'd looked back then, the little girl who'd been pushed into the brook behind the school by an older girl, Ellen Hatch. Ellen had lied about it, and Nancy hadn't tattled, had said she'd slipped and fallen in, while all the other little girls who'd witnessed the incident struggled with various moral dilemmas but none of them, including Snowy and Bev, had told the teacher. Snowy turned to that other moral dilemma, Linda Littlefield.

Linda said, "I can't believe my eyes. You two are finally attending a reunion?"

Bev said disarmingly, "We're shy."

Nancy laughed. "Oh yeah, sure. I've been reading about both of you in the newspaper these past few years, you a hotshot saleswoman, Bev, and Snowy saving the Old Man."

Linda exchanged distant embraces and air-kisses with Bev and Snowy, and then, as they all started walking toward the building, said to Bev, "I heard at our thirty-fifth reunion that you're living in Gunthwaite now?"

"Back in the old hometown," Bev said.

Nancy said, "Linda lives down in Weston, Mass. I never left Gunthwaite, which I know should bother me, but it doesn't. Me and Butch, the place suits us."

Snowy and Bev gawked at Nancy. Bev asked, "You married Butch Knowles?"

Butch had been in Tom's Class of '56, a football player, and both Bev and Snowy had dated him, and so had Darl and lots of other girls; however, neither Bev nor Snowy could remember that Nancy ever had.

"Isn't it funny?" Nancy said. "We never went out in high school, but when I came home from UNH after my freshman year, one evening I stopped at Charl and Jack's apartment to see Johnny, their first baby, and Butch happened to stop by too, and, well, it was meant. I think we had to wait to be grown-up before we fell for each other. I didn't go back to the university."

Bev asked, "Is Butch here tonight?", which Snowy would not have dared to ask, fearing the widow-widower statistics to which Dudley had alluded.

"He couldn't miss the chance to poke around the new Trask's," Nancy said. "He worked at Trask's for twenty-five years, and he can't get over what's been done to this poor old building. After Trask's closed, he went to work at the shoe factory. Our kids were grown up by then, and I got a job as a teacher's aide. Thanks to Dudley, the shoe factory hasn't been moved to Thailand or some damn place, and in three more years Butch will retire."

They had reached the front door, and as they went into the hallway, Linda asked Bev, "Is Roger here?"

Bev said, "We have a bi-state marriage, and he had to be in Connecticut this weekend."

Linda dimpled. "Come meet my husband," she said and led them into the Trask Room, where Elvis was singing about being all shook up and Charl and Darl were shooing people toward tables. At the bar, Linda introduced a lean gray-haired man who had, to Snowy's eye, the look of a runner, so impulsively Snowy asked this Dr. Sheldon Levin, internist, "Do you participate in the Boston Marathon?"

"I certainly do," he said, appaising her legs. "Do you?"

"No, I'm just a jogger." But since Kenneth Collins had been released to that halfway house, Snowy had not been enjoying her morning jogs; she kept glancing apprehensively behind her. Then Snowy remembered Puddles's orders and improvised, "Puddles sends her love to everyone. She's a nurse practitioner at a clinic on Hilton Head, and one of her twin daughters is an OB/GYN in Charleston."

"Twins!" Nancy said. "Imagine, Puddles with twins, after all her wisecracks about Charl and Darl."

Snowy added hastily, before they could start remembering those wisecracks and other gems, "Puddles is also coaching cheerleading," but this too was a sensitive subject, and she saw with relief Frankie striding over to them in his beautiful boots.

Frankie said to Bev, "Joe and I have got a table."

So Snowy found herself sitting down at one of the white-and-green tables and being introduced by Joe to a pretty woman in a batik dress: "Snowy, this is my wife, Marcy."

"Hello," Snowy said.

Joe said, "Honey, this is Henrietta Snow Sutherland. I was in love with her in junior high *and* high school."

Snowy laughed, hot with embarrassment.

Marcy looked tolerant. "Hi there."

Bev said, "Snowy, guess what, Frankie and I are in the same line of work. He's a developer out in Santa Fe."

Snowy looked at Joe. "What about you?"

"I went to M.I.T.," he said, deadpan.

Marcy said, "He always says that. Then he says—"

"—the *other* M.I.T.," said Joe, laughing. "Manchester Institute of Technology."

Marcy said, "Where my brother went. We met when my brother brought him home to our folks' house after classes and I happened to be home."

"She was a stewardess," Joe said.

Marcy said, "That's what we were called then, not flight attendants."

Joe said, "I took one look at her and asked, 'Is there an airport nearby, or is that my heart taking off?'"

"He's an electrician," Marcy told Snowy. "Very useful."

Joe said, "Got my own business."

"In the Manchester area," Marcy said. "We live in Chester. Five children, three grandchildren."

"So far," Joe said.

Marcy said, "You mean so far for grandchildren."

Everybody at the table laughed except Bev, who had been listening to Joe and Marcy's ping-pong banter, their old-married-couple overlapping voices, with a wistful look on her face.

The table seated eight. A man Snowy didn't recognize hesitated at one of the remaining chairs and asked, "Can I join you?" and Frankie said, "You bet, Norm."

Norm! This was Norm Noyes, devoted to Puddles, who had considered him a drip. Like many of the other guys here, he had lost hair and gained girth, but in Norm's case these changes were an improvement, and his old demeanor of timid doggedness had new appeal. Sitting down, he looked from Snowy to Bev and asked, "Are you in touch with Puddles?"

Snowy and Bev exchanged a quick glance. Wait'll they told

Puddles that she was still on Norm's mind!

Marcy asked, "Puddles?"

Joe explained, "Their sidekick, Jean Pond."

Bev said, "Oh yes, we're in touch all the time, via the phone. She and her husband live in South Carolina."

Norm didn't seem fazed by the mention of a husband. He said, "She never comes to reunions. I thought maybe she would, if you both were coming."

"She's awfully busy," Snowy said. "She's a nurse practitioner, and she's coaching a cheerleading squad. Um, what are you doing these days? Do you live in Gunthwaite?"

Dudley and Charl dropped into the two remaining chairs, and Dudley said, "Norm reconstructs and investigates accidents," just as a waitress approached and said, "Mayor Washburn, your table will start the buffet."

Dudley said to Snowy, "The caterer is Belanger's."

"Ah," she said, "more memories." Gunthwaite had several caterers nowadays, but instead of using Fay's services at Indulgences, or Katy's Catering Service, Charl and Darl had chosen Belanger's, which had been the one and only caterer in the old days.

Leading the way, Dudley made a joke about her appetite, just like old times. "You can take two plates, Snowy, or come back for seconds."

"Hardeeharhar." While Snowy moved down the long table's seductive arrangement of salads, casseroles, chicken, she chose dainty portions and remembered Belanger's serving other buffets or sit-down meals at various ceremonial events throughout high school, from Girls' Athletic Association awards dinners to the Class of '57's last dinner, the senior banquet, her last date with Dudley. She reached a white-coated man in a chef's hat, carving a huge hunk of prime rib, and said, "Just a sliver, please."

Dudley told him, "She's being coy. A slab off the end for our Snowy."

Oh, what the hell. She wished she could ask for a doggie bag for Tom.

When they were all back at their table, Frankie said roguishly,

"Okay, Bev, tell the tale from our misspent youth." To Joe's wife he said, "Marcy, you've got to hear about Blue Island."

Bev needed no more prompting. She began, "It was in eighth grade that Joe and Frankie and Ron Moore almost got Snowy and Puddles and me drummed out of the Girl Scouts," and as Snowy and the others dug into Belanger's fare, Bev regaled them with the tale oft-told by her in days of yore but not in recent years, about how all the town's Girl Scout troops had met for a three-day jamboree on Blue Island, and Ron, Puddles's boyfriend, and Joe and Frankie had missed Puddles and Snowy and Bev so much that on the second night, under cover of darkness, they went out to the island in Frankie's motorboat, "and they sneaked around the camping area checking tents until they found ours and we woke up with the tent nearly collapsing around us and these guys crawling in. The boat had made such a racket coming across the lake that it woke up the troop leaders, who slept more lightly than a bunch of girls full of fresh air and campfire cooking, and they embarked on a manhunt—Mrs. Simpson and Mrs. Cilley—and this woke all the girls up, while in our tent there was great commotion with Snowy and Puddles madly trying to take their hair out of pin curls while Joe was blinking his flashlight at them—"

Snowy said to Marcy, who was laughing along with everybody else at the table, "Bev always dwells on this part of the saga, because she has naturally curly hair."

"—and then," Bev said, "our tent fell down."

"Stop," begged Charl, holding her sides, "stop!"

"Please," begged Darl at the table next door, and Snowy realized that Bev had its occupants also in stitches, Darl and Bill, Nancy and Butch, Carol and her husband, and Linda's husband, all except Linda who took a sip of her wine, looking bemused, perhaps remembering how she and Puddles had been partners on JVs because they were the same height, perhaps remembering Mike Young and his blank bedroom eyes, Mike who had stopped dating her and begun going out with Puddles, Mike with his MG that had the steering wheel on the British side... Or had Bev's mention of pin curls brought back the memory of bobby pins on the stage floor?

"So," Bev said, "there we were tangled up in canvas and ropes, thrashing around, with Mrs. Simpson and Mrs. Cilley zeroing in. Finally the guys clawed their way out from under and ran hell-bent-for-leather to the boat and went zooming off, escaping across the lake, but Snowy and Puddles and I were stuck on Blue Island, left to take the blame. When we extricated ourselves from the tent, we tried to explain that this had been the guys' bright idea, all to no avail. Mrs. Simpson said we'd disgraced the memory of Juliette Low."

Culprits Frankie and Joe looked extremely pleased with themselves.

After the laugher died down, Dudley asked Snowy, "Dessert?"

As she went with him to the dessert table, she said, "Do you know what Ron Moore is doing now? Puddles wants to hear about everybody."

"He sells appliances in the Sears in Concord." Dudley handed her a plate with a piece of yellow cake frosted white and green.

"Thank you."

He held a cup and saucer under a coffee urn. "Decaf?"

"Thank you."

He gave her the coffee and poured one for himself. They stood together, looking at their classmates already beginning to table-hop. He said, "The disappeared."

Charl and Darl hurried over, and Darl said, "I think we'd better start the show."

"Right," he said.

Snowy asked, "The show?"

Darl said, "Some years we've read the Class Will or the Class Prophecy that were in the *Smoke Signal*, and other years like on our thirty-fifth we had an auction to defray the expense of reunions, and this year we're having a trivia quiz. Go do your thing, Dudley."

Sitting back down, watching Dudley step to a podium, Snowy

heaved a sigh of relief that she was being spared the Class Prophecy. She could recall putting together the Class Will with other members of the school newspaper's staff and they'd been careful to avoid insulting anyone, so it was fairly innocuous: Henrietta Snow had bequeathed the editorship of the *Smoke Signal* to the new editor, Becky Harris; Beverly Colby had bequeathed her red hair to some redheaded girl in the junior class; Jean Pond had left her cartwheels to Gail Perkins. The best one had been: "Dudley Washburn leaves his ghost to torture the teachers." But with the Prophecy they'd let themselves go, and it couldn't have been easy for Dudley at a reunion to read the prediction that he would be the youngest president in the history of the United States. Snowy shivered. They had predicted that Bev would be the toast of the town on Broadway, while Puddles would be saving lives at Mass. General Hospital (not too far-fetched, that one), and—in her mind's eye Snowy could read the exact wording of the future that the staff had given her: "Henrietta Snow will win the Pulitzer Prize for her poetry and the Nobel Prize for Literature for her earthy best-seller, *Gunthwaite Place.*"

To her surprise, she laughed, and faces turned toward her as she heard the trivia question Dudley was reading into his microphone, "Who was the first girl to drink three Awful-Awfuls at Hooper's?"

A shout went up from her classmates: "Snowy!"

Snowy stood and bowed to applause, but this accomplishment had also presented another moral dilemma, for she had cheated, throwing up the first two Awful-Awfuls in Hooper's ladies' room before returning to the counter to drink the third. The whole purpose of the feat, though, had been to get Tom to notice her.

Dudley read questions about who had owned which old car, about sports, and Charl and Darl took over with questions about recent events, such as who had the most grandchildren (Dotty Mooney) and who had come from farthest away to attend the reunion (Frankie). The attention of the audience began to wander, and the table-hopping recommenced. Snowy wished she could say something to Linda at the next table, but it would be so bumbling, so awkward, to try. Let it go; the story of her life. As Norm asked her, "Does Puddles ever visit Gunthwaite at all?", Dudley reclaimed the microphone and announced, "Now, for the grand finale, the school song, led by our peppy cheerleaders!" He beckoned to Snowy. "Come up here, Snowy. At last this year we have the captain here!"

You fucking sonofabitch, Snowy thought. She had not known about this grand finale. Long ago Dudley had said something about the twins singing the school song in each other's arms at a reunion, but she had not realized the cheerleaders were leading the goddamn thing.

Dudley said, "Come on, all you cheerleaders, Carol, Nancy, Linda, come join Charl and Darl up here rallying our school spirit!"

Carol and Nancy were on their feet, laughing, running to the front of the room. Snowy saw that Linda, standing slowly up, was no longer cool and perfect; her face was beet red, agonized. Why did she attend every reunion and put herself through this? Her husband patted her silk crepe bottom and said, "Go on, Linda," and all at once Snowy guessed that he didn't know that Linda had only cheered one year, on JVs. Linda had kept it a dark secret, it never got mentioned at reunions, and Linda was torn between fear of his discovering it and her need for his pride in this. Linda cast a terrified look at Snowy.

Snowy jumped up and put an arm around Linda and said, "Help, I've forgotten how," and they ran up together into a makeshift formation.

Of course, Snowy had not forgotten. A million times she had done this on the football field and at basketball games in the gym, on the fifty-yard line or in front of the bleachers, and at pep rallies in the auditorium. There wasn't any leaping about during the school song, thank God, just the simple arm movements to a tune borrowed from an old English drinking song, more appropriate tonight than ever before. "Rah rah for Gunthwaite High," everybody sang, and in the audience glasses were raised along with voices, "Onward to battle! Rah! Rah! Rah!" And for a few moments, belting out, "Gunthwaite High School! Rah! Rah!", she didn't even feel like a fool.

Dudley then concluded the show by thanking the twins for organizing the reunion and reminding everyone to pick up a reunion booklet at the table near the door. Bill LeHoullier turned up the tape player. Elvis asked, "Are you lonesome tonight?"

Bev swung her walk over to Snowy. "Frankie is interested in seeing Waterlight. He remembers it from the outside, going past it on the lake."

The way Tom had remembered.

"Um," Bev said, "I thought he could follow me back to the house in his rental car. We're talking about a swim. Needless to say, I can take you home as planned, but is there anyone you could maybe get a ride with, does anybody live out that way?"

Dudley said, "I'll take Snowy home, Bev."

Bev said, "Thank you!"

Snowy said, "Hey, wait—"

Frankie swaggered over, carrying a Stetson, and he and Bev went out the door.

"The party is breaking up," Dudley said to Snowy. "Are you ready to leave now?"

"I'm ready to kill you!" Snowy said. "Why didn't you warn me about the cheerleading? I know, I know, because I wouldn't have shown up. Thanks, but you and Charl don't want to drive all the way to Woodcombe. I'll give Tom a call and he'll come get me." She glanced at her watch. Nine-thirty. Nothing on TV on Saturday night. Tom might be sound asleep in bed.

Dudley said, "Charl and Darl will lock up, and Darl and Bill can take Charl home. Be right with you."

Furious at Bev, Snowy returned to their table to retrieve her little blue shoulder bag. Norm was still sitting there, just the way he used to sit and wait for Puddles while she danced with other boys. Snowy said, "I'll tell Puddles you asked after her."

"She was something else, wasn't she."

Still is, Snowy thought but didn't say out loud for fear of encouraging him. "Good to see you again, Norm."

Dudley appeared. "All organized."

As they left, she heard on the tape player "The Theme from *Picnic,*" which Tom had called the sexiest song in the world.

Since becoming mayor, Dudley had bought a car of his own so that he didn't have to show up at meetings in his sign-painting truck or Charl's Plymouth Voyager. He held open the door of the Mercury Sable for Snowy. She looked at him, then stepped in.

They drove in silence along State Avenue and Main Street, up North Main Street, to the outskirts of town.

Finally Snowy said, "It was a great reunion. You and the twins did a terrific job."

"The reunions have got more fun as we've got older."

"Forty years."

"By the next one, some of us will have started collecting our social security, some of us will be retired."

Some of us will be dead, she thought. "Is there a Mrs. Norm Noyes? Puddles is sure to ask me."

"Nope, he never married. I guess he's a one-gal guy."

They listened to what Dudley had said.

Snowy remembered that after she had seen Bing Crosby singing about being a one-gal guy in *High Society* the summer Tom broke up with her, she had wondered if that was her fate, being a one-guy gal.

She realized Dudley was making a detour, cutting east on Ridge Road, which used to run through woods and now was dotted with houses. He braked. She saw a street sign as he turned off onto what had once been a little dirt road without a sign, only a nickname given it by the teenagers who parked here: the Cat Path. She and Tom had steamed up the windows of the Chevy convertible here on their first date. Despite the houses, some with lights on, Dudley pulled over to the side of the road as if there were still just woods and it were still a lovers' lane.

Alarmed, she said, "Dudley."

He switched off the ignition and the headlights went out. Unbuckling his seat belt, he thought of all the parking she must have done here with Tom Forbes. "You and I never went parking here, did we? My special place was that dirt road behind one of the early housing developments, where houses eventually spread across it."

"Yes," she said, turning this into an observation about society's ills, "even then you were worrying about the encroachment of civilization."

"And the disappearance of places to go parking. But evidently D. J. and Ruhamah managed, that and dorm rooms and now apartments. What do you think their future holds?"

Snowy would have welcomed a discussion of their kids instead of themselves, but this subject was also full of pitfalls because she didn't know if Dudley knew about Brandon. "Kids don't settle down early, the way we did."

He couldn't stop himself from saying, "And history is repeating itself, a Washburn and a Forbes rivaling for her affections."

"It's not the same. Ruhamah and D. J. didn't play in the same sandbox. We are old old *friends*, Dudley."

"We haven't been totally platonic."

"That was an aberration."

He shouted, "Aberration?"

In the nearest house she could see the blue light of a television set downstairs and yellow lamplight upstairs. She could run there for safety. Nonsense. Dudley was not a danger. Because of Kenneth Collins, she had become too jittery. She said, "I'm sorry, I'm sorry, a stupid choice of words, I meant it was fun and full of hormones, and I do love you, Dudley, I've loved you all my life."

He banged his fist against the steering wheel. "Pals. Shit."

"I'm sorry."

"No, goddamnit, you're happy, and that should make me happy, but when you moved in with him after you'd got free of him and gone to Bev's, after you and I had that swim at that party, I just couldn't, I just can't—"

She stared at him in consternation. Dudley was trying to break up with her. When Tom had done this forty-one years ago, he had said they needed to get loose of each other or they'd go crazy, but he hadn't meant forever, just until they were grown-up. The next year when he'd wanted her back, she had said they had to get loose of each other for good. For good, that was what Dudley needed. Her oldest friend.

He said, "If you're living together, why the hell won't he support you?"

"Huh?" Then, as furious at him as she had been at Bev, she said, "Oh, right, the way a fifties girl was brought up expecting to be supported?"

"Ruhamah can handle the store. Why isn't he insisting that you give up working so you can write full-time?"

She shrieked, "*Insist?*"

"Why won't he marry you and take care of you? How can he watch you go off every morning to wait on people? You're almost sixty, Snowy, and time is running out—"

She burst into tears. "'Before my pen has glean'd my teeming brain'?"

He leaned across and grabbed her, crushing her against him. The horn honked.

She blubbered, "Get us out of here before some home owner calls the cops. The mayor arrested for—what?" For attempted adultery?

Dudley inhaled her, her hair, her skin, his drug he craved. "For making you cry. I may be fucked-up, but I did not want to do that." He let her go and started the car.

She groped in her useless pocketbook, too damn small, no Kleenex.

Dudley opened the glove compartment and handed her a packet.

As they drove to Woodcombe without speaking, she remembered their ride back from the boardwalk in his truck, singing Golden

Oldies.

He pulled into the driveway of North Country Coffins. A light was on over the small barn door beside the two big ones, and there were lights upstairs. He wondered if Tom Forbes was waiting up for her or had just left these on when he went to bed.

She said tremulously, "Thank you for the lift. Look, you've done a good job of staying out of touch this past year and a half, and now it's official. You've broken up with me. You're free. I know you're running for mayor again this fall. Good luck, Dudley."

"Thank you for coming to the reunion."

The small barn door opened and Tom stood there, in jeans and a Woodcombe General Store T-shirt. Seeing an unfamiliar car, he called, "Snowy?"

CHAPTER FOUR

MONEY MONEY MONEY.

Dudley had planted the thought in her brain. She didn't hear from him after the reunion, not even after he won his third term, but his words that August night stayed with her through the autumn, as she served apple coffee cake and pumpkin muffins to leaf peepers sitting at the tables on the back porch with their cameras at the ready, on into the winter when Tom returned to living full-time in the apartment and working full-time on coffins, working harder than ever because the usual steady orders for coffins had increased, thanks to the Web site Ruhamah had helped David create. Snowy began helping too, checking and updating the Web site; she even helped in the workshop, filling in for David if Tom was working on Sunday afternoons and needed an extra pair of hands with some step simple enough for her to do. She thought: I could retire from the store, help Tom like this, and most of the time I could work in my office. Retire? *How?* Take quarterly profits from the store? Sell the store to Ruhamah? Did Ruhamah really want it? Sell the store to someone else? There were twenty years left on the thirty-year mortgage. Money money money.

"Money," Bev said, phoning from Santa Fe on New Year's Day morning. "Here's hoping 1998 will bring some in. I have never had such a bad year as 1997."

"Happy New Year," Snowy said, thinking that everything was relative and Bev's finances couldn't be in dire straits if she'd accepted Frankie's invitation and flown to New Mexico to celebrate New Year's at his condo. Here in Woodcombe, 1998 was starting out with bright happy sunshine and zero-degree cold. "Did you have fun last night?"

"Oh God, Snowy, do you know what I did? When I had a few minutes alone, I phoned Gretchen, a friend I used to play tennis with in Ninfield, and wished her Happy New Year. Roger and I used to go to their house for their New Year's Eve party, and I could hear it in the background, and she'd already been into the champagne so she wasn't discreet, she told me that Roger was there. Not with some trophy teenybopper. It's worse, it's Amanda, another of my tennis friends. Gretchen says Amanda's divorce is final and she and Roger have been getting more and more serious. He had Christmas with her."

For the first time since Bev moved to Gunthwaite, Roger hadn't come up for Christmas with Bev and the children. He'd told her and Dick, Mimi, Leon, and Etta that he was too busy working on a very important lawsuit; he had sent checks to the children; he had had a florist deliver to Bev enough poinsettias to fill Waterlight's big entrance hallway.

Snowy said, "Well, now you know. Information is always helpful, isn't it?"

"Amanda. Yes, damnit, I *know* her, I can *picture* them together. If the girlfriend were some youngster, I'd know he was just being a dirty old man, same as Geoff is with Caitlin. But Amanda—that's an insult!"

"You've got your cowboy."

"Unfortunately, he prefers being ridden. At my age, I don't want to be on top."

Snowy giggled.

Bev said, "Okay, otherwise Frankie is fine, and he keeps saying I should move out here and make a fortune. Money! I don't think I'll even go to Geoff's stupid awards conference next weekend; I'll come down with the flu and avoid embarrassment all around—not winning any award, Geoff and Caitlin being ever so businesslike, and I sure won't miss going to the stupid meetings and Geoff's latest idea, a stress-reduction session. Stress reduction! Feh!"

Bev sounded as if she sure could use a session.

Snowy asked anxiously, "Are you actually considering a move to Santa Fe?"

"You and I grew up in a New Hampshire lakeside town, where I now have my dream home on the lake."

"Tom calls it site fidelity. A birding term."

Birds, Bev thought. Brad, the member of the Ninfield Players with whom Bev had fallen in love, had owned a shop named For the Birds, which sold birdhouses and bird feeders and such. He had flown away, with another woman to Oregon. "Site fidelity," Bev said. "That should be the title of your next collection of poems. I didn't understand how New Hampshire was in my bones until I read *Tapestry Granite.* I don't know how Puddles can live so far from home."

"Well, remember, she was born in Maine."

They laughed, and Bev said, "As always, therapeutic to talk with you, best friend. I'll call you tomorrow night to let you know I'm home safely, you worrywart."

After they hung up, Snowy went in a trance into her office. Tom had given her a Gunthwaite-green iMac for Christmas, so she was trying to switch from her typewriter, which she'd still been using for the poems. She tapped out "Site Fidelity" and spent the rest of the day working on the start of a title poem. When there were enough of the new poems for another collection, she would, she decided, dedicate the collection to Bev—if she got lucky again and it was published.

Tom, who mostly only watched football on Thanksgiving and New Year's and sometimes not even then, settled down in front of the television, faintly regretting the La-Z-Boy recliner he'd left in Newburgh.

"FUCKING NEW HAMPSHIRE!" Tom said, as the electricity went off at eight o'clock the following Thursday evening and the apartment went dark. There had been a freezing rainstorm all day, so he and Snowy were expecting the power to go off at any time, but naturally it had to be at night, he thought, grabbing the flashlight in the magazine rack beside his chair. "The goddamn New Hampshire Electric Cooperative hacks down all the trees along the road to prevent power failures but we get them all the time anyway!"

Using the little flashlight she kept in her desk, Snowy emerged from her office. "Thank God I've learned to save every single line on the computer; I didn't lose anything. I'll go check the store."

He said, as he always said, "Ruhamah will be checking the generator," but he knew that Snowy would have to see for herself. "I'll go with you."

"No need for both of us to get soaked and cold." In the kitchen, while he took an oil lamp down from a shelf and lit it, she pulled on her boots, parka, mittens, saying, "Is the phone working? You phone the power company and light the woodstove, and I'll be back in a few minutes and we can snuggle."

"Well," he said. "If you put it like that."

She took their biggest flashlight, which guided her down the staircase into the workshop. Power failures were the only times she wished she were still living over the store, so she didn't have to go outdoors and brave bad weather in order to make sure the generator had come on. She yanked up the hood of her parka and opened the little barn door. The wind roared, slinging icy rain.

The sensation was the same as the time she'd been snowshoeing across the swamp behind Hurricane Farm and the ice had cracked, plunging her knee-deep in boggy slush. The utter shock of the cold wetness. It was like being dropped into a great big frozen daiquiri.

The blackness out here felt primitive. No streetlights; no lights in the Main Street houses, which couldn't be seen, either. In the flashlight's beam, ice glittered, encasing bushes, the trunks of trees. The wind slammed into her, whipping her breath away, and the rain stung her face. She moved slowly forward, testing the driveway with her boots the way she did on a trail with her hiking boots when a ledge or rock looked slippery. The flashlight showed her the driveway's junction with the sidewalk, and she turned at the icy telephone pole. She crept past the post office. Now she could see the lights in the store. The generator had kicked in. It was safe, the store, her responsibility, her investment, her support, her millstone, her bread-and-butter.

On the store's front porch, she knocked loudly on the door before peeling off a mitten and unlocking it with her key, calling, "Ruhamah?"

Ruhamah stood on the bottom step of the inside staircase, hanging onto the railing. The fear on her face horrified Snowy.

Snowy said, "My baby, it's just me."

Ruhamah clung to the railing.

Guilt filled Snowy. Had her fears about Kenneth Collins rubbed off on Ruhamah? No, not Ruhamah, calm, sensible, self-sufficient. Snowy said, "I didn't mean to scare you. You know me, I always have to come over and check even though there's no need." From the cellar she heard the reassuring chug of the generator. She crossed to Ruhamah and took her free hand. "I'd give you a hug, only I'm so wet."

Ruhamah let go of the railing but gripped Snowy's hand as she eased herself off the last step.

Snowy said, "What's wrong?" Had something happened to Brandon, who had joined Ruhamah at Harriet's in New York during Christmas, along with Jared? Had something happened to D. J. or to any of Ruhamah's friends in Woodcombe or those who lived elsewhere?

Ruhamah chortled, "Nothing, I just got startled when the

lights went out. Which was idiotic of me, in this weather." She released Snowy's hand.

Together they went over to the cellar door. Snowy said, "Whenever we do this, I think of that Willa Cather novel, *Shadows on the Rock,* and how on cold nights the little girl got up to cover the parsley."

Ruhamah gave her a long-lidded glance. "What a funny world you inhabit."

Snowy opened the door. The generator's exhaust was piped outdoors, but there always was a whiff of fumes that threw her back through the years to Boston traffic: She was leaving her Beacon Street rooming house and walking to work at Commonwealth Publishing. Ruhamah flicked the light switch, and they went down the stairs into the old rock-walled cellar, which they kept swept clean of cobwebs and dust so that it would be as pristine as a cellar could be. It was a storeroom, too, particularly in the years since the attic had become an apartment. Down from the bulkhead ran the loading trolley, there were stacks of cases of soft drinks and canned goods on pallets on the cement floor, and along the walls were shelves with more stock as well as the store's own cleaning supplies. Ruhamah opened one of the cellar windows to vent the place, and Snowy went out through the bulkhead to check the LP gas tanks out back.

When they were once more up in the store, Snowy asked, "Are you really okay? Want to come spend the night with us?"

"It would make more sense for you two to spend the night here, with a furnace and electric lights and water."

"Would you like us to? I'll give Tom a call."

"He loves complaining and coping and playing pioneer. He'd rather be there."

"I could stay here, then."

"I'm perfectly fine. And your power will probably be back on soon. You've got your emergency jugs of water?"

"Yes." Snowy looked out the window at the blackness. "It's a horrid night. I pity the repairmen."

"Get back and into dry clothes."

Outdoors, the ferocious wind now pushed Snowy forward, making her lean backward to try to stay upright, and the ice seemed to slice right through her drenched parka. Inside the houses, faint auras of light indicated that people had found their oil lamps and kerosene lanterns; woodstoves and fireplaces would be stirred up. She slipped and landed on her ass. Christ! As she struggled up, the image of Ruhamah moving across the store tugged at her memory. Then she bent low and stomped forward, to Tom and towels and snuggling.

The next morning, the freezing rain hadn't stopped and the power hadn't come on. Glassy trees were breaking, bowing, lolling on power lines. Tom went to the store with Snowy, lugging the food from their refrigerator to put in one of the store's. Up in Ruhamah's apartment they took showers, feeling like sybarites because the rest of the townsfolk were suffering without.

Snowy phoned Cleora and asked, "Are you okay?"

"Managing fine without them cows to milk, just the chickens to tend to."

"Cleora, you didn't walk to the barn in this ice storm!"

"The chickens have to be fed, the eggs gathered, no matter what the weather is. Pete will be over to help, sooner or later, as usual. Don't you fret. I grew up doing without electricity, so I don't mind. Kind of peaceful."

Well, Snowy thought, Cleora probably *was* more familiar with austere existence than most people around here, but still, she was in her eighties. Snowy said, "If you need any groceries, phone me and Tom will deliver them," and after they hung up she phoned Rita and said, "Cleora has lost her electricity so I assume you have too?"

"Frank bought a generator, remember I told you?"

Snowy must've tuned that out. "Oh. That's great, but don't bother coming in. No need to risk the driving. Ruhamah and I can handle things. But could you or Frank look in on Cleora? Make sure Pete has brought in wood? Maybe you could convince her to have lunch or something at your house?"

"Frank will," Rita said. "I'm coming to work. I don't want to miss the excitement."

So much for being Rita's boss. Next, Snowy phoned Irene, who said she was fine, and then Snowy phoned Bev and asked, "How are things there?"

"I just bundled up and went out for some reconnaissance. A tree has fallen across the driveway so I can't get out even if I dared to try. Why didn't I have the sense to buy a car more suited to New Hampshire winters?"

"Your power is out?"

"I don't have heat except the fireplaces, no lights, no water, but am I glad I have a gas stove, not an electric. I won't starve."

"You'll freeze. Tom will go collect you and you can stay at Ruhamah's."

"Maybe they'll get the power back on soon."

"Maybe. Meanwhile, pack a few things for spending the night on the old familiar pull-out sofa, and Tom will be along. He'll shut off your pump, in case you get a freeze-up."

"Oh yes, I for*got*, you've got hot water at the store! A shower! Okay, I'll pack."

"And if there's stuff in your fridge you don't want to spoil, pack that too."

Tom took Snowy's Subaru instead of his Jeep, because of the aversion Bev had had to Jeeps ever since she used to ride to school in her stepfather's mortifying Jeep, and David went with him to help chainsaw the tree in Bev's driveway and any other trees that might be blocking the road.

The store began to resemble an emergency shelter; people made their way to its warmth, hot coffee, and food. There was a spirit of adventure as everyone speculated about the weather and the power failures across the Northeast. Snowy and Ruhamah and Rita worked like fiends, and when Tom and David returned with rescued Bev, she joined in, saying, "Just like our waitressing days at Sweetland!"

Tom and David went on to the barn, where they could do assembly work.

During a lull in the afternoon, Snowy phoned Alan's mother and located her at Margaret and Howard's house. Phyllis said, "We're managing, dear, but this is the final straw. We are discussing a move to Florida."

"They get hurricanes."

"We don't care!"

The power still hadn't come back on by nightfall.

Ruhamah was right; Tom enjoyed playing pioneer. So he and Snowy didn't have supper with Ruhamah and Bev and declined Ruhamah's invitation to spend the night. By the light of oil lamps, Snowy sliced Italian bread and on the gas stove Tom heated Chef Boyardee ravioli, which he and Snowy ate straight out of the saucepan to keep dishes to a minimum. He was rinsing them with some water from one of the big plastic jugs, when the phone rang.

Puddles said, "Well, thank God, at least your phone is working. What the hell is happening up there?"

"An ice storm. We don't remember anything like it, the power off this long. The weather forecast for tomorrow is sun, though. We're okay, and Bev is at Ruhamah's for the duration."

"How was Bev's trip to Frankie's?"

"She had fun."

"Old boyfriends. To think Norm is involved in investigating accidents. I never dreamed we'd have gory careers in common. Maybe I should've paid more attention to him, even though he was so out-to-lunch. I don't know what Guy and I have ever had in common. Opposites attracting, I suppose that's what I thought Guy and I were."

Snowy didn't say that she and Bev thought Puddles had married Guy on the rebound after discovering that her longtime boyfriend, Gene Chabot, had been unfaithful.

Puddles said, "Anyway, are you really okay? You're keeping warm?

Tom wedged another log into the woodstove. Snowy looked at his contented face, and then she looked at the open bathroom door and saw the big plastic jug of water with which to flush the toilet and wished she were over at Ruhamah's. She said, "We're fine."

"Want to know what the weather is like here?"

"No!"

Puddles laughed. "When the airports are functioning again up there, you and Bev should come down for some R&R. Bye!"

Tom and Snowy tried to read, but Tom kept getting up to shift the oil lamps for better diffusion of light and then he admitted, "It's a wonder all our forebears didn't go blind," so they went to bed early and occupied themselves with another diversion. As no doubt other people were doing. Snowy thought how nine months from this ice storm there would be a mini-baby-boom.

Next morning, the rain had stopped. The sun came out, and everywhere the ice began melting, shattering, streaming. It was very beautiful. At the store, moods were confused, cheered by the sun, hopeful about power lines being repaired, but more tense than yesterday. The adventure was over; it was time for life to return to normal, yet it hadn't. Mimi arrived from Leicester, desperate for a shower, and as Snowy worried that customers might get the same idea and storm the bathroom, Snowy remembered how during the War her mother had spoken scathingly about "hoarders." Was Snowy hoarding showers? Mimi didn't return immediately to Leicester to shiver over her looms; she stayed until midafternoon, helping in the store. Tom took Bev to Waterlight to check it and get her car, and Bev drove to the Plumley office to do paperwork but came back to Ruhamah's to spend the night. The awards conference was canceled.

After supper, the phone rang, and Tom answered it. "Oh hi, Brandon."

Snowy carried an oil lamp into her office. Think of all the poets who hadn't created by the light of electricity! She could too, longhand. After the conversation, Tom leaned in and said, "Brandon had talked to Ruhamah and knew we were okay but wanted to double-check."

"Thoughtful of him."

"He sounded—well, as if he had something more to say, but he didn't. Sounded pretty chipper, in any case."

"Another promotion in the offing?"

"We'll find out when he decides to tell us, won't we." The phone rang again, and Tom returned to the living room and answered it. "Hello, Harriet. Yes, we're doing fine." He brought the receiver to Snowy.

Harriet said, "I heard from Jared that you've all gone back to the good old days. Are you really okay?"

"Really," Snowy said.

"It's been balmy here in the city, but I've actually found myself wishing I were sharing the hardships with you."

"California girl, remember the first time you saw snow at Bennington and ran around shrieking that it was snowing and what should you wear? But this has been an ice storm, not a blizzard, so it's a little strange. And the aftermath is beginning to drag. Thank you again for entertaining Ruhamah at Christmastime."

"Oh, she and Brandon entertained themselves."

They laughed.

The next day, Sunday, was again sunny. Tempers, however, were short, and Snowy feared she might have a riot on her hands because the Sunday newspapers were delivered late. Eek, what if they hadn't been delivered at all? The disruption of routine was fraying nerves. Oh, for an end to the topsy-turvy uncertainty and a return to blessed monotony! As Bev served coffee and muffins and Snowy and Ruhamah sorted and sold the newspapers, Snowy whispered to Ruhamah, "Odd, how *tiring* this adversity gets, even for us with your furnace and water and functioning bathroom." Then she noticed that Ruhamah looked more than tired; she looked jumpy, as on edge as the most agitated customers. Snowy said, "My baby, why don't you go back to bed? Bev and I can handle things." She expected Ruhamah to refuse vehemently.

Ruhamah said, "All right," and went upstairs, gripping the railing.

Baby. Jesus H. Christ! Was Ruhamah pregnant? Snowy stood

stock-still, holding a *Boston Globe*, and to her surprise she felt delight blossoming. She squelched it. Ruhamah would be understandably upset by an unwanted pregnancy. Well, thank heavens it wasn't the catastrophe it had been in Snowy's youth, and Ruhamah knew Snowy would agree with an abortion decision. Or was Ruhamah acting strange because she didn't know if the father was Brandon or D. J.? Snowy wanted to rush upstairs and beg Ruhamah to pour out the problems, but instead she rang up the *Globe* on the cash register and kept working until the store closed at noon.

Mimi arrived again then, this time bringing Lloyd, her husband, both wanting showers. Snowy and Bev tiptoed up the stairs with them and discovered that Ruhamah hadn't gone back to bed; she was sitting at the kitchen table, watching chickadees at the bird feeder. Since Bev's arrival Friday, the state of the living-room area had made Snowy smile, reminding her of the spare room at her parents' house when Bev slept over and messed it up with strewn clothes.

Snowy asked Ruhamah, "How are you feeling? Can I make you some lunch? A cup of tea?" Decaf.

Ruhamah snapped, "Don't hover! Don't pester! I'm fine!"

Snowy went scarlet, ashamed and embarrassed in front of Bev, Mimi, and Lloyd. She gasped, "Then I'll go home," and she fled from the apartment that still technically belonged to her, down the street to Tom's barn.

He was reading in the very quiet apartment. You forgot how noisy your household equipment was until it was silenced.

He said, "Let's go out for a Sunday dinner," so they drove to Peggy Ann's Place, which was even more packed than usual, people seeking creature comforts. After they got a booth and settled down to Peggy Ann's famous baked ham, she didn't tell Tom about her suspicions or the humiliation. When they returned to the village, Mimi and Lloyd's car was still parked at the store, and so was Bev's. Jealousy seared her. Had Ruhamah confided in Bev and Mimi and were they all discussing the situation? Snowy, the superfluous mother.

The next morning, Snowy awoke exhausted by the prospect of another day of adversity, clandestine showers, irritable customers—and Ruhamah. As she reached for her bedside flashlight, there was a rumble and the entire big old barn seemed to come to life. The furnace wheezed, the refrigerator hummed. She cried, "Tom! Electricity!"

They stumbled out of the bedroom and saw that the lights that had been on Thursday evening were burning again.

Tom looked at the clock blinking on the VCR. "All good things must come to an end. Now I've got to reset forty million clocks."

Snowy laughed and ran to the kitchen sink and turned on the faucet. Water coughed out. The well's pump was working, hooray! She said, "Now that things are back to normal, I'll go for my morning constitutional."

"Be careful of the ice."

As she walked down Main Street, she saw more lights in houses than she usually did at this hour; everyone was awake and celebrating the return of civilization. She passed the store. The night-lights didn't show any activity inside. She assumed the generator had shut off. Ruhamah must still be asleep. Down the street she went, not looking over her shoulder for Kenneth Collins, enjoying the prospect of a shower in her own—well, Tom's—bathroom with everything handy. Tom would make Egg Beaters omelettes. On her way back past the store, she stopped. Shouldn't Ruhamah be up? Something was wrong. Collins had broken in, thinking she still lived here. Ruhamah had miscarried. The generator had asphyxiated Ruhamah and Bev.

She didn't have her keys with her. She started up the icy outside staircase, planning to bang on the apartment door, but then in her head she heard Ruhamah telling her not to pester her, and she heard Bev calling her a worrywart.

So she descended to the sidewalk and continued back to the barn.

After her shower, she was eating the green-pepper omelette Tom had made her when the phone rang. Tom answered it and said, "Sure, Bev, just a sec," and handed the receiver to Snowy.

Bev said, "Snowy, Ruhamah can't come out of her room. She didn't want you to know but I don't know what to do."

Denial, Snowy thought. I've been in denial.

Agoraphobia.

MANY PEOPLE IN the Northeast had it much worse, with power off much longer. Stores immediately began selling T-shirts that said I Survived the Ice Storm of '98, and Snowy sent one to Puddles as a joke, but she didn't feel that she had earned the right to wear one herself, because she had survived in the lap of luxury, comparatively.

She needed to find things funny. If she didn't, she would go crazy with worry about Ruhamah. At least she didn't think Ruhamah *was* going crazy, as she had thought about herself when agoraphobia hit; not until she had seen a *Donahue* show about agoraphobia had she realized, overjoyed, that the thing had a name and she wasn't alone.

That first morning, Snowy had stayed in Ruhamah's room with her, while Rita handled the store. Ruhamah had wept, "I thought you were weak, I thought it could never happen to me."

Hugging her, Snowy said, "Sometimes it runs in families. Now and then I wonder about my mother and the way she devoted herself to the house, her sanctuary."

Ruhamah said, "I was coming back on the bus from Harriet's, and everything started getting weird and by the time you picked me up in Gunthwaite, all I wanted to do was hide under my bed, I almost strangled trying not to yell at you to break all speed limits getting home. Home. I don't remember who I was when I left here for Harriet's. The old me."

Tentatively probing, Snowy said, "Sometime there are triggers, sometimes the cause can't be traced. In my case, I think doing a poetry reading at the Pevensay library might have contributed, and it got worse after my parents died. Um, did anything happen at Harriet's?"

"Trite," Ruhamah said.

"What?"

Ruhamah cried some more, then squashed her Kleenex and said, "At Harriet's, Brandon got talking about how he'll be thirty-eight this year and if he's going to be a father he'd like to do it before he's forty so he won't be an old geezer when the kids are growing up."

"Mmm," Snowy said noncommittally, feeling like a shrink, astonished that reticent Ruhamah was telling her this.

"And it was Christmas and everything, children and children's toys everywhere, which either can put you in the mood or quite the opposite. It put me in the mood, so we spent most of our time at Harriet's making a start on a family."

My guess, Snowy thought, had been on the right track after all.

Ruhamah said, "Oh, we were going to get married, too."

"Were?"

"Are. I don't know! On the bus trip home, away from him, I couldn't imagine what had possessed me. I'm not sure I ever want kids, and I definitely planned to wait until my thirties. But Brandon is so old!"

"Puddles had a similar problem, with Guy. She solved it fairly early and in one shot."

Ruhamah laughed shakily. "Twins."

Snowy hugged her again.

Ruhamah said, "I do know what I have to do. I'll phone Carolyn McDonald."

The psychologist for the area's schools. Ruhamah had seen her after Alan's death.

Snowy asked, "Does she take people who aren't in school?"

"I'll ask her to recommend someone. But Catch-22. How do I get to a shrink if I can't leave my room?"

"Step-by-step with me to the car, and I'll drive you."

So, the secret out, Ruhamah acted sensibly and sought help, instead of being stubborn the way Snowy had been. Carolyn McDonald suggested Dr. Pamela Keach, a psychiatrist in Concord.

Snowy and Tom began having dinner in Ruhamah's apartment, and Snowy spent nights there, on the pull-out sofa. Twice a week, leaving Rita in charge of the store, Snowy drove Ruhamah down to Concord to Dr. Keach's office, hating the drive, gritting her teeth, silently reciting Franklin Roosevelt on the subject of fearing fear but nonetheless scared stiff that Ruhamah's condition would provoke a return of her own. Hell, she should have been seeing a shrink herself, but wouldn't that take the edge off the so-called creative process and spoil the poems? She went with Ruhamah to the first session, but after that she spent the hour shopping on Main Street or at the Steeplegate Mall. Once she studied the street map and drove past the halfway house, which looked like any ordinary house.

And one morning she was killing the time reading a newspaper in a coffee shop on Main Street when a voice said, "Snowy! May I join you?" and she glanced up and saw D. J, a young rosy-cheeked attorney in a fine wool topcoat and sober three-piece suit enlivened by one of Mimi's handwoven ties, no doubt a present from Ruhamah. He folded his height onto the empty chair at Snowy's little table. It was an awkward conversation over her plain black decaf and his latte; she explained her presence in the capital by saying she was shopping; when D. J. asked after Ruhamah, saying he hadn't seen or heard from her since before Christmas, Snowy said everything had been in upheaval because of the ice storm; so they talked about the Ice Storm of '98 until D. J. tapped the headline on her newspaper and remarked, "This Clinton and the White House intern, what's-her-name."

"Monica Lewinsky," Snowy said. She'd not mentioned Dudley, but now she couldn't help asking, "What does your father think is going to happen?"

"He's rip-shit. Excuse me. But I've never seen him so angry."

"The fatal flaw."

"In my opinion," D. J. said, "Clinton won't resign, no matter how big the scandal becomes."

Driving home, Snowy said to Ruhamah, "I bumped into D. J. He says he's been getting your machine whenever he phones."

Ruhamah asked, "Did you tell him?"

"That's your business," Snowy said.

When they reached Woodcombe, Ruhamah said, "I think I'll try to work in the store a little this afternoon." She worked until closing time, and then told Snowy, "I'll be okay tonight. Go home to Tom."

Snowy didn't fuss. "Give me a call if you change your mind."

The call came at nine o'clock as Snowy and Tom were settling down to television. Ruhamah choked, "I'm not pregnant."

Snowy went running to the store's apartment, where Ruhamah was in tears. Hugging her, Snowy said, "It took me a lot of trying. My mother and her miscarriages. We Snow women have delicate constitutions."

Ruhamah wept, "I don't know how I feel. I'm relieved, I'm upset, I should phone Brandon." She carried the phone into her bedroom, but as Snowy made tea, eavesdropping without compunction, Snowy realized the call was to D. J. Ruhamah came out and announced, "I'm going to stay with D. J. for a while. That way, you won't have to keep driving me to and fro. He's coming to get me tonight."

The next evening, Snowy was surprised to receive a phone call from Cleora, who asked, "Were you eating supper?"

"No," said Snowy, bewildered.

"I didn't want to interrupt. Some people eat late."

"Oh, we're finished. How are you?"

"I've been meaning to thank you for having your Tom deliver that grocery order during the storm. I keep forgetting I have to buy milk and butter now. The times I've been in the store, Rita's running it."

"Ruhamah and I took a break. Ruhamah's still on vacation."

"Did Rita tell you I had lunch two days at her house during the storm? When she was working?"

"Yes. Is Frank a good cook?"

"He used one of them microwaves for the soup. I could've heated it up in half the time on the stove."

"I know."

"After the first lunch, I showed the little girl, that Mallory, how to make oatmeal cookies. The cookies we'd had for dessert were store-bought. After the other lunch, I showed her tapioca pudding. You ever been there since the wedding?"

"No."

"Well, just wanted to thank you. Bye, now."

Snowy replaced the receiver, wondering why she felt uneasy. Then she phoned Bev and said that Ruhamah must be making progress, if she could move from the safe haven of her own apartment to D. J.'s.

Bev said, "Good for her. Maybe my therapy should be painting the kitchen."

"Repaint over all those colors?"

"I'm thinking of redoing it in pastel greens and blues, and white. It would take a lot of coats. Maybe buy a new toaster and such. White. I'd feel as if I were a young-married again, fixing up a fixer-upper house. I did everything then, paint, wallpaper, have babies, while Roger earned the money. Those were the days."

Suddenly Snowy remembered what Bev's mother had said to Snowy, back in high school, about Bev's ambition to marry a millionaire. "That's make-believe," Julia had said. "She's never dared imagine a real marriage because she knows real men die." Bev's father had died, and Ruhamah's father had died. Was Ruhamah incapable of deciding on one man because he might die?

In February, Puddles phoned and said jubilantly, "I'm back from Orlando, and we came in third!"

Snowy had forgotten about the national cheerleading championships. "Oh wow, Puddles!"

"Of course I was dreaming that we'd win it, but my nightmare was that we'd come in last. The girls did great."

"Congratulations, Puddles," Snowy said. "Florida. Alan's mother and sister and brother-in-law didn't have a change of heart after electricity was restored to Eastbourne. They're down in Florida now, house-hunting or condo-hunting or something. They're serious about making the move."

"Will it bother you to have them gone, or will it be a relief?"

"A little bit of both, I suppose."

"How's Ruhamah doing?"

"She asked us to bring her car down to D. J.'s, so Tom drove it and I followed and we got to see D. J.'s condo. It's extremely shipshape; I guess he kept his sanity growing up in such a big family by keeping his territory neat and tidy. Ruhamah is able to drive now, if only from D. J.'s to Dr. Keach's office." Snowy didn't add that after they left, Tom wanted to drive past the halfway house and she directed him to it.

Puddles asked, "What about the other boyfriend, Tom's kid?"

Snowy hadn't told either Puddles or Bev about Brandon and the marriage talk and pregnancy attempt. "I don't know," she said truthfully. Ruhamah hadn't brought up the subject of Brandon, and Snowy forbore asking. "Again, congratulations, Puddles. This is a real triumph."

"I'm starting to dream about next year. Bye!"

At first Ruhamah had phoned from D. J.'s every evening, asking about the store, saying she was doing a lot of resting and reading. Gradually Ruhamah's calls tapered off to twice a week, and she reported that she now was seeing Dr. Keach only once a week.

Rita said snidely, "Good thing this is the slack time of year. Is Ruhamah ever coming back to work?"

Snowy refrained from throttling Rita and repeated what she'd been telling everyone, stilted though it sounded. "She is taking a well-earned break and considering her options. This store offers only a small scope for a person with an MBA."

On her fifty-ninth birthday, a Thursday, the weather presented

Snowy with snow, sleet, and, relenting, rain. That evening she and Tom drove to the Gunthwaite Inn, which, for some reason she didn't care to examine, she had a yen to revisit. The good old Gunthwaite Inn, once *the* place in town, now venerable. At fifty-nine, was she becoming venerable? Her parents used to celebrate their wedding anniversaries with dinner here. The dining room's decor hadn't changed much over the years, white linen tablecloths and napkins, old photographs of Gunthwaite on the walls, but although the menu still retained its traditional favorites like roast chicken and broiled sirloin, there were now sun-dried tomatoes and raspberry coulis. Remembering the days when dining out meant steak, Snowy chose that, while Tom had one of the newer items, ravioli stuffed with lobster, and declared it better than Chef Boyardee in an ice storm. They talked about the store and the workshop, and they speculated about Brandon, from whom Tom hadn't heard since the ice-storm phone call. Ruhamah hadn't shed any light on anything during today's dutiful birthday phone call to her mother except that she now was driving farther than Dr. Keach's office. For dessert, Snowy had the inn's rice pudding; you didn't see rice pudding on menus much anymore. Tom had tiramisu, and after the drive home, he gave Snowy a Mont Blanc pen. Expensive! Remembering the Parker pen he'd given her for her sixteenth birthday, she burst into nostalgic tears.

Bev had reported that she'd gone ahead with her notion about repainting the kitchen. One Saturday night in April she phoned, sounding nerved up but ebullient. "Come see the kitchen tomorrow afternoon! I've finished!"

"Great!" The next day was Ruhamah's birthday, but Ruhamah would be celebrating it at D. J.'s. When Ruhamah had phoned Snowy to tell her this, Ruhamah had asked, "You don't mind?" Snowy had said, "I just want you to have a happy day." Ruhamah said, "I can go into stores now," and Snowy offered a Helpful Hint: "When I first ventured into stores, I learned to have the money ready in my hand so I wouldn't shake visibly getting it out of my wallet." Ruhamah said, "It's signing a credit-card slip that's my challenge." Snowy had not even attempted such a feat during her recovery, but back then credit cards weren't used so much.

The next afternoon, a cloudy first day of daylight saving, instead of raking the lawn as she'd planned, Snowy drove off to Bev's, enjoying springtime, the trees budding pink in the woods. Yesterday she and Tom had seen their first robin of the season. She reached Waterlight. By law, bob houses had to be off the lake by the first of April, so there was no offshore colony now, just thin snow streaked with melting gray. The house still enchanted her, outside and within, and now the kitchen didn't clash with the atmosphere. The opaque light lay serenely on pale greens and blues that reminded Snowy of Monet's water-lilies paintings. But as Bev twirled around showing off all her work, Snowy sensed that her wild excitement was caused by more than redecorating. Had she heard from Roger?

"It's lovely," Snowy said. "You do a really professional job, which I learned when you painted the store's apartment."

Bev hadn't replaced the bright blue teakettle. She poured boiling water onto Earl Grey teabags in two of her loon mugs. "Sit, sit."

Snowy sat, and so did Bev. She nudged a plate of Snackwell fat-free cookies toward Snowy, who thought how horrified Cleora would be at the sight. Bev shimmered with the excitement, but she seemed unable to speak.

"Houses," Snowy continued, sociably. "Alan's mother and sister and brother-in-law decided on a condo in Clearwater. Brave of Margaret to have Phyllis live with her. So they're selling their houses, and I don't suppose they're the only folks fleeing New Hampshire after the Ice Storm of '98."

"Yes, the ice storm hasn't brought customers in droves to Plumley's. I've sold zilch so far for 1998. But Snowy—" The words burst forth. "Yesterday I got a listing that will make my fortune! Luck, you're always saying it's luck, and I had a lucky connection. The daughter saw my photo amid the other salespeople's photos in the Plumley newspaper ad, and she realized who I was, so when she phoned she asked for me because I would know the property best. Her parents bought it from Mother and Fred all those years ago. Her father died a few years back, and now her mother has died and the two children inherited the place. They have no interest in keeping it, so they're selling. When I told Geoff what I'd got, he completely forgot about Caitlin and began conferring with me about the development possibilities. We were there all this morning, looking things over."

Snowy sat turned to stone. "Julia's house?"

"The house, barn, thirty acres of fields and woods. The lake view!"

Snowy still didn't dare comprehend what Bev was talking about. "Development?"

"It has too much potential to remain the way it is, Snowy. And I need every cent I can make from it, or else I'm going to lose Waterlight."

Snowy could move now. Like a sleepwalker she rose and walked out of the pretty kitchen. In the front hall, she put on her parka and picked up her shoulder bag. As she went out the front door, she heard Bev running after her, and then she herself was running, to get away before she screamed something terrible at her. She jumped in her car and drove off, seeing in her rearview mirror Bev standing on the top step of her dream house looking after her.

Julia's house had been Snowy's dream house. It had been more home to her than her own home.

Instead of returning to Woodcombe, Snowy headed around the lake toward Julia's house, taking back roads like the native she was. She reached the road to Julia's. It still was dirt, muddy at this time of year, an old narrow road twisting up and down through the woods, across a brook, up another hill, to a field below a small white Cape with a big gray barn. She braked at the driveway. What would she do if somebody was here, Geoff Plumley or the children who had inherited it?

Fuck them. She swung up the driveway, seeing the view emerge, Lake Winnipesaukee beneath mountains. Worth a fortune. She drove around to the rear of the house. No car or cars. She got out of the Subaru. You always went in by the back door, into the kitchen with its beloved old yellow wallpaper of faded teapots, the worn brown linoleum. She walked up the path to the granite doorstep and tried the door. Locked.

In mud and wet black leaves, she walked past the barn and looked at the apple orchard, where many branches had been broken by the ice storm. She and Julia used to walk through the orchard, Julia pausing to pick up dropped apples and toss them into piles for the deer, to the path over which birches curved. The ice storm, she saw, had snapped off those birches. The path led into the woods to Snowy's favorite spot, the bog, where soon the spring peepers would be shrilling. She remembered sitting there, telling Julia how exhausted she was by high school and the prospect of four more years of trying to get the best marks. Julia had suggested Bennington, which didn't have marks. She remembered snowshoeing past the bog, into the woods, and, heartbroken, telling Julia that Tom and Joanne had got married.

Walking back to her car, she looked up at the window of Bev's bedroom, under the eaves. Snowy had spent countless nights there. Best friends.

SNOWY REMOVED HER ear protectors and said to Tom, "Bev is going to ruin Julia's place."

He was working this Sunday afternoon, so when she'd got back she threw off her parka and said she wanted to help, and he changed over from the joiner to the thickness planer to ready some more boards. While he fed the boards in, she took them as they came through and stacked them, and the concentration that even such a simple task demanded of her, because of her worry about these dangerous machines, was as much a distraction as the rasping racket of the planer. After a dozen boards were piled up, he switched it off and began helping her lug them around to be put through again, and now she thought she could describe Bev's plans with some semblance of rationality.

He took off his ear protectors and listened.

When she finished, she asked, "How can I stop her?"

"Zoning? No, Plumley Real Estate people know all about the various laws and rules and regulations." He remembered picking up Bev at that house for dates and taking her home, then taking Snowy there after dates if she was sleeping over. That dirt road had been picturesque but, in the winter and mud season, tricky, back in the days of the Chevy convertible, not four-wheel drive. He suddenly recalled waiting for Bev in the living room on what had turned out to be their last date—well, last until they started going out again after he was at Rumford. Through a doorway you looked into a dining room that didn't contain a table and chairs but a big loom and a couple of smaller ones, which he'd always been curious about. That evening, his interest had overcome any callow self-consciousness, and he'd asked Bev's mother about the weaving. Mrs. Miller—Julia—had shown him the place mats she was working on and he'd found himself telling her that, after trying the College Prep and business courses, he was transferring to shop and thinking of becoming a cabinetmaker. He said to Snowy, "Hell. I'm sorry."

"Maybe Mimi or Etta could plead with Bev to spare the place for sentimental reasons, but they don't really know or care about it. Julia and Fred were living in Florida when the grandchildren were growing up and visiting them. I've been racking my brain all the way home. The bog—wetlands restrictions? Probably no hope there. Bev knew what my reaction would be to her plans, but she's past caring. She needs to make the most money she can out of the place. Chop it up!" Snowy heard her voice rising.

Tom asked, "What about Washburn?"

"Dudley?"

"He might know some loopholes. No, Plumley will be just as expert as the mayor. Any land-conservation organization? No, they couldn't raise more money than Bev can make developing it. Shit!" Tom settled his ear protectors back on and turned on the planer.

When they stopped after that stack was done, Snowy said, "She was my best friend."

Those were, she realized, the same words she had said after she had stolen Tom back from Bev. Past tense.

Phones began ringing, on Tom's desk down here and up in the living room.

Snowy looked helplessly at Tom. "If it's Bev, I can't talk to her. Say I've gone for a walk."

He picked up his desk phone. "Hello?" He listened.

Maybe it's Ruhamah, Snowy thought. Would Ruhamah have any ideas about how to thwart Bev?

Tom said, "Take it easy, Rita. What's the problem? Calm down. Do you want me to call 911 for you? Okay, okay, I won't, we'll come right now." He hung up.

Snowy asked, "Rita?"

"She wants us there." He grabbed his parka off a hook. "She sounds hysterical."

"An accident? Fire?"

He was scrutinizing the workshop, making sure everything was turned off. "She said she didn't need 911."

In Tom's Jeep, they drove along Main Street, Snowy trying to keep her mind on Rita but veering back to the image of condos covering the orchard and the woods. As they bounced up and down the Roller Coaster Road, the jolts made her remember the very first time she'd seen Hurricane Farm. How it had reminded her of Julia's! Tom pulled into the driveway and parked and jumped out, but Snowy balked. What might Rita have done to this place, besides a hot tub and a satellite dish?

The barn door was open. Only Rita's convertible was parked in the barn. Snowy remembered running out to the barn and finding only the Subaru parked there, Alan's van gone.

She jumped down and ran after Tom, seeing a fancy swing set in the backyard.

Tom was on the side porch, knocking on the kitchen's storm door. Instead of the snowshoes and snow shovels that she and Alan kept on the porch in the winter, there were sleds and sliding saucers. "Rita? It's us!" Tom opened the storm door and tried the kitchen-door handle. Locked.

The upper half of the kitchen door was glass. Suddenly Rita appeared in it. For an instant Snowy didn't recognize what she was holding.

"Holy shit!" Tom yanked Snowy back against the porch wall, out of the line of fire.

But Rita didn't fire the rifle. She unlocked the door and opened it, looking past them at the driveway. "You didn't see him in the village?"

Tom asked, "Who?"

Rita began to sob.

Tom stepped into the kitchen and gingerly removed the .22 from her grasp. "Tell us what's wrong. Where's Frank? Is there anybody in here, an intruder?"

Snowy saw that the big low-ceilinged kitchen had been remodeled since Rita's wedding reception, the white walls painted cranberry, the old pine cupboards and cabinets replaced with some kind of shiny light wood. No more wooden countertops; soapstone had been installed. A wine cooler. Stainless appliances instead of the copper-brown ones that had been here when she and Alan bought the place. The woodstove was gone. She thought, I'm focusing on minutiae because—

As her eyes fell on a child-size table with a rose-painted toy tea set, her heart stopped. "Mallory. Where's Mallory?"

Rita threw herself into Tom's arms.

"Oof," he said, and handed the .22 to Snowy. Holding Rita, he soothed, "Come on, come on, tell us what's happening."

Snowy ran into the dining room, and it was the nightmare, the search for Alan, the dining room, the living room—some of her old furniture that Frank had bought with the house; a new cream leather sectional sofa—and the downstairs bedroom, which Frank had made into a study, and the downstairs bathroom, then up the staircase to the two bedrooms, one of which had been her office, the other Ruhamah's room. She heard voices coming from her office. She realized she was still carrying the .22, which she had no notion how to use.

The voices weren't real. A movie, movie noise. Snowy leaned around the doorway. Mallory sat on the floor of a little girl's bedroom, raptly watching a video on a television set.

Snowy said, "Hi, Mallory." How old was Mallory this year? Ten?

Mallory said, "*Cinderella,* my favorite."

"Oh yes." Snowy had seen it in the Gunthwaite theater when it first came out. "Everything okay?"

"Mmm," Mallory said, her attention on the screen.

Weak with relief, Snowy leaned against the door jamb. Then she realized Mallory was holding a pillow, on which she was detaching and reattaching some sort of shoe with Velcro—not a shoe, a slipper.

Snowy asked, "Is that Cinderella's slipper? Cinderella's pillow?"

"Mmm," Mallory said, eyes on the screen, "from the Disney Store."

Mallory's white iron bedstead had a headboard designed like a pumpkin. Cinderella's coach. The ruffly bedspread was patterned with glass slippers, the coach, the castle; the curtains too were from the fairy tale. Snowy straightened up. Across the hall, through the open doorway of the other bedroom (Ruhamah's room), she could see the view of the side hill they'd named Violet Hill because it bloomed with violets in the spring. No violets yet, but on Frank and Rita's king-size bed's duvet great rich peonies bloomed. Snowy couldn't imagine how a mattress that size had been maneuvered up the old staircase. One of the two bureaus displayed an impressive supply of cosmetics. She peeked into the upstairs bathroom. More cosmetics were arrayed on the vanity cabinet. No Chanel, though, she could tell Bev. But she would never be telling Bev anything again.

Mallory yanked the slipper off the pillow and slid Snowy a glance. "Grandma says Frank has gone away." She turned back to the video.

The .22 still clamped in her hand, Snowy ran back down the stairs. In the kitchen, Rita clung to Tom, and cried, "I thought my luck had changed! I didn't know it wasn't me he wanted!"

Snowy placed the .22 on the table. Tom looked at her questioningly over Rita's head. Snowy said, "Mallory is upstairs watching a video."

Rita sobbed, "He would watch videos with her! I thought he was so nice and caring! He took her everywhere and bought her everything! I didn't know, I didn't know, I didn't know! Not until I came home early from shopping this afternoon and found him—"

Tom said, "Oh Christ almighty."

Rita seemed to go limp. Very softly she said, "He married me to get at my little granddaughter."

Tom lowered her into a kitchen chair.

"I didn't kill him. I couldn't, not in front of her." Rita raised her face to Tom and Snowy, eye makeup smeared into huge bruises. "What do I do now?"

Snowy gave her a fistful of Kleenex from a box on a soapstone counter. As Rita was wiping her eyes, they heard a car door slam.

Rita lunged for the rifle, but Tom got to it first. Out the sink window, Snowy saw the town police car, a black Jeep Wagoneer, and she was catapulted back eleven years to the store, where she was searching for Alan when the town's one policeman found her, to tell her.

That had been Chief Danforth, now retired. Kyle Granville, the new police chief, was young, the hardware around his hips seeming too heavy for his slight frame as he came warily up the walk to the side porch. He looked shaken, sickened.

Snowy said to Tom, her voice unsteady, "It's Kyle."

Tom stood the .22 in a corner. "Snowy, would you open the door?"

Rita said, "It's my house, *I* will!" and opened the door before Kyle could knock.

Kyle asked, "Everybody all right here?" Then he saw the .22. His Adam's apple rode up and down as he swallowed. "Rita—Mrs. Barlow—is that the only weapon in the house?"

"What's wrong?" Rita asked.

"Is there another weapon in the house?"

Rita said, "Frank has a pistol. Some kind of pistol."

"Do you know where it is?"

"Frank hides it on the closet shelf in our bedroom, because of Mallory."

Kyle surveyed the kitchen. "Where's Mallory?"

Snowy thought: He isn't asking where Frank is. She said, "Upstairs watching *Cinderella*."

"If he hides the pistol," Kyle asked, "why isn't the .22 hidden?"

Not looking at Tom or Snowy, Rita said, "He thought he spotted a woodchuck out back. He forgot to put it away when he went off to do errands. I was going to put it back in the closet, but then Snowy and Tom stopped by and I forgot."

"Rita," Kyle said, "you'd better sit down. I've got some bad news."

Rita dropped into a kitchen chair.

Snowy thought: We're all there ahead of you, Kyle, and Rita is more quick-witted than I'd've believed possible. But she wondered if she should sit down too.

Kyle said, "I was off-duty today." Snowy knew from store chat that he lived alone in a converted hunting camp out on Fifield Road. "I was watching TV—" He checked his watch, which also seemed too heavy for him. "—approximately forty-five minutes ago. I heard a vehicle stop in my driveway, and when I went to see who it was—" He cleared his throat. "There was a shot."

Tom put his arm around Snowy, who remembered how some steel within her had made her press Chief Danforth for the details of Alan's death, while she still hadn't comprehended that he was dead.

Kyle said, "Rita, I'm sorry to have to tell you it was Frank. He, er, took his life."

Rita was staring at him.

"I'm sorry," Kyle said again. "I'll have to ask you some questions. Are you up to it?"

Rita turned her intent gaze on Tom and Snowy, and then Rita answered, "Yes."

"We'll get to the formal statements," Kyle said, suddenly sounding very young indeed, "but Jesus, Rita, can you tell me why you think he did it?"

That was the question Snowy had torn this house apart to try to answer.

Rita was silent, seeming to gather herself together.

Kyle faltered, "Why? In my driveway, in front of me?"

Calmly and firmly, Rita said, "He's been depressed. Despondent. I was worried he was sick and wouldn't tell me, maybe cancer. I don't know why he went to your house, but maybe he thought you'd take care of things best. Not do it here. To spare me. Me and Mallory."

THE NEXT DAY, the store was packed with townsfolk who had heard what had happened and wanted to know the details but were somewhat reluctant to cross-examine Snowy because of the circumstances. Working alone, Snowy explained that Rita's sister lived down in Somersworth, New Hampshire, and Rita and Mallory were staying with her while Rita decided whether or not she'd return to Woodcombe. Ringing up groceries, Snowy overheard somebody say, "Is there a curse on Hurricane Farm?"

Cleora hobbled in, and when she set a quart of milk and a bag of flour on the counter, she looked hard at Snowy and said, "I knew something wasn't right in that house. Felt it in my bones."

Snowy said guardedly, "It's sad, isn't it."

Tom hurried over at lunchtime, a curl of planed blond wood caught in his white curls, bringing her a sandwich he'd made, coals to Newcastle. "How are you holding up? I can let David work alone and give you a hand."

She plucked the wood curl off. "You're meeting that new big order. I'll manage." Last night they had discussed phoning Ruhamah to tell her and decided to wait until tonight when they would be under better control.

Tom said anxiously, "Phone me if you change your mind."

"I love you," she said, a seeming non sequitur.

By midafternoon, she was almost ready to phone him, as much worn out by the customers' endless speculation and having to play dumb as by waiting on them all. She couldn't recruit Irene to return to work temporarily; Gert, Irene's sister, had bought an RV after the ice storm, and they were now touring the USA. That sounded like a wonderful thing to be doing. At the meat counter weighing chicken breasts for Patsy Fletcher, Snowy answered Patsy, "No, Rita didn't know where Frank had gone. She thought he was doing errands."

Then the door opened and Ruhamah walked in, gave Snowy a half-wave, and slipped behind the cash register to wait on the next customer in line.

At six, after locking up behind the last customer, Snowy ran to Ruhamah and hugged her.

Ruhamah said, "D. J. saw in the newspaper that Frank Barlow died. He phoned me from his office. Snowy, what happened?"

So up in Ruhamah's apartment Snowy told the truth for the first time. "After Kyle left, Rita promised she'll get Mallory to a therapist immediately. She just didn't want everybody to know about Frank. Tom and I, we felt so sorry for her—this is awful, but Frank is dead, so what's the point of ruining things for Rita?"

"Won't a therapist have to report child abuse to the police or welfare or somebody?"

Snowy's perusal of the newspapers had come in handy when she and Tom were talking to Rita after Kyle left. She told Ruhamah, "I once read a discussion of this in a newspaper, and technically therapists are ethically bound to report all child abuse to the Division of Children, Youth, and Families. But when the perpetrator has already been removed from the home, the agency rarely becomes involved because the child is now thought to be 'safe from further abuse.' The therapist will probably make sure Rita agrees to keep Mallory in therapy as long as needed or else the therapist will go to the authorities. Probably the therapist will also want Rita in therapy, to deal with her guilt, her shock. Rita says she'll do anything."

"But will Mallory go back to her mother?"

"Not if Rita can help it. She is determined to atone. I guess it depends on what the therapist thinks is best."

"Is Rita coming back to Woodcombe, to live?"

"She didn't know."

"No memorial service, I assume."

They thought of the wedding in the village church, Rita's voluptuous white satin gown, Mallory with her little basket of rose petals.

Then Snowy said, "Ruhamah, you drove here by yourself?"

Suddenly Ruhamah smiled. Snowy knew the feeling.

They had supper in Tom's apartment. Ruhamah continued being practical about the situation, asking, "I assume Rita inherits everything?"

Snowy said, "She told us he redid his will when they got married. It all goes to Rita, except some to charities."

Ruhamah said, "If she decides to sell Hurricane Farm, the price will be out of sight. If you want the place, though, I bet you could convince her to let you have it at a bargain price."

"Huh?" Snowy said. Was it possible that Ruhamah was making a joke about how nobody would want to buy Hurricane Farm because there was a curse on the place? Sort of the way Mimi got a deal on that farmhouse in Leicester?

Tom gave a short laugh. "You mean we should blackmail Rita?"

Ruhamah said, "Well..."

Then Tom looked at Snowy. It hadn't occurred to him that she would want Hurricane Farm, with its ghost of her husband. "*Do* you want it?"

Her version of Julia's house. The house she'd lived in with Alan, not Tom. "Moot," Snowy said, "because we couldn't afford even a blackmail price."

Tom fell silent, doing mental math. He was renting this barn. No equity except North Country Coffins. He was almost sixty years old and he couldn't afford a house.

Snowy asked Ruhamah, "Would you yourself want it?"

Ruhamah said, "Brandon came to Concord."

To D. J.'s? That, thought Snowy, must have been cozy.

"We discussed his biological clock. How the pressure had affected me. We decided to go back to keeping things light. After all, there I was in D. J.'s condo. And Brandon goes out in Washington."

What about passion and a world-well-lost for love?

Ruhamah said, "So I don't need a house."

As Snowy got up from the table to make coffee, the phone rang, and because she was the one standing she answered it, without thinking.

Bev said, "Snowy, Rita's husband, I saw it in the newspaper, I'm so sorry. Are you all right? I mean—a suicide—I mean—"

Afterward, Snowy would tell herself that she and Tom and Ruhamah had been talking about Hurricane Farm, or otherwise she might not have said the unforgivable. At the moment, black thundering rage surged through her and she spoke with scorn, sarcasm, loathing. "Rita hasn't put the house up for sale, so there's no listing to be had, at least not yet."

She hung up.

Ruhamah asked, "Ambulance-chasing realtor?" Then she realized. "*Bev?*"

But Snowy was still too angry to explain, so Tom told Ruhamah about Julia's house.

ON TOM'S SIXTIETH birthday, he and Snowy got away from it all for three whole days. May 15 was a Friday this year; Ruhamah assured them that she could handle the store Friday on her own and announced that for the weekend she had rounded up Leon to help her.

"Leon?" Snowy said.

Ruhamah said airily, "Oh, he and Elisa have called it quits and he's living at Waterlight again with time on his hands," and she shooed Snowy and Tom off to the Kilkenny area of the north country.

During the sunny warm day, they hiked in to Rogers Ledge on a muddy trail through forests of white birches, whose new leaves were lemon-lime. As they sat on the ledge and looked out at the seemingly limitless forest, Tom remarked, "The old name for this used to be Nigger Nose."

"No!"

"Yup. Some appalled people finally got it changed in the 1960s. To honor Major Robert Rogers, of Rogers's Rangers fame."

"Good for them." But Snowy shuddered, sweat cooling. She smoothed her hiking shirt and pants. Did she need to put on her jacket up here? Name changes. In high school she had imagined being Mrs. Thomas Brandon Forbes. Then she thought of how deep into the wilderness they were, and where was the Old Man Bomber? Goddamnit, she was determined not to let him spoil this backpack, but she kept listening for a stealthy crunch of footsteps.

They set up camp on the campsite below the ledge. On the little stove, Tom cooked couscous and stir-fried chicken with vegetables.

Snowy had brought a custom-made backpackers' chocolate cake from Fay's bakery and a poem she had written for the occasion of this milestone birthday.

The next day they went on to climb the mountain called the Horn and backtracked to camp at Unknown Pond, which wasn't unknown anymore but it was still remote enough so they had it to themselves this early in the season. Weary, reeking of fly dope, they sat at the shore at sunset, watching a purple sky turn a rosy pink that lingered until dusk, the pond quiet beneath the darkening triangle of the Horn's silhouette.

Snowy thought of Bev and Dudley, friends lost. She still hadn't told Puddles about either. She'd phoned Puddles to tell her that Rita's husband had committed suicide, nothing more, and Puddles had spoken words that Snowy had never thought she'd hear from Puddles's lips: "Poor Rita, poor Rita." Then Puddles had asked, "What's this about Bev's plans to develop her dear old home? When I talked to her a while back, she was all excited about wheeling-and-dealing, and I asked her how you felt about it, and she said you weren't too happy." Snowy had replied, "It doesn't matter what I feel."

As she looked at the blurring firs, pond, mountain, Snowy tried to let her rage at Bev cool down.

Tom blurted, "I'm sorry I can't buy Hurricane Farm for you."

She jerked around to look at him. He was studying the pond. She said incoherently, "I don't want Hurricane Farm, that was a whole other life, and anyway, if I did, I'd buy it myself, only I can't. Who needs a house, anyway? We're snug where we are." But the garden, the orchard, the woods, the swamp...

"A couple more years, I can start collecting social security. What little there will be. I haven't organized very well for my old age. Hell, I haven't organized at all. From this vantage point, it appears that I have fucked things up royally."

"You created a fine small business."

"Which manages to support me and David and his family, without much left over."

"That's still quite an accomplishment." She put her hand on his arm. "And the fire-warden work, that's vital."

"Self-indulgent."

She didn't know what else to say.

He said, "I can't picture life ten years from now. If I get lucky with my health, I'll work until I drop. But it's heavy work, and how long can I keep manhandling lumber, into my seventies, eighties? If I get sick, I won't stick around—oh Christ, Snowy, I know it's a terrible subject, but—"

Snowy said, "I don't intend to stick around drooling in an old folks' home, either. Or in agony with cancer. Julia's courage; she took sleeping pills, which doctors don't hand out so merrily as they used to. I'm thinking of joining the Hemlock Society. Since Frank, I can think about these things. Odd. No rifles for me. Nor," she said, looking again at the limpid pond, "drowning."

Tom gathered her into his arms. After a while he said, "Birthdays haven't bothered me particularly until this one. See what you have to look forward to next year?"

"Let's have some more cake," she said. "Tempus fugit."

When they drove into Woodcombe late Sunday afternoon, they saw a white Jaguar with a moose bumper sticker parked in front of the store, and just as Snowy spotted Harriet and Ruhamah sitting in wicker chairs on the screened front porch, Harriet leapt to her feet and yanked open the screen door, waving and beckoning.

The first thing Snowy wanted to do was shower, but she said to Tom, "I'll hop out here and say hi. Be home in a bit." Harriet ran forward to hug, but Snowy warned her, "I've been in the woods since Friday."

Harriet hugged her anyway. "I know. I got here Friday, spur of the moment. Can't stay away from New Hampshire, particularly in the spring."

"Even with the blackflies?" Snowy asked.

"Can't stay away from Jared, either." Harriet urged her toward the porch. "Come have a beer with us."

On the porch, Ruhamah got up and asked, "A good backpack?"

"Great. Everything go okay here?"

"Fine." Ruhamah went into the store.

Why, Snowy thought, gazing after Ruhamah, why am I reminded of the cat who ate the canary?

Harriet sat back down. "This thing with Jared is turning into—well, I don't know quite what. But Friday night when he told me what had happened to Rita—I'm so sorry, Snowy—I asked him about Hurricane Farm, and he said people were thinking it might be up for sale. And all of a sudden I realized I'm ready to make a commitment. To buy a place in the country."

Ruhamah brought out a bottle of the latest beer they were auditioning, a pale ale from a microbrewery in Gunthwaite. She gave it to Snowy and sat down.

Harriet said, "So Saturday morning Jared and I went over to Hurricane Farm and walked around outside, the orchard and the woods. Then we came back here to the store to ask Ruhamah to have dinner with us, because all the implications of buying that place were something I'd have to discuss long and hard with you and her."

Harriet the owner of Hurricane Farm. Snowy tasted the beer, tasted the idea, and glanced at Ruhamah, who was examining the label on her own bottle.

"The store wasn't busy," Harriet said, "so I began to broach the subject to Ruhamah then and there, and who should come in but Rita, with her granddaughter. Rita had made a decision. They've returned to Woodcombe, to stay."

Ruhamah spoke. "Rita will be back to work tomorrow. But she doesn't want to work during school vacations anymore. We can get some college or high-school kid this summer."

Harriet said, "I'm glad she could make the decision. But I was still ready for my commitment to New Hampshire. I told Ruhamah I'd call Bev to see what she had listed, and Ruhamah mentioned Bev had a place in Gunthwaite for sale, the farm that used to belong to Bev's parents. I remembered it from when you gave me that guided tour of Gunthwaite in 1957. I remembered it was heaven.

Ruhamah said the plans were to sell it to developers. I knew that would be a crime."

Ruhamah sent Snowy a long-lidded look.

"Bev's son," Harriet said, "was working here, and Ruhamah told him to take the rest of the day off and lead Jared and me over to the Gunthwaite farm. Which he did, while phoning Bev to meet us there and show us around. It's still heaven, Snowy, isn't it. Bev and I negotiated."

Ruhamah commented, "I heard from Leon that they even said 'Feh!' and 'Vaa!'"

"And," Harriet said contentedly, "eventually we went back to her office and I signed a purchase agreement for my place in the country."

CHAPTER FIVE

HARRIET BEGAN SPENDING her weekends in Gunthwaite and Woodcombe. She was consumed by the multitude of projects that acquiring a second home, especially an old farm, embroiled the buyer in, and she relished them all, from having rotted sills replaced to choosing fabrics. She realized that she didn't have to worry about any sentimentality from Bev over the old homestead; Bev was through with the place after the sale was completed. It was Snowy she kept checking with, because in addition to wanting to remain true to that original sight she'd had of Julia's house over forty years ago, Harriet didn't want any renovation to wreck Snowy's memories. Jared did a lot of the work, which went on through the summer and fall, and he oversaw much of the rest, so she could go back to New York during the week knowing the projects were in good hands. On Sunday afternoons, she would steal Snowy away to prowl antique stores, consulting her as a New Hampshire authority. Snowy would tease her about being a summer person and advise, "Remember, don't drive like a New Yorker or, worse yet, like Massachusetts drivers, known here as Massholes. And summer people always stand too close in line; respect personal space."

Once, in a Gunthwaite antique shop they were laughing their heads off over a canvas butterfly chair just like the one they'd had in their room at Bennington except theirs had been orange while this was sun-faded aqua, an antique now, and when Harriet said, "Well, that sure won't suit Julia's house, but I'm tempted," Snowy said, "You don't have to call it Julia's house, you know. Please, call it Harriet's house, a nice alliteration, or anything you want."

With this opening, Harriet at last spoke her mind. "From what you've told me about Julia, she wouldn't have wanted the house to end your friendship with Bev, which is what Ruhamah says happened. I don't, either."

Snowy fidgeted. "Um, well, the house kind of epitomized the difference in the way we've grown to look at life."

"Friends can get past that stuff. Just avoid discussing certain things."

Snowy said, "If you don't buy this chair, I think I won't be able to resist it."

And Snowy did buy it, and put it her office.

At the store, Ruhamah was making up for the months she'd been gone, improving traffic patterns, shelving, counter arrangements, and the menu. Whenever Snowy used the computer in the store's office up in her old bedroom, she saw Ruhamah's complicated spreadsheets and wondered about spread wings. Would Ruhamah fly away or had the agoraphobia caged her?

Rita's presence in the store caused acute embarrassment at first for everyone except Rita, who was now a woman of property, reveling in having a job only as a hobby. "Her therapist," Snowy remarked to Tom, "is a miracle worker."

During the summer, Ruhamah hired Charl and Dudley's youngest child, Bernadette, a sophomore at UNH. Bernie looked like the twins, so she wasn't a constant reminder of Dudley for Snowy. Bernie fitted in so well that when she had to return to school she was signed up by Ruhamah for next summer and any other time she was home and wanted to earn some extra money.

When Thanksgiving and Christmas vacations arrived, Bernie did just that. Ah, the holidays and the obligations. Now that Alan's mother and sister and brother-in-law were down in Florida, Snowy expected Thanksgiving to consist of dinner at Lavender and David's with Tom and Ruhamah and maybe, God forbid, Joanne and Victor, but before Lavender phoned with an invitation, Harriet had decided to have an old-fashioned Thanksgiving dinner at her house in the country. Snowy and Tom and Ruhamah went there instead, greatly relieved. However, guilt about family descended, so at Christmas Snowy and Tom flew down to Florida and visited Alan's relatives while staying with Tom's mother. Although Harriet had to spend Hanukkah-Christmas in New York, Ruhamah didn't go there this year because Rita was no longer working during school vacations. Ruhamah and Bernie ran the store. Returning from Florida, Snowy hurried over to Ruhamah's apartment in the evening and found her at the computer, a mug of coffee beside her.

Snowy asked, "Everything okay?"

"Great," Ruhamah said, standing up to hug.

Snowy was struck by how lovely Ruhamah was, a young woman wearing a sapphire-blue turtleneck with her jeans, her hair in a French braid. You forgot your daughter's looks when you saw her every day. Ruhamah wasn't just cute. "Your Christmas at Lavender and David's, I hope you had a good time?" Snowy was asking if Joanne had been there.

Ruhamah replied, "Joanne and Victor were off on a skiing vacation this year. Montana. But," she added, walking into the kitchen, "Brandon joined us."

Following her, trying to absorb this, Snowy said intelligently, "Oh?"

"How was Florida?"

"What? It was hectic."

Ruhamah picked up the coffeepot and poured Snowy a mug. "Thank you for my presents. Elizabeth and Lilac and everybody had fun with theirs, too."

"Thank you for ours."

Ruhamah topped up her own mug, took a gulp, and seemed to pluck up courage. "Brandon stayed here. It was the last time, a farewell fling. He's getting married on Valentine's Day."

"Oh, Ruhamah." Snowy clunked her mug down on the counter.

"Tell Tom not to worry, it won't be a big wedding bash. It'll be small, immediate families."

"Where?"

"She lives in Arlington, Virginia. Incidentally, she's already pregnant, so Brandon will be a father before he's forty."

"Oh, Ruhamah."

Ruhamah put her chin up. Snowy had never ever seen her do this, imitate this instinctive movement of her mother's. Ruhamah said, "Speaking of weddings, Mimi says that brother Dick is engaged, and Bev is all agog. *That* will be a *huge* wedding, next New Year's Eve, the kind of wedding it takes a year to plan, and the millennium on top of everything else. Down in Connecticut. Mimi talked again about how you and Bev ought to kiss and make up."

Stiffly, Snowy said, "It's none of Mimi's business," and then she wrapped her arms around Ruhamah. Over her shoulder she saw the pull-out sofa; this apartment had been Bev's refuge, haven, during the ice storm a year ago, as Waterlight had earlier been Snowy's.

When Snowy returned to the barn and told Tom about Brandon, she said, "I'm in a muddle, I'm worried that Ruhamah will have some delayed reaction, I'm kind of shocked at her sleeping with him when she knew he was engaged to a pregnant girlfriend, and it's funny but I'm wretchedly disappointed, so I must have become used to the idea of our kids' eventually marrying after all this dillydallying."

Tom thought: If they had, Snowy and I would be related by marriage.

"In-laws," Snowy said and laughed.

Tom thought: Was Snowy implying that he and she were dillydallying and should go ahead and get married? Why the hell couldn't he take this opportunity to propose? Because marriage seemed too *formal?* Because he was afraid it would spoil what they had? Formal; informal. He said, "Even if the wedding is small, I'll still have to wear a goddamn tie."

And, Snowy thought, Joanne will be there in some beautiful mother-of-the-groom outfit. Then as she went into the bedroom to finish unpacking, she thought of how Bev must already be in a flap over what to wear to Dick's wedding. Bev had been deprived of shopping for full regalia when Mimi got married on a mountaintop. What fun she would have shopping for her appearance in Dick's, even if it was a supporting role! Snowy felt sharp regret; she missed discussing the bride and the wedding with Bev, accompanying Bev on the quest for the dress; she missed Bev. Then the rage surged again, as always frightening her, a paralyzing but liberating emotion. Betrayal, abstract and real, that's what Bev was guilty of.

When Snowy and Tom had first got home today, she had as usual checked the little fireproof safe in her office in which she kept her poems. Nowadays she also kept a backup CD of the work-in-progress there and copies in the safe in the store and her Gunthwaite bank's safe-deposit box. The manuscript of the in-progress collection was well protected during this trip to Florida. But although Snowy was still using "Site Fidelity" as its title poem because her editor liked it so much, she knew that she would not be dedicating the collection to Beverly Colby Lambert.

ON MONDAY NIGHT, February 8, Puddles phoned and said, her voice hoarse, low, sad, "I'm back from Orlando. We came in second."

Snowy started doing some cheerleading of her own. "But that's great, Puddles! Up from third last year; you're gaining on it. Congratulations!"

Puddles was sprawled prone on the cherry wood bed, too tired to sit up as she talked into the bedroom phone. Back when she and Guy were newlyweds acquiring furniture, for the bedroom set she had chosen cherry, her hilarious private joke at the time. Gullible Guy had thought she was a virgin when they started dating. "The girls are so goddamned good I really hoped we'd have a chance at winning. That old saying of my mother's, 'Don't get your hopes up.' Well, sometimes I can't help it."

Snowy changed the subject. "How *are* your folks and your brothers?"

"Okay."

"And the kids?"

"Okay. So's Guy, Snowy. Everybody's fine." Puddles heaved a sigh. She could have added that she'd reached her goal of getting the lard off right down to her high-school weight, but she didn't want to be praised by Snowy for being healthy, setting a good example for her patients and cheerleaders, and all that crap. "How did Bev do at the Plumley Awards? I bet she's back in first place. I've been so busy getting ready for Nationals that I forgot to phone her last month to ask. Those big bucks your roommate paid for her mother's place, that could've won it for her."

"Um, I don't know."

Puddles roused herself from her despair and exhaustion and sat up, alert. "You don't? Honestly, Snowy, you and Bev haven't seemed to know what each other's been doing for some time. What's going on?"

"Nothing. Except, Dick is getting married next New Year's Eve so Bev's looking forward to a big wedding, and Tom is off Friday to Brandon's wedding on Sunday, Valentine's Day."

"Brandon? He and Ruhamah are over?"

"It was never really serious."

Puddles attacked. "When did you last see Bev?"

Caught off guard, Snowy floundered, "Oh, a while ago."

"Back last year, Bev was on cloud nine about developing her old home. You're the one who loved that place. Well, she didn't ruin it, but are you still mad at her?"

"We're both just busy. Everybody's too busy. Puddles, what you've done with your squad *is* wonderful. Again, congratulations.

Now I've got to go start organizing some clothes for Tom this weekend. Bye."

After they hung up, Puddles got creakily to her feet and walked over to her cherry bureau. Amongst the pictures of Amy and Susan and grandchildren were the wallet-sized high-school yearbook photographs, framed, of Snowy and Bev.

Before Tom left that Friday, he checked with the halfway house and learned that Kenneth Collins was still in residence there. He said lightly to Snowy, "I guess this is good news. But lock up at night and all that. Be alert."

"I will, don't worry."

With Tom and David and Lavender, Snowy went in her Subaru to the Manchester Airport. Lavender seemed serene about leaving Elizabeth and Lilac with her mother for the weekend and talked happily of sight-seeing in Washington, and this made Snowy feel like a distant outsider. Despite the awkwardness, Victor would be at Brandon's wedding; he and Joanne were married. She and Tom weren't, and thus she hadn't been invited. Watching the plane take off, she waved and wept like an idiot. Instead of going directly home, she drove to the Mall of New Hampshire, but of course it wasn't any fun without Bev and she only bought a springtime jersey for Ruhamah.

Who, Snowy discovered when she got home, had left a message on her answering machine saying, "Arthur Bronson was in the store. He'd been looking for Tom at the barn, wanted to get hold of him immediately. I gave him Brandon's phone number."

Arthur? The owner of the barn, Arthur stopped in occasionally for a hunker with Tom, but there never had been any urgency about their dealings. Snowy remembered that last time the old man appeared fragile, with the red-rimmed eyes and parched skin of ill old age. Prescience prepared her for Tom's call from Brandon's that evening.

"Arthur phoned," he said. "He's throwing in the towel, going into a nursing home."

"Damn," she said. "Poor bastard."

"He's selling his house in North Woodcombe, and he's selling the barn. Back when I started renting it, remember, he and I agreed I'd have first refusal if he ever decided to sell. So the time has come."

"What are you going to do?"

"What are *we* going to do, you mean. Should we look for some other building for me to rent?"

She said, "Heavens, the address is on your stationery, your business cards, on your Web site. We'd better make sure we can stay here. Besides, what a project it would be to move the business! You've already done that once, which is plenty."

"The apartment—you don't mind it?"

"It's home. Want to go to the bank when you get back and see what can be arranged?"

Relief in his voice, he said, "Yes, but the financial arrangements will be mine. You're all tied up with the store."

She said, "How's the wedding hoopla?

"God, I hate cities."

But on Monday, when Snowy met him and David and Lavender at the airport, she thought with irritation that he looked full of vim and vigor, as if he'd enjoyed himself thoroughly. She wondered how to find out from Lavender what Joanne had worn as mother of the groom. Hell, just get her alone and ask! So in the airport rest room, Snowy asked, and Lavender said, "Joanne loves red and Valentine's Day, but red was reserved for the bridesmaid, Stephanie's sister. Stephanie, the bride, had red roses and hearts in her bouquet and lots of lace on her dress, which otherwise was plain white. Joanne just wore a suit, but it fitted in with the color scheme, sort of wine-colored, watered-down wine. Stephanie's mother had a pink dress, pink velour. Me, I never have trouble choosing what color to wear! It was a pretty wedding. David and Brandon and Tom were all very handsome. Stephanie is older than Ruhamah, in her thirties, works for the State Department. Is Ruhamah really all right?" "Yes," Snowy said.

Then, as Tom drove home, he began telling Snowy the changes

he and David would make once he owned the barn, and she realized that ownership was what had given him his fresh eagerness, his new lease on life.

He said, "And aside from the workshop, how about some creature comforts? While I'm borrowing the money for the barn I might as well borrow some extra and build a porch onto the back so we can sit outside without swatting bugs. A back porch for you to sit and relax on, instead of busting your ass as you do on the one at the store."

"Oh, Tom."

So when her sixtieth birthday arrived in March, a Friday, Tom and David had begun building the porch and also a toolshed, and she and Tom took the day off to shop for porch furniture, using David's pickup for the trip to Gunthwaite. Tom asked, "You're sure this is what you want to do on your milestone? Not something more momentous?" Snowy just wanted to get the goddamned occasion over with. Tom was right; a sixtieth birthday hit you like a ton of bricks.

She said, "This will be perfect, with lunch at Hooper's, then the Gilmore House tonight. My cup runneth over. Also my plate."

At a secondhand store they found a small drop-leaf kitchen table and a couple of kitchen chairs for porch meals; they took a break and had hamburgers and French fries at Hooper's Dairy Bar; and at a furniture store they chose a wicker armchair, a wicker rocker, and a chaise longue, Snowy reeling over the prices, remembering how she'd furnished the Pevensay front porch entirely from country-auction bargains.

Upon their return, as they began to unload the pickup, Snowy suddenly noticed across the trampled snow a big pink plastic bow hanging on the half-built shed. "What," she asked, "is that bow?"

Tom grinned. "Good, David remembered to do it. A surprise. This isn't really going to be a toolshed, Snowy. It's a potting shed. I'll till up a garden this spring, big enough for salad stuff. Happy birthday."

"Tom."

Once again Snowy and Tom were kissing for all the village to see.

In the mail was a sixtieth-birthday card from Charl and Dudley, addressed and signed by Charl. In yesterday's mail there had been a similar card from Alan's mother and a raunchy one from Puddles. Mimi sent one of the cards that her husband designed and Mimi decorated with woven strips, the latest item in her shop. Nothing from Bev. No phone message from her either, and when Snowy and Tom got home from dinner at the Gilmore House that night, the only message was from Puddles, singing "Happy Birthday to You," complete with the "How old are you now?" verse.

Snowy thought: Then that's that. I won't send Bev a birthday card on her milestone next month or go to any party Mimi throws for her.

And she didn't. Mimi sent an invitation card to Bev's sixtieth birthday celebration, and in longhand Snowy RSVP'd with regrets; she didn't return an answering-machine plea from Mimi to come.

SNOWY WAS TIDYING tables during the afternoon lull before the end-of-day rush on a Tuesday in the beginning of May, with a delayed April shower outdoors at last turning lawns green after a springtime drought, when the store's phone rang.

At the cash register, Rita answered it. "Hi there, Puddles—" She stopped, shrugged, and held the receiver out to Snowy, saying, "It's Puddles, in some great big hurry."

Snowy took it. "Puddles?"

Puddles said, "Brace yourself, I've got bad news. Guy had a heart attack yesterday. They did an angioplasty and he's okay, but I'm unraveling. I need a support system. Could you and Bev come down and help me?"

Ten thousand thoughts raced through Snowy's mind. She said, "Oh my God, Puddles, I'm so sorry. How did it happen?"

"Typical. Chest pains, which he said were indigestion. I checked him and called 911. I'll phone Bev now and tell her. Don't fly down. It'll only take you three days, two nights, and since you haven't ever seen anything south of Washington except in the air, Snowy, you should broaden your horizons. Bev can drive you both. You give her a call in a couple of minutes. Get directions to my house from Ruhamah, or if she's forgotten, call me. I'll expect you for dinner Friday. Bye."

"Puddles, *hold on a minute—*"

But Puddles had hung up.

Rita now was waiting on a customer. Ruhamah came out from behind the meat counter and looked at Snowy quizzically.

Snowy stared at the receiver. Puddles was assuming too much. What if Bev couldn't leave? *I,* she thought, can't leave! Puddles had two daughters down there, one of them a doctor, for Christ's sake; she had parents and brothers. They could rally. Puddles did not need a couple of old friends.

Puddles's husband had almost died. Puddles complained about Guy, had even been unfaithful to him, but they had been married almost forty years.

Snowy remembered receiving, in Pevensay, a phone call from the Gunthwaite hospital telling her that Mother had died of a massive heart attack. Instantly.

She said to Ruhamah, "Puddles's husband has had a heart attack."

"Shit," Ruhamah said. "What's his condition?"

"An angioplasty. Puddles says he's okay, but she asked me to come down. Me and Bev. I should go."

Ruhamah said, "Pam says to substitute 'want' for 'should' on our to-do lists."

Advice from Ruhamah's shrink. Snowy said, "I'm going upstairs."

In Ruhamah's apartment a phone had been put in Snowy's

old bedroom when it became an office. Snowy went instead to the more familiar kitchen phone. She tapped Bev's Plumley number.

Bev's voice sounded distraught. "Yes?"

"It's me. Did you get a phone call from Puddles just now?"

There was a silence.

Then Bev said, "What do we do?"

Snowy said slowly, "She needs us. I guess we start packing."

"I can only be away a week at the most, including travel time, and she wants us to drive down so you can see the USA, or some of it."

"We can ignore that order, and fly."

Another silence.

"No," Bev said, "I'll pick you up at seven tomorrow morning," and hung up.

Snowy phoned Tom at the fire tower and told him.

Tom said, "Dangerous thing, retirement. I hope Guy will really be okay. Go, go, don't worry about anything here. But don't forget to come back."

WEDNESDAY MORNING WAS sunny, chilly. Bev pulled up in front of the barn in a new car. By God, she had a Subaru! A luxury-model Outback, with leather seats and plenty of sunroofs, but still a sensible car for New Hampshire. Bev's outfit, however, was Western, a carved leather vest (expensive!) over a denim shirt and jeans, with turquoises in her ears. Snowy had thrown on one of the new Woodcombe General Store sweatshirts, jeans, and grabbed her blue Polartec jacket, as confused about clothes as she was when packing for Florida. Last week, she had still been wearing long underwear during her morning run!

The car radio tuned to NPR, they traveled without talking as

Bev took the routes she knew so well from trips to visit Etta, I-89 over into Vermont and then down the Connecticut River valley on I-91 into Massachusetts past umpteen colleges, including Mount Holyoke. When they neared Springfield, Bev thought how long it had been since she'd continued south down this interstate into Connecticut. She turned west onto the Massachusetts Turnpike.

Snowy thought how different this was from their drive to Camden.

Bev asked, "Time for a bathroom and some food?"

"Sure," Snowy said.

Bev brought a road map with her into the rest area's Burger King and studied it while they ate their burgers, which they'd paid for separately. "I'm taking an inland route, the way Roger used to when we drove with the children down to see Mother and Fred. Avoid Philadelphia and Washington and all that mess."

Snowy thought of everything they hadn't discussed this past year. She assumed Bev knew via Mimi that Brandon had got married and Tom had attended a Washington-area wedding. She ventured, "How is Roger?"

"He came to the birthday bash Mimi threw for my sixtieth,"

Snowy ignored the birthday reference and ventured further. "What about Roger's girlfriend—Amanda, was it?"

Bev refolded the map and stood up, handing it to Snowy. "We'll take the Taconic State Parkway. You navigate."

"I can do some of the driving."

"No need."

Bev headed back toward her car.

As they continued on the Mass. Pike, they went under a bridge on which "Appalachian Trail" was lettered, and Snowy found the AT's dotted line on the map. Tom had walked across that bridge.

Bev drove off the Mass. Pike, onto the quiet parkway. Snowy looked out the window at green countryside, dandelions, a red barn. Warmer climes already! She navigated, and they crossed the Hudson River. Cows, farmland, pear and cherry trees in blossom.

Then on into Pennsylvania they went, and the traffic became thick and hectic through Scranton to Wilkes-Barre, where Bev said, "That's enough for today," and pulled off the turnpike.

Snowy said, "It goes without saying that we'll split the motel costs."

"But of course." From the clamor of signs Bev chose a Red Roof Inn. "I like to be able to park in front of my motel room, not walk down corridors." The nonsmoking room they were given smelled of smoke, so Bev demanded and got another, and they sank onto the two queen-size beds, Snowy very impressed by Bev's travel-smarts and very, very tired even though it was Bev who had done the hard work.

Bev said, "We'd better find some dinner."

Snowy couldn't imagine getting in a car and going anywhere ever again, but they went back out and Bev drove through the tangle of traffic, appraising the offerings. "T.G.I. Friday's," she decided and swung into the parking lot.

After they were seated and Bev had ordered a veggie platter and Snowy a Cobb salad, Snowy looked around and said conversationally, "I've seen commercials for this chain but I've never been in a T.G.I. Friday's before."

"I've stopped occasionally with one or another of the children."

"The 'waitstaff' itself seems to consist of children." Snowy smiled at the young people's outfits, striped tops, suspenders, a top hat here, a derby there. "Some different from our Sweetland uniforms."

They watched these kids until the meals arrived and watched them while eating.

Then Bev put down her fork, bent her thumbs backward, and asked, "How do you gauge the situation? Do you think Puddles really meant that Guy is going to be all right?"

"You know Puddles; she doesn't pull punches. If he were at

death's door, she'd tell us. But the scare must be awful for her, even though she's a nurse."

"Maybe it's worse *because* she is a nurse and aware of all that can happen."

"Yes."

"Guy must be fairly fit, playing golf all day. I mean, it's only golf, but it's better than nothing."

"Nevertheless, he's sixty-nine years old."

"Roger still plays tennis, but he works too hard at his firm; he's a prime candidate for a heart attack or a stroke. God, how did we ever get to this point in our lives? Do you want any dessert?"

"I guess not." Snowy took her wallet out of her shoulder bag and slid out her Visa card. "Let me pay for the meals. You're paying for the gas. It'll be easier for us—and for the waitstaff. We former waitresses have great consideration for present ones."

Bev hesitated. "Okay, but if we take Puddles out, we'll split it."

In the motel, they unpacked some clothes. Snowy noticed that tomorrow Bev would be forsaking the Wild West for a short-sleeved green jersey and khakis; Snowy would be wearing a short-sleeved pink-checked shirt and clean jeans. Bev opened the map and showed Snowy tomorrow's route down I-81 into the Blue Ridge Mountains, saying, "I'm guessing we'll be ready to stop for the night in Roanoke." Then they washed up and put on night cream, remembering the Noxzema of their youth, and in their nightgowns they got into their beds to watch some television. Instead, they conked out, sound asleep immediately.

The next morning, Snowy was in the shower by five o'clock, Bev by six, and after they'd grabbed coffee and bagels at a Dunkin' Donuts, they were off, down the interstate. Pennsylvania. Snowy wondered if those were really coal heaps along the way. Aha, one definitely was; it brought back memories of the coal cellar in her parents' house, with the little window down which the delivery truck would dump a roaring avalanche of coal for the furnace. Later, her father had turned the coal cellar into a rumpus room.

Near Harrisburg, they pulled off the turnpike for a break and found themselves in trucker-land. In the gas station handy to the exit, at first they could only see diesel pumps amid the giant trucks, before they located a regular self-service island. Then as they went into the restaurant across the street, Snowy saw that part of it was a store full of necessities for truckers, from auto equipment to—wonderful!—audio books. Greeting cards declared trucking sentiments, and Snowy bought "I Miss You over the Miles" to send to Tom. In the dining section, all the customers seemed to be using cell phones. The menu was not for dainty appetites. Snowy noticed sausage gravy and biscuits listed on it, and because she'd never had sausage gravy before, she ordered this, with scrambled eggs.

For the first time on the trip, Bev laughed. And although she'd been planning on an English muffin toasted dry, she ordered instead scrambled eggs and bacon.

Snowy tasted the sausage gravy. "Oh lord, I can feel my arteries hardening. I'll be in the hospital beside Guy. Oh, this is good! Want some? Another milestone."

They listened to the words, thinking of their many milestones.

Bev said, "I've had sausage gravy, white gravy, before." But she scooped up a sample.

So they were sharing food.

"Yum," Bev said. "We're going to be waddling home."

Onward, toward Puddles, across the Susquehanna River on a looooong bridge, and then out into flat green farmland, where beige-white silos with white tops made Snowy think of giant mushrooms, different from New Hampshire silos. The big farms had a cloying chemical-fertilizer smell. Crab apple trees bloomed pink. Cows. The dandelions down here were already gone to fluff. Bev left Pennsylvania behind, and signs said Maryland Welcomes You and Mason-Dixon Line. Then they were across the Potomac into West Virginia, and Bev remarked, "Looks pretty normal, doesn't it. I don't see a still anywhere."

Snowy gave a giggle. "The scenery is reminding me of our Girl Scout trip to Washington."

And then they were in Virginia. The weather was summerlike when they stopped at the Welcome Center to use the bathroom, and when they continued onward, daisies polka-dotted the green fields. In the distance, mountains were hazy. Snowy located the Appalachian Trail on the map. Tom had hiked through this territory. She was seeing new sights, in a car if not on foot, and she began to think that Puddles was right; making this trip by car was a good idea. It would've been even more so back in the days before interstates when roads had personalities, but nevertheless, wasn't she watching the countryside change as she and Bev progressed south? The restaurant signs at the exits were beginning to be different. It was at a Subway, however, that they stopped for lunch. Disappointment in Bev's choice of a familiar chain changed to delight when she discovered that this Subway had another new delicacy, Krispy Kreme peach pies, which of course she had to try.

Snowy said, "The Shenandoah Valley. I keep wanting to burst out singing 'Shenandoah.' Don't worry, I won't."

"I don't mind. I've listened to a carload of my children singing it."

But Snowy restrained herself. She didn't again offer to drive, either. As they continued on, the mountains became dramatic folds and crinkles to the left, then drew in close on both sides. The scenery was now luxuriant green, the trees in full leaf. She felt the connection to home stretching taut.

"Roanoke," Bev said.

They checked into a TraveLodge. Snowy assumed Bev would be staying in more elegant places if she didn't have to take Snowy's finances into consideration.

Bev said, "Did you see that Cracker Barrel nearby? Shall we go there for supper?"

"I saw the sign. What is it?"

"A chain. You'll get a kick out of it."

When they entered, Snowy thought Bev had made a mistake and this was a gift shop. But Bev led the way through the country-quaint shop into a restaurant, where Snowy proved to herself she had crossed the Mason-Dixon line by ordering grilled catfish, fried okra, and turnip greens, all of which she described to Tom when, back in their room, she phoned him at his cabin atop Pascataquac. Then she asked, "Is everything okay?"

"Fine. Quiet up here, and still not too buggy. You'll get to Hilton Head tomorrow?"

"Yes, I'll phone you from Puddles's. You're down at the barn the next three days? Give Ruhamah my love. Love you."

"I love you."

"Um, remember to lock doors."

The next morning, after her shower Snowy put on another pair of jeans and a short-sleeved blue shirt she'd bought from L. L. Bean's traveler catalogue for last Christmas's trip to Florida. No wrinkles! Wish I could say the same myself, she thought as she checked her Chanel in the motel mirror. It had been eleven years since she and Bev had had their get-together with Puddles in Camden. How much had they aged? Bev looked as beautiful as ever, today in white pants and a black-and-white jersey.

On the television, as they repacked, there was an interview with a banjo player, who performed a snappy rendition of "Darling Nelly Gray," and at a nearby Waffle House they had pecan waffles, and when Snowy paid, the cashier said, "Y'all have a good day." It was certainly a Southern start to this Friday.

South, south out of the mountains into North Carolina, poppies in the median strip, and cannas, and a butterfly. Bev pointed out that the Southern look of the houses seemed to be caused by their being set right on the ground, without cellars.

They both realized this subject came dangerously close to real estate. Snowy didn't change it. "And brick ranch houses," she said. "Brick!"

"Maybe people down here say, 'She's built like a brick ranch house.'"

They laughed.

"Jesus!" Snowy said. "Jesus! Jesus!"

Bev shot her an alarmed glance.

Snowy said, "I'm not swearing, I'm reading all these fucking signs." Religion was loud and insistent here, on church signs, on billboards.

In the women's room of a gas station, there was a machine with four types of condoms, including French ticklers. The traffic was a madhouse in Charlotte, the worst yet, and Snowy's admiration for Bev's driving increased even more. At last, South Carolina! Columbia had a ring road around it, whew. They turned onto I–26, which was more like a parkway, and stopped at a Cracker Barrel, where Snowy couldn't resist a dessert of Coca-Cola chocolate cake, another first. After a field blooming with pink and white flowers that Bev and Snowy agreed must be dwarf cosmos, they reached I–95, and Bev put her foot to the floor. Snowy was reminded of watching a Kentucky Derby or some such race on TV, when a horse comes up on the outside and starts passing all the others. She held her breath and didn't say a word, not even an eek.

Then finally she gasped, "The exit ahead, that's us," and pulled Ruhamah's jotted directions out of her shoulder bag.

White fencing. Gated communities. Lush green opulence. Palm trees at a mall! A golf club. Hilton Head Factory Stores. Over a curving bridge they drove, past marshes, through a tollgate. Snowy strained to see street signs in the fast four-lane five-thirty traffic. "Keep going, keep going, at the stoplights up ahead I think we turn right off the main drag. Yes." She directed Bev down streets through various green and woodsy neighborhoods until—the house looked just like the photographs, earth-tone taupe, under Southern pines—"Here we are!"

Bev braked to a stop in the driveway, in front of a two-car garage beneath the house. The garage doors were up, and Bev and Snowy gawked agape at Guy lifting a bag of golf clubs out of the trunk of his car.

He glanced up at them and waved. He appeared to be fit as a fiddle.

The front door slammed open, and down the stairs hurried Puddles, who had lost a lot of weight since they last saw her and was wearing white shorts and a sleeveless jersey of horizontal red-and-white stripes that called deserved attention to her boobs, just as her tight sweaters had in high school. She cried happily, "Welcome!"

Snowy and Bev looked at each other.

Puddles had always been crazy. How could they have forgotten that?

AND PUDDLES WAS unrepentant. Hugging them, she said, "I had to trick you. Extreme measures were necessary. Now we'll celebrate our sixtieth birthdays and the upcoming millennium all at one swell foop!" To her husband she shouted, "Guy, get their suitcases!"

Speechless, dizzy from travel, Snowy tottered after her up the stairs. Bev followed, estimating the price of this very desirable split-level, saying, "Jean Pond Cram, I cannot believe it, you made us drop everything and drive almost all the way down the entire eastern seaboard worried sick about Guy, and there's nothing wrong with him?"

Puddles opened the front door. "Aren't you glad he's okay? He even offered to do his Low Country cookout for you tomorrow night, but I'm shooing him off to visit Susan and the grandchildren tomorrow." She turned and yelled at Guy, "I'm telling them how we girls are going to be alone here this weekend!"

Snowy looked back at Guy, laden with suitcases, and saw distinct relief on his face.

Puddles said, "The reason I have to holler is, when he took his shower after golf yesterday he neglected to remove his hearing aids. They're not ruined, he jumped out and dried them off, but they have to stay in his nighttime dehumidifier jar for a while. So I get to exercise my lungs." She ushered them into a foyer. "Want a bathroom?"

In photos of this house and their previous house, Snowy had seen their elaborate Southern furniture, some of which Guy had acquired from his grandparents when he and Puddles got married, the rest inherited when his parents died, and now in person she saw it here in the foyer and down a step in the dining and living-room area, against white walls with family portraits, on the pale gold wall-to-wall carpet Puddles had insisted upon. The effect was gorgeous—and far away from the house Puddles had lived in on Gowen Street in Gunthwaite, New Hampshire, that brown house with the high screened front porch sticking out as if it were pregnant, the living room of slipcovered chairs and a pull-out sofa where the triumvirate slept when Snowy and Bev were staying over.

"A bathroom," Bev said, "if you please."

Puddles headed down a hall hung with photographs of groups of cheerleaders and pointed at doorways. "A guest bathroom for you two. Guest bedrooms—Snowy, that's yours; put her stuff in there, Guy; and this bedroom's yours, Bev."

Snowy saw that Puddles had shown unusual tact, giving her instead of Bev the guest room obviously used by the grandchildren. If Bev had had to sleep in one of the twin beds under either the NASCAR bedspread or the Strawberry Shortcake bedspread, surrounded by toy chests, a dollhouse, toy trucks in many sizes and varieties, and a bookcase of kids' books, board games, videos, video games, she would have been constantly reminded that she didn't yet have those grandchildren she unfathomably wanted. The bedroom Puddles assigned to Bev was for grown-ups.

"Join me in the kitchen after," Puddles said, heading back down the hall. Bev scooted into the guest bathroom. At the end of the hall, Guy went into what must be Puddles and Guy's bedroom, and before he shut the door behind him, Snowy glimpsed New England reigning there, white ruffled curtains and chenille bedspread, braided rugs—and, for God's sake, on one wall the Gunthwaite High School pennants that Snowy remembered from Puddles's bedroom at home!

In her room, Snowy unzipped her suitcase. She was so tired, she wanted to lie right down on Strawberry Shortcake. Just as the thought of Puddles's audaciousness sent a jolt of adrenaline through her, Bev knocked on the door and came into the room saying, "How *dare* Puddles!"

"Do we turn around and start back tomorrow?"

Bev walked over to a toy chest, opened the lid, and looked inside. "I don't know. It's so maddening."

"I can't really imagine getting on a turnpike again tomorrow, and I haven't been doing the driving."

Bev picked up a baseball mitt, then returned it to the toy chest. "Yes, I suppose we should unkink our muscles for a day. Start home Sunday."

They went down the hall to a blue-and-white kitchen, where Puddles was plunking ice into insulated highball glasses decorated with tropical fish. Puddles said, "If I forgot to put anything in your rooms you need, just tell me. Come out to the porch and meet Pom-Pom." She handed them each a glass and hustled them down into the living room and out through a sliding glass door onto a taupe unscreened porch, a shaded retreat where the ginger cat with black paws lay on a dark green wicker hassock lazily watching a bright red cardinal who was keeping a safe distance, Snowy hoped, in a nearby tree.

"Sit, sit," Puddles said, and they did, in the dark green wicker chairs. She continued, hostessy, "How was your trip?"

Snowy sipped gin-and-tonic. "A mission of mercy."

Bev said, "A headlong dash to comfort our dear friend on the brink of widowhood."

Puddles stroked Pom-Pom, looking from Snowy to Bev and back. They might not have become best friends again yet, but they must have declared a truce on the way down, and now they were united in being pissed off at her. Good.

Snowy said, "However, I did see some new sights, and I did eat sausage gravy, amongst other new treats."

Puddles said, "Tonight I'm making you shrimp scampi, real

South Carolina shrimp I've learned to love. Tomorrow we'll see the sights of Hilton Head."

Bev said, "You're quite a sight yourself, Puddles. You look great."

Suddenly shy, Puddles stood up. "Well, I finally had to get the tonnage off my arthritic hips and knees, with diet and the coaching and would you believe tai chi. Sit and unwind. I'll send Guy to fetch you when supper's ready." She went indoors.

Snowy said to Bev, "Tai chi? Puddles?"

They giggled. Then in the peaceful warm air, they dozed. They snapped awake when Guy, his sparse hair wet from his shower, leaned out onto the porch and said in his accent, "I hate to disturb you ladies, but Puddles says I have to. Incidentally, my apologies for not having had a heart attack. Y'all know how it is when Puddles takes a notion."

Snowy said, "Oh heavens, don't apologize," but Bev was clearer, miming extravagant relief that he was indeed all right. He laughed.

At the ornate Cram dining table, they ate Puddles's light and spicy supper, Snowy and Bev recounting tales of the road, Guy trying to follow the conversation. Snowy hadn't consumed anything made by Puddles since high-school pizza, and because Puddles had been such a fussy eater, Snowy figured she would have become an indifferent cook. She hadn't. "You and Bev," Snowy said, "are gourmet chefs."

Puddles blushed.

Guy asked her, "Did you tell them yet?" and poured everyone more wine.

Bev asked, "Tell us what?"

"Well," Puddles said, "Ashley, the head coach, got offered a better-paying coaching job, thanks to our second-place win at Nationals, so she's moving on to another school. I was offered her job."

Bev applauded, and Snowy said, "Puddles, congratulations!" Guy raised his glass and said, "Here's to the head coach!"

As they toasted her, Puddles said giddily, "Me, age sixty in July, getting a job offer, who'd have thunk it. I'll cut back at Palmetto Family Medicine, but I won't retire from nursing, I couldn't do that. Snowy, I'm looking for an assistant coach. Do you want a new job at age sixty?"

Later, Snowy carried Puddles's kitchen phone into her bedroom, phoned Tom, and told him about Puddles's deception.

"Sonofabitch," he said admiringly. "She is a piece of work."

"So Bev and I will head back Sunday. Everything okay up there?"

"Everything's just fine. See you Tuesday."

When they hung up, she wondered if she really had heard a fractional pause before he answered her question.

The next morning she awoke to the sound of birds outdoors; she could identify cardinals and mourning doves but the rest had Southern accents. She pulled back a vertical blind and looked out at a sunny Southern day. Puddles already had impatiens blooming in a border, something she hadn't noticed in the shock of their arrival. After her shower, in her room she got dressed in the most summery clothes she'd brought, a short-sleeved coral jersey and lightweight denim pants, and when she stepped back out into the hall, Bev emerged from the bathroom, showered, in a white-and-turquoise bathrobe, and said, "Doesn't it look beautiful out? It's summer! I've forgiven Puddles. Yum, coffee, I'll be right along."

Snowy went slowly down the hall toward the aroma of coffee that wafted from the kitchen. Had she and Bev also forgiven each other? But she no longer knew what forgiving meant, if she ever had; it seemed too simple. She examined the hallway photographs of cheerleaders in terrifying pyramids, flipping, flying, tumbling, dancing—dancing? What the hell? In one of the photographs, the girls were jitterbugging!

Puddles was stirring something in a saucepan on the stove. She wore khaki shorts and an orange T-shirt that said If Cheerleading Were Easy, More Boys Would Do It. "I've already sent Guy on his way," she announced, and beamed at Snowy. "I can't believe it. At long last, you're down here!"

"Those hall photos—did my eyes deceive me? Are your cheerleaders jitterbugging? I supposed they'd dance to rock music."

Puddles made an attempt to look modest and failed. "That was my idea when we were choreographing for this year. At first the girls complained, but pretty soon they loved the routine, and it sure got attention. Shake, rattle, and roll!" She pointed with a wooden spoon at the breakfast bar set for three. "Sit."

Snowy obeyed, hopping onto a bar stool, but protested, "Can't I help? I'm all discombobulated. I should be at the store right now, not sitting around."

"Snowy, there is such a concept as vacation." Puddles banged down a mug of coffee in front of her and grabbed a platter of cut-up fruit out of the refrigerator. "Did you sleep okay in a strange bed? I assume you chose Jean's, not Little Guy's? Did I tell you that Jean is going to be cheering next year? They have these junior squads now."

"How old is she, seven? So young."

"Some girls start even younger. Susan has a few misgivings about letting her daughter do it—Susan just cheered in high school, the way we did—but as I told her, Jean can always change her mind if she doesn't like it. Is Bev up?"

Bev said, "That's my cue," and made her entrance wearing a sleeveless jade jersey and beige jeans.

So here the triumvirate was, in Carolina in the morning, in their summer duds. Puddles even had on sandals.

Bev said, "I peeked and found your laundry room. Is it all right if I do a wash later?"

"Make yourselves at home." Puddles poured coffee for Bev, slammed down the toaster lever, and poured Egg Beaters into a skillet, saying, "Isn't this a dream come true, you two here! At first I was planning to get Amy and Susan and the grandchildren to come meet you, and invite my folks too, the more the merrier, and then I thought what the hell do we want with all those people underfoot, this is *our* visit."

"The photos in my bedroom," Bev said, settling onto a bar stool.

"Twins down through the ages, a cavalcade of Susan and Amy! I feel they're right here. Is Amy still living with that man who fixes shopping carts?"

"Yup," Puddles said, tipping the skillet, stirring the saucepan, "I think he's Mr. Right. They just aren't bothering to get married. Aren't they smart?"

Snowy laughed and said to Bev, "Is Puddles reminding you too of Jimmy at Jimmy's Diner? Remember how when he was working fast at the grill, he looked like an octopus?"

Puddles giggled. "Can't show you an octopus on our tour, but I hope to find a Hilton Head alligator for you. And here's this." She plopped a spoonful of pale mush onto a plate and shoved it at Snowy.

"Cream of wheat?" Snowy said.

"Grits," said Puddles, dumping scrambled Egg Beaters onto their plates as toast leapt out of the toaster.

Snowy said, "I've never had grits," and tasted.

"That's what I figured. Guy loves them, natch, but even after all these years I'd still rather eat wallpaper paste. Did you notice how he's treating my coaching with respect now that I'm going to be the head coach, not just the assistant? Men."

Bev said, "We left in such a rush we didn't get you a hostess gift, but tonight we'll take you out to dinner to celebrate your new job as well as our reunion. We insist, don't we, Snowy."

Snowy nodded, mouth full.

Puddles said, "Well, I was going to take *you* out. But okay. Now, did you both bring your vitamins? If not, ours are on that shelf; help yourself. You're still on HRT? I've cut my dosage in half, and I'd advise you to think of doing the same."

Bev said, "Long-term use. We're still guinea pigs."

Snowy asked for seconds of grits.

After breakfast, they went out to Puddles's Toyota, Puddles announcing, "Snowy, you sit in back; Bev, you need more legroom, so you sit up front. Speaking of anatomy, Hilton Head is shaped like a foot, and we'll start with a visit to the toe."

As Puddles drove, Snowy couldn't help asking constant questions from the backseat, like an irritating child. "What are those trees?" she asked. Puddles answered, "Live oaks." "Is that Spanish moss?" Puddles answered, "Yes, Spanish moss." "Are those magnolias?"

Bev asked, "Do all the houses have to be done in earth tones?"

"Just about," Puddles said. "But here we are in Harbour Town, lots of colors." She parked.

They walked past tropical-hued shops to a red-and-white striped lighthouse, which might have inspired Puddles to wear that striped jersey to welcome them yesterday.

Snowy said, "Do I see hibiscus in these flower beds? Do I smell jasmine?"

"You bet," Puddles answered patiently.

They walked out on the dock and looked at all the expensive boats sparkling in the sun. The sun! Snowy realized she was sweating, flushed, reeling.

"Shit," Puddles said, "I forgot you're not used to this kind of heat in May. You *are* wearing sunscreen, aren't you?" She inspected Bev. "How are you feeling?"

Bev said, "Fine. I adapted some, thanks to my visits to the Southwest."

"Frankie! I've got to hear all the details. But right now—" Puddles dragged Snowy off the dock and into a shop. "Both of you, buy hats."

Bev chose a flattering straw one, while Snowy couldn't resist a baseball cap with an embroidered mosquito and an inscription that read Bite Me, which she thought would make Tom laugh when he saw it on her, and then of course she had to buy a Hilton Head T-shirt for him and a shell bracelet for Ruhamah, and oh why not, a set of insulated glasses like Puddles's for the new porch. When they left the shop, both Snowy and Bev were wearing their hats and carrying large pink shopping bags.

Back behind the wheel, Puddles continued the tour and continued answering questions from a Snowy revived by shopping and air-conditioning. "Yes, those are marsh grasses, and baskets are made from them." As she recited Hilton Head's population figures, permanent and seasonal, she decided to shut Snowy up with food.

At a South Beach restaurant, sitting at an outdoor table, Snowy felt again as if she were melting, despite her cap, whereas Bev seemed to be blossoming, and Puddles still looked cool as a cucumber. The restaurant was busy, with people commenting on the lovely hot weather. Snowy ordered a grilled grouper sandwich and hush puppies, all new to her, and listened to Bev tell Puddles about Frankie and Santa Fe. Hush puppies turned out to be round fried corn muffins, sort of.

Bev said, "Frankie's sister—do you remember her? I don't; she was a senior when we were in junior high—she married a guy in the air force, and they were stationed out in Arizona, and when Frankie was at UNH he would save up his money and go out there during Christmas vacations to get away from winter. He loves the Southwest. He married a UNH classmate and they settled in Santa Fe. He's involved in developing 'spec' houses, of the exclusive variety."

Puddles set down her glass of iced tea. She prompted, "And?"

"We reminisce a lot. We talk shop a lot."

"And?"

Bev studied a sign that said No Crabbing Allowed. "Well, it's fun to have an excuse to go to Santa Fe, sight-seeing, shopping. I don't miss him madly between visits, if that's what you mean, and I'm glad he isn't around all the time."

"Sounds like what you have going with Roger, or at least before that Amanda. What's with Roger now?"

"He showed up at my birthday party. Afterward, I checked with my friend Gretchen in Ninfield, and she said that he and Amanda are still together but Amanda is getting tired of waiting for him to make a commitment."

"Where did he spend the night, after the party?"

Bev said complacently, "At Waterlight, wishing me happy

birthday," and soaked up their reaction the way she was soaking up the South Carolina sun. Puddles laughed so loudly that people turned to stare; Snowy raised an eyebrow. Bev asked Puddles, "Can you really locate a Hilton Head alligator for us? I've only seen Florida ones."

They drove off in search, along a lagoon on one side of the road, on the other side the ocean and sumptuous houses. Snowy asked, "What does 'Leisure Trail' mean? A sidewalk?"

Puddles stepped on the brake. "There's one!"

In Florida, Snowy had been pleased to see that alligators looked just the way they should, and so did this eight-foot specimen floating in the lagoon, lazy and sinister.

That sight taken care of, Puddles drove to Coligny Beach, where they walked out onto the long stretch of sand that disappeared into the distance. People were seriously sunbathing or cavorting in the ocean. "Swimming in May," Snowy marveled. "Alan used to say that New Hampshire's ocean would freeze the balls off a brass monkey on the hottest day of the summer."

Then they stopped at an ice-cream shop for cones, and Snowy chose peach, because they were so near Georgia.

Puddles said, "I wish you could stay longer. We could go to Savannah, make a pilgrimage to Juliette Low's house like good Girl Scouts."

Bev said, "But alas, we all should be back at work Monday."

Feeling the visit nearing its end, they returned to Puddles's house, where Bev and Snowy used her washing machine and dryer and went sight-seeing through the rooms, getting weepy over their graduation pictures on her bureau, laughing over the golf paraphernalia in Guy's study, reading the spines of books in the living-room bookcases (not surprisingly, Puddles had what must be Patricia Cornwell's entire oeuvre to date), even investigating her cupboards to find out what groceries Southerners kept on hand.

Bev said wonderingly, "Canned boiled peanuts?"

Puddles grumbled, "Guy loves them."

Snowy shrieked, "Piggly Wiggly! Puddles, you actually shop

at a Piggly Wiggly? Do you actually say, 'I'm going to the Piggly Wiggly to pick up some bread'? Don't you die laughing?"

"Believe it or not," Puddles said, giggling, "I got used to it. Now you've set me off again. Well, if you're through snooping, let's go have dinner. You'd better bring a sweater or jacket; it'll be chilly."

Chilly? To Snowy, the evening was still sweltering. Puddles drove them to a restaurant at a marina, waved at friends on whose sailboat she and Guy occasionally went sailing, and chatted with the waiter, who seated them at a window table. Amongst the other diners, there was a spirit of revelry, the good life.

"Guy is happy," Puddles reflected. "I'm glad we moved here, after all. He worked hard, so he deserves to play. Whenever I feel guilty about—" She gestured at the room, the ocean. "—I remember the lean times we went through. And at my practice, I've got the real world, and to offset *that,* I've got the cheerleaders and teenage trials and tribulations. Okay, Bev, what's this about your number one son's big wedding? Tell all!"

So Bev told the story of how Dick, who was such a New York Mets fan—"So quixotic!"— that he always bought a season ticket, had met last summer in the seat beside him a young woman who was also a die-hard fan—"and they fell in love as the Mets lost another game, *so* romantic!"

Snowy listened, sipped wine, ate her crab cakes, watching night come on and the dock lights, wondering if Tom was eating supper now too.

"Her name is Jessica Hopkins," Bev concluded, "and she works in Manhattan, in public relations. Roger has met her parents, says they're pleasant and they dote on Dick." Then Bev added, "During my birthday, Roger and I kept going over our part in the wedding plans, and we kept talking about our own wedding. Funny. I even dug out our wedding album and we looked at the pictures. *God,* we were young!"

"Love," said Puddles. "Is Snowy the one of us still really in love?"

Luck, Snowy thought. I am in love with the person I fell in love with when I was a girl, and he loves me; my daughter is healthy; I am doing work I love, and it's being published.

And she would be dedicating *Site Fidelity* to Bev after all.

TOM SAID, "RUHAMAH and I didn't want to tell you and spoil your fun."

In the late Tuesday afternoon, he and Snowy were inspecting the garden behind the barn. After hugging him, this was the next thing she wanted to do upon her arrival home. Ruhamah wasn't around to be greeted, for Tom had reported that Ruhamah sent welcome-home wishes to Snowy but was off to Concord to spend the night at D. J.'s.

"What?" Snowy looked up from admiring the pea fence Tom had built. He had said the garden would just be big enough for growing salad ingredients, but of course they hadn't been able to resist planting peas last month on Fast Day, a New Hampshire tradition on a New Hampshire holiday "Tell me what?"

"Cleora Thorne died. Last Friday. Well, sometime during Thursday-Friday night, in her sleep. When Pete went to the farm Friday to do chores, he realized the chickens hadn't been fed. He fed them, went in the house, and found her."

Snowy put her face against Tom's chest, the old chambray shirt soft.

He folded his arms around her. "The service, a graveside service, is tomorrow. Rita wants to go, too, so Ruhamah asked Lavender to handle the store; they worked out the timing about Elizabeth and Lilac in school and all."

Snowy said, "Cleora was determined to die at home, like Isaac. Thank heavens she did."

Late the next morning, Snowy stood in the neighborhood cemetery at the end of the Roller Coaster Road (Thorne Road) with Tom, Ruhamah—and D. J., who, to Snowy's surprise, had taken this Wednesday off to accompany Ruhamah to the funeral of somebody he didn't know. The day was sunny but nice and *cool.* While she'd been away, the trees had leafed out very fast and the grass was thickly green, everything in a rush after the drought. Cleora and Isaac's children and grandchildren and great-grandchildren were standing near the grave. Snowy remembered watching Louis, the oldest son, help Cleora hobble toward Isaac's grave beside this one in the Thorne plot, at the springtime service after Isaac's wintertime death.

The minister prayed, "He maketh me to lie down in green pastures; he leadeth me beside the still waters; he restoreth my soul."

D. J. handed Ruhamah his handkerchief.

Snowy heard an oriole.

After the service, they stopped at the Thorne farm for coffee, sandwiches, pies and cakes, in the living room that Snowy had only entered after Isaac's service. It was dominated by a massive recliner and big television set, both fairly new and presumably presents from the kids. The rest of the furniture, scabby, rump-sprung, would no doubt make an antique dealer salivate, even the nifty-fifties blond coffee table gouged with cigarette burns. A framed faded old photograph was the original of one Snowy had seen in the historical society, showing the Thorne farm set on wide rolling fields, before the woods began to return, the land cleared halfway up Pascataquac. As Snowy and Tom made small talk with one of the Thorne daughters about the delicious rhubarb pie Cleora had given Tom after he helped round up the cows that time they got loose, Snowy saw across the room Ruhamah and D. J. in earnest talk with Louis.

Snowy glanced at her watch. Time to go relieve Lavender. She caught Ruhamah's eye, and Ruhamah said something to D. J., then joined her and Tom, saying, "May I hitch a ride with you?

D. J. wants to stay." Ruhamah and D. J. had driven to the service in D. J.'s Jeep Cherokee.

"Sure," Tom said, but there was curiosity in his tone. And in Snowy's mind.

They said their good-byes.

Ruhamah climbed into the backseat of Snowy's Subaru, and as they bumped and bounced down the Roller Coaster Road, she leaned forward between the front seats and said, "Here's the thing. Are you two interested in buying the Thorne farm?"

Snowy and Tom looked at each other.

Snowy said, "Tom just bought our barn. That's where we live."

"Well, if you aren't interested, D. J. and I are."

Snowy swung her head around to look at Ruhamah, and jounced. "Ruhamah!"

"D. J. is planning to run for Congress next year. He wants a more solid home setting than a condo. His commute to work would be only forty-five minutes, an hour."

Snowy mustered all her self-control and did not ask if the politically-correct setting included a wife. "Yes, people do commute from Woodcombe to Concord. A rare few commute to Boston. By Congress, you mean the U.S. House of Representatives?"

"I know, I know, a Democrat, a long shot." Ruhamah suddenly laughed, a throaty chortle. "He won't quit his day job. And yes, Snowy, if he's getting further into politics, we'd better not live together. We'll be getting married. I know you think formal weddings are silly, so don't worry. Tom, you definitely will not have to wear a tie."

Snowy thought: Dudley.

Later, when Snowy and Ruhamah were alone at the store, Ruhamah asked, "You haven't been wearing your wedding and engagement rings since you moved to Tom's. You've kept Alan's wedding ring in your safe-deposit box all these years. I told D. J. I would like them, if you would like us to have them. Oh, Snowy, I knew you'd cry sooner or later."

THESE WERE PRACTICAL kids. D. J. and Ruhamah met with Louis Thorne, the executor, and with the Thornes' lawyer, and not until the details of settling the estate were worked out and all the paperwork was done to D. J.'s and Ruhamah's satisfaction, the red tape taking until July, did they suddenly inform their families that they would be getting married the following Sunday afternoon, the wedding and reception to be held in the *store,* which had better facilities than Ruhamah's apartment or Tom and Snowy's for handling a bunch of people, because even though the ceremony was just for the families, in the Washburn case that meant a multitude of D. J.'s brothers and sisters—and the whole town was invited to the reception, along with Ruhamah's and D. J.'s friends. By choosing a Sunday afternoon, Ruhamah told Snowy, they didn't lose any business because the store was closed anyway, and inviting all these people generated goodwill for the store and for D. J. Ruhamah also explained that Harriet had wanted to give her and D. J. a trip, but they had declined, with much gratitude, because they were too busy. Their honeymoon would consist of moving into the Thorne farm; Ruhamah had plans, too, for expanding the office in the apartment over the store, with the eventual acquisition of other general stores someday; and of course there was the planning of D. J.'s campaign.

Filled with whirling emotions, very proud of Ruhamah's keeping the wedding simple, Snowy did wish to hell she and Ruhamah had time to go shopping for new outfits, no matter how informal, but they didn't, so that Sunday afternoon she found herself the mother of the bride in one of her summer book-signing outfits, cotton slacks and short-sleeved jersey whose colors had been called respectively, on their tags, wheat and butterscotch. Ruhamah wore an embroidered skimpy sexy sundress she'd bought on that trip to Portugal five years ago. D. J. wore a polo shirt and khakis.

Although Alan's mother wasn't up to a short-notice trip to New Hampshire, she had wanted to be part of the ceremony and had ordered flowers. On the checkout counter Snowy had set the big arrangement of white roses and irises. In front of the counter one of D. J.'s colleagues, a judge, looked amused as he performed the casual ceremony, and Charl wept tears that were happy despite her regrets that this wedding wasn't taking place in a Catholic church, while Snowy kept gulping and blinking, gripping Tom's hand, thinking of Alan, images from the past pelting her thick and fast. She felt Dudley's eyes on her.

In all the phone calls to and fro after Ruhamah and D. J. announced their intentions, Snowy and Charl had done the rejoicing and talking. Dudley hadn't joined in; he hadn't phoned her himself. He must, she thought, really be hating this enforced proximity.

The ceremony ended, short and sweet, sealed with Snowy's and Alan's wedding rings. It was done; her daughter had chosen and married Dudley C. Washburn, Jr. The store was in an uproar, the hordes of Washburn children hugging Ruhamah and D. J. and Snowy and Tom—they definitely took after Charl! Snowy saw Bev's car pull up outside. Bev wasn't going to be fashionably late to the wedding reception of her best friend's daughter. Then came other cars, including one driven by Ruhamah's UNH roommate, and then Jared in his pickup with Harriet in the passenger seat, and village neighbors were walking down the street, converging on the store. "Eek," Snowy said to Tom, "break out the champagne!", but he was lost amid Washburns, so she hurried over to the cooler, casting glances at the store's front and back porch tables where she'd arranged little centerpieces of roses.

"Let me, in-law." Behind her, Dudley opened the cooler door and began taking out an armload of the many champagne bottles within.

Snowy didn't look at him but at, in the cooler, Fay's present from her bakery. The sight of this traditional tiered wedding cake, glossy with butter-cream frosting, made Snowy burst out, "Oh, Dudley, I'm so happy it's D. J."

He leaned down and kissed her cheek. Platonically. "I'm so sorry I've been so stupid about things. What can I say? I thought you were just my first love, but you turned into my midlife crisis. A late midlife crisis, at that."

"I thought a decision about your political career was the crisis."

"The realties of that were easier to face. A medium frog in a little pond. Well, it was good training for D. J. and Ruhamah."

Ruhamah skipped up, not looking at all practical. "Snowy, did you tell Dudley what Puddles sent? A ton of shrimp!"

Dudley said, "Then let's party, dude."

AS THE SUMMER WENT on, Snowy got a kick out comparing the way Ruhamah and D. J. attacked the Thorne farm with the way Harriet had made Julia's place her own. The difference wasn't simply a matter of money. Harriet was playing house, acting younger than these newlyweds who, already rooted in New Hampshire, were establishing a home, setting down deeper roots—although if by some wild chance D. J. won the House seat, he at least would be living part-time in Washington. Ruhamah and D. J. had lists of priorities, the first ones being: apply elbow grease to the house, and start saving the barn. In lieu of a trip, Harriet had given them a new barn roof, which Jared and his crew were putting on. Snowy assisted in the barn project by removing the manure piles; this wasn't altruism, for she used to haul manure from the Thornes' to her Hurricane Farm garden and she had been coveting the stuff. Sometimes when she was shoveling manure into the Thornes' old pickup that Ruhamah and D. J. had bought with the farm, or when she was driving it to Woodcombe or shoveling the manure off beside her garden, incongruous memories preoccupied her and she would be spending her Commonwealth-Publishing lunch hour browsing in the housewares department of Jordan Marsh, daydreaming over pots and pans. She saw her young self riding the escalator, looking at everything, and instead of embarrassment she felt affection for that person.

One August evening, Tom got a phone call from Brandon, and Snowy heard Tom saying, "Great, that's terrific, I'm glad they're both okay. Oh? Well, it's a family name," and when he hung up he told her, "Stephanie had the baby, and the ultrasound was right, he's a boy. She has decided to name him Brandon, but he won't be a junior."

Snowy said, "I didn't know it's a family name. I don't know what I thought."

"My mother's maiden name. Are you going to tell Ruhamah?"

"She can do math. She must know the baby is due around now." But Tom shouldn't be looking worried after his good news, so Snowy dived at him, tickling and saying, "Aren't you relieved, Grandpa? A baby boy after all that sugar and spice? Come on, 'fess up!"

The next morning, Ruhamah came to work carrying egg cartons. She and D. J. had decided to keep Cleora's chickens, and they'd got poultry-tending lessons from Pete, and now Ruhamah was promoting these local eggs sold at the store.

"Hi, Ruhamah," said Bernie, D. J.'s youngest sister, already hard at work, filling the new coffee carafes, concentrating on the job.

Snowy followed Ruhamah to the big refrigerator and said in a low voice, "Tom is a grandfather again. Do you want the details?"

"Everybody healthy?"

"Yes."

"That's enough."

Whenever Tom was working at the fire tower on Sundays, Snowy hiked up in the afternoon, after the store was closed and her chores were done. As the day ended and the summit emptied, they would sit on the cabin porch, and it was as though they were an old retired couple on vacation, looking at the view, which of course became even more beautiful—and too fucking symbolic—as autumn progressed in reds and yellows, the forest floor tawny with fallen pale pine needles, the ferns the color of tea leaves. In the mornings, she would awake to heaped pink clouds and the rosy apricot of foliage on the surrounding mountains, above the silvery mist rising from Woodcombe Lake. She could look at Woodcombe Lake now without always thinking of Alan. In the farther distance lay Lake Winnipesaukee.

This evening in October, sitting on the cabin porch, Snowy told Tom, "On the early TV news this morning, there was a piece about the foliage, and a New Hampshire native, an old woman probably my age, was asked her opinion." Snowy slid into her best New Hampshire accent, imitating her mother. "She replied to the interviewer, 'I think now is pretty hard to beat for beauty.'"

"Ayah," Tom said, and reached for Snowy's hand.

As was usual with their Monday routine up here, the next morning Snowy hurriedly dressed in yesterday's hiking pants and shirt while Tom made coffee, of which she had a quick slug while packing her rucksack. She would get home in time for a shower before work. Putting on her Polartec vest and the rucksack, she asked, "You've got Wednesday and Thursday off, right? You'll be home tomorrow evening?"

He nodded. "Tell David I'll be phoning him about the new order."

"Tonight I'll go over the manuscript one last time before sending it to Kara." She kissed him, grabbed a granola bar and her trekking poles, and opened the door. A round sun was coming up, so orange it looked like a harvest moon. "I'll miss you."

"I'll miss you."

She walked down the porch steps onto the dewy gray grass, across ledges, and ate the granola bar as she went down the trail through the spruces and firs into the hardwoods, thinking about the *Site Fidelity* manuscript. When she heard footsteps behind her and turned to see a man running down the trail, her mind was far away and he seemed part of the glowing morning woods. And when she recognized him, her first thought was to thank him for getting her work published. Then she was seared by a fear hotter than any hot flash had ever been.

Kenneth Collins had gained weight since his Appalachian Trail exertions, and his bulkiness was increased by a big backpack, which looked new. His beard was gone, and a buzz cut had replaced the ponytail. But his eyes held the same Ancient Mariner glitter.

Since that episode at Gordon Pond, she carried a Mace gun in her rucksack. Could she get at it?

He said, "The New Hampshire primary is four months away. This time we'll succeed, we'll change the course of history. Come along, now, quick down the trail. We're going to the Old Man of the Mountain."

"Kenneth," she began, trying to sound reasonable.

"It's better than before." He smiled. "This time it will be for the millennium election! This time I've read all your books, Henrietta Snow. Snowy. I read about us, you and me, in the newspapers on the library computer. I know all about you now, where you live, what you do, what you think. I know for sure you agree with me, and this time Thomas Forbes won't interfere."

Hadn't Kenneth Collins comprehended that she was the one who'd hit him, before Tom tackled him? Her mouth was so dry she could hardly ask, "Why won't he?"

"Because his cabin is on fire." Kenneth Collins reached for her. "And he's in it. Let's go, let's go."

Snowy raised her trekking poles to stab Kenneth Collins. He wrenched them away. She dodged around him and ran, not down the trail but up, her heart thudding louder than her footsteps. Tom, oh Tom, oh Tom. She stripped off the straps of her pack to rid herself of the weight, dropping it, hearing Kenneth Collins stumble over it in his pursuit. He was twenty years younger than she, he was taller, longer-legged. Had she no advantage but weight? She weighed a hundred pounds less than he did even without his backpack, and a glance over her shoulder showed her that he hadn't discarded his pack. Did it contain dynamite, as that other one had? Tom, oh Tom.

Kenneth Collins made a lunge and caught the hem of her vest. She shoved the vest off her shoulders and felt him lurch away, and suddenly she remembered the old service road, the old direct route to the summit. It was somewhere over there through the woods, to the right. She swerved off the trail and aimed east at an uphill angle, bushwhacking now but the undergrowth slowed Kenneth Collins down more than it did her. She tore through invisible clinging cobwebs, crashed through bushes—oh shit, a swamp. Why had she ever thought she loved Julia's bog? She didn't stop. She dashed right into the murky water, and it was the agoraphobic sensation, a floor wavering, the ground gone liquid, and she would die.

Kenneth Collins shouted, "Snowy!"

The mud sucked at her boots, the water soaked her pants to the knees, thighs. She tripped over slippery sunken branches, but she didn't fall, and when she floundered out onto the other side she saw the ghostly path, the overgrown trace of the service road. She looked back. Kenneth Collins was wobbling and staggering through the water, sinking deeper than she had. Was he mired? She *did* love swamps, bogs, wetlands! Her lungs straining with the effort, she ran straight uphill on the road, up into the spruces and firs. Smoke! She smelled smoke. If Tom was dead, it didn't matter if she died. She heard herself making a sobbing noise.

Then there was a roaring sound. She surged onto the summit. The cabin blazed, flames shot up, shimmering. "Tom!"

She couldn't get near. But her pants were still dripping from the swamp. She started to unzip the ankle zippers.

"Snowy!"

She ignored the voice. She would slide her pants off over her boots, wrap them around her face, and storm that cabin.

"Snowy!"

It wasn't the voice of Kenneth Collins. Tom was scrambling down the tower's zigzag staircase. He shouted, "Are you okay? Where is he?"

She would die, die of relief. "Tom."

He ran over to her, grabbed her. "Where is Collins?"

"You're bleeding. You're cut."

"Where is Collins?"

"Down there. Coming up the service road or in a swamp. Tom, his backpack—dynamite again?"

"We'll go down the trail." He pulled her toward the woods. "Are you all right?"

"Yes, but your face is bleeding."

"Let's go. I called it in. The fire department's on its way."

Snowy and Tom ran pell-mell down the trail they knew every inch of, and when they stopped to pick up her dropped rucksack, they saw firefighters with back pumps ascending fast, these volunteer men and women from Woodcombe, one of whom was Jared. He said, "You two okay? Get down to the base. A couple of helicopters have been dispatched to drop water. Tom, you need first aid."

Tom told him, "The guy who started the fire is still on the mountain. The Old Man Bomber."

Snowy gasped, "Be careful, he's got a backpack, and that's what he was carrying dynamite in at Gordon Pond—"

They heard an explosion on the summit.

LATE THAT AFTERNOON, when Snowy and Tom had the apartment to themselves after Tom had been treated at the Gunthwaite hospital, after the police and reporters and townsfolk had left, after Tom had convinced Ruhamah and D. J. (summoned from Concord by Ruhamah) and Lavender and David it was okay to leave them even though Snowy was still shaking, and after she had reassured Bev over the phone, Tom said, "Let's plant the garlic."

This was to be their experiment this year. Neither of them had ever grown garlic in their previous gardens, because supposedly you planted garlic in October for harvest the next August, and they simply had never been able to believe that those little cloves would survive a New Hampshire winter. They had decided it was time to find out, but it seemed so unlikely they kept forgetting.

The helicopters and the firefighters had got the fire under control before it spread. Kenneth Collins was dead. How had the dynamite exploded? Had he bungled an attempt to blow up the fire tower? The authorities would try to find out, and everyone said that the damaged tower would be repaired and the log cabin would be rebuilt, but all that mattered to Snowy was that Tom was alive.

Now they went down into the workshop and out the back porch, to the potting shed. The garden was mulched with the old hay from Ruhamah and D. J.'s barn, except for the area left for garlic. Tom churned up the soil with a hoe and mixed in manure. Snowy lined up three rows with string on stakes. Then, crouching side by side, they began breaking apart the garlic bulbs and pushing cloves into the earth. Snowy's cloves trembled.

Snowy said, "The Stockholm syndrome. Is that what I mean? When Swedish hostages began to identify with their captor? I wonder if I was feeling a version of that. Because he got me published."

"No," Tom said, "he *didn't.*"

"He's dead. He's dead." And, she thought, Tom wasn't. As he'd explained to Kyle, the town cop, he'd been sucker punched by Kenneth Collins upon emerging from the outhouse—how's that for heroic—and Collins must have dragged him into the cabin and set it on fire, but by luck, *luck,* he regained consciousness and crawled out before the fire got fierce.

"Duty," Tom muttered, jabbing a clove in. "I was so damn groggy I acted like a fool. I should've gone after you immediately, but what do I do? I automatically drag my ass up the tower to do my duty and call it in. I guess I really didn't come to until that was done, and then I almost went berserk, and then you walked out of the woods. " He took her dirty hands in his dirty hands and held them until they steadied. He turned over her left hand. "Would you like a ring on this?"

She had thought about it for so long, but still she didn't know what she would answer until she heard herself say, "I don't think we need one, do you?"

SNOWY AND TOM had been pretty sure that even with coffee instead of booze they wouldn't last until midnight at Ruhamah and D. J.'s combination millennium New Year's Eve party and housewarming party, and sure enough, by ten o'clock they were signaling each other through the crowd of friends, relatives, and useful political people. When they sidled into the spare room downstairs where coats had been put on the old iron bedstead, they discovered that Ruhamah and D. J.'s new puppy felt the same way they did and had collapsed, utterly exhausted, in the dog bed Tom had built for her, snoring into her paws. Snowy had thought that Ruhamah hadn't paid any more attention to Tom's few references to his border collie, Bonnie, than she had to Snowy's tales about Annie Laurie, the Sheltie, but Ruhamah had chosen a female border collie and for her name had chosen the Gaelic word for get-together, céilidh, pronounced "kaylie," and she and D. J. were talking about maybe acquiring a few sheep to keep Kaylie occupied, but meanwhile Kaylie was trying to herd chickens.

Tom said, "Kaylie isn't worrying about any Y2K computer bugs."

As he helped Snowy on with her parka, they heard Dudley's voice above the din, declaiming Tennyson:

> "'Comrades, leave me here a little, while as yet 'tis early morn,
> Leave me here, and when you want me, sound upon the bugle horn.'"

Snowy started laughing, and Tom said, "'Locksley Hall' and the vision of the future?" and they moved back through the living room, looking for Ruhamah. They found her in the kitchen throng, refilling a bowl of hummus.

"We're off." Snowy set their coffee mugs on the counter. "Bedtime for parents."

Ruhamah chortled, "Not for Dudley and Charl."

Tom said dryly, still none too fond of Dudley, "He's a century and a half behind."

"Happy New Year," Snowy said, hugging her. "Happy New House."

Dudley was delivering:

> "'For I dipp'd into the future, far as human eye could see,
> Saw the Vision of the world, and all the wonder that would be;
> Saw the heavens fill with commerce, argosies of magic sails,'
> Dum dum dum dum dum dum dum—
> 'Heard the heavens fill with shouting, and there rain'd a ghastly dew
> From the nations' airy navies grappling in the central blue,'
> Dum dum—Hey, Snowy, help me out!"

Her hand on the back doorknob, Snowy recited,

> "'Till the war drums throbbed no longer and the battle flags were furled
> In the Parliament of Man, the Federation of the world—'"

Tom said, "And lotsa luck with that. Happy New Year, Dudley, Charl."

As they drove away, jouncing up and down past Hurricane Farm, Snowy said, "At New Year's, I'm more apt to think of Edwin Arlington Robinson's writing about the futility of regret.

I expected that a millennium New Year's would get me onto that train of thought, all the what-ifs, and now that the view from the caboose is lengthier than the view from the engine—to strain the metaphor—I expected a train wreck of regrets."

"I regret the summer of 1956."

The summer he broke up with her. She was astounded he remembered the date. But was he just being gallant? Tom, the charmer. His greatest regret must be his knee on Mount Daybreak. No, that must be far beyond mere regret.

They drove along the lake. If only, she thought, I had pulled my share of the load when Alan bought the store; if only I had sat up with Alan the night after the Fabulous Fifties party.

As they neared the village, Tom remarked, "There's Huxley's admonition to avoid emotionally-charged memories. Easier said than done." He took one hand off the wheel and rubbed the nape of her neck. "Let's think about the garlic. Want to make a bet on whether or not it'll survive?"

She laughed. "Okay. I bet it will."

"It's like that bumper sticker that says 'There's No Hope. But I May Be Wrong.' I want to bet it will, too."

"Then this isn't a bet."

"So we'll wait and see."

Up in the apartment, they found a message on the answering machine. Phoning from her Manhattan apartment, Harriet exclaimed, "Happy New Year, see you next month in the next century!" and behind her, Jared's voice called, "Happy New Year, you guys, stay the fuck out of the woods!"

Tom took down from a cupboard the bottle of Oban Whisky, the very expensive single malt scotch he had bought at Gunthwaite's New Hampshire state liquor store, figuring this was what a millennium New Year's demanded, and Snowy got out her best glasses. The phone rang.

She asked, "Do I let the machine answer it?"

"It'll be somebody else wishing us Happy New Year."

The machine answered, and through hubbub Bev said, "Snowy,

Snowy, I know it's late, but it's New Year's Eve and I hoped you'd still be up, are you up?"

The racket in the background must be the wedding reception! Snowy ran into the living room and grabbed the receiver. "Yes, we're up, how did Dick's wedding go?" In the past months, Snowy had accompanied Bev on fruitless searches for a mother-of-the-groom outfit that would be perfect for a big millennium New Year's Eve wedding, in malls in Manchester and Nashua, at the Rare Essentials store in Concord. They were considering Boston next, but when Snowy was getting some shopping done in Gunthwaite one Sunday afternoon, as she drove down Main Street she stomped on the brake at the sight of a new dress shop with an old name: Yvonne's Apparel. In the window was *the* dress. Competing with malls, the shop was open on Sunday. She used her new cell phone to call Bev, who came tearing back from showing a property, and they stood together in front of the window the way they had gazed as teenagers at Yvonne's displays of dresses and, in season, prom gowns. Going inside, they learned that the proprietor was one of Yvonne's daughters, who had been a buyer for a Boston department store but had always wanted a shop like her mother's and had finally taken the plunge, lured back by Dudley's "revitalization" of downtown. The dress was tinsel-silver, with a flocked green pattern. Yvonne's daughter had it in Bev's size.

Bev said breathlessly, "The ceremony went without a single glitch, and as you can hear, the reception is a tremendous success. But best of all, Snowy, I had to call and tell you—there's going to be another wedding."

"Etta? Not *Leon?*"

"Roger and I have decided to renew our vows!"

Snowy almost fell down laughing. Luckily she didn't, because at that moment Tom handed her a glass. He raised his to her, she raised hers, and he turned on the television. She carried the phone to the kitchen area.

Bev was saying, "We'll have the ceremony at Waterlight, and of course you and Tom are invited. Would you believe Roger is doing what I never really thought he'd do, he's retiring—what?" She turned away from the phone. "Yes, yes, Mimi, I will." Back into the phone she said, "Mimi wishes you Happy Millennium. We aren't telling the children until after the wedding is over. Roger learned his lesson about making announcements at weddings. He apologized, Snowy, he at last apologized for his antics with my real-estate certificate." She sniffled. "I keep weeping, and everybody thinks it's because of Dick! And partly it is."

Snowy knew her hilarity was about to brim over, and she mustered decorum. "This is remarkable. After all these years. It's wonderful."

"Could you call Puddles and tell her she's invited? I'll call her myself when I get back to New Hampshire."

"I will. Happy New Century, Bev."

"Bye!" said Bev, sniffling.

Snowy laughed and laughed, and as she tapped Puddles's number she said to Tom, "Bev and Roger are going to 'renew their vows.'"

"Holy shit," he said.

Now, thanks to the South Carolina trip, when the phone was answered she could picture exactly Puddles's blue-and-white kitchen. Or, oops, maybe it was the bedside phone; maybe Puddles and Guy had been asleep.

"Happy New Year," said Puddles, "whoever the hell you are."

"It's me, did I wake you?"

"You didn't wake Guy. He's the one who's gone to bed. Pom-Pom and I are in the living room watching the tube, seeing in the millennium together, and we have noisemakers because with his hearing aids out Guy wouldn't hear the trumpet of doom, and we even have pom-poms to wave. You didn't hang in at Ruhamah's party? I figured you wouldn't."

"Puddles, Bev just called from the wedding reception, and I'm relaying her news. She and Roger have got back together, he's moving back to Gunthwaite, and they are going to renew their vows."

Puddles hooted. "With orange blossoms and the whole works?"

"I don't know. I wouldn't be surprised. It'll be at Waterlight, and Bev will be phoning you to give you the details. Do come!"

"I might," Puddles said. "Maybe I'd bump into Norm Noyes somewhere in Gunthwaite. But I'll only come up if it doesn't interfere with Nationals. We are going to win in the year two thousand."

"Happy New Century, Puddles."

"Happy New Century to you and Tom, you sinners."

Laughing, they hung up. Snowy carried her glass into the living room and as she went past his chair Tom slid his hand over her hip and she just naturally toppled onto his lap. Together they watched the Times Square celebration.